I think you should know I kill people.

But don't be alarmed. I am one of the select few, executioners who operate within their own concepts of legality, justified—although not officially acknowledged or recognized—by the United States of America . . .

Tor books by Brian Freemantle

Betrayals
The Choice of Eddie Franks
O'Farrell's Law

O'FARRELL'S LAW

BRIAN FREEMANTLE

TOR

A TOM DOHERTY ASSOCIATES BOOK
NEW YORK

This is a work of fiction. All the characters and events portrayed in this book are fictitious, and any resemblance to real people or events is purely coincidental.

O'FARRELL'S LAW

Cover art by Les Katz

A Tor Book
Published by Tom Doherty Associates, Inc.
175 Fifth Avenue
New York, N.Y. 10010

Tor ® is a registered trademark of Tom Doherty Associates, Inc.

ISBN: 0-812-58254-3

First edition: February 1990
First mass market printing: May 1993

Printed in the United States of America

0   9   8   7   6   5   4   3   2   1

O'FARRELL'S LAW

ONE

EVEN IN the guaranteed security of his Alexandria home, it was instinctive, far beyond any training, for Charles O'Farrell to awaken as he did: eyes closed, breathing deeply as if he were still asleep, listening first. Always essential to listen first, to be sure. Around him the house remained early-morning quiet, the only sound the soft, bubbled breathing of Jill, still genuinely slumbering beside him. Safe then. O'Farrell opened his eyes but did not move his head. It wasn't necessary for the initial ritual.

The bedroom cabinet with the photograph was directly in his line of sight. Except when he was on sudden overseas assignments, when it would have been unthinkable to risk such a prized possession, the photograph was invariably O'Farrell's first sight in this unmoving, safety-checking moment of awakening. Just as at night, usually while Jill was making dinner, he went to the den to look over the cracked and yellowing newspaper cuttings of the archive he was creating. With just one martini, of course, the one a day he allowed himself. Well, normally just one. Sometimes two. Rarely more.

The way the newsprint was deteriorating worried him, like the fading of the photograph from brown sepia into pale pink worried him. It would be easy enough to get the cuttings copied, although a lot of the special feeling—the impression, somehow, of *being* there—would go if they were transferred onto sterile, hard, modern paper. Essential that he do it, though, if he were to preserve what he had

.so far managed to assemble. He'd need advice on how to save the picture. Copied again, he supposed. O'Farrell was even more reluctant to do that: there would definitely be a loss of atmosphere if the treasured image were transferred to some glossy, up-to-the-minute print.

There was no detail in that stiffly posed souvenir of frontier America that O'Farrell did not know intimately, could not have traced, if he'd wanted to, with his eyes shut. Sometimes, on those foreign assignments, that was precisely how O'Farrell did conjure into his mind the picture of his great-grandfather, allowing his imagination to soften the sharp òutlines, even fantasizing the squeak of ungreased wagon wheels and the snorts of impatient horses and—only very occasionally—the snap of a shot.

O'Farrell knew there would have been such snapping echoes (why did a pistol shot never sound the way it was supposed to sound, always an inconsequential pop instead of a life-taking blast?) because the cuttings from the Scott City journal that at the moment formed the basis of his archive recorded six shoot-outs from which the man had emerged the victor. There would have been much more shooting, of course; the six had been reported because people had died, but O'Farrell knew there would have been other confrontations. Had to have been. Law was rare and resented in Kansas then, and anyone attempting to enforce it was more likely to be challenged than to be obeyed.

Objectively, the aged photograph hardly showed a man to be obeyed. There was nothing in the background of the photographic studio to provide a proper comparison, but the man appeared to be quite short—maybe just a little shorter than O'Farrell himself—and slightly built, like O'Farrell again. The stature was accentuated in the picture by the long-barreled Colt. It was holstered high and tight against his great-grandfather's waist, a necessary tool of his trade, not low-slung and thonged from the bottom around his leg, like those in preposterous Hollywood portrayals. Properly carried, as it was in the photograph, it appeared altogether too large and heavily out of proportion. But for the gun, it would have been impossible to guess what job the man held. He'd obviously dressed for the portrait: the trousers of his waistcoated, high-buttoned suit worn over his boots, tie tightly knotted into a hard-starched collar, hat squarely, almost comically perched on his head. Why, wondered O'Farrell, hadn't his great-grandfather worn his marshal's badge? It was a recurring question that O'Farrell had never resolved. He doubted his late father's suggestion that it had been a retirement photograph. Currently the last of the fragile cuttings, an obituary of his great-grandfather's peaceful death—in bed—at the age of seventy-six, also reported his quitting as a lawman when he was sixty. And he certainly didn't look sixty in the photograph; somewhere between forty-five and fifty. Maybe forty-six. My age, thought O'Farrell; he liked to think so. Personal comparisons were very important.

O'Farrell moved at last, turning away from the bedside cabinet to look at Jill. She shifted slightly with his movement but didn't awake. A skein of hair, hairdresser-blonded now because of the hint of grayness, strayed across her forehead. Very gently O'Farrell reached out to push it back, but paused with his hand in front of himself. No shake, he saw, gratefully. Well, hardly; no more than the minimal twitch to be expected from his lying in such an awkward position; wouldn't be there at all when he got up. Continuing the gesture, O'Farrell succeeded in rearranging his wife's hair without disturbing her. Worrying over nothing, he told himself. Which *was* the problem. Why was this feeling of uncertainly constantly with him? And growing?

He eased cautiously from the bed, wanting Jill to sleep on, but hesitated before the cabinet. It was definitely impossible without the gun to imagine his ancestor as a lawman. Even more difficult to believe him to have been someone to be obeyed. Or capable of shooting another man. But then it was never possible to judge from appearances whether one man could kill another.

Charles O'Farrell knew that better than most.

Until the official opening by President Kennedy in 1961 of its headquarters at Langley, just off the Washington Memorial Parkway, America's Central Intelligence Agency was housed piecemeal at 2430 E Street NW, in barracks alongside the Reflecting Pool and in wooden buildings behind the Heurich Brewery. Not everything was brought conveniently to one location by that 1961 presidential ceremony, however.

The security needs of the Agency's most secret divisions actually dictated that they should remain outside its identifiable headquarters, and its most secret division of all was kept in Washington, on two floors of an office building just off Lafayette Park, to maintain a physical distance between the CIA, a recognized agency of the U.S. government, and a part of that agency determinedly unrecognized. Its existence was known only to a very few men. Required under oath to admit that the Agency possessed such a facility—at congressional inquiries, like those, for instance, that shattered the morale of the CIA in the mid-1970s—those men would have lied, careless of perjury, because their questioners were insufficiently cleared at the required level to receive such intelligence. The division, created after those mid-seventies congressional embarrassments, fit the phrase that became public during those hearings. It was "plausible deniability."

The division came under the hidden authority of the CIA's Plans Directorate. It was run by two men who worked on completely equal terms, although George Petty was accorded the title of director, with Donald Erickson defined as deputy. Each was a third-generation American who believed implicitly in the correctness and the morality of what they did, an essential mental attitude for every constantly monitored employee.

"It's O'Farrell's medical today," Erickson said. He was a tall, spare man with hair so thin and fair that he appeared practically bald. By standing at the window of their fifth-floor office suite, he was just able to look across the park to the White House he considered himself to be protecting. It was a favorite stance and an unshakable conviction.

"I know," George Petty said.

"Have you spoken to the doctor?"

Petty was a heavy, towering man who appeared slightly hunchbacked from his tendency to bring his head forward, like a turtle emerging from its shell. He did not reply at once, making much of filling the ornate bowl of his pipe with a sweet-smelling tobacco and tamping it into a firm base once he got it lighted. He said, "I didn't consider it wise."

"Why not?" asked Erickson, turning back into the room.

"It has to be his opinion, without any influence from us," Petty said.

Erickson nodded. "Probably right," he agreed at once.

"O'Farrell's a good man."

"One of the best," said Erickson.

TWO

It was more a mansion than a house, a huge granite-fronted building with Colonial pillars set back in at least three unfenced acres off one of those tree-lined roads that wind up through Chevy Chase toward the border with Maryland. The doctor personally admitted him, so quickly the man might have been waiting on the other side of the door. There was no noise anywhere to indicate anyone else in the house: there never had been, on any of the visits. O'Farrell followed the other man familiarly across the black-and-white marbled floor to the side consulting room. There was no medical staff here, either, unlike the man's downtown clinic, which was one of the most comprehensively manned medical centers in Washington. But then that was public and this was private: very private indeed.

"How's it going?" the doctor asked. His name was Hugh Symmons. He was a thin, prominently boned man who had conducted O'Farrell's three-monthly examinations for the past four years. Despite having one of the highest security clearances as a CIA medical adviser, Symmons was kept from knowing O'Farrell's real function, merely that it was a position imposing the maximum mental and physical stress. O'Farrell was aware there were other psychologists and psychiatrists with even higher clearances, the real tidy-up-your-head experts, who would be allowed to know his job: the fact that he was still at Symmons's level proved that no one had discerned his uncertainty.

"Fine," said O'Farrell.

Symmons waved him to an accustomed seat and opened a thumbed file and sat reading it, as if O'Farrell were a first-time patient. O'Farrell, who was used to the routine, gazed through the picture window to the expansive lawn. There were a lot of carefully maintained trees in the garden, several long-haired gray firs with branches sweeping down to touch the grass. Groups of squirrels scurried around their bases and there were others in the branches, and O'Farrell was surprised. He understood squirrels damaged trees and would have expected Symmons to employ some sort of pest control. O'Farrell, whose training had involved extensive psychological instruction, was glad of the reflection: just what he should be doing, musing unimportant thoughts to minimize the risk of anxiety. Was Symmons taking longer than usual? There was no benefit in posing unnecessary questions. O'Farrell checked his watch. Jill would be at the remedial center by now. A busy day, she'd predicted, at breakfast: eight patients at least. O'Farrell was glad his wife had gone back to physiotherapy now the kids had left home: gave her a proper outside interest and prevented her becoming bored. More unimportant musing, O'Farrell recognized, gratefully: not that he considered Jill unimportant in any way. He sometimes believed that was how she regarded him, though: secretly, of course, never any open accusation. He wished she didn't. But it must be difficult for her to accept his supposedly being an accounts clerk, knowing as she did of his Special Forces beginning.

O'Farrell turned away from the window as Symmons looked up at last. "Time to play games," the man announced.

O'Farrell got up and went to the side table, wondering what the sequence would be today: it was necessary for Symmons to vary the psychological assessment to prevent his being able automatically to complete the tests. O'Farrell realized it was to be physical coordination and judgment as Symmons began setting out the differently shaped blocks and wood bases.

"Three minutes," the doctor said.

Two less than normal. Why the reduced completion span? No time to speculate: he only had three minutes. O'Farrell curbed the nervousness, feeling out in apparent control to fit the shapes correctly into their receiving places. They were different from any he had used before, again necessary to prevent his becoming accustomed. More difficult, he determined; he was sure they were more difficult. Some were carved and shaped almost identically and he made three consecutive mistakes before matching them to the board, in his frustration once almost dropping a piece. Careful, he told himself. Stupid to become frustrated and panicked. *Exactly* how the test was devised to

make him behave. So *exactly* why he had to do the opposite. There were still two pieces unconnected when
Symmons said, "Stop!"

He had failed before to complete fully, O'Farrell reassured himself. On several occasions, in fact: but not for a
long time. It didn't matter: by itself it didn't matter at all.

"A bitch this time, eh?" Symmons suggested.

O'Farrell knew there was no remark, no apparent aside,
that was insignificant during these sessions. He smiled and
said, "Next time we'll set up side bets." That sounded
good enough, someone unworried by a minor setback.

"Let's try some words now."

O'Farrell folded one hand casually over the other,
crossing his legs as he did so, wanting to appear relaxed.
It gave him the opportunity to feel for any wetness in his
palms. No sweat at all, he decided, relieved.

"Mother," set off Symmons, abruptly.

"Disaster." Why this beginning? Symmons knew the
story, but they hadn't talked about it for a long time.

"Violence."

"Peace," responded O'Farrell, at once. Why violence,
of all words?

"Death."

"Dishonor." The trigger words were not supposed to be
connected but there was a link here, surely?

"Water."

"Boat." Easier, thought O'Farrell.

"Money."

"Debt." Why the hell had he said that! He wasn't in
debt—had never been in debt—but the answer could indicate he had financial difficulties.

"Country."

"Patriot." Which was sincerely how he felt about himself: the justification—no, the solid basis—for much of
what he did. *All* of what he did, in fact.

"Dog."

"Bone." Nothing wrong that time.

"Fuck."

"Obscenity." Another change from normal: O'Farrell couldn't remember Symmons swearing before.

"God."

"Devil."

"Right."

"Wrong."

"Plastic."

"Cup." It caught O'Farrell as absurd and he came dangerously close to laughing, only just managing to subdue a reaction he knew to be wrong. Nothing insignificant, he thought again.

"Boy."

"Son." Saturday tomorrow: the day for the weekly call to John. Stop drifting! No room now for inconsequential intrusions.

"Car."

"Engine."

"Oppressor."

"Russia." It *had* to do with his mother!

"Murder."

"Crime." Another link, to the first two words, surely!

"Gun."

"Weapon." And again! O'Farrell thought he could feel some dampness on his hands now.

"School."

"Class."

"Capital."

"Punishment." Damn! The man had meant "capitol."

"Birth."

Death was the first word that entered O'Farrell's mind, the reply he should have given according to the rules of the examination. Cheating, he said, "Baby."

"Age."

"Retire."

"Rat."

"Enemy." Could have done better there.

"Accuse."

"Defend."

"Traitor."

"Spy."

"Hang."

"Kill" was the word but O'Farrell didn't say it: his mind wouldn't produce a substitute and Symmons said, "Quicker! You're not allowed to consider the responses! You know that! Hang."

"Picture."

"Sex."

"Wrong." Why the hell had he said that; it didn't even make sense! O'Farrell hoped the perspiration wasn't obvious on his face.

"Gamble."

"Streak."

"Family."

"Life."

"Wife."

"Protector." Better: much better.

"Sentence."

"Justice." Damn again! Why hadn't he said something like "words" or "book"!

"Evil."

"Destroy." How he felt. But maybe there should have been a different reply. It sounded like a piece of dialogue from one of those ridiculous revenge films where the hero bulged with muscles and glistened with oil and could take out twenty opponents with a flick of his wrist without disarranging his hairstyle.

"Dedication."

Once more O'Farrell stopped short of the instinctive response—"absolute"—but without the hesitation that had brought about the previous rebuke. He said, "Resolution."

Symmons raised both hands in a warding-off gesture and said, "Okay. Enough!"

Enough for what or for whom? queried O'Farrell. He

wasn't sure (careful, never decide upon anything unless you're absolutely sure) but he had the impression of another change from their earlier encounters: before this Ping-Pong of words had always seemed to last longer than it had today. Continuing the analogy, O'Farrell wondered who had won the game. He wanted desperately to ask the psychologist how he had done, but he didn't. The question would have shown an uncertain man and he could never be shown to be uncertain. O'Farrell said, without sufficient thought, "You sure?"

Symmons smiled, a baring of teeth more than a humorous expression. He said, "That's the trouble. Ever being sure."

Don't react, thought O'Farrell: the stupid bastard was playing another sort of word game. What the fuck (obscene, he remembered) right did this supposedly scientific, aloof son of a bitch have to make judgments on the state of someone else's mind? Didn't statistics prove that these jerks—psychiatrists or psychologists or whatever they liked to call themselves—had the highest mentally disordered suicide rates of any claimed medical profession? Important to present the correct reaction, O'Farrell thought: glibly confident, he decided. He said, "Your problem, doc: you're the one who's got to be sure."

"You're right," agreed the other man, discomfortingly. "My problem; always my problem."

Symmons smiled, waiting, and O'Farrell smiled back, waiting. The silence built up, growing pressure behind a weakened dam about to burst. Mustn't break, O'Farrell told himself. Mustn't break; couldn't break. It had to be Symmons who spoke first: who had to give in.

He did. The psychologist said, "How do you feel about colors?"

O'Farrell smiled again, enjoying his victory, and said, "Why don't you find out?"

O'Farrell considered the color test—matching colors, identifying colors, blending colors into the right sections of a spectrum divided into primary hues—easier than the verbal inquisition and finished it feeling quite satisfied that he had made no errors; done well, in fact.

The physical examination was as complete as the mental probe. O'Farrell, well aware of the procedure, stripped to a tied-at-the-back operation gown and subjected himself to two hours of intense and concentrated scrutiny. Symmons put him in a soundproof room for audio tests and plunged it into absolute blackness for the eyesight check. Before putting O'Farrell on a treadmill, the man took blood samples, as well as checking blood pressure and lung capacity. The man gradually increased the treadmill speed, pushing O'Farrell to an unannounced but obviously predetermined level. O'Farrell was panting and weak-legged when it finished.

O'Farrell was weighed and measured—thighs and chest and waist as well as biceps—and touched his toes for Symmons to make an anal investigation and spread his legs and coughed when Symmons told him to cough.

O'Farrell dressed unhurriedly, wanting some small redress for the indignities. He fixed and then refixed his tie and arranged the tuck of his shirt around a hard waist to spread the creases and carefully parted and combed his hair. The reflected image was of a neat, unobtrusive, unnoticed man, fading fair hair cropped close against the encroaching gray; smooth-faced; open, untroubled eyes; no shake or twitching mannerisms visible at all. All right, thought O'Farrell, actually moving his lips in voiceless conversation with himself; you're all right, so don't worry.

"Will I live?" he demanded as he emerged from the dressing area, caught by the cynicism of a further attempt at glibness. That was all right, too: Symmons didn't know. Only a very few people knew.

Symmons stayed hunched over the formidable bundle of files and documents and folders that constituted O'Farrell's medical record. Symmons said, "A shade over one hundred and forty-eight pounds?"

"I saw it register on the machine."

"The same as you were twenty years ago." Symmons smiled up at him. "That's remarkable at forty-six: there's usually a weight increase whether you like it or not."

"I suppose I'm lucky."

"Still not smoking?"

"Hardly likely I'll start now, is it?"

"And still only one martini at night?"

"No more." That was near truth enough.

"What about worries?"

"I don't have any."

"Everyone has something to worry about," challenged the man.

But what precisely was the *something*—the doubt—making him feel as he did? O'Farrell said, "Lucky again, I guess."

"That makes you a very unusual guy indeed," Symmons insisted.

"I don't think of myself being unusual in any way," O'Farrell said. Didn't he?

"What about money difficulties?"

Damn that reaction to the financial question. O'Farrell said, with attempted forcefulness, "None."

"None at all?" pressed Symmons.

"No."

"What about sex? Everything okay between you and Jill?"

They did not make love with the regularity or with the need they'd once had, but when they did, it was always good. O'Farrell said, "Everything's fine."

"What about elsewhere?"

"Elsewhere?" O'Farrell asked, choosing to misunderstand.

"Any sudden affairs?"

It was a fairly regular question, acknowledged O'Farrell. Getting satisfaction from the reply, he said, "None."

"You've said that before," the doctor reminded him unnecessarily.

"It's been true before, like it is now."

"Not a lot of guys who say that are telling the truth."

"I am," said O'Farrell, who was. He'd never ever considered another woman, knew he never would.

"Jill must be a very special lady."

"She is," said O'Farrell, bridling.

The psychologist discerned the reaction at once. "It worry you to talk about her?"

"It worries me to talk about her in the context of screwing somebody else." Where was he being led? "Jill hasn't got any part of this," he said.

"Any part of what?"

"What I do." Fucked you, you self-satisfied bastard, he thought, knowing that Symmons couldn't ask the obvious follow-up question.

"That worry you, what you do?"

O'Farrell swallowed at the ease of the other man's escape. "No," he said, pleased with the evenness of his own voice. "What I do doesn't worry me."

"What does worry you?"

"I told you already: nothing."

"Been to the graves lately?"

It had been a long time coming. "Not for quite a while."

"Why not?"

"No particular reason."

"That used to worry you," the psychologist said.

O'Farrell felt the slight dampness of discomfort again. "Wrong emotion," he insisted. "It was sadness that something that happened to her so young made her later do what she did."

"Lose her mind, you mean?" Symmons was goading him.

"That. And the rest."

"Never feel any guilt? That you could have done more but didn't?"

"No," O'Farrell insisted again. "No one knew. Guessed."

"Looks like that's it, then," Symmons said abruptly.

O'Farrell had not expected the sudden conclusion. He said, "See you in three months then?" The squirrels were still swarming over the trees. O'Farrell had an irrational urge to ask the man if they damaged his garden but decided against it: he couldn't give a damn whether they chewed up everything.

"Maybe," Symmons said, noncommittal.

He would be expected to respond to the doubt, O'Farrell realized. So he didn't. He let Symmons lead him back across the coldly patterned hallway and at the entrance gave the perfunctory farewell handshake. Because he guessed the man might be watching from some vantage point, he did not hesitate when he got into the car, as if he needed to recover, but started the engine at once. He carefully controlled his exit, not overaccelerating to make the wheels spin but going out as fast as he could, an unconcerned man wanting to get back to work as quickly as possible after an intrusive disruption. Which he actually didn't want to do. He was only about thirty minutes—forty-five at the outside—from Lafayette Square, and Petty would expect him to come in, but O'Farrell decided on unaccustomed impulse not to bother. A call would do. Start the weekend early, instead: that was what half the people in Washington did anyway.

O'Farrell drove without any positive goal, the road dropping constantly toward the capital. He *had* done all right, he decided, repeating the dressing-room assurance. But he'd been stupid to try to find significance in Symmons's questions: he'd have to avoid that next time. There'd been one or two moments when he'd come near to making mistakes by wrongly concentrating upon what

the psychologist meant rather than upon what he was saying, but nothing disastrous.

Jill wouldn't be home yet. And she might think it odd
if he were in the house ahead of her, because it hardly ever
happened. Maybe he should go to Lafayette Square after
all. No, he rejected once more. What then? O'Farrell
started to concentrate on his surroundings and realized he
was near Georgetown and made another impulsive decision. If he were going to goof off, why not really goof off?

O'Farrell got a parking place on Jefferson and walked
back up to M Street, choosing the bar at random. Inside,
he sat at the bar itself, selecting with professionally in-
stilled instinct a stool at its very end, where there was a
wall closing off one side. He hesitated only momentarily
when the barman inquired: the martini was adequate but
not as good as those he made at home.

Why was he doing this? It was out of pattern, a definite
break in routine, and he wasn't supposed—wasn't
allowed—to do anything contrary to pattern or routine.
But where was the harm! He was just goofing off a couple
of hours early, that's all. It wasn't as if he were on assignment: never took risks on assignment. No harm then. Have
to call Petty, though. But not yet: plenty of time to do that.
From along the counter the barman looked at him ques-
tioningly, and briefly O'Farrell considered another drink
but then shook his head. Only one, he'd assured the psychologist. What about when he got home? So maybe it
would be one of those nights when he'd have another. No
reason why he shouldn't have more than one, like he did
occasionally. Just a small pattern break, still no harm.

O'Farrell lingered for another fifteen minutes before going to the pay phone further into the bar, glad that temporarily there was no music. He dialed the number of Petty's
private telephone, the one on his desk. The man answered
without any identification, and O'Farrell didn't name himself either.

"Where are you?" his controller asked.

"Thought I'd go home early," O'Farrell said. Now he'd told Petty, he wasn't even goofing off anymore.

There was a momentary pause. "Sure," the man agreed. "How did it go?"

"Like it always does."

"Was he happy?"

You get the official reports, I don't, O'Farrell thought. He said, "Seemed to be."

"Have a good weekend then."

"You too."

O'Farrell used the Key Bridge and chose the Washington Memorial Parkway instead of the inner highway, wanting to drive along the Potomac. He did so gazing across the river, picking out the needle of the Washington Monument and the Capitol dome. The word stuck in his mind, from that day's assessment. And then others. Country. And patriot. Which really was how he felt: he was a free man in a free and beautiful country and it was right that he should feel—that he should *be*—patriotic toward it. And he was; O'Farrell reckoned it would be difficult to find many other men prepared to take their patriotic duty as seriously as he did.

Jill was already home. He kissed her and asked about her day and she complained it had been busy and asked about his, and he said his had been, too. She believed him to be a financial analyst at the State Department with particular responsibility for the budgets of overseas embassies, which provided a satisfactory explanation for those sudden foreign trips; when he was not employed in his true function O'Farrell actually did work on accounts, those of the CIA's Plans Directorate. Of everything, O'Farrell found the pretense with his wife the most difficult to maintain: she trusted him absolutely and every day of their married life since joining the Agency he'd lied to her.

The martini he made for himself was a proper one, with a bite that caught in the throat; he slightly overfilled the shaker, so he had to take a sip to make room for the remainder. Two and a half, he thought as he did so. No harm at all.

O'Farrell took the glass to the den, placing it carefully on the side table away from his desk, where there was no danger of anything accidentally spilling on the clippings. He kept them in a thick book, covered in genuine Moroccan leather. He opened it familiarly but at random, eyes not immediately focusing on the words. It was the obituary. It was practically a eulogy, running almost to two columns: THE MAN WHO BROUGHT LAW TO THE TERRITORY was the headline. O'Farrell became conscious of the words shifting and realized his hands were shaking, very slightly. Just the weight of the book, he told himself, trying to concentrate upon the account again but finding it difficult because of another intrusive thought.

O'Farrell forced himself to confront it. Had his great-grandfather ever questioned what he had to do, been unsure whether he could go on doing it? The way O'Farrell was starting to question what he was called upon to do?

There was one part of the diplomatic bag, a specially sealed and marked satchel, which no one but the ambassador was allowed to open, and the ambassador, upon strict orders from Havana itself, always had to be available instantly to receive it.

José Gaviria Rivera recognized the necessity for such precautions but was frequently inconvenienced by them. As he was tonight. He'd allowed a two-hour fail-safe between its expected arrival and the time he had to be in the reserved Covent Garden box alongside a mistress about whom, almost disconcertingly, he felt differently than he'd felt about any other. But because of fog the damned aircraft had been diverted to Manchester. So he couldn't make the curtain. She'd said she understood when he'd telephoned, coquettishly insisting she would punish him for it later, but Rivera actually enjoyed *La Bohème*; this

was an acclaimed production and he had wanted to see all
of it, not merely a segment. So it was at the moment difficult to convince himself that the system really had the
highest priority. Not that Rivera would ever have neglected business for pleasure, even for someone as plea-
surable as Henrietta. Internal as well as external spying
was an important function for those members of the
Dirección Generale de Inteligencia posing under diplomatic cover within the embassy. Because of the special demands being made upon him, Rivera had succeeded in
putting himself above any sort of prying whatsoever. He
was fully aware how much those specific orders from Havana were resented by the local station chief, Carlos
Mendez. And how very anxious the man was to send an
adverse report back to Cuba.

Rivera sighed, striding back and forth in front of the
window of his office. Perhaps he should be philosophical
in another way: perhaps the sexual punishment for one act
would make up for missing the first of another. Had he allowed himself to consider the emotion, which of course
was unthinkable, Rivera might have imagined himself in
love with Henrietta.

It was almost an hour before the diplomatic bag arrived
and his personal "Eyes Only" satchel was hurried to him.
Rivera let the breath go heavily from himself, forming a
whistle, as he read the demand. It was far greater than ever
before, far beyond the usual small arms and handguns and
low-caliber ammunition, although they were included. This
time he had to supply ground-to-air missiles and sophisticated communication equipment; there was even a request
for tanks, if they could be supplied.

Rivera sat back, gazing sightlessly at the door, momentarily curious. Where was it all destined to go? Nicaragua
was an obvious recipient, despite the supposed peace ac-
cord with the Contras. Maybe Honduras. Or Panama, perhaps; the government there might, after thumbing its nose
at Washington, consider an arms buildup a sensible insur-

ance. What about the guerrillas in Colombia, the country upon which it all depended anyway?

Rivera shrugged. It did not really matter, wherever it was. His part began and ended with European arms dealers. And even before making the most preliminary of inquiries, Rivera knew the cost would be incredible. He smiled. And not all of that incredible expenditure was actually going to be spent upon the weaponry he was being ordered to buy.

Rivera knew precisely his importance in Havana's drugs-for-arms—arms-for-drugs chain: without him there wouldn't even be a chain. So it was right that such expertise be properly rewarded. Ten percent was the usual fee he awarded himself, but this was a much bigger consignment than any he'd handled before. It was going to take a lot of organizing. He considered that his unofficial commission should go up commensurately. He didn't doubt that those at the other end of the chain, those Cuban diplomats entrusted through embassies and legations and missions with the drug distribution, were making far greater personal profits than he was. Not that Rivera was jealous. He knew he would not have enjoyed being a money raiser, actually dealing in cocaine. That would have been much too dangerous.

THREE

O'FARRELL'S OBSERVANCE of order and routine extended into his private life. It was a Saturday, and on Saturdays his first job was to clean the cars. He always did it early because it meant backing the vehicles out of the narrow garage onto Fairfax, with a view of the Old Presbyterian Meeting House. By midmorning, particularly in the spring and summer, Alexandria became thronged with tourists, and he liked to finish before they arrived. Not that he wasn't proud to live in such a historic township. The reverse. O'Farrell got real pleasure from residing in a township where George Washington and Robert E. Lee had once lived; he knew all its history and its landmarks and talked knowledgeably on the few occasions when he had been trapped by early visitors. But those occasions had been very few; O'Farrell shunned casual contact, even with anonymous tourists: certainly with anonymous tourists carrying cameras that might record him.

Today there was an additional reason for wanting to be outside. After the two and a half martinis of the previous night he'd awoken with an ache banded like a cord around his head, and he needed to get out into the air.

It was warm, despite being early, and apart from the headache O'Farrell was comfortable in jeans and shirt sleeves. There was, of course, a pattern to the cleaning. He hosed the car down first, to soften the dirt and dust, washed it off with soapy water, and then hosed it down again before toweling away the excess water. He completed the drying with a chamois cloth and finished off by polishing with more toweling.

O'Farrell enjoyed engines. They performed to predetermined orderliness, dozens of independent parts making up a complete whole. He supposed that tinkering with the workings of his car and Jill's had been his only hobby until he'd started upon the ancestral archive. He greased them and balanced them and tuned them, and as he finished off the cleaning O'Farrell decided that the care and attention paid off. The paintwork of both had practically the same showroom sheen, which they wouldn't have had if he'd stop-started them through some plastic-brushed car wash. There wasn't any rust, not so much as a warning stain behind any of the decorative metalwork. O'Farrell reckoned he would easily get another four years out of each vehicle before trading them in.

By which time he would be fifty, O'Farrell calculated, reversing the Ford back into its garage. Retirement age; another word association from the previous day. Not slippers and pipe and walking-the-dog sort of retirement. He'd have to wait another ten years for that, patiently reviewing and assessing the Plans Directorate finances full-time. But spared that other function, that other function he increasingly felt unable to perform. Dear God, how much he wanted to be spared that again! What were his chances? Impossible to compute. The last time had been more than a year ago—the first occasion he had felt nervous and hesitated and almost made a disastrous mistake—and between that assignment and the one before there had been an interval of almost three years. Always possible, then, that he wouldn't be called upon again: possible but unlikely, he thought, forcing the objectivity. So why didn't he simply quit? Go to Petty and Erickson and tell them how he felt and ask to be taken off the active roster? He knew there were others, although naturally he wasn't aware of their names. Not as good as he was, according to Petty, but O'Farrell put that down to so much obvious bullshit, the sort the controller doubtless said to them all.

So why didn't he just quit? Had his great-grandfather ever backed down? O'Farrell wondered, attempting to answer one question with another. Bullshit of his own now. Until these handshaking doubts, O'Farrell had always found it easy to consider himself a law officer like his great-grandfather, merely obeying different rules to match different circumstances. Now he acknowledged that if he made the analogy with objective honesty, what he did and what his ancestor had done in the 1860s were hugely different. So that answer didn't wash. What did? O'Farrell didn't know, not completely. There was a combination of reasons, not sufficient by themselves but enough when he assembled them all together, the way the individual parts of an automobile engine came together into something that made functional sense. Different though his job might be from that of his great-grandfather, he *was* enforcing justice. It was something very few people could do. (Would want to do, echoed a doubting voice in his mind.) And he genuinely did not want to back down, submit to an emotion he could only regard as weakness, although weakness wasn't really what it was.

There was also the money to consider, reluctant though he was to bring it into any equation because he found the self-criticism (blood money? bounty hunter?) too easily disturbing. For what he did he was paid $100,000 a year, $50,000 tax-free channeled through CIA-maintained offshore accounts. The system enabled him to live in this historically listed house in Alexandria and help John now that he'd quit the airline to go back to school for his master's. It enabled him and Jill to fly up to Chicago whenever they felt like it to visit Ellen and the boy.

He *wouldn't* quit, O'Farrell determined. He'd get a grip on himself and stop constantly having such damned silly doubts and see out his remaining four years. If he were called upon to take up an assignment, he'd carry it out as successfully and as undetectably as he'd carried out all the others in the past. Not that many, in fact. Just five. Each justified. Each guilty. Each properly sentenced, albeit by an unofficial tribunal. And each performed—albeit unofficially again—in the name of the country of which he was a patriot.

Jill's car was smaller than his, a Toyota, and it did not take O'Farrell as long to clean as the Ford. He did it just as meticulously, seeking rust that he could not find, and regained the house before the tourist invasion.

O'Farrell was relieved by the decision he'd reached. And his headache had gone, like his inner tension.

O'Farrell and Jill drank coffee while they waited for

eight o'clock Arizona time, knowing that John would be waiting for their call. In the event it was Beth who answered, because John was upstairs with Jeff. O'Farrell, immediately concerned, asked what was wrong with his grandson, and Beth said "nothing," and then John came on the line to repeat the assurance. He thanked O'Farrell for the last check but said he was embarrassed to take it. O'Farrell told his son not to be so proud and to keep a record so that John could pay him back when he got his degree and after that the sort of job he wanted. It was not arranged that they call their daughter in Chicago until the afternoon and when they did, they got her answering machine, which they didn't expect because Ellen knew the time they would be calling; it was the same every weekend. Always had been and particularly after the divorce. They left a message that they had called and hoped everything was all right and tried once more before going out that evening and got the machine again, so they left a second recording.

"That's not like her," said Jill as they drove into town. They used her car because, being smaller, it was easier to park.

"It's happened before," said O'Farrell. It had become so ingrained over the years in his professional life not to overrespond (certainly never to panic) that O'Farrell found it impossible to react differently in his private life. Or did he?

"Why didn't she call us? She knows we like to speak every week."

"There's all day tomorrow," O'Farrell pointed out, going against his own need for regularity. He wished Jill had adjusted better to the collapse of Ellen's marriage; she found it difficult to believe their daughter preferred to make her own life with her son in faraway Chicago rather than come back to Alexandria or somewhere close, where they would be near, caring for her.

"I wonder if something has happened to Billy," said Jill, in sudden alarm.

"If something *had* happened to Billy, she would have gotten a message through to us."

"I don't like it."

"You're getting upset for no reason." Routine sometimes had its disadvantages, he thought.

There was some roadwork on Memorial Bridge but the delay wasn't too bad and they still got into town in good time, because O'Farrell always allowed for traffic problems. He found a parking place at once on 13th Street and as they walked down toward Pennsylvania he said, "We've time for a drink, if you like."

Jill looked at him curiously. "If you want one."

"It's practically an hour before the curtain," O'Farrell pointed out. "The alternative is just to sit and wait."

"Okay," she said, without enthusiasm.

They went to the Round Robin room at the Willard and managed seats against the wall, beneath the likenesses of people like Woodrow Wilson and Walt Whitman and Mark Twain and even a droop-mustached Buffalo Bill Cody, all of whom had used it in the past. O'Farrell got the drinks— martini for himself, white wine for Jill—and stood looking at the drawings. Had his great-grandfather encountered William Cody? he wondered. The martini could have been better.

There had been a lot of noise from a group on the far side of the small room when they'd entered and it became increasingly louder, breaking out into a full-blown argument. There were five people, two couples and a man by himself; the arguers appeared to be one of the couples and the unattached man was attempting to intervene and placate both of them. O'Farrell heard "fuck" and "bastard" like everyone else in the room and the barman said, "Easy now: let's take it easy, eh folks?" They ignored him. The would-be mediator put his hand on the arguing man's arm and was shoved away, hard, so that he staggered back toward the bar and collided with another customer, spilling his drink. The barman called out, "That's enough, okay!" and the woman said, "Oh, my God!" and began to cry. O'Farrell gauged the distance to the only exit against the nearness of the disturbance and decided that the shouting group was closer. Better to wait where they were than attempt to leave and risk getting involved. The man who'd staggered back apologized and gestured for the spilled drink to be replaced and went back to his group, jabbing with outstretched fingers at the chest of the man who'd pushed him. Waste of effort, thought O'Farrell: at least three inches from the point in the chest that would have brought the man down, and the carotid in the neck was better exposed anyway. The bridge of the nose, too. And the temple and the lower rib and the inner ankle. The killing pressure points that he'd been trained so well how to use—but only in extreme emergency, because the absolutely essential rule was always to avoid possible recognition by an intended victim—reeled off in his mind until O'Farrell consciously stopped the reflection. It was prohibited for him to become involved in any sort of dispute or altercation, to attract the slightest attention, official or otherwise.

"Why doesn't someone do something!" Jill demanded, beside him. "Look at her, poor woman!"

"Someone will have sent for security," O'Farrell said, and as he spoke two uniformed guards came into the room and began herding the group away, ignoring their protests.

Jill shuddered and said, "That was awful!"

"Embarrassing, that's all," O'Farrell said. "They were drunk."

"I didn't like it." Jill shuddered again.

It wasn't being a very successful day, O'Farrell thought. He said, "Do you want another drink?"

"No," she said, at once. "Surely you don't, either?"

"No," said O'Farrell. There would easily have been time. "We might as well go, then."

They emerged from the hotel through the main Pennsylvania Avenue exit and immediately saw the group continuing their argument. The crying woman was still weeping and her hair was disarrayed. The other woman was trying to pull her male companion away and he was making weak protests, clearly anxious to get out of the situation, but not wanting to be seen to do so. As O'Farrell and his wife looked, the man who appeared to be at the center of the dispute lashed out; the disheveled woman somehow didn't see the movement and the open-handed blow caught her fully in the side of the face, sending her first against the hotel wall and then sprawling across the sidewalk. When she tried to get up, he hit her again, keeping her down. Neither of the other two men attempted to intrude. One allowed his companion to pull him away, and the other, the one who had made an effort in the bar, visibly shrugged off responsibility.

"Do something!" Jill insisted. "Somebody do something! He's going to hit her again."

The man did, and this time the woman stayed down. Distantly O'Farrell thought he heard the wail of a police siren. He took Jill's arm, forcibly leading her back into the hotel toward the long corridor that bisected the building to F Street.

"We can't walk away!" Jill said. "She could be hurt."

"It's okay," O'Farrell said. "It's all being taken care of."

"What are you talking about!"

"Didn't you hear the sirens?" She'd expected him to intervene, he knew. And was disappointed that he hadn't.

"No!"

"I did. They're coming."

On the pavement outside, on F Street, Jill stopped, head to one side. "I still don't hear anything."

"They'll have gotten there by now: police, ambulance, everyone." O'Farrell wondered why he was shaking, and why his hands were wet, as well. Jill would think him weak, a runaway coward.

"He could have killed her."

"No," O'Farrell said.

"How do you know?"

How do I know! Because I'm an acknowledged and recognized expert, O'Farrell thought: that's what I do! He said, "It was one of those lovers' things, matrimonial. An hour from now they'll be in the sack, making up."

"Can you imagine anyone capable of hurting another human being like that!"

"No," O'Farrell said again, more easily now because he'd learned to field questions like that. "I can't imagine it."

The show was at the National Theater so they cut down 14th Street, pausing at the Marriott corner to look back along the opposite block. O'Farrell saw, relieved, that the ambulance and police vehicles were there. "See?" he said, snatching the small victory. The fighting couple were side by side now, the woman shaking her head in some denial or refusal, the man with his arm protectively around her shoulder.

"I can't imagine that, either," Jill said.

"Probably even turns them on."

The play was a regional theater company's far too experimental performance of *Oedipus* that had been under-rehearsed and mounted too soon. O'Farrell insisted on their going to the bar during intermission—switching to gin and tonic this time, because he wasn't prepared to risk the martinis—and when they went back into the auditorium a lot of people, practically an entire row at the rear of the orchestra, hadn't bothered to return. O'Farrell wished he and Jill hadn't, either. Throughout, Jill sat pulled away from him, against the far arm of her seat.

Afterward, certainly without sufficient thought, O'Farrell suggested they eat, and at once Jill said, "Ellen might have called."

In the car she continued to sit away from him, as she had in the theater. Neither spoke until they'd crossed the river again, back into Virginia.

"It wasn't very good, was it?"

"Dreadful."

"So much for the *Post* review." An altogether bad day, O'Farrell thought again.

"I still don't care," Jill blurted suddenly.

"Care about what?"

"If it were a lovers' quarrel or what the hell it was: I couldn't understand no one going to help that woman."

It was the nearest she'd come to an outright accusation, he guessed. It wasn't a good feeling, believing Jill despised him. He said, "It would have been ridiculous for me to have become involved. He might have had a gun, a knife, anything. You really think I should have risked being killed?"

"I wasn't thinking of you," Jill said, unconvincingly.

Overly defensive, O'Farrell said. "There's you to worry about, and John and everyone in Phoenix to worry about, and Ellen and Billy to worry about. You think I'm going to endanger so many people I love!" Hadn't he endangered them too many times? he asked himself.

"It just upset me, that's all."

"Forget it."

"I'm sorry. I know you're right. You're always right."

"I said forget it." What would she have thought if he had gone in, reducing the bullying bastard to blubbering jelly? Another preposterous reflection: he never entered an unarmed combat training session—and he still went through two a month—without the prior injunction that his expertise was strictly limited to what he did professionally and should never be employed in any other circumstance.

Ellen's call was waiting on their machine and he let Jill return it, very aware of her need. He sat opposite her in the living room, near the bookshelves, smiling in expectation of his wife's smile of relief at whatever explanation Ellen gave. But a smile didn't come.

Instead, in horror, Jill exclaimed, "What!"

There was no way O'Farrell could hear Ellen's reply but his wife apparently cut their daughter off in the middle, telling the girl to wait for O'Farrell to get on an extension.

O'Farrell actually ran to the den, snatching up the telephone to say, "What the hell is it!"

"Nothing," said Ellen, in a too obvious attempt at reassurance. "No, that's not quite true. It's important, but Billy isn't involved, isn't in any trouble."

"What!" repeated O'Farrell.

"It was a special meeting of the PTA today," their daughter said. "Very special. All the parents and all the teachers. Like I said, Billy isn't involved; he says he hasn't been approached and we've talked it through and I believe him. But there have been quite a few seizures, so there's no doubt that drugs are in circulation in the school."

"What sort of drugs?" Jill asked.

"Everything," Ellen said. "Even crack. Heroin, too."

"Billy's not nine years old yet!" O'Farrell said.

"Nancy Reagan sought no-drug pledges from nine-year-olds," Ellen reminded them. "And no one's gotten to Billy yet."

"Get out of Chicago," Jill implored. "Come back somewhere around here, near to us."

"You telling me it's any better in Washington?"

"You'd be safer here."

"We're not in any danger here. You asked me where I'd been, and I told you. If I'd imagined this sort of reaction, I might have lied, to spare you the worry."

"We'll come up next weekend," Jill announced.

There was a question in her voice directed toward O'Farrell on the extension and he said, "Yes, we'll come up."

"What for?"

"Because we want to," said her mother decisively. "We haven't been up for a long time; you know that."

"A month," Ellen corrected. "I'm not going to escalate this into a bigger drama than it is, Mother; let Billy imagine it's some big deal that'll attract a lot of family attention if he tries it."

"We won't escalate anything," Jill promised. "We just want to come up. See how you are. That's all."

"I'm fine. Really I'm fine."

"Please let us come up, Ellen," O'Farrell said, requesting rather than insisting.

"You know you don't have to ask," the girl said, softening.

"You sure Billy's all right?"

"Positive."

"What's happening to the people doing it? The dealers?" O'Farrell demanded.

"There haven't been any major arrests yet. Just kids, pushing it to make money to buy more stuff for themselves."

My beautiful country—the country of which I'm proud to be a patriot—being eroded internally by this cancer, O'Farrell thought. He said, "So what *is* going to be done?"

"That was the purpose of the meeting: telling us how to look out for signs. We've set up a kind of parents' watch committee."

For kids not nine years old, thought O'Farrell. He said, "You take care, you hear?" and was immediately annoyed at the banality of the remark.

"Of course I will."

"Tell Billy he can choose whatever treat he wants for next weekend."

"You shouldn't spoil him like you do."

"Call us at once if anything happens," Jill cut in.

"Nothing's going to *happen*, Mother!"

That night, in bed, they lay side by side but untouching,

insulated from each other by their separate thoughts. It was Jill who broke the silence. She said, "I'm sorry, about tonight."

"What about tonight?"

"You were right not getting involved in that scene in the bar. An awful lot of people *do* depend upon you. It would be ridiculous to put anything at risk."

"I won't, ever," O'Farrell said. It did not actually constitute a lie, he told himself, but it was still a promise he could never be sure of keeping.

Petty was engulfed in so much tobacco smoke from his pipe that his voice came disembodied through it; Erickson thought it looked like some poor special effect from one of the late-night television horror movies to which he was addicted.

"Well?" Petty asked, wanting the other man to volunteer an opinion first.

"Certainly appears to go some way toward confirming the impressions Symmons formed three months ago," Erickson said.

Petty picked up the psychologist's report, concentrating only upon the uppermost précis. "But this time Symmons considered it a challenging encounter, that O'Farrell was fighting him."

"Why would O'Farrell want to challenge the man?" the deputy asked. The psychologist hadn't reached a conclusion about the attitude.

"I wish I knew," the controller said, refusing to give one. "I really wish I knew."

"Then there's the preoccupation with violence," Erikson pointed out, going deeper into the report where Symmons had flagged a series of word associations.

"And he talked to himself when he was dressing," Petty added. They knew because a camera was installed behind the mirror into which O'Farrell had gazed, arranging and rearranging his tie and mouthing to himself the assurance that he'd come through the interrogation successfully.

"It happens," Erickson said, with a resigned sigh. Today across Lafayette Park some protesters were marching up and down outside the White House; the angle of the window made it impossible for him to see what the protest was about.

"I don't think we should be too hasty," Petty cautioned.

Erickson turned curiously back into the room. "Use him again, you mean?"

"He *is* good," the huge man insisted.

"*Was*, according to this." Erickson gestured with his copy of the psychologist's report.

"It would be wrong to make a definite decision just on the basis of two doubtful assessments," Petty argued. "There's never been the slightest problem with any operation we've given O'Farrell."

"Isn't that the basis upon which the decision should be made?" Erickson queried. "That there never can be the slightest problem."

"We'll wait," Petty said. "Just wait and see."

For a long time after it happened, Jill used to accompany him to the cemetery, but today O'Farrell hadn't told her he was coming; there hadn't seemed to be any reason for doing so. He guessed he would not have come himself but for the session with Symmons. O'Farrell gazed down at the inscription on his parents' grave, easily able to recall every horrific moment of that discovery, his father blasted beyond recognition, his mother too. And of finding the note, the stumbled attempt of a tortured mind to explain why she was killing the man she loved—and who loved her—and then herself. Oddly, she had not mentioned Latvia and what had happened there: the real explanation for it all. Carefully O'Farrell brushed away the leaves fallen from an overhanging tree and placed the flowers he'd brought, caught by a sudden awareness. He had not real-

ized it until now, but his mother's running amok with a
shotgun coincided almost to the month with his decision to
find out as much as possible about the origins of his settler
great-grandfather, the man who'd become a lawman. The
psychologist would probably be able to find some significance in that if he told the man. But he wouldn't, O'Farrell
decided. He didn't believe there was any relevance.

FOUR

EARLY IN his assignment José Rivera had regretted
that the Cuban embassy was in London's High Holborn
and not one of the impressive mansion legations in Kensington. Estelle, he knew, remained upset, but then his
wife was a snob and easily upset; she considered it reduced them to second-grade diplomats.

Rivera didn't regret the location of the embassy anymore. Carlos Mendez, the resentful local head of the
Dirección Generale de Inteligencia, maintained close contact with the KGB *rezidentura* attached to the Soviet embassy in Kensington, and from Mendez, despite their
limited contact, Rivera knew of the intensive surveillance
imposed there by British counterintelligence. And intensive surveillance was the very last thing to which Rivera
wanted to be subjected. For that reason, once he'd been
given the arms-buying role in Europe, Rivera had persuaded Havana to free him from Mendez's prying. The
given excuse was that arms dealers wouldn't trade if they
thought their comings and goings were being recorded.

The real reason was Rivera's determination to restore a family fortune lost when Fidel Castro came to power.

There was nearly two million dollars so far on deposit in a numbered account at the Swiss Bank Corporation on Zurich's Paradeplatz, all unofficial commissions creamed off previous deals. He was impatient for today's meeting to gauge by how much that amount was likely to increase from the latest huge order from Havana. It would be huge, he calculated; it was a comforting, satisfying feeling. Rivera liked being rich, and wanted to be richer.

Rivera was confident he had established the way. It was always to obtain everything demanded, in less time than was allowed, from men whose names were known only to himself, but no one else. Which made him absolutely indispensable. More than indispensable: unmovable, which was very important.

Rivera liked London. He liked the house in Hampstead and the polo at Windsor. Hardly any part of Europe was more than three hours' flying time away—Zurich even less—and by his upbringing Rivera always considered himself more European than Latin American. Until, like the survivors they were, his family realized Batista's Cuban regime was doomed, they had been among the most fervent supporters of his dictatorship; certainly the family had been among the largest beneficiaries of Batista's corruption. That wealth had ensured Rivera's Sorbonne education and the introduction to a cosmopolitan and sophisticated existence. They'd had to lose it, of course, when Castro came to power. And the teenage Rivera had loathed every minute of the supposed socialist posturing, actually wearing ridiculous combat suits, as if they were all macho guerrillas, and reciting nonsense about equality and freedom.

The life he led now was Rivera's idea of equality and freedom. Realistically he accepted that it would, ultimately, have to end. And with it, he had already decided, would end his diplomatic career. By that time the Zurich account would be larger than it was now—many times larger. At the moment, although he was not irrevocably committed, he favored his boyhood Paris as the city in which he would settle.

It would mean a fairly dramatic· upheaval, but he was preparing himself for it. Rivera cared nothing for Estelle, as she cared nothing for him. They'd stayed together for Jorge, whom they both adored. But Paris would have to be the breaking point. It had taken Rivera a long time to admit the fact but now he had, if only to himself. He loved Henrietta and wanted her in Paris, with him. There wouldn't be any difficulty getting the divorce from Estelle, any more than for Henrietta to divorce her aging husband. The only uncertainty was how Jorge would react. The boy would come to accept it, in time: learn to love Henrietta. There was no question, of course, of Jorge living anywhere but in Paris, with him.

All possible from the biggest arms order he'd ever been called upon to complete.

The ambassador strode across his office to greet the chosen dealer as the man entered, retaining his hand to guide him to a conference area where comfortable oxblood leather chairs and couches were arranged with practised casualness around a series of low tables.

The size of the order had decreed that Pierre Belac had to be the supplier, because he was the biggest Rivera knew. Belac was a neat, gray-suited, gray-haired, clerklike man, in whose blank-eyed, cold company Rivera always felt vaguely uncomfortable. Sometimes he wondered how much profit Belac made from his dealings and would have been staggered had he known.

Observing the preliminary niceties, Rivera said: "A good flight?" Although he knew Belac's English to be excellent, Rivera spoke in French, in which he was fluent: it pleased him to display the ability.

Belac shrugged. "Brussels is very efficient: I suppose it's having NATO and the Common Market headquarters to impress."

"I appreciate your coming so promptly," Rivera said. He thought, as he had before, that it was difficult to imagine this soft-spoken, unemotional man as one of the largest arms dealers in Europe. Rivera did not think that Belac liked him much.

"I am always prompt where money is involved," Belac said. Which was the absolute truth. Belac was obsessive about money, consumed above all else in amassing it. He was unmarried and lived in a rented, one-bedroom, walk-up flat near the main square in Brussels. When he wanted sex he paid a whore, and when he was hungry he used a restaurant, usually a cheap one like the prostitutes he patronized. He thought he had a very satisfying life.

Rivera offered the other man the list that had come in the special satchel. Unhurriedly Belac changed his glasses and took from the waistcoat pocket of his suit a thin gold pencil, using it as a marker to guide himself slowly through the list. He gave no facial reaction but his mind was feverishly calculating the profit margin. It was going to be a fantastic deal, one of the best. He smiled up at Rivera once, thinking as he did so how he was going to lead this glistening, perfumed idiot like a lamb to the slaughter. Rivera smiled back, curious how difficult it would be to outnegotiate Belac as he intended to outnegotiate him. That's all he would do, decided Rivera, nothing more than gain a temporary advantage to profit by. It might be dangerous to consider anything more.

Belac was expressionless when he finally looked up. He said, simply, "Yes."

Rivera guessed that showing no surprise was an essential part of the carefully maintained demeanor. He said, "So it is possible?"

Belac's face broke into the closest he could ever come to a smile. "Everything is possible."

Negotiations were beginning without any preamble, Rivera decided. He said, "But not easy?"

"No difficulty at all with the small arms, rifles, and ammunition. Most of it is available through Czechoslovakia, with no restrictions," said Belac dismissively. "The guidance systems all contain American technology. COCOM, the committee of all the NATO countries, with the addition of Japan, denies official export to communist bloc countries of dual-use technology, meaning anything that could have military application, which this has. Washington—the Commerce and State departments—keep a very tight lid on that."

"How can it be done unofficially?" Rivera demanded. Remaining indispensable—and unmovable—required that he knew in advance any problem likely to arise, no matter how small.

"There are companies in Sweden, with the advantage of its neutrality, through which such things can sometimes be arranged," said Belac. "There will have to be adjustments to End-User Certificates. I have several *anstalt* companies established in Switzerland that can place the Swedish orders; it will still be difficult to find the necessary end-user destination."

Trying to show that he was not completely unaware of backdoor channels, Rivera said, "What about Austria?"

"As a cutoff, perhaps," said Belac, unimpressed but content to let the posturing fool indulge himself if he wished. "But it's become known to the Americans as a door all too often ajar. I have a situation in Vienna we could utilize, maybe. But for this I think we might have to consider repackaging and transporting through the Middle East. There are a number of accommodating states in the Arab Emirates where smuggling is considered a profession of honor."

Rivera paused. Was the man proposing the circuitous routing for reasons of security, or to establish the highest price because of its intricacy? To get a higher price, he decided. He said, "What about the communication items?"

"Exactly the same COCOM barrier as with the guidance systems," the arms dealer said. "Everything listed here contains American technology for which no export license could possibly be obtained." Which made them for Belac the most difficult and dangerous part of the order, particularly as there already existed in America two criminal indictments against him for evading the restrictions upon such items. Belac decided to delay doing anything about them; he would string Rivera along and maybe not attempt them at all.

"The same routing, then?" the Cuban diplomat asked carelessly.

"I don't think so, do you?" Belac said at once. "The English have a proverb warning that if all one's eggs are kept in the same basket, they risk being smashed in an accident."

Damn! thought Rivera, resenting the lecturing, patronizing tone. He said, "How, then?"

"Japan," Belac said. "Very discreet, very efficient. We'll move the communication stuff through Japan. Place the orders direct through the *anstalt* companies but make sure there's alternative, disguising cargo carried at the same time. . . ." The man hesitated, performing his version of a smile again, his mind already calculating the final purchasing figures. "Alternative cargo which you, of course, would have to underwrite. Once at sea, the Swiss holding company will sell the innocent cargo—"

"To a company in Japan," Rivera said. "So in midvoyage the ship will change destination from Europe to the Far East and any forbidden cargo will disappear?" Belac *was* patronizing him! The realization did not annoy Rivera. Rather, he was pleased. Play the gullible customer, the Cuban decided.

Belac nodded in agreement. "It will achieve the purpose, but I do not expect we will be able to dispose of the genuine cargo at anything like a profit. A loss is practically certain."

A loss that Cuba would have to finance to the benefit of the Japanese buyer, Rivera thought; and that Japanese buyer would inevitably be yet another company controlled by Pierre Belac. The grasping pig deserved to be outnegotiated; in its personal, self-rewarding way it would be a fitting penalty for the man's avarice. Luring the Belgian on, Rivera said, "I accept that a loss would be unavoidable. But then, losses are always budgeted for in business. Which leaves the tanks to be discussed."

What the hell did this soft-handed poseur know about business! Belac nodded in agreement once more. "Awkward things, tanks. Cumbersome. Practically impossible to break down into any sort of discreetly transportable size. The shell has to be solid, you see?" Belac was enjoying himself, mainly because he knew how much money he was going to make, to within a thousand dollars. Spurred by his greed, Belac had on occasions taken chances and come close to disaster, although he'd always managed, just, to pull back. There wasn't going to be any danger here. This looked like the easiest deal with which he'd ever become involved. He continued, "But they are available. The United States had a lot mothballed, the majority in the Mojave Desert. The climate is perfect for preservation. Virtually no metal or engine deterioration at all."

"Available?" queried Rivera.

"Periodically," the Belgian said. "Fortunately for us, there is to be a surplus sale in the next two or three months."

Everything seemed to be very easy, Rivera reflected, happy for the man to make his sales pitch. He said, "Fortunate indeed."

"Providing the interest is not too intense," Belac qualified. "There hasn't been any sort of release on the market for more than a year. Most of the important dealers throughout the world will be there, bidding."

"And the bidding will be high?" Rivera guessed the profit Belac was writing in for himself would be huge.

"It will be a seller's market, won't it?" Belac said, answering question with question.

"You'll need to be able to outbid anyone else?" Rivera asked in apparent further anticipation. He found it difficult to believe that Belac was leading the bargaining precisely in the direction he wanted. It was almost too simple.

"If you are to get what you want," the Belgian agreed. "Substantial funds in advance, in fact?"

"Yes," Belac said. It was too early to start talking figures yet: there was more he could get. Picking up the shopping list, Belac said, "And there would seem to be an omission."

"Omission?" He would not remain indispensable and unmovable if things were left out, Rivera thought, immediately alarmed.

"Spares," Belac said. "The stipulation is for a maximum of fifty tanks but nowhere is there a mention of spares for them. You know that something as inconsequential as a failed spark plug can incapacitate a vehicle costing a million dollars?" Appearing at once to realize his error, Belac quickly added, "Probably a lot more than a million dollars."

"Yes," Rivera conceded. "I suppose it would. So there must be an additional allowance for spares?"

"Essential," the Belgian said. "A tank that won't work is a useless piece of metal, isn't it?"

Rivera guessed the man had a scrap-metal business to accommodate that eventuality as well. "Spares should be added to the list," he agreed.

"A very substantial list," mused the Belgian, shifting the responsibility for guiding the conversation onto Rivera.

"How long, to provide everything?" the diplomat demanded.

Belac humped his shoulders, reluctant to be trapped too easily into a commitment. "Three months," he said. "Maybe four."

"There would need to be a completion date," Rivera pressed. The letter accompanying the order, a letter only

Rivera had read, had insisted on six months as a maximum.

"Four," Belac said.

The moment for which he'd been patiently waiting, Rivera recognized. "This is not the business of legally binding contracts," he said. "What guarantees will exist between us?"

"Mutual, reciprocal trust," Belac said easily.

Horseshit, thought Rivera. "Would it not be better, perhaps, if I took some of the smaller items elsewhere, spread the order among lesser dealers?"

"No!" Belac said, greedily and too quickly. "I can handle it all. It's far better to keep it all simple, just between us two."

"You can guarantee the four months then?"

"My word," Belac said. He couldn't be forced to keep it.

"We haven't yet discussed price," Rivera said, spread-eagling himself upon the sacrificial stone.

Belac went through the charade of examining the list again, as if he were only then making his calculations. Rivera guessed he had nearly everything priced practically down to the last half-dollar.

"Ninety million," Belac announced. Hurriedly again, he added, "But that would merely be for the purchases. In addition there would have to be allowances for transportation. Money will also have to be paid out for the switching of the End-User Certificates. So there will need to be provision for extensive commission payments. Say another ten million."

Most definitely the need for extensive commission payments, thought Rivera; the euphoria swept through him. Even if he modestly maintained his own personal commission at ten percent on the purchase price, that would mean ten million. Keeping any excitement from his voice, Rivera said, "Won't there also need to be a substantial, instantly available sum to enable the on-the-spot bidding for the tanks?"

"A further fifty million," Belac declared at once.

Which meant a further five million for him, mentally echoed Rivera, feeling another flush of excitement. He would keep his share to ten percent: on such figures it would be greedy to think of more. On a profit of fifteen million he'd definitely quit, when the deal was completed. "There will be a need to consult, of course," he said. "But I don't see the slightest problem with those figures."

Immediate anger surged through Belac. He'd thought a clear twenty-million-dollar profit, which was what he'd allowed himself, to be as high as he dared push it, but from the other man's reaction he could have gone even higher! "That's good to hear," Belac said, although it hadn't been good to hear at all.

"I would expect a response within a week."

"Let's meet again in a week, then?" The Belgian sat with the complacency of a winner in everything, the anger going. There still might be ways to edge the profit up. And twenty million was a lot of money anyway.

"And this time let me come to you in Brussels," Rivera offered. The man would feel more confident in his own surroundings.

Belac hesitated briefly. "As you wish."

Rivera worked for an hour after the Belgian's departure, setting out accurately everything about the encounter until it came to Belac's estimate for transportation costs and the necessary bribes. To the Belgian's figure of ten million Rivera added the majority of the fifteen million he intended diverting to himself. He attached a separate sheet setting out the implacable insistence of his unnamed supplier that all finance and communication should channel through him, in London, with the unnecessary reminder that it was how every successful transaction had been conducted in the past. He personally sealed the communication in the special satchel and personally again ensured it was safely placed within the diplomatic bag. Back in the seclusion of his office, Rivera stood looking out over High Holborn, satisfied with his day's work. With his personal commission added to the price set by Pierre Belac, the whole deal amounted to $165 million.

How much cocaine would be needed from Colombia for worldwide sales to raise such a sum? Whatever, Rivera knew it would be available. It always was just as there were always buyers. He thought once more how glad he was not to be involved at that end of the chain.

The investigation into Pierre Belac's illegal movement of American hi-tech prohibited under the Export Administration Act of 1979 was originally begun by the U.S. Customs Authority, the regulatory body for such policing. When the scale and enterprise of the Belgian's activities were realized, the operation was necessarily extended to include the Federal Bureau of Investigation to work within the United States, and the CIA to liaise externally. It was therefore a CIA task force that monitored the man's flight from Brussels to London and followed him from Heathrow Airport to the door of the Cuban embassy at 167 High Holborn. A number of photographs were taken of Belac entering the building and more of his leaving. He was followed back to the airport, and on the returning aircraft a CIA officer sat just two rows behind in the economy-class section.

A complete report was included in that night's diplomatic dispatch from the U.S. embassy in the Belgian capital to Washington. A cross-reference noted that the report should be considered in conjunction with a report upon José Gaviria Rivera that was being separately pouched from London that same night.

FIVE

At the end of the O'Hare concourse there was a liquor booth and O'Farrell stopped and bought a bottle of Bombay gin and some screw-topped tonic.

Jill stood apart from him, frowning, and when he went back to her she said, "What did you do that for?"

"Ellen doesn't usually have any drink in the apartment."

"So?"

"So I thought it might be an idea to take some in."

"Why? We never have before. Who needs it?"

"It might be an idea, that's all." O'Farrell's voice was weary rather than irritated; trained always to subdue any extreme emotion—and certainly anger—he never fought with Jill. In the early days of their marriage she'd sometimes tried to provoke arguments, to blow off steam, but he'd never responded, and over the years she'd stopped bothering. She'd never openly said so, but he guessed she despised him for that, too. Another clerklike weakness, unwillingness to fight on any level.

He'd set up the car rental ahead of time, so all the documentation was ready. O'Farrell started to put the luggage on the rear seat but then changed his mind, stowing it in the trunk, so the plastic bag containing the liquor was out of sight.

They drove for a long time without speaking, and then Jill said, "You all right?"

"What sort of question is that?"

"The sort of question a wife can ask her husband."

"Of course I'm all right. I'm fine. Why?"

"I just wondered."

"There must be a reason." That had been the time to drop it, not persist with any further challenge.

"You've just seemed kind of strange a couple of times lately, that's all."

"Strange like what?" Stop it! he thought, let go!

Beside him the woman shrugged. "Nothing I can point at. Why don't we forget it?"

O'Farrell opened his mouth and then closed it again, taking her advice. Damn the stupidity of buying the booze. She was right; who needed it?

Ellen had a ground-floor apartment on the Evanston side of Chicago, not quite close enough to the lake to be cripplingly expensive but not far enough away to be reasonable, either. She and Billy must have been watching through the window, because they both came running out before O'Farrell and Jill got completely from the car. There were kisses and hugs, and Billy kept thrusting an electric toy into O'Farrell's face until he paid attention. Closer, O'Farrell saw it was a spacecraft that worked off batteries, and that it could be manipulated to turn into a space figure as well. Billy said there was an entire fleet of different designs.

Inside the apartment, O'Farrell offered his daughter the plastic bag and announced, "Supplies!"

Ellen accepted it without any surprise and said, "Great!" and O'Farrell was relieved.

Ellen had moved the boy into her room. O'Farrell hung up his garment bag and stored Jill's small case where Billy slept, a bedroom festooned with posters and with toys neatly in a box, a catcher's mitt uppermost. There was a plastic cover over the video machine and its game-playing keyboard. O'Farrell guessed Ellen had tidied up the room before their arrival.

Outside Billy was on the living-room floor, squatting with his legs splayed beneath him but actually sitting, the way kids his age were able to do. Jill and Ellen were in the kitchen, talking soft-voiced by the coffeemaker. As O'Farrell entered, he heard Ellen say, "Mother, I've told you: you're panicking about nothing!"

"I don't regard it as nothing!" Jill said.

"There've been incidents and so there was a precautionary meeting, that's all!" said Ellen. "The school has behaved very responsibly and I'm grateful."

O'Farrell stood without intruding into the conversation, comparing the two women. They were very similar, unquestionably mother and daughter. And Jill stood up to the comparison very well, O'Farrell judged, proudly. Maybe just a little thicker around the hips but still pert-breasted, as firm as her daughter. Stomach was as flat, too: she worked out at the clinic, he knew, practicing the fitness exercises with which she treated others. Certainly as clear-skinned and practically as facially unlined as Ellen, and only he knew that Jill needed a hairdresser's help now to keep her hair matchingly blond. Very beautiful; very beautiful indeed. He felt a positive jump of emotion, a stomach churn: he loved her so much.

"What are the police doing about it?" Jill persisted, setting out the cups.

"The best they can."

"What's that?" O'Farrell came in.

Ellen gave her father a sad smile, wishing he had not asked. "Just that," she conceded lamely. "One of the drug officers talked at the meeting. Said it was easy enough to pick off the street pushers—which they do, of course—but that they're replaced the following day. It's like a pyramid, he said: if they get lucky, they might catch the guy from whom the street dealer gets his supplies, but rarely the one above him. And hardly ever the real organizers, the guys who are making millions . . . billions."

"You know what I think!" Jill said with sudden vehemence. "I think they ought to kill the bastards! Make it a capital offense and execute them; no appeal, no excuse, nothing. Dead!"

"They do in some parts of the world, apparently," said the younger woman.

O'Farrell supposed it was easy for Jill to feel as she did. He said, "Is there anything we can do?"

Ellen smiled at him again, gratefully this time. "Nothing, in a practical sense. Just knowing you're around always helps."

"We're always around," O'Farrell said sincerely.

Ellen said she still hadn't done any grocery shopping, but Billy protested he didn't want to do something as boring as that, so the two women went off in the rented car, with Jill driving, and O'Farrell used Ellen's car, another Toyota, to take Billy to the theme park nearer into town. He chose Lake Shore Drive because it was a more attractive route than remaining inland, and at the traffic light at its commencement he had to snatch up the emergency brake as well as pump the footbrake to get it to stop. He gasped, frightened, only inches from the car in front. When the lights changed, he set off carefully, taking the inside lane and testing the footbrake again when he was clear enough of following traffic. The only way to stop satisfactorily was to start pumping a long way from where he wanted to halt. He pulled over into a bus stop and got out, able without lifting the hood to hear the whine and shuddering unevenness of the engine.

Back in the car he said to the boy, "Things don't seem too good with the car."

"Mom says she's going to get it fixed," said Billy.

"When?"

"Soon."

O'Farrell drove very slowly, ignoring the horn blasts of protest, and found a service station just at the beginning of the high-rise area. The manager insisted the work would be impossible to do at such short notice, and O'Farrell said it was an emergency and that he guessed it would involve overtime working on the weekend, and after thirty minutes of persuasion the man agreed to take it in. It took another thirty minutes for them to check through the work necessary, the manager clearly impressed with O'Farrell's knowledge of engines.

"Four hundred is only an estimate, you understand?" the mechanic warned.

"Whatever," said O'Farrell. It gave them carte blanche to rip him off, but so what? The only consideration was getting the vehicle roadworthy over the weekend.

They took a cab to the theme park and O'Farrell indulged Billy on whatever ride he wanted and then let himself be tugged to a store practically next door to be shown the range of electric space vehicles. He bought one that changed from a vehicle to a warrior, like the one Billy already had.

On the way to the park, O'Farrell had seen a restaurant with an open deck stretching toward the lake, so he took Billy back there to eat. They sat outside, the silver-glinting lake to their left, the upthrust fingers of the Chicago skyscrapers to their right. Billy chose a cheeseburger and fries with a large Coke and insisted his new toy should remain on the table between them. O'Farrell ordered gin and tonic and tuna on rye; by the time the food came his glass was empty, so he ordered another.

"Hear there's some nasty things going on at school," O'Farrell said.

"Huh?" The child's mouth was full of fries.

"Mommy had to come to talk to some people this week?"

"Oh that," Billy said dismissively.

"What was it about?"

"Drugs," the boy announced flatly. He moved the toy along the table, toward the Coke container, making a noise like explosions.

"You know what drugs are?"

"Sure," Billy said, attention still on the spacecraft.

Not yet nine, thought O'Farrell: long-lashed, blue-eyed, red-cheeked with uncombed hair over his forehead and his shirttail poking curiously over his belt, like it always did, and he knew what drugs were. And not yet nine! He said, "What?"

"Stuff that makes you feel funny."

"Who told you that?"

"Miss James."

"Your teacher?"

"Uh-huh." He was biting into his cheeseburger now, ketchup on either side of his mouth.

"What did she say?"

Billy had to swallow before he could reply. "That we were to tell her if anyone said we should try."

"Would you tell her?"

"Boom, boom, boom," went Billy, attacking the Coke container. "Guess so," he said.

"Just guess so! *Has* anyone ever said you should do it?"

"Nope. Can I have a vanilla ice cream with chocolate topping now?"

O'Farrell summoned the waitress and added another gin and tonic to the order. "You know anyone who has tried it?"

"Couple of guys in the next grade, I think."

Ellen had talked about Nancy Reagan seeking pledges from nine-year-olds, O'Farrell remembered. He said, "What happened?"

"They sniffed something. Made them go funny, like I said." The toy ceased being a spacecraft and was turned into a warrior so that it could attack from the ground.

"What happened to them?"

"They had to go to the principal. Now they're in a program."

"You know what a program is?"

"Sure," Billy said, letting his warrior retreat. "It's when you go and they keep on about you not doing it."

It was a good enough description from someone so young. O'Farrell said, "You love me?"

Billy looked directly at him for the first time. "Of course I love you."

"Grandma too? And Mommy most of all?"

"Sure. Dad too."

What about Patrick? O'Farrell thought for the first time. He'd have to ask Ellen. "I want you to make me a promise, a promise that you'll keep if you love us all like you say you do."

"Okay," the child said brightly. The warrior became a spacecraft again.

"If anyone ever comes up to you, at school or anywhere, and tries to get you to buy something that will make you go funny, you promise me you'll say no and go at once and tell Miss James or Mommy? You promise me that?"

"Can I have another Coke? Just a small one."

O'Farrell caught the waitress's eye again and insisted, "You going to promise me that?"

" 'Course I am. That's easy."

"And mean it? Really mean it?"

"Sure."

O'Farrell felt a sweep of helplessness but decided against pressing any further. Maybe he shouldn't have tried at all. He hadn't suggested to Ellen that he should discuss it with the child; perhaps there was some established way of talking it through—something evolved by a child psychiatrist—and he was being counterproductive by mentioning it at all. He felt another sweep of helplessness.

O'Farrell considered stopping at the service station on the way back to Ellen's apartment, but decided against it; there did not seem to be any point. The women were already home, hunched over more coffee cups at the kitchen table with the debris of a sandwich lunch between them.

"Steak for dinner, courtesy of Grandma!" Ellen announced as they entered.

"Great!" Billy said. "I got a new spaceship! Look!

Gramps bought it for me. And a vanilla ice cream with a chocolate top!"

"Looks like our time for being spoiled, Billy boy," Ellen said.

The child scurried into the living room to locate the previous toy and begin a galactic battle; almost at once there came lots of *boom*, *boom*, *booms* and a noise that sounded something like a throat clearing.

O'Farrell said, "Your car's in the garage."

"You had an accident!"

His daughter's instant response caused a burn of annoyance. Never get mad, always stay cool, he thought. He said, "I could have. It's a miracle you haven't. That car's a wreck: at least five thousand miles over any service limit! Didn't you know that?"

"Been busy," said Ellen. She spoke looking down, her bottom lip nipped between her teeth, and O'Farrell recognized the expression from when she'd been young and been caught doing something wrong.

"Darling!" he said, perfectly in control but trying to sound outraged despite that, wanting to get through to her. "On at least one wheel, possibly two, there are scarcely any brake shoes left at all. Which is hardly important anyway because there was no fluid in the drum to operate them anyway. Two plugs aren't operating at all, your engine is virtually dry of oil, and the carburetor is so corroded the cover has actually split. Both your left tires, front and back, are shiny bald, and your alignment is so far out on the front that any new tire would be that way inside a month."

"Intended to get it fixed right away," Ellen said, head still downcast. "The brakes are okay, providing you know how to work them."

"That car's a deathtrap and you know it!" O'Farrell insisted. "So when was it last in the shop?"

"Can't remember," Ellen said, stilted still.

"It hasn't been serviced, has it? Not for months!"

"No."

There was a loud silence in the tiny kitchen. Remembering something else, O'Farrell said, "What about Patrick?"

"What about Patrick?" his daughter echoed.

"You told him about this scare at Billy's school?"

"No."

"Why not?"

"Because that's all it is, a scare," Ellen said. "Nothing's happened to Billy."

Don't be sidetracked, thought O'Farrell. "Patrick's got visitation rights, hasn't he?"

"You know he has."

"Tell me the custody arrangement."

"You know the custody arrangement!" Ellen said angrily.

"Tell me!"

"Alternative weekends," Ellen said. "Vacation by arrangement."

"So Billy was with his father last weekend?"

"No," Ellen admitted tightly.

"And the time before that?"

"No." Tighter still.

"Why not?"

A shrug.

"Why not!"

"Patrick's got problems; he got laid off."

"From the loan company?"

Ellen shook her head. "That was the job before last. He was working on commission, with a group of guys, trying to sell apartments in a renewal development downtown."

"But he got laid off?"

Ellen nodded.

"When?"

She shrugged uncertainly. "I'm not sure. Three months ago, maybe four. I'm not sure."

Jill had been listening, her head moving backward and

forward like a spectator's at a tennis match. She said abruptly, "Honey, we've been up here twice in the last four months! Why didn't you tell us?"

"My business," Ellen said, little girl again.

"No, honey," Jill said gently. "*Our* business."

"It was all right at first. He kept seeing Billy and . . ." she trailed away.

"And what!" demanded O'Farrell, guessing already.

"And the payments," Ellen finished.

"How much is he behind?"

There was another uncertain shoulder move. "Two months."

"Alimony *and* child support?" O'Farrell pressed.

Ellen nodded. "Actually it's three months."

"And when did he last want to see Billy?"

"It's not that he doesn't want to see him! He and Jane have two kids of their own now; he's got a lot of priorities."

"You and Billy are his prior commitments!" O'Farrell insisted. "He married you first. He had Billy first. He owes you first."

"He asked me to give him a little time, just to sort himself out. Jane's still jealous of me, he says."

"She's jealous of *you*, for Christ's sake!" Jill erupted. "She was his mistress for a year before she became pregnant to make him choose between the two of you. And you're doing her favors! Come on!"

"Leave it, Mom. Please leave it!"

"You could have died in that car," O'Farrell said. "Been badly hurt at least."

"I was saving, to get it done. But I didn't want to fall behind with the mortgage."

"Have you?" O'Farrell asked. He'd put up the down payment for Ellen for the apartment, believing she could manage the monthly installments.

There was a jerking nod of her head. "Only this month."

"You still make the same?" O'Farrell asked. Ellen worked as a medical receptionist; she'd cut short her training to be a physiotherapist like her mother in order to marry Patrick. Billy had been born nine calendar months later.

"It averages around a thousand a month; sometimes I work overtime and it comes to a little more."

"You can't afford to live here on a thousand a month!" Jill said. "You can't afford to live anywhere on a thousand a month. You've got to get Patrick's payments going through the courts, like you should have done in the first place."

"You can't get what's not there."

"How do you know it's not there?" O'Farrell asked.

"I know."

"Tell me something," Jill said. "You surely don't think there's a chance of you and Patrick getting back together again, do you? He's got two other children by her!"

The girl's shoulders went up and down listlessly. "I don't know."

"Would you get back together if he asked you?"

Another shoulder movement. "I don't know."

O'Farrell and Jill frowned at each other over their daughter's head, shocked by the lassitude. Each tried to think of something appropriate to say and failed.

It was Jill who spoke, with forced briskness, trying to break the mood. "Why don't I make supper?"

Without asking either woman O'Farrell fixed drinks for all three of them. Jill took hers without any critical reaction and didn't comment or even look when he made himself another before they sat down. Largely for the child's benefit, they made light conversation during the meal, and afterward O'Farrell played spacemen with Billy while the women cleared away. The boy was allowed to watch an hour of television, and while Ellen and Jill were bathing him before bed O'Farrell made a third drink, a large one, and kept it defiantly in his hand when Jill came back into the room. She didn't appear to notice it.

By unspoken agreement Ellen's problems weren't raised again during the evening, but the subject hung between them, like a room divider, all the time.

That night, in Billy's bed, lying on her back in the darkness, Jill said, "Christ, what a mess!"

"It's not too bad, not yet," O'Farrell said, trying to be realistic.

"It's not too good, either."

"I tried to talk to Billy at lunchtime about drugs."

He felt her head turn toward him in the darkness. "And?"

"He spoke about it," O'Farrell tried to explain. "This little kid tried to speak about it like he knew what we were talking about and all the time he was playing fucking Star Wars!"

"She's got to go to an attorney, get the proper court payments set up," Jill insisted. "I don't give a damn how bad his own situation is. I don't see why Ellen and Billy should suffer because of it; he created it all."

"Yes," O'Farrell agreed.

"She married too young," Jill said abruptly.

"The same age as us."

"I got you; she got a bastard."

What words would she use if she really knew? O'Farrell said, "Maybe we were wrong, making it possible for her to buy the apartment. It's a hell of a drain on what she earns."

"What can we do, apart from pressure her about a lawyer?"

"I don't know," admitted O'Farrell.

"What about money? Couldn't we make her some sort of allowance?"

Not if he went to Petty and said he wanted to quit. "Yes," O'Farrell promised. "If we can get her to accept it, we could make her an allowance. We'll definitely do that."

"I love you," Jill said.

Would she if she really knew? he wondered again.

CIA surveillance picked up the Cuban ambassador the moment he left High Holborn. The alert that he was probably making for London airport was radioed from the trailing car when the official vehicle gained the motorway and confirmed when it turned off onto the Heathrow spur. The observer risked following closely behind Rivera at the check-in desk, to discover his destination, but it was the driver who took over to purchase a ticket and board the plane to Brussels, to avoid any chance recognition. Before the aircraft cleared English airspace watchers were already assembling at Brussels, waiting: the CIA officer from London headed back immediately upon arrival, again to avoid possible identification.

Rivera took a taxi into the center of the capital and went through an effort at trail clearing that earned the professionals' sneers, it was so amateurish. They kept him easily under observation until he entered Pierre Belac's nondescript office. The Agency had not risked installing any listening devices there. Had they done so, they would have heard Belac ask for a downpayment of thirty-five million dollars and Rivera agreeing without any argument, with an added, entrapping assurance that if Belac had any additional expenditures in excess of this advance sum he would be immediately recompensed. Even with a listening device, they could not have picked up Belac's reaction, a repeat of his earlier and intense irritation at not having pitched the demand higher at their embassy meeting.

At least, Belac reasoned at once, he had the authority to buy in addition and in excess of his thirty-five-million-dollar advance. Which he resolved to do; he would purchase a vast amount of Czech small arms and ten of the fifty tanks that were not coming from America but from a German arms dealer who had them available for sale. They were far cheaper than he'd have to pay for the American vehicles; Belac guessed $10,000 a tank, although, of course, he wouldn't tell Rivera that. Belac reckoned that as he was taking the risk, by using his own money, then his should be the unexpected and unshared profit.

Rivera remained with the arms dealer for less than an hour, walking back to the center of town, where he caught a taxi to the airport, boarding the midafternoon plane to London. There he was followed back into the city. He did not go to his Hampstead home but to a mews house in Pimlico that was already logged on the CIA's watch list. It belonged to an aging, self-made English newspaper magnate named Sir William Blanchard. Inquiries showed that he was in Ottawa negotiating fresh newsprint prices with Canadian manufacturers. Lady Henrietta Blanchard, twenty-three years her husband's junior, was at home, though.

It was nine A.M. the following morning before Rivera left.

SIX

THE HEAD of the CIA's Plans Directorate was a barrel-chested, bull-necked Irishman named Gus McCarthy. He was thickly red-haired and had a heavily freckled face, with freckles on the back of his hands as well; they were also matted with more red hair. He looked like a barroom brawler—and was able to be—but his looks belied the man. He was a strategist capable of intricate and manipulative schemes, never concentrating upon an immediate operation to the exclusion of how it could be extended and utilized to its fullest advantage. He was perfectly matched by his deputy, Hank Sneider, a precise, slight man who had the ability to recognize the direction of McCarthy's thoughts almost before the man completely explained them, and correct and improve upon the details. Their nicknames within the Langley headquarters were Mutt and Jeff. They knew it and weren't offended; there were benefits to being underestimated.

"So what have we got?" McCarthy demanded, not seeking an answer. "One of the largest arms dealers in Europe, a Cuban ambassador who likes the good life, and a British newspaper owner."

"I think to include the newspaper owner is confusing," Sneider said. "Blanchard isn't involved. Rivera's just humping the wife is all."

"Maybe not all," McCarthy mused. "Couldn't we use that? Blanchard's got a hell of an empire: television stations and newspapers and magazines here as well as in Europe. Get ourselves a corner there and we'd have an incredible outlet for whatever we wanted to plant."

They were in McCarthy's seventh-floor office in the CIA building, high enough for a view of the Potomac glistening its way through the tree line. Sneider ignored the view, pouring coffee for both of them from the permanently steaming Cona machine. McCarthy consumed a minimum of ten cups a day. Sneider carried McCarthy's mug back to the man's desk and said, "It's worth thinking through. But we could only achieve that by pressuring the old guy. The shit we've got is on the woman."

"How much of a lever does she have on her old man?"

"Get things published the way we want, darling, or hubbie gets to know all the sordid details?" Sneider suggested.

"Something like that," McCarthy agreed, appreciatively sipping. "Be nice to get a picture of her with her ass in the air."

"Rivera's too, in tandem."

"They discreet?"

"Don't appear to be, particularly. Rivera shacked up at the family home when the old guy was in Canada and she often accompanies him to polo matches. That's his sport, polo."

"So what's that?" McCarthy asked, another rhetorical question. "Sheer couldn't-give-a-damn carelessness? Arrogance? What?"

"Maybe Blanchard knows and doesn't mind either," Sneider speculated. "You know how it is with some old guys: all they want is a decoration on their arm and maybe an occasional feel in the sack to make sure it's still there and working and the rest of the time the bimbo can party with whom she likes."

"Difficult to turn that into an advantage," McCarthy complained.

"What about cutting the deck a different way?" Sneider asked.

"Rivera?"

"Not exactly leading the life of José the Cane Cutter, is he?"

"What's the objective?"

"Spy in the court of King Castro?"

"To be that Rivera's got to be back in Havana," McCarthy said. "Won't work. To maneuver his recall we'd have to spread the word about his high life. So he goes back in disgrace and wouldn't be in a position to give us anything anyway. And when we show him the pictures of himself and the lady, he says, 'She was a good lay, so what?' "

"So?"

"We divide it," McCarthy decided. "Let's message London to get as much dirt as possible on the two of them but not to spook Rivera. And run him and Belac quite separately."

"Parallel surveillance is going to tie up a lot of manpower."

"Belac's big; the biggest. It could be worth it."

"We going to seek British help?"

"No," McCarthy said at once. "If it's going to be big, let's keep it nice and tight, just to ourselves."

"Then the way in is through Belac," the other man said. "There's already a bunch of stuff on the guy; we've got a good handle on his sources. If we can find out what he wants, then it'll give us an idea what Rivera could be ordering."

"Belac's the biggest?"

"Yes," Sneider said, trying to tune in to the direction of McCarthy's thinking.

"So logically whatever Rivera—whatever Cuba—wants is substantial," McCarthy said. "If it were just the usual run-of-the-mill stuff, there's a dozen smaller guys they could have bought from. Belac means it's a huge order and that it's the latest state-of-the-art matériel."

"You talking Apocalypse?"

McCarthy got up to pour his own coffee this time, looking inquiringly toward his deputy, who shook his head in refusal. McCarthy returned to his high-backed chair and said, "The days of missile crises are over. I think Havana's looking south, not north. We won't know until we get some idea just how substantial, but it's got to be more than continuing support in Nicaragua; much more."

Sneider gestured to indicate the building in which they were sitting. "Time to start spreading the news?"

"Not yet," the Plans Director said. "There's not enough news to spread; just speculation. But it's definitely worth expending the manpower."

"Most definitely," agreed Sneider, all doubt gone now.

"And when we get it, we make the most extensive possible use of it," McCarthy said. "Ripples upon ripples upon ripples."

O'Farrell had expected his offer of financial support to meet a stronger argument from Ellen and decided with Jill that their daughter's almost immediate acceptance showed just how desperate she had become. They agreed on $400 a month, and Billy had clung to his mother's leg and wanted to know why she was crying. The car repairs cost $550, and before they left Chicago Jill went grocery shopping again, stocking up the cupboards and the deep-freeze. During their last conversation, after Sunday-morning church, Ellen said she'd see her lawyer before the month was out.

They wrote as well as telephoned now, and that first week O'Farrell sent a long letter to John, in Phoenix, aware that the boy would not be able to offer Ellen any financial support but suggesting that his sister might like support of another kind, like a call or a letter. He didn't say it outright but hoped his son would infer that the occasional checks would not be quite as much as they had been in the past. There was a reply practically by return. John said that what was happening in Billy's school was nothing unusual and that they weren't to worry. Jeff had actually come home one day and talked about being offered marijuana; he and Beth were pretty sure he hadn't tried it but couldn't be one-hundred-percent certain. John promised to write to Chicago every week, the way they were doing now, and added a postscript that the checks had always embarrassed him anyway and in the future he wouldn't expect anything at all from his father.

To establish—and hopefully to go on improving—his great-grandfather's archive, O'Farrell had written to still-existing newspapers throughout Kansas that had been publishing during the man's lifetime and even wrote further afield, to papers in Colorado and Oklahoma. In addition he approached as many historical societies and museums as he could locate, asking them to publicize his on-going search for information about his ancestor in any newsletter or publication they issued.

By coincidence there were two responses within two weeks of his returning from Chicago. A historical society in Wichita said one of their researchers had come across references to a Charles O'Farrell as a teenage scout in a wagon train and asked if he were prepared to spend fifty dollars on a more specific investigation. O'Farrell replied at once that he was, enclosing his check.

An Amarillo dealer in early-American weaponry wrote saying that he was on the mailing list of every historical society in five nearby states. The man had a mint-condition Colt of the model and caliber he believed O'Farrell's great-grandfather would have used. Did O'Farrell want to buy it to form part of his collection?

O'Farrell replied to that by return as well, politely rejecting the offer. Even before the manner of his parents' death, he'd considered it unthinkable to have a gun in his house, even an antique from which the firing pin had probably been removed.

At church that weekend, O'Farrell prayed that Billy would be kept safe, knowing that Jill would be praying the same. Additionally O'Farrell prayed for himself, asking to be excused any more assignments. He was made uncomfortable by the reading, which was from St Luke: "Judge not and ye shall not be judged."

SEVEN

It HAD been Rivera's father who'd been the sports fisherman, pursuing the blue marlin and the other big-game fish off the Keys and the Grand Bahama Bank. Rivera had fished, too, quite competently, but he'd never gotten the pleasure from it that the older man had. He'd learned the principles, of course; the use of the proper bait to catch the best fish. And carried that principle on. Which was why he'd initially, unquestioningly, advanced so much money to Belac, with the assurance that any additional personal expenditure would be instantly recompensed. And Belac had responded fishlike. But not like a marlin. Like a greedy, eat-all shark. His father had despised shark as game fish.

The unscheduled meeting was at Belac's request. The arms dealer came confidently into the London embassy office and at once, proudly, announced, "I want you to see what I've achieved." He produced a list but read from it himself. "Two hundred Kalashnikov rifles, with six thousand rounds of ammunition. One hundred Red Eye missiles and two hundred Stinger missiles. Three hundred assorted Czech handguns and three thousand rounds of matching ammunition. There are five hundred grenades and two hundred antipersonnel land mines. . . ." The man looked up, giving a self-satisfied smile. "And ten tanks. All en route, aboard ship, without the need to go through Japan or the Arab Emirates." He smiled further. "Your original request only listed five armored personnel carriers. I have secured fifteen, if you wish to increase the order." He'd already put down a deposit, from his own money again.

"I will check back with my people," Rivera promised. By how much, he wondered, had Belac overextended himself?

"And not just that," Belac continued briskly. "I have two thousand jungle-camouflaged uniforms and three thousand of the latest type of army boot. Also practically an unlimited supply of infantry matériel—webbing, field equipment, stuff like that."

"Again, I'll check." Gently prompting, Rivera said, "What about the remaining tanks?"

"The auction is still to come," the Belgian said. "I will be bidding, of course, through an agent."

"And the electronic systems?" pressed the diplomat.

"I have already established through a Swiss *anstalt* the purchasing route with a company on the outskirts of Stockholm—"

Rivera refused him the escape. "We discussed the method at our first meeting."

Belac nodded, in apparent recollection. "An order has been placed through Stockholm," he assured. "Which brings us to the point of my coming here today—"

"Money?" cut in Rivera, again.

"The request is for a VAX-11/78," Belac said, in another unnecessary reminder. "That's the system employed within the U.S. Pentagon itself! It is going to be very expensive; maybe more than we first budgeted for."

"It's precisely *because* the VAX is the Pentagon system that we want it," Rivera said.

"Expensive, like I said," repeated Belac.

"How much?"

"I have committed a great deal of my own money, on the basis of our understanding," Belac said generally. "I shall need another thirty-five million working capital at least." He spoke as if the sum were unimportant. He looked at Rivera in open-faced, almost innocent expectancy.

Rivera smiled back just as innocently. "I am surprised at the need for such a large payment, so quickly after the first advance of thirty-five million."

The arms dealer faltered, just slightly. He gestured toward the list between them and said, "I have just told you what has been purchased and shipped. Three vessels have had to be chartered. Commissions paid. Deposits made, for other material you want."

"Like the VAX communication equipment?" Rivera persisted.

There was a further hesitation. "I may need the full time allowance there," Belac conceded.

"Wouldn't you agree that on my part I have been very generous in the agreement we have reached?"

"Yes," Belac allowed doubtfully, unsure of the direction the ambassador was taking, but not liking it, whatever it was.

"Particularly in not insisting upon there being a penalty clause understood between us, in the event of nondelivery of any of the items you've guaranteed to supply," Rivera continued, laying more bait.

"Yes," Belac said again. The Cuban was performing for his own benefit. In what public court did the fool imagine suing to recover any penalty sum?

"I think one should be established," Rivera announced. "Here, today."

"What have you in mind?" Belac asked, tolerantly going along with the diplomat.

"A percentage," Rivera said. In the excitement of the moment Rivera was unable precisely to calculate the additional, interest-earning profit to himself, through whom all funding had to flow and in whose account any withheld money would remain, if Belac failed to keep to his own established timetable.

"I don't understand," Belac complained, his complacency wavering.

"Our agreement was upon an expenditure of a hundred and fifty million?"

"Yes," accepted Belac, fully alert now.

"Of which thirty-five million has already been advanced?"

"And spent," Belac insisted at once. "Not only spent but greatly exceeded."

"I propose there should be a ten-percent withholding upon all future advances, that sum to be paid as and when the articles for which it is committed are delivered."

Belac was too urbane a negotiator to burst out with an instant rejection but it was very close. Icily controlled, he said, "That's not acceptable, under any circumstances, Excellency. As I have made clear, I have already gone to considerable personal expense and effort, committed myself to great expense with other people. In the business I follow, everything depends upon personal reputation."

And why you've no alternative but to agree, thought Rivera. He said, "Which was why the thirty-five million was advanced, surely!"

"An advance on account," Belac said, unsettled now. "And from it I have extended other advances on account, accounts that my suppliers expect me to honor in full and on time."

"Exactly!" Rivera said as the hook jarred upward. "Your suppliers expect you to fulfill your commitments on time, I expect you to fulfill your commitments on time. We're in agreement then!" It was the moment for the patronizing attitudes to be reversed. It was the overextended Belac who would have to dance to the tune he played, accepting what payments he chose to advance. Rivera knew from other deals how these men worked, interchanging and swopping weaponry, the word-of-mouth agreements having rigidly to be met. And how violently disputes were resolved, if they weren't. He remained curious at Belac's apparent hesitation over the VAX equipment, feeling a stir of unease. Did the Belgian intend to supply it? Or merely to provide enough of the other things to make a substantial profit but leave him exposed for the difficult but essential computer? A further, essential reason to withhold the money.

He'd been too confident of the limitless money continuing, Belac admitted to himself. Now he was trapped, with timed deliveries that had to be paid for. Desperately, vowing somehow to repay in kind the smirking bastard sitting opposite him, Belac said, "Without another advance of thirty-five million, everything collapses. My suppliers simply won't deal with me."

His voice had lost its smooth, imperturbable tone. He waited, but the Cuban said nothing. Practically pleading,

Belac said, "I have given personal guarantees. Payments are arranged on fixed dates. We agreed you would immediately cover any additional, necessary expenditure, for God's sake!"

Make up the shortfall from your own funds; you're rich enough, thought Rivera. He said, "I'll advance the next thirty-five million, less the ten percent withholding, to protect my delivery being on time. . . ." He allowed just the right degree of hesitation. "Or would you have me change the whole arrangement? Withdraw some of the requirements from you and spread them to other dealers: the VAX computer particularly, if you are finding that difficult."

"No!" Belac said too quickly. If that happened, some of the subsidiary dealers with whom he'd made arrangements would realize the purchases were being spread and would imagine him to be in difficulties, which he was. And would be in greater difficulty when they demanded their money immediately, frightened he had a cash shortage. What Rivera was allowing him—$31,500,000—would just be enough to cover the commitments for which he'd given his word. Still too quickly, he went on, "I agree to the arrangement."

"I'm glad we've had this meeting," the ambassador said. "I feel it has clarified a number of points." The main one being that you can't contemptuously treat me like some cigar-chewing peasant.

"I think so, too," Belac said, wanting to recover. "I think there are other points that maybe need clarifying, too."

"Such as?"

"That mutual trust we spoke about," Belac said heavily. "I think it would be very unfortunate if there stopped being mutual trust between us."

"So do I." An open threat, Rivera recognized, uneasily.

"It would be regrettable for any other sort of penalties to be considered by either of us, don't you think?" Belac said.

"I'm not sure I'm following this conversation," Rivera said. His voice remained quite firm, he decided, gratefully.

The Belgian sat regarding the other man without speaking for several moments. He said, "It is important that we understand each other."

"There's no misunderstanding on my part," Rivera assured him. "I sincerely hope there's none upon yours."

"There won't be, from now on," the Belgian said.

The encounter concluded, Belac's departure duly noted by the CIA surveillance team, with Rivera firmly believing himself to be the victor.

Which he had been, far more than he knew.

Belac had done nothing about obtaining the American-manufactured, American-equipped computer system listed among the top ten items barred from export to any communist country.

Belatedly Belac approached a hi-tech consultant in California through whom he had previously dealt—always by telephone or letter—for technical advice upon such things. And upon the consultant's advice Belac finally did approach Sweden. The company was named Epetric, was headquartered in the very heart of Stockholm, and was regarded as the most amenable to rule bending as well as one of the best hi-tech corporations in the country.

Precisely because it was such a state-of-the-art organization as well as being so amenable to rule bending, Epetric was prominent on the list of suspected technological infringers not just in the CIA but in the U.S. Customs Service as well. The combined pressure of both agencies resulted in Washington warning Stockholm that unless they did more to control the technology flood, Swedish industries, and particularly companies like Epetric, would be denied by federal legislation the legal American computer exports upon which the industry, worldwide, depended.

Stockholm resented the threat but could not deny the hemorrhage, and the cabinet decided that the country had to show itself a less open technological doorway.

Nine months before Belac approached Epetric—months, in fact, before there had ever been contact between the Belgian and José Gaviria Rivera—Swedish customs investigators had succeeded in suborning an informant within the contracts and finance department of the Epetric company.

His name was Lars Henstrom.

Paul Rodgers felt life was sweet; sweet as a little nut. Sweeter in fact. What was sweeter than a little nut? Angie maybe. She sure as hell was sweet; tits she had—no silicone, either—made those bimbos in the skin mags look like grandmothers or bag ladies. And not just the tits. Rodgers, who'd bucked a few in his time flying in Nam and then for Florida, before it went bust, reckoned there hadn't been a trick invented in the sack that Angie didn't know; guessed she might have invented a few of them.

And not just the joy of Angie, since he'd wised up. There was the paid-for-cash condo in Naples, as an investment, and the paid-for-cash beach house where they lived at Fort Lauderdale, and the paid-for-cash Jaguar XK6, the latest convertible model, and those discreet safe-deposit boxes in Miami and Tampa and Dallas and New York, everything nicely spread around, solid as those unquestioning banks. Yes sir, life was sweet; sweet as a little . . .

Rodgers didn't bother to finish the thought, frowning at the cumulus buildup ahead, a boiling, churning foam of blackened cloud already split apart by lightning. The forecast—the best he could get, that was, before lifting off from the dirt strip outside Cartagena—had warned of occasional seasonal turbulence. Sure as fuck this wasn't occasional seasonal turbulence. This was a full-blown storm, the kind that every so often strutted the Caribbean, blowing down the tarp shacks and uprooting a tree here and there and giving those vacationing jerks paying $300 a day the hurricane story of a lifetime when they got back to Des Moines or Billings. Except that it wasn't a hurricane. Just an awkward fucking storm just when he didn't want one, right in the way of where he wanted to go.

"Shit!" Rodgers said with feeling. Briefly—but only briefly—life wasn't quite so sweet anymore.

The wise money said to fly around it. The engines of the DC3 were already chattering like they had teeth and twice he'd thought they were going to cut out altogether. Rodgers bet the entire fucking aircraft was held together with no more than string, spit, and chewing gum.

If he went head-on into what was up ahead, he was going to end up in the matchstick-making business and that wasn't the business he was interested in building into a career. Which course, then? Wise money again said even more abruptly to go eastwards, over Haiti, and hope he could get around the blockage and still cut westward to come down on the Matanzas airstrip.

Except the bastard Colombians had short-changed him on the fuel, knowing the gauge was faulty and that he couldn't really challenge them. It was fucking amazing: every run worth a minimum of $50 million, and they had to cheat on nickels and dimes.

Westward then? Less chance of being driven out into the Atlantic, with nothing between him, paella, and the bullfights of Spain but three thousand miles of empty ocean. But the Americans were shit-hot around the Gulf: not just radar on the ground but AWACs planes in the air and spot-the-druggie training forming a permanent part of all air-force and naval exercises.

The DC3 began to buck and shudder, the stick sluggish in his hands and the rudder bar spongy underfoot. Decision time. Rodgers turned west; there might be a lot of guys in white hats, but this way there was also Mexico, and if the fuel got crucial, there were more safe illicit airstrips than fleas on a brown dog.

Rodgers had always had a nasty feeling about having to ditch in the sea and get his ass wet. Besides, there was the cargo to think of: almost five hundred kilos of high-purity cocaine could be better used on dry land—even if it weren't the dry land upon which he was supposed to put down—than to clear the sinuses of the sharks and barracudas.

He still intended, if he could, to deliver in Cuba.

Rodgers kept right against the storm edge—able to see clear sunlight to his left, rain-lashed blackness to his right—riding the up and downdrafts, teeth snapping together with the suddenness of the lifts and drops. The ancient aircraft groaned and creaked in protest, those sounds overwhelmed by the crashing of the storm outside.

One of his wipers quit—fortunately not that of his immediate windshield—and then he went too close and was engulfed in the cloud, and the crack of the lightning strike was so loud it actually deafened him, making his ears ache. On the panel his instrumentation went haywire; the compass was whirling like a roulette wheel and the artificial horizon showed him falling sideways, although the altimeter had him at two thousand feet. If that were his correct height, then he'd been driven too low, Rodgers realized: dangerously too low. Not necessary to worry too much. He'd be difficult to detect, mixed up in this sort of shit.

Rodgers had the cans off his ears, held by the headpiece around his neck; through them came the occasional screech of static and in a sudden but brief moment of absolute clarity he picked up Miami airport sending out a general warning of a severe and unexpected storm in the Caribbean basin, setting out its longitude and latitude.

"Thanks a bunch, fella!" Rodgers said aloud. If anything in the goddamned airplane worked and he had any charts, he might have been able to find out how far, and how deep, he was into the storm.

The bright sunshine to port dazzled Rodgers, making him blink, and he turned out toward it, wanting to clear the cumulus and prevent the plane breaking up. The transition, from practically uncontrolled bucking to level-flying calm, was startling, and Rodgers heard his own breath go from him, unaware until that moment how tense he had been.

He watched eagerly for the instruments to settle, wanting a positive bearing, uncomfortably aware that by taking the course he had he had placed the storm—the storm that was still raging and growling to starboard—between himself and Cuba. And if it didn't dissipate, which it showed no signs of doing, he was going to put himself dangerously close to the American mainland by flying around it.

He'd fucked up, Rodgers decided. The storm was stationary, a positive barrier. If he'd gone eastward in the first place, he could have come easily up over the Grand Bahama Bank, made a perfect three-pointer at Matanzas, and by now have been drinking the first rum and lime with the $100,000 delivery fee snug in the arm-strap money wallet that now hung empty and waiting, like a shoulder holster, beneath the sweat-blackened shirt.

"Son of a bitch!" he said bitterly. And then, when he saw it, he said "Oh fuck!" even more bitterly.

The first plane was a jet, a spotter, which circled and buzzed and tried to come close for a look-see but wasn't able to because it couldn't go that slowly. Very soon the rest of the squad, the smaller propeller-driven aircraft, swept in from the north and swarmed around him like killer bees. There were three; two pulled up close, either side, and although he couldn't see, he guessed the third was above and behind, ready for any unexpected avoidance routine. The two alongside had U.S. Customs markings, as well as their government insignia. At an obvious signal each plane gave the wing-wobble follow-us instruction, and just in case he'd misunderstood, the pilot to starboard mimed the hand gesture.

"Fuck you," said Rodgers, hoping the man had understood what he'd said. To himself, looking away, he said, "Sorry guys. What I ain't got, you can't find." It seemed a criminal waste, dumping nearly half a ton of coke into the sea.

Rodgers put the controls into auto and groped his way toward the rear of the aircraft. The drug occupied very little of the cargo space, all easily accommodated near the port door. Such a waste, he thought again. He tugged at the handle. The bar was unlocked but it didn't budge. He yanked again, feeling the sweat break out on his forehead, looking around for something solid with which he could smash at it. There wasn't anything. It was only the fact that he was holding on to the handle, making another attempt to open it, that saved Rodgers from being hurled the complete length of the aircraft. It suddenly went nose-up, when the auto pilot slipped out, then began pitching downward. Rodgers let go, allowing the angle of the plunging aircraft to slide him back to the cockpit, snatching out for the controls to pull it back level. The sea was so close he could see the silver glint of the sun on the wave tops and make out a startled couple in a yellow and blue cruiser. Momentarily he was alone and then the escorts were alongside again; they would have thought he was trying to evade them, Rodgers realized. He put the auto on again, waiting, and at once it disengaged. He tried again. It disengaged again. It was a pretty simple choice, Rodgers recognized: death—injury at least—or discovery. From either side there was another wing wiggle and a hand gesture and this time Rodgers raised his hand in acknowledgment.

They put down in Tampa. By the time they landed the radio-alerted Customs had the airfield prepared, civilian as well as official vehicles blocking him the moment he stopped.

Rodgers sat where he was after turning off the systems; they had to hammer, too, to get through the jammed door. A stream of investigators came into the aircraft, some immediately coming up to the flight deck, others staying around the cargo.

"Well lookee here!" said one, in a thick, southern accent. "Why didn't you dump it, you stupid bastard!"

Rodgers sought out the man who looked to be in charge. "I think we've got things to talk about," he said.

EIGHT

IT WASN'T getting any better; worse, in fact. O'Farrell knew that he was still outwardly holding himself together—almost literally—and that no one, not even Jill, had guessed how his nerves were tightening up, but inwardly that was just how he did feel, stretched tight as if he were being gradually pulled apart on some medieval rack.

O'Farrell would definitely have gone to Petty and ended it, but for how things were going at home. That was worse, too. Not actually worse—it seemed important, as strained as he felt, to get the words accurate—but not as good as he would have liked. During a second visit to Chicago, Ellen admitted that she hadn't gone to an attorney yet and there had been a shouted argument in front of Billy, which had been a mistake. They'd all ended up in tears, only O'Farrell staying dry-eyed, and that with difficulty. And then John had flunked a course in Phoenix. It was not an outright disaster, just a setback that was going to mean maybe an extra nine months before he graduated. And nine months was a rather apposite period, because in his last letter his son had announced that Beth was pregnant and they were all very happy about it. So were Jill and O'Farrell, although they realized it meant Beth was going to have to quit her job selling advertising space in the local Scottsdale newspaper, which had provided most of their income, apart from what O'Farrell sent and had intended to reduce.

It would not have been so difficult if O'Farrell hadn't years before gone in for the sort of insurance he had, guaranteeing a tremendous death benefit but with matchingly high payments he was locked into, without any possibility of renegotiating. At the time he'd felt—he still felt—that it was the responsible thing to do to protect the unknowing Jill and the kids if anything did happen to him on an assignment, but in the changed circumstances it monthly absorbed more of his available cash than was convenient. And then there was the heavy mortgage on the Alexandria house. So there were nights in the den now when O'Farrell hunched over rows of figures, not his ancestor's archive, working out how much he could afford to send to Arizona, on top of the allowance for Ellen, when Beth did have to stop work. He discussed it with Jill, of course, because they discussed every domestic situation together, and decided that the best they could manage for Phoenix was $300 a month; John had a part-time job in a garage anyway and they both agreed, without much discussion, that Ellen's needs were greater. O'Farrell had been relieved, during the last telephone call two days ago, to hear that Ellen had at last gone to her attorney and that the lawyer had already written to Patrick. And even more relieved to hear that three pushers had been rounded up near Billy's school without others appearing to have taken their place and that the feeling was that there had been an overreaction to the drug scare in the first place. O'Farrell hoped it were true.

The Wichita addition to his archives provided a welcome respite. The material came a month after the initial letter from the historical society and built up an appreciable amount about his great-grandfather's early life. It stopped short of answering one of O'Farrell's major questions—whether the man had been an immigrant or whether there had been an American O'Farrell before him—but it put him at eighteen on a westbound wagon trek and recorded his swearing in at Wichita as a sheriff's deputy. Earlier than I started, reflected O'Farrell, the second martini already half-drunk and dinner still an hour away; years earlier in fact. But the ruling (by whom? O'Farrell wondered) decreed that a person had to attain a reasoning and balanced maturity before being inducted into the specialized section of the CIA to which O'Farrell was attached.

He finished the martini and topped up his glass with the overflow that seemed invariable these evenings, pleased that it practically filled his glass for a third time. The assessment wouldn't be a problem, he was sure; he'd get through it, like he'd gotten through all the others. And not just the sessions with Symmons—any psychologist. Since his last, successful, encounter with the man, there had been range practice—not just fixed but moving targets—and his score had only been a point below his usual average, so the twitch in his hands wasn't a problem in an important situation. And he'd isolated and evaded the watchers on each of the mandatory surveillance exercises and that wasn't easy because shitty-shift penalties were imposed upon the tracking professionals if they failed. So he was still as good as ever. Almost. Just a bit under par, that's all; distracted by the children's difficulties.

Wrong, though, to let it all get to him like it had. So okay, they weren't having an easy time—Ellen more than John—but objectively (always be calm and objective) they were a damned sight better off (and certainly better protected) than a lot of others their age. Had that been when it started, this uncertainty of his, around the time of Ellen's problems? Near enough, O'Farrell thought; within days at least. Christ, these martinis were good! O'Farrell decided he could win drink-making contests with them. He studied the glass seriously, extended before him. Not a difficulty, he told himself. He'd increased from one to two—and sometimes a half more, so what!—a night but that was still a very moderate intake and it didn't affect him at all. Still steady as a rock. Almost. Hadn't he thought that word before? Not important. What was important was that he didn't need it. That afternoon on the way back from Chevy Chase had been the last time he'd taken a drink before getting home and after that he'd set himself the test and passed, because he didn't think of booze or need it during the day. Didn't need it now; just a way of relaxing while Jill fixed the meal and he looked over the cuttings.

He hadn't done anything about getting them copied, he realized. Or preserving the photograph upstairs. He really had to do that. Maybe he'd take the whole lot into Washington the following day and get it done, there and then. Then again, maybe he should wait and ask around; he couldn't risk the slightest damage. Who could he ask? Someone in one of the libraries or archives, he supposed; Washington was knee-deep in records so it shouldn't be difficult. He seemed to remember that the Library of Congress had a photographic section, too, so he could ask there about the fading print. He'd definitely do it the very next day. Not a lot of work on, after all. He was up to date with the accounts and Petty hadn't—O'Farrell determinedly stopped the direction, unwilling to consider Petty and what a summons from the man would mean. Perhaps there wouldn't be one anymore, he thought, the perpetual hope. With it came the other hope to which the first was always linked. There were others in the department after all—although he had no idea of their identities, of course, any more than they had of his—so it was not automatic he would be the one chosen.

With the third martini almost exhausted (no, he wouldn't make anymore: that would be ridiculous) O'Farrell hunched over his glass, forcing the examination upon himself. Why? Why was he feeling like this, nervous like this, flaky like this! It couldn't be any moral uncertainty. Every sentence he had carried out had been one hundred and one percent justified, absolutely, unquestionably, and unequivocally; all the evidence examined and checked, all the benefits and doubts allowed in the defendants' favor. Proven guilty beyond doubt or appeal. Why then! Age; some midlife hormonal imbalance? Preposterous! What did age have to do with anything! The three-monthly physical examinations would have picked up any bodily fluctuations. And mentally he'd been trained far beyond this sort of infantile self-questioning. What about fear? The word presented itself in his mind, like an unwelcome guest whose shadow he had already picked out beyond a door but hoped would not intrude. Fear of what then? The roles being reversed? Had he become frightened of the tables being turned, of there one day being a mistake—the simplest, easiest error—and of himself becoming the victim, the hunted, rather than always the victor, the hunter?

Had that been how his great-grandfather felt when he retired? But at sixty, O'Farrell remembered, not forty-six. He shuddered the question away, not able to answer it anyway. There was something he *could* answer, positively resolve. Now that he'd let the unwelcome shadow take a form—present itself—O'Farrell was sure he could defeat it. As long as he didn't make a mistake—and wasn't that the thrust of all the training and retraining and exercises?—he didn't run the risk of becoming a victim. There was a slight lift of relief, but very slight, not as much as he wanted. Enough, though. He'd isolated the problem, and having isolated it, he could easily defeat it. He hoped that really was his problem.

O'Farrell responded at once to his wife's call, curious when he stood to see that his glass was empty, because he couldn't remember finishing it. He carried it with him to the kitchen and smiled at Jill, who smiled back.

"I was writing to Ellen and I burned the meat loaf," she apologized.

O'Farrell became aware of the smell. "I like my meat loaf well done."

"You got it!"

The gin and vermouth were still on the counter, where he had left the bottles after making his martini. He put his empty glass beside the sink, away from them. With his back to his wife, O'Farrell said, "Would you like a drink with dinner?"

"Drink?"

"I bought some California burgundy—Napa Valley—on the way home."

"No," said Jill, very definitely.

"Then I won't, either," he said, turning and smiling at her again. Another proving test, showing (showing who?) that he didn't need it.

They sat with their heads lowered and O'Farrell gave thanks, wondering for the first time ever if there were an hypocrisy in how easy he found it to pray. Why should there be? Were more regular lawmen—FBI agents and CIA officers and sheriffs and policemen and marshals and drug enforcement agents and Customs investigators— precluded from acknowledging God because of the occasional outcome of their vocation?

"I told Ellen we'd go up next weekend," Jill announced, serving the meal. "I haven't sealed the letter, though; just in case you didn't want to."

"Is that likely?"

"I didn't want to take it for granted."

"I love you," O'Farrell blurted. And he did. He felt a physical warmth, a surge of emotion, toward her; he could have made love to her, right there, and decided to, later.

Jill smiled across the table at him, appearing surprised. "I love you, too," she said.

"There's something I want to tell you—" O'Farrell started to say, and then jerked to a stop, horrified at how close he'd come to bringing about an absolute disaster. He'd actually set out to explain to her—the words were jumbled there, in his mind—what he truly did! The incredulous awareness momentarily robbed him of any speech, although his mind still functioned. What was the right order of words?

I think you should know, darling, that I kill people. But don't be alarmed. I am one of a select few, executioners who operate within their own concepts of legality, justified—although not officially acknowledged or recognized—by the United States of America to rid it (and the world) of men who deserve to die but are beyond the reach or jurisdiction of any normal court of justice. Think how many lives would have been saved—assassination actually saves lives, you know—if someone had removed Hitler or Stalin or Amin. I just thought you should know and the meat loaf isn't burned too badly at all!

"What?" prompted Jill.

"Nothing . . . I . . . nothing . . ." O'Farrell mumbled.

"But you started to say—"

"I wasn't thinking. . . ."

"Darling! You're not making sense! And you're sweating! The sweat's all over your face. What is it!"

"Nothing." He was still groping, seeking an escape. What were the words! The explanation!

Jill laid down her knife and fork, staring at him across the table. "Are you all right!"

"Hot, that's all," he said, mumbling. "Maybe a fever." Could he get away with something as facile as that? She wasn't stupid—and she worked in a medical environment, for Christ's sake!

"Can I get you anything?"

The meat loaf was dry in his mouth, the ground beef like sawdust blocking his throat. He gulped at the water she'd set out, wishing it were the red wine he'd brought (better still, a strong gin). "It was an odd feeling, that's all. It's gone now. I'm all right. Honest." Why had he done it? What insanity had momentarily seized him and carried him so close to the cliff edge like that?

"So?" Jill prompted.

"So?" O'Farrell was stalling, still without the proper words.

"You started to say there was something you wanted to tell me?" she reminded him gently.

"The money," O'Farrell said desperately. "I made some calculations in the den tonight. I think we can afford to go on making the kids the sort of allowance that we are at the moment."

Jill frowned at him. "But we already decided that."

"I wasn't sure," O'Farrell said, a drowning man finding firmer ground. "That's why I made the calculations. Now I am. Sure, I mean."

Jill stayed frowning. "Good," she said curiously.

"It *is* good, isn't it?" O'Farrell started to eat again, forcing himself to swallow.

"Very good," she agreed, still doubtful.

That night they didn't make love after all. O'Farrell remained awake long after Jill had fallen asleep beside him, his body as well as his mind held rigid by the enormity of his near collapse. His body was wet with the recollection but his mouth was dry, parched, so that he lay with his mouth open and had the impression that his lips were about to crack. He desperately wanted a drink but refused to get out of bed, fearing that if he went to the kitchen for water, he would change his mind and pour something else. Didn't need it, he told himself. Didn't need it. Couldn't give in. Wouldn't give in.

"Sweet Jesus!" exclaimed McCarthy. "Holy sweet Jesus!" He was given to blasphemous outbursts when he was excited and he was excited now.

"Quite a picture," Sneider agreed, seeking a lead from the other man.

"We can close down Belac," the CIA department head said. "Lure the bastard here, have the FBI arrest him, and then hit him with so many indictments he won't know which way is which."

"What about the ambassador, Rivera?"

"Which is what he is, an ambassador," said McCarthy, with logic that would have been absurdly obscure to any other man.

"He's not committing a crime within the jurisdiction of any American court. And he can always cop a plea of diplomatic immunity if we save it up for later."

McCarthy nodded in agreement. "He's got to be stopped, though."

"No doubt about it." Sneider knew the way now.

McCarthy used the private telephone on his desk, one that was security-cleared but did not go through the CIA switchboard. "George!" he greeted when Petty answered. "How are things?"

"Good," said Petty, from his office near Lafayette Park.

"Busy?"

"Not particularly."

"Thought we might meet?"

"You choose."

"How about tomorrow?"

"Tomorrow's good."

"Twelve-thirty?"

"Fine."

The summons to Charles ·O'Farrell came twenty-four hours after that.

NINE

PETTY DECREED a meeting in the open air, which he sometimes did, and which O'Farrell regarded as overly theatrical, like those movies about the CIA where people met each other without one acknowledging or looking directly at the other. The section head chose the Ellipse, at noon, but O'Farrell intentionally arrived early. He put his car in the garage on E Street, which meant he had to walk back past the National Theater and the Willard, where he and Jill had endured the embarrassment of that face-slapping row. Momentarily he considered the Round Robin again but almost at once dismissed it. Instead he cut around the block to the Washington Hotel, choosing the darkened ground-floor bar, not the open rooftop veranda overlooking the Treasury Building and the White House beyond. It was more discreet, anonymous; he certainly didn't want to encounter Petty and Erickson taking an early cocktail themselves. He didn't know if either of them drank; didn't know anything at all about them. Just that they were the two from whom he took his orders. In the first year there had been three. Chris Wilmot had been an asthmatic jogger who'd died on a morning run down Capitol Hill. O'Farrell never knew why the man hadn't been replaced.

He ordered a double gin and tonic, but poured in only half the tonic, briefly staring into the glass. Okay, so now he was drinking during the day. Not the day; the morning. Needed it, that's all. Just one, to get his hands steady. He studied them as he reached forward for the glass; hardly a movement. He was fine. Just this one then. Wouldn't become a habit. How could it? Other times he had an office to go to and accounts to balance. Nothing at all wrong in taking an occasional drink this early; quite pleasant in fact. Relaxing. That's what he had to do, relax. Get rid of the sensation balled up in his gut, like he'd eaten too much heavy food he couldn't shift, the feeling that had been there since the telephone call.

More movie theatrics. "There's a need for us to meet." No hello, no identification, no good-bye, no kiss-my-ass. O'Farrell openly sniggered at the nonsense of it. The barman was at the far end, near the kitchen door, reading the sports section of the *Washington Post*, and didn't hear.

O'Farrell took a long pull at his drink. Tasted good; still only 11:20. Plenty of time to cross over to the park. To what? He made himself think. There was only one answer. Who would it be? And why? And how difficult? The method was always the most difficult; that's what made him so good, the time and trouble he always took over the method. Never any embarrassment, never any comeback. It would be the sixth, he calculated, the same number now as his great-grandfather. Who'd retired after that. No, not quite. The man had stayed in office for another five or six years at least. But he'd never been forced into another confrontation. Six, O'Farrell thought again. All justified, every one of them. Crimes against the country, against the people; his country, his people. Verdicts had not been returned by a recognized court, that's all; no question of what those verdicts would have been, if there had been an arraignment. Guilty every time. Unanimous; guilty as charged, on all counts.

Eleven-thirty, he saw. Still plenty of time. Some tonic left. He made a noise and the barman looked up, nodding to O'Farrell's gesture.

The barman set the fresh glass in front of him and said, "Time to kill, eh?"

"Something like that."

"Visiting?"

"Just looking around," O'Farrell said, purposely vague. Never be positive, never look positive, in any casual encounter; always essential to be instantly forgotten at the moment of parting.

."Great city, Washington. Lot to see."

A great capital for a great country, thought O'Farrell, the familiar reflection. "So I hear."

"Where you from?"

"Nowhere special."

The barman appeared unoffended by the evasion. He said, "Austin myself. Been here five years, though. Wouldn't go back."

"Never been to Texas," O'Farrell lied, unwilling to get entangled in an exchange about landmarks or places they both might know. There was a benefit, from the conversation. It was meaningless, empty chitchat, but O'Farrell looked upon it as a test, mentally observing himself as he thought Petty and Erickson might observe him later. He was doing good, he assured himself. Hands as steady as a rock now, the lump in his stomach not so discomforting anymore.

"All the sights are very close to here," offered the barman. "Smithsonian, Space Museum, Washington Monument, Lincoln Memorial . . ."

And the Museum of American History, thought O'Farrell. It was his favorite, a place of which he never tired; he'd hoped, a long time ago, that he might find some reference to his ancestor in Kansas but the archivist hadn't found anything; perhaps he should try again. He said, "Thanks for the advice."

"You feel like another?" The barman indicated O'Farrell's empty glass.

Yes, he thought, at once. "Time to go," he said.

"See you again, maybe?"

"Maybe," said O'Farrell. He wouldn't be able to use the place anymore, in case the man remembered.

The bar had been darker than he realized, and once outside he squinted against the sudden brightness, wishing he'd brought his dark glasses from the car. He hesitated, looking back toward the parking garage and then in the direction of the Ellipse, deciding there was insufficient time now, nearly five-to as it was. O'Farrell was lucky with the lights on Pennsylvania and again on the cross street but still had to hurry to get to the grassed area before the hour struck, which he wanted to do. Petty was a funny bastard and absolute punctuality was one of his fetishes.

He heard the chime from some unseen clock at the same time as he saw both of them on one of the benches opposite the Commerce Building, and thought, Damn! He wasn't late—right on time—but it would have been better if he'd been waiting for them rather than the other way around.

They saw O'Farrell at the same time and rose to meet him, walking not straight toward him but off at a tangent into the path, so that he had to change direction slightly to fall into step.

"Sorry to have kept you," he said at once.

"You weren't late," the section head assured him. "We were early." Petty was using a pipe with a bowl that seemed out of proportion to its stem; the tobacco was sweet smelling, practically perfumed.

"It was a pleasant day to sit in the sun," Erickson said.

O'Farrell still had his eyes screwed against the brightness and hoped he didn't get a headache. He experienced a flicker of irritation. The three of them knew why they were there, so why pussyfoot around talking about the weather! He said, "What is it?"

"Difficult one," Petty said. "Bad."

Weren't they all, O'Farrell thought. He scarcely felt any apprehension; no shake, no uncertainty. "What?"

"Drugs and guns, two-way traffic," came in Erickson.

"Cuba working to destabilize God knows what in Latin America."

"Drugs!" O'Farrell said at once.

"Massive shipments," said Petty. "That's how Havana is raising the money."

O'Farrell had the mental image of little Billy playing space games in the Chicago cafe. And then remembered something else. *I think they ought to kill the bastards! Make it a capital offense and execute them; no appeal, no excuse, nothing. Dead!* Jill's outburst that day in Ellen's kitchen: the dear, sweet, gentle Jill he didn't believe capable of killing anything, not even a bug. He said, "There can't be a federal agency in this city not connected in some way with drug interdiction." It was not an obvious attempt at avoidance. The rules were very clear, very specific: he—and these two men walking either side of him— only became involved when every legal possibility had been considered and positively discarded.

"They would if they could," Petty said. He stopped and the other two had to stop with him while he cupped his hand around his pipe bowl to relight it: briefly he was lost in a cloud of smoke. "It's being done diplomatically," he resumed. "After the initial delivery in Havana, it's all moved through diplomatic channels. Nothing we can do to intercept or stop it."

"Moved everywhere," said Erickson. "Europe, then back to here, according to one source."

"Who is?" O'Farrell demanded at once. Another clear and specific rule was that he was allowed access to everything—and everyone, if he deemed it necessary— connected with an operation, to assure himself personally of its validity. Increasingly over the years, he had come to regard what he'd initially considered a concession to his judgment to be instead a further way for the CIA to distance itself from the section.

"Supply pilot," Petty said. "Got caught up in a storm.

An AWAC zeroed in on him and some of our guys forced him to land in Florida."

They came to a bench near a flowered area and Petty slumped onto it, bringing the other two down with him; the section leader's self-consciousness about his size meant he sat with his head hanging forward, almost as if he were asleep.

"This is just the spot on July Fourth," Erickson said. "Fantastic view of the fireworks. You ever been here on July Fourth?"

"Yes," O'Farrell said. Ellen must have been around eleven, John a year younger. He wondered why they'd never brought the grandchildren; he'd have to suggest it to Jill. "Why's he talking?"

Erickson snickered. "The plane was packed with almost half a ton of coke, ninety-two percent purity, that's why he's talking. He wants a deal."

"He going to get it?" Letting the guilty escape justice in return for their informing on others was a fact of American jurisprudence with which O'Farrell could never fully become reconciled. It made it too easy for too many to escape. His hands were stretched in front of him, one on each leg; very calm, very controlled. They really could have been talking about the weather or the July Fourth fireworks.

"It's a Customs bust, not our responsibility," said Erickson.

What, precisely, was their responsibility? O'Farrell wondered. He couldn't imagine it ever having been defined, within parameters. Well, maybe somewhere, buried in some atom-bomb shelter and embargoed against publication for the next million years. "Which means the bastard might!"

The moment O'Farrell had spoken, he snapped his mouth shut, as if he were trying to bite the remark back, abruptly conscious of both men frowning sideways at him.

Petty said, "You got any personal feelings about this?"

Nothing is personal; never can be. If it becomes personal, withdraw and abort. The inviolable instructions. Always. O'Farrell said, "Of course not! How could I?"

"You seemed to be expressing a point of view," Petty pressed.

"Isn't a person allowed a point of view about drugs?"

"We comply, we don't opinionate," Erickson said.

The logic, like the word choice, was screwed, O'Farrell thought. How could they do what they had to do—but much more importantly, how could *he* do what he was required to do—without coming to any opinion. It was the same as concluding a judgment, wasn't it?

"Just as long as it isn't a problem," Petty said, almost glibly.

"The courier isn't who we're talking about," Erickson added.

"Who then?" O'Farrell was glad to escape the pressure. Still no shake, though; no problem. He felt the twinge of a headache. Not the booze; goddamned sun, blazing in his face like this.

"The ambassador in London. Guy named Rivera. Glossy son of a bitch." Petty began to cough and tapped the pipe out against the edge of the bench. "Doctor says I shouldn't do this."

The dottle made a breeze-blown, scattered mess and it didn't smell perfumed anymore. O'Farrell found it easy to understand why pipe smoking was banned in practically every public place: it was a filthy, antisocial habit. He said, "What about the arms supplier?"

"The FBI can get him," Erickson said. "They're setting up a scam to get him within American jurisdiction. Then . . . snap!" The man slapped his hands together sharply, a strangely demonstrative gesture, and O'Farrell jumped, surprised. He wished he hadn't.

"London's the target then?" He looked from one man to the other. Neither spoke. Petty gave the briefest of affirmative nods. Arguably deniable, if the shit hit the fan, thought O'Farrell. "There's a file?"

"Of course," Petty said.

"What's the time frame?"

"Linked to a move against the supplier," Erickson said.

"I need to be sure."

"The usual understanding," Petty agreed at once.

First one, then the other, recognized O'Farrell. Like a vaudeville act. Except that this wasn't the sort of act to raise a laugh. Deniable again. Brought before any subsequent inquiry, each, quite honestly and without the risk of perjury, could deny a chain of command or instruction. *I may have said this, but I categorically deny saying that. No, sir, I cannot imagine how the impression could have been conveyed for this man to believe he was operating under any sort of official instruction. Yes sir, I agree that such an impression is impossible. Yes sir, I agree that the concept of taking the life of another without that person having been found guilty by a properly appointed court of law is inconceivable. No sir, I did not at any time.* . . . Was that another fear, O'Farrell wondered urgently, that he was so completely exposed, without being guaranteed—no, not even guaranteed—without any official backing in what he unofficially did for his country? Close, he thought; not a complete explanation but coming close. He said, "If the arms dealer is caught, then surely the ambassador, Rivera, will be publicly implicated?" Again it was not an obvious attempt at avoidance; rather the question of a professional properly examining what he was being called upon to do, examining all the angles, all the pitfalls.

"Of course," Petty said, glib again. "But so what! There can be a denial from Havana. He'll invoke diplomatic immunity. And go on trafficking."

"So what about the coincidence of something happening to Rivera at the same time as the arms dealer is busted?" O'Farrell persisted.

"Examples—and benefits—to everyone!" Erickson said, embarking again on their vaudeville act.

"All the innocents, on the outside, imagine some sort of feud between the two," Petty began.

". . . thieves falling out," said the other man.

". . . Cuba privately gets the warning it deserves," mouthed the section chief.

". . . and so do all the other arms suppliers, against becoming involved again."

". . . all the angles covered . . ."

". . . all the holes blocked . . ."

". . . discreet . . ."

". . . effective . . ."

Petty smiled, the star of the show, confident of another consummate display. "How we always like to be," he said in conclusion. "Discreetly effective."

It *was* a virtuoso performance, O'Farrell conceded. He wished he were able to admire it more. "Anyone else involved?"

"Peripheral people . . . shippers, stuff like that," said Erickson. "They'll get the same private message."

"England is pretty efficiently policed," O'Farrell pointed out. More than any other country in which he had so far operated, he acknowledged to himself for the first time.

"We accept that," Petty said, rising up on the verbal seesaw again.

"Usual understanding," Erickson descended.

". . . Yours is always the right . . ."

". . . to refuse . . ."

Now! thought O'Farrell. Now was the moment, the agreed-upon, accepted moment, when he was allowed to decline. Before he became irrevocably committed by that one further step, going forward to access the topmost classified files, after which there was no retreat, no escape. Easily done, supposedly. No requirement for an explanation or reason. He'd immediately come under suspicious scrutiny, he guessed; practically tantamount to resigning. Wasn't that precisely what he wanted, to resign! Just continue with a recognized official job? The halt came with the continuing thought: a recognized official job with a recognized official salary, to which his pension would be linked. Couldn't afford that now, not while he was helping Ellen and John. Blood money, he thought; bounty hunter. He said, "I'd like to interview the pilot first."

The men on either side smiled, and Petty nodded at the acceptance. The section chief said, "It's a very necessary operation."

They wouldn't be sitting here in the blinding sunlight if it hadn't already been judged that, O'Farrell thought, irritably; so why the apparent justification? "Where is all the documentation?"

"At the Lafayette office," said Erickson.

"I'll look that over afterward."

"The pilot is being held in Tallahassee; name's Rodgers, Paul Rodgers."

"Be careful," Erickson said.

O'Farrell turned to look directly at the man, genuinely astonished.

Erickson appeared embarrassed, too. He lifted and dropped his hands in a meaningless gesture and said, "It's never easy," which was neither an apology nor an improvement.

"Is there anything else?" O'Farrell asked curtly.

"In London . . . anywhere else you have to go . . . you'll keep in touch through the embassy's CIA channels," Petty said.

Why did they keep on saying things that were routine! Careful, O'Farrell thought; it would be wrong to overreact and read into remarks significance that was not there. Routine or not, they had to be said. There could be no misunderstanding or mistake. "Of course," he said.

"And we'll pouch anything technical you need in the diplomatic bag," Erickson said.

Just like Cuba pouched its cocaine, thought O'Farrell; things to kill with, one way or the other. He stood, looking down at the two seated men. "I wonder if it really will be taken as a warning?"

"That's the message," Petty said. "It'll be heard, believe me."

The two remained on the bench, watching O'Farrell walk back toward Pennsylvania Avenue.

"Well?" Petty asked.

Erickson made an uncertain rocking motion with his hand. "Okay, I think."

"Symmons isn't often wrong."

"There's always a first time."

"There can't ever be a first time."

"Sorry," Erickson apologized. "Figure of speech. Sorry about telling him to be careful, too. That was stupid of me."

"Yes," Petty said, unforgiving. "It was. Very stupid. Did you smell booze on his breath?"

"Before noon! You've got to be kidding!"

"That's why I put the pipe out, to be sure."

"Were you?"

"Pretty sure."

"I didn't get it myself; I would have expected to."

"Yes," Petty agreed. "Perhaps I was mistaken."

"That final remark was interesting," the deputy suggested.

"About being taken as a warning?"

Erickson nodded. "You think that indicated any doubt, about the validity of what he does?"

"It sometimes happens. I would have thought he was pretty straight about the morality, though."

"There was a sharp reaction when he heard drugs were involved," Erickson said. "His kids ever get mixed up with any shit?"

Unknown to O'Farrell—although suspected by him because it was obvious—everything in his background and family had been examined by the Agency. Petty shook his head. "Squeaky clean, both of them."

"Maybe just a natural response to narcotics."

"I think we should take precautions," Petty decided.

"More than usual?" There was always surveillance.

Petty nodded. "Just to cover ourselves."

"Probably wise," Erickson concurred.

"You were right," Petty announced.

"Right?"

"It's a great day to sit in the sun."

That night O'Farrell deliberately made three full martinis, which he drank unseen in the den, and he insisted upon opening the Napa Valley wine to drink with the steaks. Jill only had one glass and O'Farrell limited himself to two, wanting to prove to her—and to himself—that he could leave some in the bottle for another occasion.

He took her abruptly in bed, without any foreplay, and she was obviously startled and then responded, and it was good for both of them.

Afterward she said, "That was practically rape!"

"I'm sorry."

"I didn't say I minded."

"I might have to go away for a while."

"Where?"

"Something to check out down south first. Then Europe, possibly."

"How long?"

"I don't know." As quickly as possible, he thought. Get it over with.

"I've got some time coming," said Jill. "I might go up to Chicago."

"Why don't you do that?"

"I'm glad that thing with drugs at Billy's school was a false alarm."

"So am I, if it really were a false alarm."

"You want to know something?"

"What?"

"I'm so very happy and content. You happy?"

"Of course," O'Farrell said. Dear God, how he wished that were true.

TEN

O'FARRELL REMEMBERED the first time very well. He could recall, vividly, every operation, of course, but the first most clearly of all. He had not been with the Agency then. Seconded to it from his special-duty unit in Vietnam, he had been on a deep penetration probe over the border into Cambodia, just himself and two other full-time CIA officers, checking a report that the village headman near Vinh Long was a primary intelligence source for North Vietnamese coming down the Ho Chi Minh Trail. And actually come upon the bastard huddled among his communist contacts, identifying American positions on a map on the ground between them.

It was O'Farrell's introduction to the importance of forethought; his aptitude test, as well, for the job that the Agency would offer when he finished his army tour, although he was never to know it had been such a test. He'd actually moved, without the slightest sound, in the bamboo thicket from which they were watching, bringing up the M-16 to wipe out every one of the motherfuckers. And then felt the restraining hand upon his arm and looked up to see the CIA supervisor, Jerry Stone, shaking his head and then gesturing for them to pull back.

It had been the following day when he killed the headman, without any compunction. It was a war situation and people were killed in wars. And he knew, unquestionably, that the man was guilty. He'd carried out that execution in front of the man's own villagers as a warning against co-operating with the enemy. And Stone had found the map in the man's hooch, and they'd set up the ambushes at every U.S. emplacement they knew to be targeted by the North Vietnamese and the Vietcong and shot all sorts of shit out of them when they hit. The body count had been thirty-five. He'd been awarded a Bronze Star for distinguished service.

As a professional serving soldier, O'Farrell had never had any difficulty over Vietnam. He'd been proud to go—*wanted* to go—and serve his country. He saw it as a simple black-and-white conflict, the way his father had seen the war in Korea, freedom versus communism. It had been easier for him, he supposed, and easier still for his father, because they knew about communism, the way it should be known about. Personally. His mother had only been a child, little older than nine, he guessed, when she'd been smuggled out of Latvia, but she'd been able to recall what it had been like and tell him about it—every detail—when she'd felt he was old enough. She told him how Soviet soldiers had come into Klaipeda and raped her mother and how they would have raped her, although she was only a child, if the woman hadn't refused to tell them her hiding place, in the chimney inglenook. How she'd crouched there, hearing it happen, and afterward heard her mother murdered in their anger at not being able to find a girl they knew to be there somewhere, even though they practically ripped the house apart. And the less personal stories. How anyone bravely stupid enough to oppose the Soviet annexation was either deported or slaughtered, all freedom crushed underfoot. Of the secret police and the all-too-eager informants and the forcible induction of all the able-bodied men into the Russian army, an induction from which her father had escaped only by taking her on an apparently suicidal rowboat voyage across the Baltic to Karlskrona.

The opposition to Vietnam that arose at home had bewildered him; still did. He had never been able to understand why the draft dodgers and the flag burners and the protesters couldn't comprehend the reality. America's mistake had not been *fighting* in Vietnam. It had been not fighting enough, making it a limited war that stopped at a dividing line instead of going right on up into Hanoi. If Johnson or Nixon had done that, hundreds, thousands, of lives would have been saved, just as thousands of lives were saved by what he did. Vietnam would now be unified and free. And the war would have ended years earlier than it had, and without that humiliating claptrap about peace with honor, which had been nothing of the sort, but rather America being ass-whipped by a bunch of peasants in lampshade hats and black pyjamas.

The FASTEN SEAT BELTS sign came on at the same time as the announcement and O'Farrell obeyed, gazing through the window at the flatness of Florida. Why the doubts then? Why the doubts and the need for a quick drink to steady himself and the constant self-examination? Intellectually— although he never conceded it emotionally—he had difficulty with the Hitler and Stalin and Amin analogy. But he *sincerely* believed, he told himself, that a lot of lives, and suffering and hardship and misery, had been saved by what he'd done. After all, he'd carried out his own investigation every time and studied every piece of information. And a lot of lives would be saved if he were satisfied with this and took out a diplomat abusing his privileges by trafficking in drugs and guns. It would be difficult, for Christ's sake, to come up with any combination that caused more deaths and suffering and hardship and misery than drugs and guns.

You know what drugs are? he'd asked Billy.

And the answer: *Stuff that makes you feel funny.* Boom, boom and the Coke container was breached by the space invader. Easy, he told himself; don't make it personal. He shouldn't have reacted so vehemently in front of Petty and Erickson. Got away with it, though; still, not a mistake he should make again. Shouldn't make any mistakes; couldn't make any mistakes.

O'Farrell became conscious of the stewardess in the aisle and looked toward her. She was a milk-fed, apple-cheeked blonde and professionally pretty, like a doll; there had to be a factory somewhere producing five hundred such girls every week, already clad in the uniforms of the world's airlines.

"I need your tray table up in the seat in front of you, and I need to take your glass," she said. The teeth were capped and perfect, like everything else about her. He wondered if she were still a virgin and was surprised at the turn of thought.

O'Farrell restored the tiny table and handed her the glass; three but it had been a boring trip, although there had been time to think. And the gin hadn't touched him at all. Sober as a judge. Wasn't that what he was, a judge appointed to carry out a full and complete inquiry and to reach a verdict properly befitting the crime? No, he thought, in immediate contradiction. His responsibility was the sentence, not the verdict. The verdict had already been reached. Another contradiction. Returned. But still to be carried out.

O'Farrell was working professionally, which imposed many patterns. An important one was untraceable invisibility. So he disdained any thought of a hotel, cruising around the town until he located a motel on Apalachee Parkway and limiting his association with any staff to the single act of checking in.

He was at the detention building fifteen minutes ahead of the Washington-arranged interview. There was a bar opposite, and he knew he had time, but he entered the government building, pleased with his self-control. O'Farrell endured the expected affability of the local officer, agree-

ing that drugs were a bitch and the shortages of enforcement resources were a bitch and changing policies were a
bitch and that the constant infighting between the various
federal agencies was a bitch, but that this was a good bust
and there was going to be a lot of promotional mileage out
of it.

O'Farrell insisted on entering the interview room first
so that Rodgers had to be the person coming to him. He
didn't stand when the man entered. When the escort asked
if he should stay, O'Farrell barely shook his head so that
the prisoner would see the contemptuous dismissal of the
idea that Rodgers might be any sort of physical risk.

Because he was still on remand, Rodgers had been allowed to retain his own clothes, a cut-to-the-skin black
shirt, open at the neck, and designer jeans that O'Farrell
guessed had been additionally tailored, so perfectly did
they fit. The loafers were Gucci. All the jewelry had been
impounded, but there was a thin white ring marking the
skin around the man's sun-bronzed neck. There was also a
wider band of white on his tanned wrist and the pinky finger of his left hand. Everything would have been gold,
O'Farrell guessed; heavy gold. Rodgers was exercise lean,
tightly curled hair close to his scalp.

"You my man?" Rodgers said, still at the door. The
teeth were white and even, like the stewardess's on the
plane.

"Sit down!" O'Farrell ordered, gesturing to the seat on
the other side of the table.

Rodgers did but reversed the chair to straddle it like he
was astride a horse, arms crossed over the round of its
back. Christ! thought O'Farrell. Then: Don't get upset,
personally involved. Then: *Stuff that makes you feel funny.*
Just feet away—six or seven feet away—was one of the
bastards providing shit to make kids feel funny.

"So, you my man?" Rodgers's nails were perfectly
manicured.

"Can you count?"

"What sort of question is that? 'Course I can count!"

O'Farrell splayed his right hand in front of the other man's face and said, "So count," opening and closing his fingers seven times. If the asshole wanted it played macho-man rules, it was all right by him.

"Thirty-five," Rodgers said.

"Years," O'Farrell added. "That's the max: thirty-five years. I checked with the District Attorney. And that's what they're going for, the maximum, no parole, because you haven't got a defense that Perry Mason would even consider. You're thirty-three. I checked that, too. So you're sixty-eight when you get out. You any idea how difficult it is to get any pussy when you're sixty-eight?"

"What the fuck are you talking about?"

"Facts," O'Farrell said. "I'm talking facts."

"Haven't they told you, for Christ's sake?"

"Told me what?"

"I want to *cooperate*! Do a deal!"

"They told me."

"So what . . . ?" Rodgers faded away, confused.

"I want you to understand from the beginning," O'Farrell said quietly. "You're going to tell me everything true, no bullshit, no fucking around. True from the very word *go*. Because I'm going to check and double-check and if I find just one thing wrong—" O'Farrell narrowed his thumb against his forefinger, so there was practically no space between—"just that much wrong, I'm going to dump on you. I'm going to go back to the DA and I'm going to say that Paul Rodgers is a scumbag and I don't deal with scumbags and you can throw the book at him. Sixty-eight years old and trying to get pussy . . . Just think of it."

"Jesus!" the drug runner exclaimed, physically recoiling.

It had been overdone, O'Farrell conceded; theatrical, just like Petty and Erickson. "You understand?"

" 'Course I understand!" Rodgers said. "You think I don't know what I got to lose!"

The bombast and swagger had gone, O'Farrell thought; so it had been worthwhile. "Good. So what is it you've got to tell me?"

The smile came back, a sly expression. "Haven't we got something to tell each other?"

Careful, thought O'Farrell. He said, "Like what?"

"Like the exchange. What I get for what you get."

"You don't listen, do you?" O'Farrell said. "I'm not offering you shit. You're looking at thirty-five years, and you're going to go on looking at thirty-five years until I'm convinced you've leveled with me. On everything."

"This way I got nothing! I'm dependent on you all the way!"

"Don't you forget it," O'Farrell said. "Forget that for a moment and you're screwed."

"I dunno," Rodgers said, shrugging and looking away. "I dunno this is such a good idea."

Would he personally be off the hook if this bastard withdrew cooperation? Probably not; Petty talked of there being a file at Lafayette Square. He said, "So what other shot you think you've got?"

"I need a guarantee."

"You need a miracle."

The man's lower lip was going back and forth between his teeth, like Ellen's had, in Chicago. "I just didn't expect it to be done this way, is all."

O'Farrell exaggerated his sigh of impatience, moving as if to stand. "Okay, so you've nothing to tell me! I've wasted my time and that makes me mad, but you're the guy digging the grave. Enjoy life in the slammer, jerk."

He actually began to rise and Rodgers said, "No! Wait!" He made a lowering gesture with his hand. "Okay, we'll talk. . . . I'll talk. Just don't go."

For several moments O'Farrell remained neither standing nor sitting, appearing unsure whether to agree. Then he sat and said, "Okay. So talk."

Rodgers swallowed and looked away, assembling his

thoughts. "Been doing it for quite a while," the man began awkwardly. "Years. Had a good run. Because I was careful, see. Word got around. Made a reputation."

"Flying from where?" O'Farrell asked.

"Colombia, always Colombia." Rodgers extended his hand, palm cupped upward. "They got the trade like that. Bolivia and Peru might be bigger growers, but Colombia controls the trade."

"In what?"

"Coke, man! Marijuana too. And pills. Methaqualone."

O'Farrell thought the man spoke like a salesman, offering his wares. *Stuff that makes you feel funny.* He said, "Whereabouts in Colombia?"

"All over. I guess Medellin more than most."

"And to where?"

"All over again, in the early years," said Rodgers. "Bahamas, Turks and Caicos, Mexico. Couple of times—three actually—I even flew into Florida. Too dangerous, though. Had to abandon the airplane every time because I couldn't refuel."

"Dates!" O'Farrell insisted at once. There would be an official record of abandoned aircraft.

"Dates?"

"The month and the year when you abandoned aircraft in Florida."

Rodgers frowned with the difficulty of recall. "June . . . I think it was June . . . 1987. Then again in September that year. January eighty-eight. I'm sure about that; the nearest I came to getting busted—"

"What about later?"

"They came to me in eighty-eight," Rodgers said. "February. I got a place on the beach just outside Fort Lauderdale. Guy comes there one day. Latin, prefers to speak Spanish. Very smooth. Says he had a proposition and I think it's a setup, and I tell him to go to hell, that I'm a property developer and I don't know what he's talking about. He laughs at me, says he admires my caution.

But not my business ability. Says that flying one way with cargo but back again empty is a wasted commercial opportunity, which I know it is, but what's been the alternative? I still think he's sucking me, so I go on playing wide-eyed and innocent. Then he asks if I'm curious how he found me, and I say I am, and he tells me it was on the personal recommendation of Fabio Ochoa—"

"Who is?" interrupted O'Farrell. He already knew but wanted Rodgers to tell him.

"One of the big guys in Colombia . . . and I'm talking *big*. An actual member of the Cartel. I'd flown for him a few times, out of Medellin," Rodgers said. "But it still don't mean a thing, right? It could still have been a come-on. So I say ho-hum, diddly-dee, admitting nothing. And then he knocks me sideways. Tells me his name is Cuadrado and he knows I am doing a run the next week for Ochoa—which I was—and that when I get into Medellin, Ochoa is going to meet me personally and tell me what a one-hundred-percent guy he, Cuadrado, is. Which is exactly what happens, and now it can't be a setup with any of you guys, right?"

"What did Ochoa tell you?"

"That business was expanding. There was going to be a two-way traffic, drugs outward, weapons inward. And that the risk factor was going to be cut to nil because from now on there would only be one customer, Cuba. That it was all official, right up to Castro's crotch in Havana, so there'd be no hassle. And that Cuadrado was in the government and I was to do everything he said."

"You went to Cuba?"

"That collection from Ochoa was *for* Cuadrado," said Rodgers. "The airstrip is at Matanzas and it *is* official. Government planes, government officials, all the right stuff. Cuadrado drives me into town and gives me a fat steak and a Havana cigar and sets out the whole deal. Says they've hit upon the perfect enterprise, giving the capitalists—he actually said that, the capitalists—what they want and with the money from the capitalists they're going to give the oppressed in Latin America what they want, the way to gain their freedom. All bullshit—but what the hell, I'm making more money, so he can spout crap all he wants. . . ."

Freedom! thought O'Farrell. What did this oily son of a bitch know about freedom! Or those other sons of bitches in Havana! Freedom to them was maneuvering countries into becoming client states, dependent for arms or money or both, and then treating them like satellites. The Soviet Union had been doing that since 1917. He said, "We're talking truth, agreed?"

Rodgers looked at him warily. "So what's the matter?"

"Cuadrado is in the government?"

Rodgers smiled. "Works in their Export Ministry! Isn't that a kicker!"

"And you're a drug runner?"

The grin on Rodgers's face faded. "So?"

"So what's an official of the Ministry doing setting out the whole deal—your words—to the delivery boy?"

Rodgers's face went tight at being dismissed as a delivery boy, but he cleared it quickly. "Ochoa guaranteed me. And Cuadrado has a personal problem."

"Personal problem?"

Rodgers put an outstretched finger beneath his nose and inhaled noisily. "He got too fond of sampling his own supplies."

"So he was high when he told you this?"

"At thirty-five thousand feet. Feeling no pain."

There should be photographs of Cuadrado in CIA files, O'Farrell calculated. And the Agency should have sources in Havana to provide some background material as well. "So what else did he tell you?"

"That the scheme was foolproof. All the ordering—the drugs too, after delivery to Cuba—would travel as diplomatic cargo; get that!" Rodgers laughed.

"How did the weaponry come, loose or crated?" O'Farrell asked.

"Crated; nearly always crated."

"That couldn't be diplomatic cargo."

"Sea," Rodgers said at once. "Like the man said, it was perfect. The majority of the supplies came from Europe, by ship. Sometimes they were rerouted during the voyage. But always to somewhere safe, where there was no hassle."

From the Cuban—the communist—point of view, it was perfect, O'Farrell conceded. "So that's how it happened?"

"Smooth as silk," Rodgers said.

"How many trips did you make, running guns?"

There was another frown, for recall. "Thirty," the man said. "It has to be thirty at least; more I guess. I didn't really count."

The switch, from past to present tense and then back again, was all part of the finger-snapping, macho shit, thought O'Farrell. *You my man?* Black jive, in addition. Christ, what an asshole Rodgers was! Scum. Scum that got scoured out, cleaned away. Everything fumigated afterward. *Stuff that makes you . . .*

No. Wrong. And for more than one reason. He was trying to shrug off the responsibility for what he was now committed to do, shrug it off onto another offense, onto something vaguely involving his family and an innocent, gullible, long-lashed, round-cheeked little guy who played with plastic spacemen. Billy, the risk to Billy, couldn't be his shield, his excuse. He'd made his own decision, in a brown-dirt village square with squawking chickens and crying, pleading villagers in front of two calm-eyed, calm-limbed CIA officers. Black and white: wrong and right. Like this was wrong. He said, "Where?"

A vague shrug. "Everywhere."

"What do you mean, everywhere?" The voice almost too loud, too demanding.

"Just that, man."

Man. O'Farrell said, "You got a bad memory? Forgotten what we talked about, maybe?"

"What the hell do you want?"

"Where! That's what I want! *Where!"*

A shrug started, then stopped. "Colombia itself, a lot of times. There are guerrilla groups there, you know? FARC and M-19 . . ."

"I know," O'Farrell said shortly. "Where else?"

The hesitation this time was not for recall, O'Farrell gauged. This time the fucker was running the other delivery places through in his mind, trying to calculate which would cause least offense.

"I did a run to Brazil, place near Porto Alegre." Rodgers appeared proud of the choice; the evasion.

Brazil was a drug-producing country; it would have been small-time stuff, a few handguns to allow the local traffickers to strut their stuff, bang-bang you're dead. "And?" Very quiet, like it didn't really matter, but looking directly at Rodgers to show he wasn't impressed by this bullshit.

"Mexico! Two or three to Mexico!"

Another producer. A border country, though, where there were frequent shoot-outs and investigating agents—Americans—had been blown away; blown away by weapons this shithead had flown in. "And?"

"Other places."

"What other places!"

Another half shrug. Then, reluctantly: "Matagalpa."

"What about Managua?"

A full shrug this time. "Okay, man! So what the fuck!"

"You supplied the Nicaraguan government!"

"I flew a plane down, I flew a plane back. I'm a delivery boy; you said that. Who the fuck knows who I supplied?"

"It's a communist government; this country is supporting the rebels."

"And in Chile it supports the government of Ugarte

Pinochet, who makes Adolf Hitler look like a wimp! And
in Uruguay it supported a Nazi who ran the fucking country! And in the Philippines we supported—for how many
years, man?—a guy who peed his pants all the time he
watched blue movies and a wife who had more pairs of
shoes than the world's got feet! Come on! We talking ac-
tuality here or we talking fairy tales!" Rodgers had to stop
for breath. "Don't give me philosophy, okay? I did Nam
and I learned my philosophy: smart guys survive, dumb
guys die. That's all you gotta know. Aristotle and Plato?
Forget 'em. Off the wall, all of them. Only one philosophy
in life. Number one: *número uno.* Everyone else—all the
governments, all the leaders—are out to fuck you, because
you know what their philosophy is? Number one, that's
what. The smart guy's philosophy of life. You do Nam?"

No, thought O'Farrell, I didn't *do* Nam. I served in
Vietnam, served three extended tours. He said, "I was
there."

"You ever know such shit?" Rodgers's hands were out,
palms again, an inviting gesture. "You ever know such shit
in your life! I mean what the fuck were we there for?"

"A principle," O'Farrell said, and wished he hadn't.

"Principle! What fucking principle!" Rodgers erupted.
"You know what the South Vietnamese were doing while
our guys were getting blown up and killed or maimed or
losing their minds because they couldn't understand what
the fuck they were there for? The South Vietnamese were
cheating us and robbing us and laughing their balls off at
us and having the greatest fucking time of their lives,
that's what they were doing! Same philosophy, Asian version. *Número uno.*"

"I believed—believe—it was important."

"You wanna tell me the final score? Like, was it a win,
or a loss, or a draw?"

Peace with honor, thought O'Farrell, remembering his
reflections on the way to Florida. Not reflections; very
much the sort of cynicism that this bastard was offering,

but from a different side of the fence. He had lost control of the interview; he didn't know, at that moment, how to continue it. Hurriedly he said, "Ochoa supplies the drugs?"

"Usually. The stuff I got caught with came from the Milona family, in Cartagena."

"And the guns come from Europe?"

"That's what Cuadrado told me," Rodgers said. "And when we really got the thing under way, I several times saw crates brought from the port to Matanzas with Czech lettering."

No proof, O'Farrell thought, in an abrupt flare of hope. He'd heard a fairly convincing story of a drug-and-gunrunning enterprise, but so far there was nothing tying in the Cuban ambassador to Britain. And without that proof, he didn't have to proceed; wouldn't proceed. He said, "What was the system? Where did the drugs go? Who got paid the money after the drug sale?"

"Europe," Rodgers said at once. "America too. Everywhere."

"A city. Give me a city," O'Farrell said.

"London," Rodgers said finally. "That's what Cuadrado told me, that London controlled the European arms sellers who were reliable and who could get everything. He boasted their guy was in the government, too, just as he was. I tell you, Havana's put a lot of thought into this."

"Does London handle the drugs as well?"

Rodgers frowned doubtfully. "Never quite understood that," he admitted. "I got the impression that wasn't how it was done, but I don't know."

"What about the guy in London?" O'Farrell pressed. "What about a name?"

Rodgers shook his head. "No name, ever. Just that their man knew the business. Was highly respected."

"Like you did," O'Farrell said carelessly.

"Got unlucky, is all," Rodgers said, equally careless.

Shithead, O'Farrell thought. He said, "You ever think about what you were doing: worry about it?"

"Why the hell should I?" Rodgers came back. "I was making big bucks; free enterprise, the American way. You ever worry about what you do?"

As soon as he'd posed it O'Farrell had regretted the question, but he regretted the response even more. Yes, he thought; increasingly. Every day and every night I worry about what I do. "Cuadrado ever say anything more specific about the arms suppliers? Any names?"

The shoulders went up and down. "I told you already, they were using a lot of different suppliers. I never heard no names."

"There must have been some lead about London," O'Farrell insisted. "Some lead to who it was." If Rodgers could provide it, then this was his moment of commitment, O'Farrell acknowledged; his stomach felt loose.

Opposite him Rodgers sat with his chin on his hands, leaning forward on the chair back. His brow was creased and O'Farrell wondered if he were trying for genuine recall or trying to invent something that might help him get the special treatment he was seeking. "Not really," the man said emptily at last.

"What does 'not really' mean!"

"We were eating, time before last . . . we kinda got into the habit of going out together every time. Some guys are like that, they get a buzz out of hanging around sky jocks. I didn't mind, what the hell—"

"What happened!"

"It was when Cuadrado was talking about electronic equipment," Rodgers said. "Said it was going to be high-class stuff, the best. Fixed up by whoever was handling it in London. And then he says, 'He's a real hotshot but that don't matter.' "

" 'A real hotshot but that don't matter,' " O'Farrell echoed. "What's that mean?"

"No idea," Rodgers said. "Just thought it was a funny remark."

Would a Cuban in his country's export ministry consider an overseas ambassador a hotshot? Maybe. And then he remembered Petty's description during that theatrical briefing in the Ellipse. *Glossy son of a bitch.* Similar, but still not a positive enough connection, not positive enough for him to carry out the sentence with which he had been entrusted. He said, "That all?"

"That's all," Rodgers said. "You satisfied?"

"Not by a long way. We're going to need to meet again."

"When?"

"What's your hurry?" O'Farrell said, intentionally bullying. "You got all the time in the world."

Before leaving the building, O'Farrell requested material he wanted from Washington and received the immediate assurance that it would be provided the following day. He ate, early and without interest, in the motel coffee shop, and afterwards went directly to his room. By coincidence a segment of "Sixty Minutes" was devoted to Nicaragua, with a lot of footage of American troop exercises in neighboring Honduras. Cut into the report was film of protests throughout America against the United States's involvement. O'Farrell was curious: How many Americans were already in-country, "advisers" or "aid officials," working with the Contras? There'd be quite a lot, he knew, despite congressional objections and protest marchers with banners.

After "Sixty Minutes" O'Farrell turned off the television, wishing he'd bought a book or a copy of the *Miami Herald* at least. He'd noticed a liquor store two blocks away on his return from the interview and determinedly driven past. It meant he hadn't had even his customary martinis. It would be a five-minute walk, ten at the outside; not even necessary to cross the highway. Nothing wrong with a nightcap, hadn't had anything all day. Well, just those on a plane on the flight down. Only three. Long time ago. Hardly counted. O'Farrell stretched out both arms before him, pleased at how little movement there was.

Determinedly—as determinedly as he'd driven past the liquor store—O'Farrell undressed and put out the light and lay in the darkness, sleepless but proud of himself. He didn't need booze; just *proved* to himself that he didn't need booze.

The file arrived the next day as promised. There was confirmation that a Rene Cuadrado held the post of junior minister in Cuba's export ministry and a sparse biography putting his age around forty. He was believed to be married, with one child. He was said to live in Matanzas. There were three photographs. The file upon Fabio Ochoa was far more extensive and obtained mostly, O'Farrell guessed, from Drug Enforcement Administration sources. There were five photographs of the Colombian. O'Farrell chose the best picture of each man and intermingled them among fifteen other prints of unnamed, unconnected people shipped at his request in the overnight package. In addition to what had been sent down from Washington, local authorities confirmed the three abandoned aircraft landings Rodgers had talked about. So he'd told the truth there; but then he'd had no reason to lie.

Rodgers sat correctly on the chair this time, sifting through the photographs, laying out each print as he'd studied it as if he were dealing cards. He made a first-time, unequivocal identification of both Cuadrado and Ochoa.

"You sure?" O'Farrell persisted, nevertheless. That was what he had to be, sure; one-hundred-percent sure.

"You think I don't know these guys!" He extended his hand, forefinger against that next to it. "We were that close!"

There was something he'd forgotten, O'Farrell realized. He said, "Just you? Or were there others?"

The question appeared to disconcert the other man. "There were others," he conceded dismissively. "But I was the one." The fingers came out again. "We were that close, believe me!"

So Rodgers's seizure hadn't stopped the traffic. *Stuff that makes you feel funny.* O'Farrell collected the photographs and said, "All right."

"What now?" Rodgers smiled, knowing he'd done well.

"You wait some more," O'Farrell said, slotting the prints into the delivery envelope.

"Hey man!" protested the smuggler. "I've cooperated, like you asked! How about a little feedback here! How long I gotta wait!"

Man. O'Farrell felt himself growing physically hot. "As long as it takes," he said. Maybe longer, he thought.

Both encounters were recorded, on film as well as tape, and Petty and Erickson considered them, comparing them with the earlier transcripts of Customs and FBI interviews.

"I think he was too aggressive," Erickson said. From his spot by the window he could see the protestors against something, but could not hear their chants to discover what it was.

"I don't know." Petty pointed to the film. "Look at Rodgers; pimp-rolling son of a bitch. He needed to be knocked off balance, and O'Farrell certainly did just that. And by doing so he got more than anyone else."

"Anything particular strike you?" Erickson demanded pointedly, looking back into the room.

" 'You ever think about what you were doing, worry about it,' " quoted the section leader at once. "Of course I noticed it."

"So?"

Instead of replying, Petty fast-forwarded the video, stabbing it to hold on a freeze-frame at the moment of O'Farrell's question. Petty said, "There's no facial expression to indicate it meant anything to O'Farrell himself."

"It didn't have a context," Erickson said.

"It might have produced an angry reaction; got the bastard to say something he was holding back," Petty suggested.

"I've got an uneasy feeling," Erickson said.

"I've always got an uneasy feeling until an assignment is satisfactorily concluded," said Petty.

ELEVEN

O'FARRELL COMPLETED the files in the Lafayette Square office by midmorning. To ensure his success in the argument with Petty he carefully went through everything again, intently studying the photographs as well as the case reports. *A real hotshot*, he thought; then, *glossy son of a bitch*. José Gaviria Rivera certainly appeared that. The photographs were not just the snatched, concealed-camera shots of the ambassador with Pierre Belac. There were some posed pictures, at official diplomatic functions— sometimes with his dark-haired, statuesque wife—and others taken at various polo functions, several showing the man with an equally statuesque but fine-featured woman whom the captions identified as Henrietta Blanchard. From the accompanying biography O'Farrell knew the diplomat to be fifty-two years old; the photographs showed a man who kept in shape, and who dressed in clothes designed to accentuate that fitness, like Rodgers. There was another similarity in the perfect evenness of the teeth. The ambassador seemed to smile a lot. Although the circumstances of his studying both men were different, and it was difficult for him to reach a conclusion without seeing how Rivera moved and behaved, O'Farrell did not get the impression that Rivera was flashy, like Rodgers was flashy. Glossy, certainly, but the gloss of someone accustomed to luxurious surroundings and fitting naturally into them. O'Farrell decided that although the word hardly seemed appropriate for a representative of Cuba, the man's stance and his demeanor appeared aristocratic, the chin always lifted, the arm and the frozen gesture invariably languid.

The second examination finished, O'Farrell reassembled the file and restored it to the safe, thinking about what he was going to do. He was right, he told himself; he was unarguably right. And *they'd* made the rules, not him. He was merely—but quite properly—obeying them. To the letter, maybe, but wasn't that how rules should be obeyed, to the letter? Of course it was. His decision. Always his decision. Another rule. Theirs again, not his.

Petty would see him immediately, O'Farrell knew, but he held back from making the contact at once. Lunchtime, after all. And he'd finally brought the sepia photograph and the cuttings in from Alexandria and made appointments at the copiers recommended by the helpful archivist at the Library of Congress. The afternoon would be fine for seeing Petty. Not that O'Farrell was avoiding the confrontation. He was giving the evidence he had studied the proper consideration it deserved, not rushing anything. Was there a chance of his changing his mind? Unlikely, but there was nothing to lose by thinking everything through again. The sort of reflection they would expect, would want from him.

At the copy shop O'Farrell impressed upon the manager the importance of the cracked and flaking newspaper cuttings, and the man assured him that he would personally make the copies. The discussion took longer at the photographic studio. The restorer there offered to touch up the original, assuring O'Farrell that it would be undetectable, but O'Farrell refused, unwilling to have it tampered with. There was then a long conversation about the paper and finish of the copy. The man suggested the heaviest paper and a high-sheen reproduction, which was precisely what O'Farrell did not want. He listened to various other suggestions and finally chose the heaviest paper but a matte finish, which he thought most closely resembled the photograph taken all those years ago. Not the same but close.

O'Farrell completed everything with almost an hour to go before he was due to return to Lafayette Square. He found a bar on 16th Street, near the National Geographic Society building, a heavily paneled, dark place. It was crowded, but O'Farrell managed a slot at a stand-up shelf that ran around one wall. Because the jostle was so thick at the bar he'd ordered a double gin and tonic and wondered when he tasted it if the man had heard him, because it did not seem particularly strong.

Would he still be called upon to make a recommendation about Paul Rodgers, now that he had reached a decision about Rivera? O'Farrell supposed the man could give sufficient evidence before a grand jury to get an indictment against Rene Cuadrado. In practical terms that would not mean much, because of course Cuadrado would remain safe from arrest in Cuba, but the media coverage would expose the Havana government as drug traffickers and Congress or the White House might consider that useful. What happened before a grand jury wasn't his concern, O'Farrell recognized. It was the district attorney who would have to decide what deal to offer Rodgers in return for his cooperation. So what was he going to say, if he were asked? *Stuff that makes you feel funny,* he thought. Fuck him. Fuck Rodgers and his shoulder swagger and finger-snapping jive talk. *Coke mainly, of course. Marijuana too. And pills. Methaqualone. Just* like a salesman, offering his wares. How many kids—how many people— had been destroyed by the shit brought in by the bastard? Impossible to calculate, over the period he'd boasted—yes, actually *boasted!*—of operating. So he could go to hell. Literally to the hell of a penitentiary and O'Farrell hoped it would be for thirty-five years, which was a figure he'd made up at the interviews, just wanting to frighten the man. Perhaps the sentence could be longer than that. O'Farrell hoped it was. Clear the scum off the streets for life. *Hey, you my man?* No, thought O'Farrell. I'm not your man. If I'm asked, I am going to be the guy who screws you.

O'Farrell went to the bar and ensured this time that the man knew he wanted a double, and not so much tonic this time. He supposed he should eat something but he didn't feel hungry. He'd wait until dinner, maybe cook himself a big steak. If he were going to do that, then he'd have to stop off on the way home and get some wine. It was becoming ridiculous, constantly buying one bottle at a time. Why didn't he get a case: French even, because French was supposed to be superior, wasn't it? Ask the guy's opinion and buy something decent and lay it out like you were supposed to in the cellar. Ask about that, too; get the right temperature and ask whether to stand it up or lay it on its side. All the pictures he'd ever seen had the wine lying in racks, on its side. Okay, why not buy a rack then? Nothing too big. Just enough for say a dozen bottles, maybe two dozen, so he wouldn't have to keep stopping.

He'd tell Jill about it when he telephoned that evening. She'd seemed okay when he called last night, although she was worried that Ellen's payments still hadn't been straightened out. Ellen was being silly about Patrick, holding back from taking the bastard to court. He'd try to talk to Ellen about it this weekend, when he went up, make her see that it wasn't just herself and how she felt— although he could not conceive her retaining any feeling for the guy—but that she had to consider Billy now. That Billy, in fact, was more important, far more important, than her own emotions.

Just time for one more, O'Farrell decided. The lunchtime crowd was thinning, and when O'Farrell reached the bar and got the drink, he decided to stay there. He hoped the copier wouldn't screw up and damage the cuttings. The

Library of Congress archivist had been very helpful, talking of special acid-free storage boxes that sealed hermetically, cutting down on the deterioration caused by exposure to air. O'Farrell wondered if he should get some. He didn't have a lot of stuff, so one would probably do by itself; two at the outside. He decided to call the man again to ask about it. Maybe this afternoon. No, couldn't do it this afternoon. Had something else to do this afternoon. Soon now; less than an hour. Time for. . . ? No. Had to get back. Make his argument. No problem. Knew the file by heart.

O'Farrell was sure he could get a taxi, so he didn't hurry over the third drink, but there weren't any cabs cruising 16th Street when he left the bar. He moved impatiently from one foot to another on the curb, looking both ways along the street, then started to walk, which was a mistake, because when he glanced back he saw someone get a cab from where he had been standing. When he finally picked one up, his watch was showing only five minutes from the appointment time, and two cars had collided at the junction with L Street, so there was a further delay getting through.

He was twenty minutes late reaching Petty's office. The section head was tight-lipped with irritation, and Erickson, from his window spot, looked pointedly at his watch when O'Farrell entered.

"Sorry," O'Farrell said. "One car rear-ended another on L; caused a hell of a tie-up."

"That's all right," Petty said.

From the man's tone O'Farrell knew perfectly well that it was anything but all right. What the hell? he thought. He said, "I've read the file."

"And?" Erickson said.

"I don't think it's sufficient," O'Farrell declared bluntly. He felt empty-stomached and there was a dryness at the back of his throat; he was glad at the strength that appeared in his voice.

"What!" Erickson exclaimed, just ahead of Petty.

"I think it is too circumstantial," O'Farrell said. "The requirement, surely, is that there is enough evidence to convince a court if a prosecution could be brought? Having talked to Rodgers and read all that's been assembled, I am not satisfied a jury would return a verdict of guilty." There was still no difficulty with his voice, no indication of his uncertainty.

"Now let's just go through this again!" Petty leaned forward on his desk in his urgency. "We've got a drug smuggler testifying that Cuadrado told him about the use of diplomatic channels. We've got London positively named. And then we've got the Cuban ambassador to Britain provably associating with a known arms dealer. You call that circumstantial!"

"There is no direct link to Rivera, no definite identification, from anything Rodgers told me. Or from what Cuadrado told him," O'Farrell insisted. "And there's no proof that Rivera is obtaining arms from Pierre Belac."

"You think it's a social friendship, for Christ's sake?" Erickson demanded.

"I think there's insufficient proof, as I said. It might be different if we had separate testimony, from Belac."

"He's a professional arms dealer!" Petty said. "He's not likely to volunteer anything even if we manage to bust him. And Commerce isn't ready to make a case yet."

"I'm sorry," O'Farrell said, with what he hoped was finality.

"You got anything else to tell us?" Erickson challenged openly.

"Like what?" O'Farrell asked, avoiding an immediate response.

"You having problems beyond the evidence you've seen?" Petty asked.

"Justifying things to yourself?" Erickson suggested.

There were reverting to their pitter-patter style of debate, O'Farrell realized. He said, "Not at all. I am just following procedure."

"I think there's sufficient evidence," Petty said.

"The assignment would not have been proposed if there weren't," agreed the deputy.

"I have to be sure personally," O'Farrell insisted. "I'm not."

"So you're refusing?" Petty said.

"No!" said O'Farrell at once. "I'm seeking further evidence."

"I don't see how we can provide more than we have already," Petty said.

"Then I'm sorry." O'Farrell wondered who else would be assigned to the job. It didn't matter; not his concern anymore.

"So am I," Petty said heavily.

"Would you like to go through everything again? Reconsider?" Erickson offered.

O'Farrell shook his head. "I've studied everything. I don't think I need to reconsider."

"Without stronger evidence?" Petty asked pedantically.

"Without stronger evidence," agreed O'Farrell.

Petty made a production of lighting his pipe, speaking from within a cloud of smoke. "Then we'll have to get it, won't we?"

O'Farrell had begun to relax, imagining he had maneuvered himself away from an assignment without either refusing or resigning. Abruptly—sinkingly—he realized he had not done anything of the sort. The operation wasn't being abandoned or switched to someone else: it was simply being postponed.

José Rivera hesitated outside the Zurich bank, stretching. He'd picked up a cramp hunching over the statement of the working account he'd opened to handle the transactions with Belac. He'd done well, negotiating the interest-bearing facility. As well as he had done in outnegotiating

Pierre Belac. Certainly the account would not remain at $60 million because Belac was due another $30-million installment for another shipload of weaponry on its way to Havana. But the account included the full $15 million Rivera had added to the price Havana was being charged, on the entire deal. He'd decided to leave it in the interest-bearing account for a few more weeks before transferring it to his private account. Rivera was glad he had taken the trouble to come to Zurich on his way to Brussels, awkward though the detour was: by putting all the money in a controlled withdrawal account he had obtained an extra half-point interest and at these sorts of levels that was a worthwhile increase. It was a good feeling, being a rich man.

On his way back to the airport, Rivera considered taking a further detour after the Brussels meeting, spending a day or two in Paris making preliminary inquiries among housing agents there. He had more than sufficient money and it made economic sense to buy at the current market prices rather than wait for some indeterminate period by which time the cost would undoubtedly have increased. Or should he go straight back to London, instead, and make the Paris trip later, perhaps bringing Henrietta with him? That might be an altogether better idea; make it more of a pleasure than a business trip.

There was no delay on the flight, and Rivera was in Brussels by midafternoon. Belac produced documentation showing that all the small arms and ammunition had been dispatched, along with half the missiles. He'd made preliminary approaches to Epetric, a Swedish company, about the VAX and intended confirming the order as soon as Rivera advanced the next allocation of funds necessary for a deposit.

"Thirty million?" suggested the ambassador, fresh from studying the Swiss accounts and sure of the amount.

"I know that's what we discussed," said Belac. "But as well as back settlement for what's on its way to Havana, there are deposits for the VAX and a fourth ship to charter, to carry the tanks. I need fifty million to allow for the ten-percent withholding. Transferred direct to the *anstalt*, BHF Holdings."

If he kept back the ten percent from the latest demand, he'd have five million gaining interest, Rivera calculated. He said, "I know the name well enough by now."

So, of course, did Lars Henstrom, the Swedish inform-ant within the Epetric contracts and finance department, when Belac placed the confirmed order two days later. Henstrom passed the information on at once, and within two days it was transmitted to both the U.S. Department of Commerce and Customs Service.

Under an American–Swiss treaty, Berne had agreed that the country's traditional bank secrecy laws can be abro-gated and accounts made available to investigators if Washington satisfactorily proves that such accounts are benefitting from the proceeds of drug trafficking. The CIA used the sworn statement of Paul Rodgers to seek access to BHF Holdings' accounts, from which they learned of the multimillion-dollar transfer the day after a meeting they had observed in Brussels between Pierre Belac and José Rivera. They learned, however, about more than just the transfer. Against it was recorded the number of Rivera's account in the Swiss Banking Corporation on Zurich's Paradeplatz. The CIA made a further access re-quest, and it was granted, giving them complete details of Rivera's secret deposits.

Petty reached O'Farrell at the Alexandria house. "You wanted better proof," the section head said. "We've got it. It's time we talked again."

Petty merely held down the lever to disconnect the call, keeping the receiver in his hand and dialing again imme-diately. Gus McCarthy, director of the Plans division, an-swered at once.

"We need to talk, just the two of us," Petty said.

TWELVE

McCARTHY AVIDLY followed the social columns and the Style section of the *Washington Post* and chose Dominique's restaurant for the meeting. He arrived early and was already at the ledge away from the tiny bar, the whiskey sour half-finished, when Petty appeared. Petty ordered beer, a Miller Lite, instead of the milk he should have had, hoping his ulcer wouldn't act up; it had been at least six years since the doctor had allowed him any spirits. Sometimes, like now, he ignored the order.

"You read the writeup about this place last Sunday?" McCarthy asked at once.

"No," Petty said. He had, but he didn't want to indulge the other man's pretensions.

"Got a hell of a recommendation," McCarthy said. "Know something else about it?"

"What?" Petty asked, knowing he had to.

"Don't allow pipes at all." The planning chief grinned. He was a nonsmoker and always tried to avoid any encounter with Petty where the man could light up. McCarthy looked around the bar, which he dominated by his size. "What's the problem?"

"I'm not sure there is one, not yet," Petty said. "It could be worrying, though."

"O'Farrell?"

"Yes," Petty said shortly. He followed McCarthy's examination of the wall-to-wall crowd and for the same reason said, "Lot of people here."

"Been promised a good table inside," McCarthy assured him. "So why don't we have another drink first?"

"I'll stay with this." There was so far no protest from the ulcer but Petty knew it was too soon to tell.

McCarthy went to the bar and returned with his drink and menus. Petty studied his and said, "You really think it is rattlesnake they serve here?"

"Speciality of the house. What's Erickson think?"

"Unsure, like me," Petty said. "I think I'll take the lamb; can't risk anything too exotic with my stomach."

"Lamb's good, too. Unsure enough to change our minds?"

"That's why I thought we should meet," Petty said. "And maybe melon to start."

"How about some wine?" McCarthy offered.

"Not more than a glass," said Petty. "You didn't mind me raising it, did you?"

"Glad you did," McCarthy said. "I think I'll take the rattlesnake and then the lamb, like you. They cook it pink. You mind it pink?"

"That's the way it should be cooked," Petty said. "I thought it was important we talk it through."

"Sure." McCarthy asked, "You like burgundy?"

"Only a glass," Petty repeated.

McCarthy's signal got an immediate response, and as he had promised, their table was discreetly in a corner and far enough away from anyone else to avoid any sort of eavesdropping. McCarthy nodded his approval of the wine and they pulled back for the first course to be served. Once the waiter had left, McCarthy said, "What was his reaction to the Swiss stuff?"

"Yes."

"That's all he said?"

"Just that," the section head confirmed. "So I asked him if there could be any doubt, anymore, and he said no, not anymore. That he was satisfied."

"When's he due to go?"

"Monday. He asked for the weekend to pack and I warned him everything had to be coordinated with the move against Belac, that he might have to wait."

"What's Symmons say?"

"Nothing definite," Petty reported. "Just general unhappiness about the last two assessments."

"This rattlesnake really is quite unusual," McCarthy said. "You want to try a piece?"

"I'd better not, but thanks." Petty had drunk less than half the wine, but already he was feeling the vaguest sensation from his stomach; not actual pain but a hint that it might come.

"Why the uncertainty?" McCarthy demanded.

"Symmons's doubts, initially," Petty said. "That, coupled with other things. The initial refusal, most of all. Both Erickson and I think that was quite inexplicable. Erickson thinks he was too heavy with the runner, Rodgers, but I don't go along with that. Seemed fine to me."

"Nothing else?"

"We've run tight surveillance on him. The watchers report he's been drinking a bit. He's been buying more gin than usual, to take home. Wine too. By the case."

"Any sign of it affecting him?"

"None."

"Perhaps he was giving a party?"

"We checked. He wasn't," Petty said.

Both men stopped talking while their lamb was served. McCarthy said, "Doesn't that look terrific?"

"Terrific," Petty agreed, declining the waiter's offer to refill his glass.

"So that's it?"

"The watchers discovered he's tracing his ancestry. Found a great-grandfather who was an early lawman, out West."

"How do they know?"

"He's having some copying done, preserving some original newspaper clippings. A photograph too."

"Nothing so unusual in that," McCarthy said. "Lot of people are interested in their origins."

"It was the tie-in with the lawman that intrigued me," Petty said. "That's the basic psychological justification, that what we do is always valid. That our people are surrogate lawmen."

"Sure you don't want any more wine?"

"Perhaps half a glass." There hadn't been any further discomfort.

"So it's a coincidence," McCarthy said. "How else do you read it?"

"Symmons can answer that better than I can."

"Except that he can't be asked the question without being told the reason."

"I know that."

"You want something else? Dessert maybe?" McCarthy, the considerate host, asked.

"No, I'm fine, thank you." Petty still felt okay but guessed he'd suffer later. He wished—his hands almost itched!—he could light up his pipe. "Coffee would be good."

"Regular or decaf?"

"Decaf." Regular coffee would have killed him.

McCarthy summoned the waiter and then, with unexpected insistence, said, "Run something by me again. What was all that business about with his mother and father?"

McCarthy knew as much about it as he did, Petty thought, curious at the demand. Obediently he said, "All pretty straightforward, really. His mother was Latvian; underwent some traumatic experience when she was a kid. Her mother was raped by Russian soldiers, then killed when they'd finished with her. The girl was brought here by her father, who became a drunk. Why not? Seems he thought himself a coward because he'd run away when the soldiers came into their village; hadn't done anything to protect her. Kid married O'Farrell's father when she was eighteen—he was a brewery worker in Milwaukee, two or three years older—and got involved in the Latvian protest movement against the Soviet Union, which to be charitable in the extreme isn't worth a bucket of spit. In psychiatric treatment for depression by the time she was thirty; in and out of institutions, for a while. Declared completely cured by the usual bunch of jerks when she was forty. By then hubby has fought in Korea, got a Bronze Star and the Purple Heart, but has difficulty pinning them on because the war cost him his left arm. They scrimp by on his pensions, putting O'Farrell through college. He goes to Vietnam, exemplary conduct, which is how he comes to our notice. Been with us for seven years when one day she picks up this old gun, somehow loads the cartridges, and blows hubby away while he's dreaming of better things. Then herself. But before she does that, she leaves a note saying it's because she's failed to make people realize what it had been like to be overrun by the Soviets."

McCarthy appeared deep in thought, gazing sightlessly into his wineglass, but not drinking. All around, the aviary of the restaurant chattered and chirped, but the silence between them lasted so long that if Petty had not seen that the other man's eyes were open—and that he occasionally blinked—he would have imagined McCarthy somehow to have fallen asleep or even into a coma. At last, his voice distant with continued reflection, the director of Plans said, "She was a Russian dissident, then?"

"Hardly," Petty said, momentarily forgetting McCarthy's legendary hatred of the Soviets and implacable distrust of the Gorbachev freedoms. "You know what these nationalist groups are like—a small room with a copier, lots of cigarette smoke, all the men with beards and all the women in cardigans talking about how different it would all be if they could get their hands on just one atom bomb. The reality is that they don't count a bucket—"

"I heard you the first time," McCarthy interrupted. "And I don't disregard or sneer at genuine nationalist activity against Moscow." Still to himself, but insistently, he said, "A dissident."

"I don't understand."

"No," McCarthy said, without offering to explain further. Sneider would have understood by now; seen the direction, at least. McCarthy doubted, though, that he would talk it through with his immediate deputy; better to keep things compartmentalized. He already knew it was a brilliant idea, if all the strands could be knitted together as they had to be. Makarevich, he remembered: that had been the name. Perhaps he would talk it through with Sneider after all. It was going to be a tricky one; tricky as hell.

The coffee arrived and McCarthy said, "Would you like a liqueur with that? Brandy or something?"

Petty heard a dismissive tone in the other man's voice and decided he had made a mistake in requesting the meeting. He said, "We don't seem to have gone any further forward."

Petty expected some definite response, a decision even, but instead McCarthy turned the remark back. He said, "How much further could we take it at this stage?"

"You think we should proceed?" Petty asked openly, wanting to shift responsibility if anything went wrong.

Again McCarthy turned it back. "What do you think?"

He hadn't shifted the responsibility at all, Petty saw. But then, how could he? There was no protection—no protection at all—in getting any sort of verbal assurance from this man. Petty said, "I think we should proceed."

McCarthy grinned, the same sort of triumphant grin he'd shown earlier about pipe smoking. He said, "I'm glad that's your recommendation."

"It would be yours?" Petty asked, relieved.

"Unquestionably," McCarthy said. "Absolutely without question."

"I'm glad we agree," Petty said, sincerely.

"But keep those watchers in place," McCarthy said. "Particularly when the operation starts and he's abroad."

"Of course." Petty's relief was turning into a feeling of satisfaction.

"How's Elizabeth and the kids?" McCarthy asked, in another abrupt shift of direction.

"Very well. Ann and your children?"

"Couldn't be better," said McCarthy. "Judy's gotten into Miami University. Gus junior wants UCLA but I don't know if he's going to get in. It isn't easy, I understand."

"Kids are a worry, aren't they?" Petty commiserated.

"Always a worry," McCarthy agreed. "I've enjoyed the lunch."

"Me too," Petty said, knowing it was not a casual remark.

"We should do it again."

"I'd like that."

"Particularly when this gets under way. I want to be kept in close touch, all the time."

McCarthy had never made such a direct request before. Petty said, "Of course."

"Regards to Elizabeth," McCarthy said.

"And mine to Ann."

O'Farrell knew he should have gone up to Chicago, had known even when he'd made the excuses to Jill and then to Ellen, saying that there were too many things to do, when all it had amounted to was packing a suitcase, the work of an hour at the most. And he'd finished that a long time ago. In under an hour. There were the cars, of course; both his and Jill's. He hadn't cleaned them last weekend, either. He really didn't feel like it. Too late now, anyway. Alexandria was packed with tourists at this time of the day, swarming up and down the streets. He'd leave them. For how long? An unanswerable question. As long as it took in London, however long that was. The file was very detailed, Rivera's movements and habits charted, all the routine available. Shouldn't take long. *England is pretty efficiently policed.* Who'd said that? He had,

O'Farrell remembered. That day of the briefing at the Ellipse, with Petty and his stinking pipe and Erickson with his bald head that wasn't really bald at all. Maybe not so quick then; dangerous to rush it and risk a mistake. He'd take his time, only move when he was absolutely sure. Certainly he had no doubt about Rivera's guilt, now that the banking records were available. Guilty as judged, beyond any appeal; sentence duly returned to be carried out. For *him* to carry out. His job.

O'Farrell wished he had something else to do, to think about. He regretted now taking the archive to be copied. Jill could have done it while he was away, and it could have been waiting for him when he got back. Except that he'd wanted to do it himself, to explain how important it was that nothing was damaged. Jill could have done that just as well, of course. But the responsibility would have been hers then if anything had gone wrong. So it wouldn't have been right, putting the burden on her. He would still have liked it to be here, though. Given him something to do: taken his mind off other things. No, not other things. Just one thing. He'd have to remember to ask Jill to pick the archive and the photograph up for him so it would all be here when he got back.

The martini pitcher was near at hand, still half-full because he'd made a big batch, and he topped up his glass. How was he going to do it? A premature question. Never able to decide until he'd carried out his own reconnaissance, trained better than anyone else to see the possibilities. What was there to think about then? Nothing. Should have gone up to Chicago. Except that he hadn't wanted to, hadn't wanted to do anything but sit here in the den, hidden away, safe. But only for another few hours. Had a plane to catch in a few hours; less than a day. From National Airport, too. Not more than thirty minutes up the road. All so easy, so simple. Except . . . O'Farrell blinked, momentarily confused at the blurring in front of his eyes. And then the confusion became embarrassment and he was

glad he was alone, hidden away, because he'd never want
anyone to know how he'd broken down.

Lawmen didn't cry, ever.

THIRTEEN

THE PROBLEM of being alone had always been just
that. Being alone. Even when he was at home in Alexandria, apparently leading a normal life with Jill, there was
always a feeling of being cut off, part of himself isolated
and alone. Because it had to be that way. Always. He had
not acknowledged it in the early days; he had certainly
never understood how permanent the feeling would become. It was as if, in fact, he were two men. Charles William O'Farrell, faithful, loving husband and caring, loving
father. And Charles William O'Farrell, unofficial, unrecognized government executioner. Neither knowing the other;
neither, realized O'Farrell, extending the thought, *wanting*
to know the other.

Of course he'd been aware of solitude in those early
days, those assignments after Vietnam, after the careful,
circuitous CIA suggestion that he quit the regular army
and serve his country another way.

Vienna the first time. January 1974. A bad month, op-
erationally, because of the weather. Thick snow everywhere and the temperature hovering around freezing
during the day and well below it after about four P.M.,
which made the necessary surveillance a problem because
no one hung around on street corners or in doorways in
conditions like that. His name had been Mohammad

Mouhajer, and there had not been any doubt about his guilt, about why the sentence should be carried out, because the man had been paraded as a hero in Tripoli, leader of the PLO extremist group that hijacked a TWA plane and slaughtered ten Americans before blowing the aircraft up in front of selected television cameras. A freedom fighter, he'd been called. At a press conference he'd pledged himself to continue fighting to bring attention to the Palestinian cause. O'Farrell could even recall the translated phrase at that bombastic Libyan media event. *It is inevitable that people must die.* Inevitable, then, that Mouhajer had to die. His case was classic proof, in fact, of the doctrine preached at those top-secret training sessions at Fort Pearce and Fort Meade. *Assassination saves lives.* O'Farrell had spent two weeks watching the man's every move, tracing his every contact. Mouhajer *had* been boastful, oversure of himself, never taking any precautions. A single shot from the car—a Kalashnikov rifle, a provable Soviet bullet—as the man walked along the Naglergasse near midnight, the weather now a positive advantage because it was five degrees below and no one was on the street.

Alone then, but not a difficulty. Only away three weeks. He'd taken a leather purse back for Jill, a dirndl-dressed doll for Ellen, and a mechanical car for John.

How was Vienna, darling?

Pretty. I'll have to take you sometime.

I'd like that.

There'd been a connection with Vienna the second time: March 1975. Paris. The name this time had been Leonid Makarevich, although they discovered at least four aliases during the investigation. A KGB major, the guns-and-bombs delivery man for the terrorist groups. A similarity with the current operation, O'Farrell supposed. The proof was that Makarevich had supplied the explosives for the TWA bombing and O'Farrell recognized the Russian immediately from the photographs; he was the man with whom Mouhajer had conducted three meetings in Vienna. *Assassination saves lives.* True. Always true. He wouldn't be doing it, if it weren't true and justified, would he? Ridiculous self-doubt. A more complicated operation evolved when O'Farrell disclosed the Vienna information. More planning was necessary, too, because Makarevich was a professional who took no chances, always trying to clear his trail, aware of everything around him. The rule was that the method should be left to O'Farrell, but now a shooting was ordered, because the death had to tie in with Mouhajer's. On the street again, as Makarevich left the Hotel Angleterre, the weapon and the bullet as before: it had to appear tit-for-tat. O'Farrell had nothing to do with the anonymous telephone call to the hotel, supposedly from the PLO, talking of revenge. Or the planted stories in the CIA-controlled media—not in America, but in Italy and France itself—which were picked up and reported in the rest of the world's press, recounting a supposed feud between Moscow and the PLO. In fact, a rift actually did develop, because neither believed the other's denial of involvement in the two killings.

A Hermes scarf on this occasion for Jill, another nationally dressed doll for Ellen, a penknife for John.

Is Paris prettier than Vienna, darling?

I think so.

I'd like to see that, too.

One day we'll go.

They never had, though. Would he ever bring her here to London? O'Farrell wondered, as the airport bus left the motorway to become clogged in the morning rush-hour traffic. He doubted it. The decision to avoid all the operational places had been unconscious, until now. He never wanted to return anywhere he'd worked professionally, never wanted to be reminded by a street he'd walked, a building he'd passed, a restaurant where he'd eaten. Alone.

He was alone now. Had to be. The unseen, never-there man. Coming into the city by bus was the necessary initial move, mingling with a crowd and not risking a taxi. From the city terminal, garment bag in hand, he walked three streets before hailing one, changing transport this time because a person boarding a town bus with a suitcase is remembered. He paid the cab off in Courtfield Road and waited until it disappeared into Earls Court before setting out again to lose himself, crossing the Cromwell Road in the direction of Kensington but soon stopping short, locating the ideal guest house just past Cottesmore Gardens. The owner was a thin-faced, weak-eyed man who greeted O'Farrell in shirt sleeves and offered him the choice of a front or back room. O'Farrell chose the back and paid in cash for three nights, saying that he was on an economy vacation and would be going north, to Edinburgh, by the middle of the week. He was asked to enter his own registration, in an exercise-book type ledger. He used the name Bernard Hepplewhite, the first of the four aliases that had been decided upon, and said he would not be needing any food, not even breakfast.

The room was basic but clean and the bed linen fresh, for which he was grateful; it was always necessary to use anonymous places like this, and sometimes they'd been dirty.

It had, of course, been an overnight flight—from New York, not Washington, a further security detour—and O'Farrell had not slept at all. He attempted to now. Tired, overly fatigued people made mistakes he couldn't make . . . O'Farrell lay wide-eyed for an hour and then reluctantly took the prescribed pill, which gave him relief for four hours. He awoke just after midday, clog-eyed and dry-mouthed and unrested. Water, that's all; all he'd take was water. Didn't need anything else. A lot to do. Not Rivera yet, though. One of those first lessons: *Think backward, not forward.* Plan escape routes before looking the other way.

He ignored the bars and restaurants and hotels on Kensington High Street and others in Kensington Church

Street and Earls Court Road, noting instead the name of a boardinghouse in Holland Street and another in Queen's Gate Terrace. He found an unvandalized telephone booth back on Kensington High Street from which he called both boardinghouses, setting up consecutive reservations for when he left Courtfield Road. *Always move on; never remain long enough to be remembered afterward.*

O'Farrell used a map of the London underground to cross the city and locate another boardinghouse in Marylebone—in Crossmore Road—and a fifth, a small commercial hotel, two miles to the west off Warwick Road. It was more difficult this time to find a telephone box that worked but he managed it at last, in Porteus Road, and made three-night reservations to continue from those he'd already secured in Kensington.

By 5:30 he felt exhausted, heavy-eyed and heavy-limbed, aching everywhere. And thirsty; very thirsty. Carefully he chose an unlicensed coffee bar, where the actual coffee was disgusting, and ate chicken coated in a glutinously cold sauce and papier-mâché peas.

Completely drained as O'Farrell was, he still had to observe other professional necessities before he went back to Courtfield Road, but it was a halfhearted performance for the watchers he knew would be in place.

He walked to Marble Arch underground station, several times using doorway reflections and crossing streets abruptly to check for pursuit. He passed by one entrance to the subway and turned into Oxford Street before darting sideways to enter the system. O'Farrell remained on the Central line for only two stops, getting off at Oxford Circus to pick up the Victoria line but going north instead of south. Too tired and disinterested to do anything else, he caught a cruising taxi at Euston and rode it all the way to Gloucester Road. So tired was he that he was aware of his feet scuffing, too heavy to lift into a definite step. Didn't matter how tired he was. Not yet. Not even reconnaissance at this stage. Basic groundwork, that's all. Which he still had to complete. Plenty of time tomorrow. The day after that, if it were necessary. No hurry, no panic. Always wrong to hurry and panic. Dangerous.

The weak-eyed man was still in his shirt sleeves when O'Farrell pulled himself up the worn steps of the board-inghouse, nodding at him but not smiling.

"Too late for dinner," he challenged at once.

"I said I didn't want to eat," O'Farrell reminded him.

"There's the bar, though; not really a bar. You tell me what you want, and I get it for you and bring it into the lounge." He nodded toward a closed door to his right. "It's very comfortable. There's television."

O'Farrell clenched his hands again. "No, thank you," he said. "Nothing."

"Seen all you wanted to, the first day?"

"I think so," O'Farrell said.

"This is a shitty job. You ever think what a shitty job this is?" The driver's name was Wentworth. He was bulged from junk food and sitting around, the necessities of a watcher's life.

"All the time," Connors agreed. The observer was a music enthusiast; the personal stereo and earphones were in his lap now, the Tchaikovsky tape twice exhausted. He disconsolately lifted and then dropped the stereo in his lap and said, "I can't believe I forgot the other fucking tapes!"

"You think he's in for the night?"

"How the fuck do I know!" demanded the observer. "It's only nine."

"So we gotta wait?"

" 'Course we gotta wait."

"What do you think?"

"About what?"

"About how he's behaved so far, that's about what!" Wentworth said. "What else do you think I mean, for Christ's sake!"

Connors considered the question. Then he said, "By the book. Everything he should have done so far."

"Didn't lose us on that runaround, did he?" There was a triumphant note in Wentworth's voice.

"He was only going through the motions," Connors guessed, groping around and beneath the seat yet again for the mislaid cassette carrier. "I don't think he was really trying."

"Would you have admitted it if he had lost us?"

" 'Course not, asshole!" the observer said.

"We could have been suspended," the driver said.

Connors stopped searching, grinning sideways. "Almost worth lying over, on a shitty job like this," he agreed.

FOURTEEN

BARNEY SHEPHERD wore a baseball cap backward, with the rim covering his neck, an apron declaring "Ole King o' the Coals" over his bermuda shorts and sweatshirt, Docksiders without socks on his large feet, and a grin of complete contentment on his smooth, round face. He stood in the expansive barbecue area to the left of the pool, surrounded by marinated ribs, ground beef patties, and more dissecting tools than an average surgeon in an average operating room, waiting for the cue from the magic man that the act had just ten more minutes to run. That would be the time to start cooking. Janie was in front of the performer, jumping up and down with the demands of a birthday girl, whooping with delight when she got the candy stick for winning whatever the game had been. Shepherd

smiled and waved, but she was too absorbed in the party
to notice him. Beautiful, he thought; genuinely beautiful.
Blond, like Sheree, and blue eyes like her mother's, too.
Beautiful mother, beautiful daughter. He looked beyond
the screaming kids, over the landscaped garden and the
shrubs and trees to the silver glitter of the Pacific, and then
back to encompass the sprawling California ranchhouse
that he'd had built to his detailed specifications, including
the Jacuzzi and the sauna and the tennis court and the
four-car garage. Everything beautiful. Shepherd knew—
guessed, at least—that some people thought it ostenta-
tious but he didn't give a damn. It was a symbol—*his*
symbol—of achievement, and he deserved it. It was good,
not having to give a damn, ever again.

The problem was keeping things that way, now that the
slump had hit Silicon Valley. Shepherd's firm had so far
ridden out the recession better than most other hi-tech
companies in Santa Clara county. But he'd had to cut
some corners and not ask as many questions about some
orders as he should have asked. Shepherd wished he could
have avoided that, because he didn't want to risk those all-
important Defense Department contracts. The shortcuts
were necessary, to maintain cash flow, but it was the long-
term defense stuff that mattered for the prestige of the
company. And guaranteed the real heavy profits. The sort
of profits that enabled him to have a house overlooking
Monterey Bay, with a live-in maid and a Rolls as well as
a Mercedes in the garage (Sheree had a 928 Porsche and
a Golf GTI runaround) and to take time off for the cookout
for Janie's tenth birthday.

Shepherd was still looking expectantly toward the
magic man, so he wasn't immediately aware of Sheree
emerging through the patio doors, salad bowl before her.
He turned at the movement. So very beautiful. Except for
her ass, maybe. Not as tight as it used to be; the definite
suggestion of a sag, in fact. He'd have to suggest she get

it lifted. Use Dr. Willick again. He'd done her tits and her eyes and her chin and made a good job of all of them.

"Good party, eh?" he said when she reached him.

"I thought I'd leave the Jell-O and the ice cream in the kitchen refrigerator rather than bring it out here yet," she said, nodding to the cabinet set apart from the barbecue pit. An outside refrigerator had been one of Shepherd's specifications: it meant the wine was always chilled.

"Good idea." Definitely a sag; he'd talk to her tonight about getting it fixed.

"There's some men to see you."

"What?"

"Two guys." Sheree jerked her head back toward the house. "From the government."

"I do business at the office!" Shepherd erupted, annoyed. "Didn't you tell them that? It's Janie's birthday party, for Christ's sake!"

"I asked them if you expected them . . . whether they had an appointment . . . and they said no, but they thought you'd see them—" The woman broke off, looking toward the magician. "You see that! Janie got the dove out of the guy's hat and it's sitting on her arm!"

"They say who they were?" Shepherd felt a vague stir of unease.

"Uh-huh. Customs and FBI."

For a moment Shepherd made no response, his mind refusing to function. He said, "They say what they want?"

"Look at that!" Sheree said, ignoring her husband. "The bird's actually eating corn out of her hand now! This is going to be Janie's best party yet!"

Shepherd forced the patience. "Did they say what they wanted?" he repeated.

She turned back to him, smiling, innocent-faced. "Just to see you. They said they didn't think you'd mind."

Something that he couldn't immediately identify registered with Shepherd, and then he remembered the arranged signal in the act to tell him to start the barbecue. "Shit!" he said. "I gotta put the food on."

"They said it was important."

Briefly Shepherd looked between the house and the concluding magic show. "You'll have to take over; hamburgers to the right, ribs to the left. Coals are cooler on the left, for when things cook through. Don't forget to keep brushing the sauce on." '

He hurried across the expansive patio, threading his way between the umbrellaed furniture. He'd been careful; bloody careful. They couldn't hang anything on him.

Two men were standing in the panoramic room, the one that extended practically the rear width of the house and looked out over the pool and the ocean beyond. They turned as he entered, one young, full-haired, the other older, balding but trying to disguise it by combing what was left forward. Both wore Californian lightweight suits and ties, and Shepherd looked down at his King Coal apron and felt foolish. Self-consciously he took it off and threw it over the nearest chair and said, "What's this all about?"

The elder man moved, coming forward and offering his shield. "Hoover," he said. "U.S. Customs. My colleague here is Morrison, Federal Bureau of Investigation."

The younger man offered his identification and Shepherd glanced briefly at the wallet, not knowing what he was expected to confirm. Mother of Christ! he thought, looking up again.

"We've been admiring your house while we waited," said Morrison. "It's fantastic, absolutely fantastic."

Shepherd realized that the younger man had an eye defect, the left one skewed outward. Don't panic, Shepherd thought; nothing to panic about. Hear them out first. He said. "Thank you. I designed most of it myself."

"You're a lucky man," said the Customs investigator.

"You come here to admire my house?" Shepherd demanded. It was important to strike the balance, stay calm but not take any shit, not yet. He supposed he should suggest they sit, offer them a drink, but he did neither.

"You carry a few government contracts?" Hoover said. "High-security electronic stuff?"

"Yes," Shepherd said cautiously.

"Your corporation is highly regarded," Morrison said.

"I like to think so," Shepherd replied.

"You know the reason for the COCOM regulations, Mr. Shepherd?" asked Hoover.

"To prevent restricted, dual-use hi-tech material and development going to proscribed countries, usually communist," replied Shepherd. What the fuck was it? He kept a personal handle on orders that might be questionable and was sure there hadn't been one.

Hoover smiled and nodded, patronizing. "And you observe the Export Controls List?"

"I keep right up to date with it," Shepherd said.

"You know anyone named Pierre Belac?"

"No, I don't know anyone named Pierre Belac. Should I?" They were serving shit. Who the fuck *was* Pierre Belac?

"No, Mr. Shepherd, you definitely shouldn't know him," Hoover said.

The floor-to-ceiling windows were double-glazed, so there was no sound, but Shepherd could see the kids clamoring around Sheree for food. She was looking anxiously toward the house, seeking assistance. He yelled out toward the kitchen, "Maria! Go out and help Mrs. Shepherd, will you?"

Morrison smiled in the direction of the patio. "Looks like a great party. My boy was eight, two weeks ago. Took them all to Disneyland."

"Why don't we sit down?" Shepherd suggested. "You guys like a drink? Anything?"

Speaking for both of them, Morrison said, "Nothing."

"Couldn't we be a little more direct about all this?"

Shepherd asked. The air-conditioning was on high and he felt cold, dressed as he was.

"Pierre Belac's an arms dealer operating out of Brussels," Hoover disclosed. "Very big. Gets things they shouldn't have for people and countries who shouldn't have them. Sneaky as hell: false passports, stuff like that. We've been trying to pin him for years. Come close but never close enough."

"What's this got to do with me?" He was clear, Shepherd thought hopefully. There was nothing in his books or records connected with anyone called Pierre Belac.

"You make the VAX 11/78?" Morrison said. "Your biggest defense contract at the moment, in fact?"

"You know I do."

"What would you say if I told you that Pierre Belac, a leading illegal arms dealer, was buying a VAX 11/78 from your corporation to supply a communist regime?" Morrison demanded.

Shepherd actually started up from his chair but was scarcely conscious of doing so, eyes bulging with anger. "Bullshit!" he said vehemently. "I keep a handle on everything that goes on in my company—" He broke off, stabbing his own chest with his forefinger. "Me! Personally! And particularly defense contracts. I don't deal with companies I don't know, and I don't deal with mysterious intermediaries. Your contract buyers know that, for Christ's sake! That's why I *am* a government supplier!"

Both men stared, unmoved by the outrage. Hoover said, "You familiar with a Swedish company called Epetric?"

"Yes," he said. He was dry-throated and the confirmation came out badly, as if he had something to hide. Slowly he sat back in his chair.

Hoover stood up, however, coming over to him with a briefcase Shepherd had not noticed until that moment. From it the Customs investigator took a duplicate order sheet. Shepherd looked, although it was not necessary.

"A confirmed and acknowledged order for a VAX

11/78, from Epetric, Inc. of Stockholm," Hoover said, even more unnecessarily. "That is your signature, isn't it, Mr. Shepherd?"

"Epetric is a bona fide company, incorporated in Sweden," Shepherd said, with pedantic formality. "There is no legal restriction against my doing business with such a company: Sweden, incidentally, is not one of the countries that are signatory to the agreement observed by the Coordinating Committee for Multilateral Export Controls. My contract is with Epetric, not with anyone named Pierre Belac."

A silence developed in the room as chilling as the air-conditioning, and Shepherd wondered if they expected him to say more. He couldn't, because there was nothing more to say. How deeply had they already investigated him? He'd tried to calculate how many deals he'd taken to the very edge, and perhaps sometimes over it. Enough, he knew. More than enough to be struck off the Pentagon list. But at the moment he was still ahead. Which is where he had to stay.

"We know that Pierre Belac placed that Epetric order through a shell company in Switzerland," Hoover said.

"Your advantage, not mine," Shepherd said. "My dealings thus far are absolutely and completely legitimate. This evidence? You could make it available to me?"

"You want proof?"

The resolution would be very simple, Shepherd realized, the relief flooding through him. He said, "My lawyers will, because inevitably there will be a breach-of-contract suit."

Hoover frowned. "I'm afraid I don't quite follow here."

Shepherd said, "I don't really see that we have a problem. No problem at all. The Epetric order is less than a third filled. I'll throw it back at them tomorrow, and that will be the end of it."

"The kids are in the pool," Morrison said. "Is it heated?"

Shepherd glanced through the window, then back at the Bureau agent, frowning. "Of course it's heated."

"Great house," Morrison said, echoing his initial admiration.

"What the hell's going on!" Shepherd demanded. Easy! he warned himself. Take it easy!

"We've taken legal advice on what we've got," Hoover said. "If we presented the evidence before a grand jury, we'd get an indictment against you and your company for conspiring to evade the requirements of the Export Administration Act, as amended."

"Wait a minute!" said Shepherd. "Now just wait a goddamned minute! That's bullshit and you know it. You'd never get a conviction in any court, not in a million years. And I'd fight you every inch of the way."

"But that's not how it works, is it, Mr. Shepherd?" said Morrison, with that infuriating mildness. "A grand jury isn't a court. It's an examination of evidence to see if there's a case to answer, leading to an indictment. Which, as I say, our legal people feel confident we'd get. Only then do we actually get to court. Where, probably, you'd be acquitted."

Shepherd felt numb from trying to comprehend the riddles this bastard was weaving. "I don't understand," he confessed desperately.

"You'd have been named in the indictment," Hoover pointed out. "There'd be a loss of confidence, among suppliers, customers . . . customers like the Pentagon . . ." The man smiled invitingly. "Can't take any chances with our national security, can we?"

"Guilt by association, even if I'm ultimately found innocent of every accusation and charge." Shepherd grasped the argument at last. A steady guaranteed flow of Pentagon orders bringing in a steady, guaranteed flow of profits, he thought, profits that provided Maria and bought the Rolls and the Mercedes and the Porsche and the pool with its Jacuzzi—the pool in which he could see Janie and the kids playing, right now—and an uninterrupted view of Monterey Bay.

"Ever hear the expression 'shit sticks,' Mr. Shepherd?" asked Morrison.

"Yes," Shepherd said. "I've heard it."

"Fact of life. Unfair fact of life."

"I think you'd better tell me what you want," Shepherd said. Were they trying to shake him down? He'd have to be careful. Maybe it was an entrapment. He'd demand time to consider or to raise the money and talk it through with his lawyer. What if it wasn't an entrapment, just a simple case of bribery? Of course he'd pay. Whatever they wanted would be cheap, to avoid losing everything he had. It was easy to see now why there had been all that crap about the house and the pool. No point in fucking around. He said, "So okay, let's get down to the bottom line. How—"

"We want Belac," Morrison said.

Shepherd had just—only just—pulled back from the lip of the precipice, but felt as if he might still be in danger of toppling over. "Want Belac?" he managed, with difficulty.

"Here, in the United States of America," Hoover said. "Where we can arrest him and arraign him on grand-jury indictments we've already got. Belac's a wanted man."

Shepherd strove to keep up, seeing the tightrope stretched in front of him, the tightrope he had to balance on, cooperating with these guys but keeping them very firmly away from anything they shouldn't see. "What do you want me to do?"

The two men exchanged glances. Morrison said, "Bring him to us."

"How can I possibly do that!"

"Don't actually refuse to complete the VAX order— although you won't send anything more, of course," Morrison said. "Tell Epetric you're not satisfied with the

End-User Certificate or the bills of lading for ultimate destination. Whatever."

"And they'll send their own man," Shepherd argued. "Or deal with it by letter."

"No, they won't." Hoover smiled. "The Swedish authorities have had just the sort of conversation we're having here with all the directors of Epetric. They're willing to cooperate, just like you."

They were assholes, both of them, thought Shepherd. He said, "This man, Belac, he'll never fall for it."

"He's got an important customer to supply; we know it's a big order," Morrison said. "We think it's worth a shot."

Time for him to bargain, Shepherd decided. "So what if I get him here? What about all that"—he almost said crap but decided against it at the last minute—"talk of a grand jury?" He had to avoid that at any cost.

"We were just setting out all the possibilities," Morrison said easily. "If we get Belac, then publicly you'll be the loyal American who did his duty, and everyone will admire you."

Patronizing bastard, Shepherd thought. He said, "Fuck the public. What about the Defense Department?"

"Customs will make sure the Pentagon knows the contribution you made," Hoover said.

"So will the Bureau," Morrison said.

"Not enough," Shepherd said. This was a two-way deal, despite all the macho talk. "What if Belac doesn't jump as you expect?"

Hoover shrugged. "So the shot didn't work."

"But you can still move against me, to get Belac named on another indictment in his absence," Shepherd said astutely. "So you've still got something and I've got nothing." He thought he caught a nod of apparent admiration from Morrison but wasn't sure.

"What do you want, Mr. Shepherd?" Morrison asked.

"A legal document dated before my notification to Sweden, deposited with my lawyer, setting out what I am doing."

"Very cautious." Hoover smiled.

"Very necessary," Shepherd said. He accepted a card with a San Francisco address that Morrison offered and put it in the pocket of his shorts. He said, "It wasn't necessary, you know. All those heavy-duty threats. I'd have cooperated from the beginning if you'd told me then what it was all about."

"We just wanted to set out the options," Morrison said. "Be sure ourselves."

So they did suspect him. Shepherd said, "I'm glad you are now."

"This time we're going to get Pierre Belac," Hoover said, with quiet confidence.

The two men had reached Route 208, on their way back to San Francisco, before Hoover spoke. He said, "What do you think?"

"About Shepherd? He's dirty," Morrison said. "Dirty and worried."

"But about Belac?"

"Maybe not. I think the surprise was genuine there."

"What do you think we should do?"

The other man was quiet for several moments. Then he said, "Let this run, see how it works out. We can pick up Shepherd anytime. He's not going anywhere from that awful house."

O'Farrell used public transport, buses and the underground trains, to crisscross London. He needed small garage businesses with just a few rental cars—and those cars not current models—instead of the big agencies like Hertz or Avis or Budget with access to international computer links that could run checks at the touch of a few terminal keys. Not that the credit cards or driver's licenses he was using would have thrown up any problems; all the aliases were supported through a carefully established set of addresses in Delaware, that discreet American state most favored by the CIA for its secrecy codes, which practically matched those of any offshore tax haven.

He traveled north from Kennington to Camden and westward from there to Acton only to backtrack eastward to Whitechapel, seeking out the sidestreet hirers. From each he received matching agreements that they'd take the credit-card imprint as a guarantee of the vehicle's return, but the final settlement would have to be fully in cash, which meant they had a tax-free, no-record transaction and he could destroy the credit-card slips. Further, habitual protectiveness.

The Kennington car was a three-year-old Vauxhall. O'Farrell guessed the odometer had been wound completely back at least once and possibly twice. It was misfiring on one cylinder, and the unbalanced wheels juddered at anything over forty-five miles an hour. There was rust in the rear fender and the tire treads were only just legally permissible. O'Farrell regarded it as completely anonymous and therefore perfect.

He approached Rivera's Hampstead home from a mile to the north and drove by without slowing or paying any obvious attention, reserving the more detailed surveillance until later and merely noting as he passed that the house front was near the road, shielded only by a moderately high wall and ornate double gates. He clocked at twenty-five minutes the distance to the High Holborn embassy, but knew there would be differences depending upon times and traffic congestion. He did not pause at High Holborn, either. It took longer, another fifteen minutes, to reach the Pimlico home of the Cuban's mistress, and again he drove by. But in Chelsea O'Farrell stopped, deciding it was necessary to record the timings. He found a pub on the Embankment, overlooking the Thames, and carried the gin and tonic outside; it was warm and pleasant to sit on the bench, although he could not actually see the water because of the river wall. Both sides of the road were marked with double yellow lines, which meant parking was illegal; a car did stop with one man who remained at the wheel, and O'Farrell watched it without apparently doing so until a girl emerged from a house farther up the road, was enthusiastically kissed, and then driven away in the direction of the city. There were five metered parking bays, all occupied but every vehicle empty. The only other occupant of the river-bordering benches was a tramp absorbed by the unseen contents of a Safeways carrier bag. He was on his own, O'Farrell decided.

He'd seen the double measure put into his glass from the approved jigger used in English pubs, but it seemed weak, and then O'Farrell reflected that they often did these days in American bars, too. The only way to get a decent drink seemed to be to make it himself. Not that he intended taking a bottle to Courtfield Road or any other of the boardinghouses. No booze yesterday, he remembered proudly. He wouldn't have more than one or two drinks today.

He entered the times into his pocketbook but without any designation of what they represented so they would be meaningless to anyone but himself. He had a second drink—considering and then rejecting the idea of eating— and then a third because it was still comparatively early and it was pleasant, sitting in the sun. So he had a fourth. It was then that he was sure he spotted the watchers monitoring him—two men in a Ford that had gone three times along the same stretch of the Embankment. Fuck them, he thought belligerently.

It took O'Farrell an hour and fifteen minutes to reach the Windsor ground where Rivera customarily played polo, which was out of season just now, and even longer to get back into London, because by then the evening rush hour was at its height. He decided to utilize it, going to the embassy again and then stopwatching himself back up to Hampstead and the ambassador's residence on Christchurch Hill. The journey took an extra ten minutes.

It was more difficult than the previous night for O'Farrell to find an unlicensed restaurant, but he did, and decided the search had been worthwhile because the food was better. He'd parked the car away from Courtfield Road, of course. He didn't want the boardinghouse owner, whose shirt that morning had been the same as the previous day, to make any connection between himself and the vehicle. Walking back from the restaurant, O'Farrell passed two hotels and three pubs and studiously ignored every one. Made it, he thought, in his room; knew I could make it.

Connors and Wentworth, who'd drawn the dogwatch again, slumped in their observation car outside. Connors had located his cassette case and was happier than the previous night, the Walkman loose against his head.

"You like Mahler?" he asked the other man.

"Gotta tin ear," Wentworth said. "What do you think of today?" They'd picked up a full report from the day team.

"Careful guy," Connors said. "Covering all the angles."

Two hundred yards away, sleepless in his darkened room, O'Farrell forced himself to confront the awareness he had been avoiding throughout the day. It hadn't been necessary to cover the routes as thoroughly as he had, filling up the entire day, certainly not to drive all the way out to Windsor and back again.

He was putting it off, O'Farrell knew, putting off what he had to do.

FIFTEEN

THEY WERE together so rarely as a family that the evening had an odd formality, a gathering of polite strangers intent upon doing nothing to offend the others. Rivera was smilingly solicitous to Estelle, who smiled a lot in response. And Jorge, whose twelfth birthday it was, gave each parent his open-eyed, respectful attention, alert to intervene at the first sign of discord between them, as he had learned to divert arguments before, when enough feeling had remained between them to stimulate arguments. It wasn't there any longer, but the child didn't know that.

Rivera had given some thought to planning the treat, going as far as discussing it in advance with Estelle, who agreed that an entire evening would be difficult for the two of them and thought the revival of *South Pacific* would be ideal. Before setting off from Hampstead for the theater, Jorge was given his presents while Rivera and Estelle made a conscious effort and sipped champagne. It was not the first effort either had made. An element of competition remained between them, and each had tried to outdo the other with the choice of present. Estelle had gone for the traditional, an elaborate designer bicycle heavy with every available extra—which certainly gave her the contest in actual appearance. Rivera explained to Jorge as he handed over the document that it was a contract for success-guaranteed hang-gliding lessons, and that the hang glider was too bulky to get into the drawing room but was waiting in the garage. The experienced child reacted with precisely the same level of enthusiasm to both, but Rivera considered himself the winner.

They had box seats at the musical, which turned out to be an excellent choice for Jorge. The boy sat enraptured, applauding loudly. Rivera found his seat uncomfortable in his boredom and guessed Estelle did, too. Occasionally he glanced across at her but she studiously ignored the attention, instead gazing fixedly at the stage as if she were as enthralled as their son.

Whose fault had it been that their marriage had turned out the disaster it was? Hers, he decided instantly. There'd never been love but he'd been prepared to make some attempt, establish a relationship in which they could both exist comfortably. But Estelle, who was eighteen years younger, had turned shrew almost from the moment the ceremony was over, practically gloating over her success in snaring a grateful middle-aged diplomat whose vocation would get her away from Cuba and into social strata where she felt she belonged; like Rivera's family, Estelle's had suffered by Castro's accession to power, but it had been slower to recover. Rivera brought his attention closer, to the boy. Part of that ensnarement, Rivera was sure, conceived the moment Estelle discerned his disinterest and feared he might end the marriage. Certainly he'd never believed she'd wanted to become pregnant; it was maneuvered, like the marriage itself. And it had been an absurd nine months, Estelle demanding nearly daily attention from the gynecologist and exercising constantly to maintain her figure. After the birth she'd been more concerned with regaining her waist than she seemed to be with Jorge, whom she immediately handed over to a nurse. No matter, thought Rivera philosophically; they were both making the best of it.

He wondered sometimes about Estelle's men: whether she slept with one particular lover or many. He pitied them, compared to the experience of sleeping with Henrietta. With whom he would have rather been now—even *out* of bed—than enduring a blaring musical on a seat built for dwarfs with a woman he didn't like anymore and who disliked him just as much in return. He felt far differently about Henrietta than he ever had about Estelle. Actually missed her; thought about her constantly.

Rivera chose the Caprice for dinner afterward, specifically because it was not a restaurant he and Henrietta often frequented and he didn't want intrusive headwaiter recognition. It appeared, however, to be a favorite of Estelle's, who was greeted as familiarly as he was examined curiously. There was even an offer of a better table, made as much to Estelle as to him. Rivera said they were content with the one they had.

"Do I need to order the aperitif, or will they know automatically?" said Rivera.

Estelle frowned at the petulance, surprised, and Rivera regretted the remark, surprised at himself. She said, "They'll probably know if you ask for the usual, but if the normal man is having the night off, it's a vodka martini with an olive," and Rivera regretted it even more. To avoid the test, Rivera ordered Roederer Crystal, the champagne they'd had earlier.

Aware of her advantage in the exchange, Estelle spoke to Jorge but directed the remark at Rivera, as a continuing taunt. "The liver is always very good. That or the lamb."

It had been his own stupidity, Rivera knew; she had every right to use the ammunition he'd supplied. He said, "I think I'll go for fish," and recognized that as a mistake, too; he should have taken one of her recommendations.

Estelle smiled at him. "That's what I often have, too," and stayed waiting for him to react.

He had to back off, Rivera realized. It offended him to do so, because he didn't like losing even the most inconsequential exchange with her, but he was conscious of Jorge's apprehension and refused to let a ridiculous sparring match over a restaurant menu mar the child's evening.

Straining, as always, for impartiality, the boy chose chicken. Estelle had the lamb.

The musical formed the safest subject of conversation and Rivera guided it easily along, pleased that Jorge genuinely seemed to have enjoyed it. When they exhausted that subject, they talked about hang gliding, which Rivera decided gave him the victory in the present-buying contest. Estelle offered no more challenges. Rivera was careful about everything he said, before he said it, so there was nothing against which she would feel she had to fight back.

They drove directly from the restaurant back to the Hampstead house, where Rivera had to park outside because of the hang glider. With the evening over and with it the risk of any confrontation, he opened the garage doors to show the apparatus to Jorge. It was still packed but Rivera made holes in the covering for the boy to see the color, and there was some excited talk about buying a trailer to transport it. Jorge wondered, when he was qualified, if he could fly from Hampstead Heath itself and Rivera said he didn't know but he expected it was possible, and anyway he'd find out.

Inside the house Jorge thanked him for what he called a wonderful evening and they kissed and Rivera made gratefully toward the drawing room again, unsure if it were too late to call Henrietta; it was a simple code, when her husband might be home, leaving the telephone to ring three times before disconnecting, allowing a few minutes for her to get near a receiver, and then dialing again. It *was* later than he usually telephoned, but Rivera decided to do it; they'd spoken that afternoon but Rivera wanted very much to talk to her again, although there was nothing to say.

Rivera stopped short immediately inside the door, not expecting Estelle to be there. She was in one of the fireside chairs, a brandy snifter already cupped between both hands.

"What's he think of his hang glider?" Estelle asked conversationally.

Rivera went to the liquor tray and poured brandy. "He's excited about it." Too weary to bother with more contests, he said, "He's delighted with the bike, too."

Estelle was smiling when he turned back to her, but it was not the usual contemptuous expression. "I'll concede if you want me to: yours was the better gift."

"I don't want you to concede anything," Rivera said, honestly. How long before she went to bed! He couldn't remember the last time she'd joined him for an after-dinner drink—the last time she'd even been home at this hour, which for Estelle was early.

"It was juvenile tonight, wasn't it?"

Still conversational, practically friendly if that weren't impossible, Rivera judged. He was confused. Go along with the discussion until the point emerges, he thought, the professional diplomat. He said, "Yes, very juvenile."

"Don't you think it's time we did something about it?"

"Something about it?" Rivera's confusion worsened.

"Why don't we get divorced?" she blurted. "There's absolutely no purpose in making the pretense anymore. We only did it for Jorge, and did you see him tonight? Poor little bastard was tighter than a spring, trying to please both of us. Ready to act as a mediator, if necessary. It's crueler to stay together than it would be to break up. . . ." The nonchallenging smile came again. "I know what he means to you, what having a son means to you. I'd agree to your having permanent custody, with my having visiting rights. Let's be civilized about it."

Rivera had fully recovered, his mind grasping and placing everything she'd said in order of priority. Adjusting his own priorities, his own necessities, too. Irrespective of his thoughts in the theater that night—and all his previous reflections—Rivera had never contemplated the breakup being at Estelle's instigation. Not that Cuba mattered, because he had no intention of ever returning there, but a divorce at her instigation would make him a laughingstock there. He could imagine the gibes: *Rivera, the man with no cojones.* She must be mad, imagining it was even a subject for discussion between them. Not a subject for her to initiate, anyway. But what about him and Henrietta? He'd already thought about it, after all.

"I see," Rivera stalled. Estelle had clearly rehearsed what she'd just said. And revealed a lot in her eagerness. He said, "Does he want to marry you?"

Estelle blushed, obviously, something he could never recall her doing before. She said, "He's telling his wife tonight as well."

"Who is he?"

"His name's Lopelle, Albert Lopelle. He's the military attaché at the French embassy."

"Military attaché" almost automatically meant French intelligence. Certainly there'd be an investigation by Cuban counterespionage which would create an excuse to extend that probe into his own private affairs. Rivera didn't want that, any more than the spotlight of newspaper publicity on a divorce. He said, "How long?"

Estelle shrugged, as if it were unimportant, which it was. "Almost a year. We met at a Foreign Office reception celebrating the Queen's birthday. You were there."

Rivera couldn't remember the event, but it was the sort of social occasion that was important to Estelle. He was fairly confident he knew how to handle it now, although he wished he were better able to gauge Estelle's reaction.

"No," Rivera said bluntly.

"What!" Estelle blinked up at him, clearly shocked.

"I said no," Rivera repeated. "Under no circumstances will I consent at this time to a divorce between us."

"But . . ." Estelle stumbled, and stopped. "You must!" she started again, disclosing how readily she had expected his agreement. "There's nothing between us, except dislike! There's no *point* in going on!"

"At this time I need a wife, a hostess, officially," said

Rivera. "Which is what you will remain, my official wife. I'll make no other demands upon you, apart from that. You can come and go, spend as much time with this man Lopelle as you want, providing it does not clash with any official function we have to attend together—"

"But that's precisely what we do now," she cut in.

"If you try to force any sort of divorce action upon me, I shall see that you are returned to Havana and that all travel permission is withdrawn. You'll never see Lopelle again."

"Why!" Estelle wailed.

"I said 'at this time.' "

"Please explain that," Estelle said, subdued.

"To my timing and to my choice you can have your divorce," Rivera said. "It's the timing to which I object."

"When?" she asked eagerly, smiling hopefully.

"I don't know, not specifically. Not a long time." The current deal with Belac should be over before the year's end, Rivera thought. Which was when he'd already decided to quit and find that Paris home. In passing, Rivera was caught by the coincidence of his deciding to live in France and Estelle choosing a French lover. "Well?" he said.

"It's hardly a choice, is it?"

"I think so," Rivera said. "My way gives you everything you want with just a delay, that's all."

The smile came again, not as easily but still a smile. "I suppose it does, really. You do mean it, don't you?"

"I promise you," Rivera said.

"Not long?" Estelle pressed.

"That's what I said," Rivera reiterated. "And during that time, perhaps we could have a little less hostility."

"I'd like that, too," Estelle said sincerely. "And thank you."

The idea of having Estelle returned to Cuba and held there had come suddenly to Rivera, without any forethought, but considering it more fully, he decided it would be an excellent ploy when he decided to leave London. His planning would have to be precise, officially informing his intelligence people about her association with a French spy to absolve himself from any suspicion, but it shouldn't be too difficult. He certainly didn't intend to be cast aside publicly at her whim, in favor of another man. She was stupid not to know better.

O'Farrell had moved into the second guest house toward evening and afterward went to the Christchurch Hill house to try to spot any obvious security precautions, like guard dogs or patrols. He was startled to see Rivera emerging with his family and on impulse followed them to the theater. It was impossible for him to get a ticket so late, but he had their car as a marker and spent the time in a pub from which he could see it, strictly rationing himself to three drinks. He was ready a good half hour before they left, and he followed them again to the restaurant.

For a long time after they entered, O'Farrell remained undecided in the rental car, his reluctance to enter after them shaking through him, so that he actually cupped one hand over the other for control. Eventually he did go in, declining a table but sitting at the bar, where he risked a martini, which was surprisingly good.

Rivera was maybe ten feet away. All the words like "glossy" and "smooth" and "hotshot" applied to the man, O'Farrell decided. The woman was very beautiful and the kid polite and attentive, but it didn't appear a particularly happy trio. It was a brief speculation because O'Farrell's professional concentration was upon Rivera. The man's movements *were* languid, as they had seemed in the photographs: very self-assured, expecting every attention without having to ask, but interestingly not bothering at all with his surroundings. Not someone who felt in any personal danger, then.

O'Farrell ordered a second drink, assuring himself it was necessary for the observation he was conducting, remaining for a further thirty minutes without adding anything to his impressions of the ambassador. The shaking threatened him again, and so he left, getting to Hampstead ahead of them, intent upon what he'd first come to the house to discover. There was no barking, and no guards appeared, when the family returned, no hesitation when the woman entered first to indicate the switching off of any alarm system. For a full ten minutes Rivera stood clearly identifiable in the brightly lighted garage, showing something very large and wrapped to the boy before the two followed the woman into the house. As he watched, O'Farrell established the time sequence of the police foot patrols, two men who paid no particular attention to the ambassador's residence.

The surveillance had been worthwhile, O'Farrell decided as he was driving away. Difficult though it was to believe, it seemed that Rivera had no security precautions or alarms at all at the house.

O'Farrell took a wrong turn on his way back but was unworried, knowing the names of the central districts by now and using them as a guide until he recognized the streets again. He joined a road he knew and saw an off-license on the corner. He made a decision, stopping the car and going in. Gin would require mixes and create too bulky a package, he decided. So he bought brandy.

At the guest house he rinsed out the bathroom glass and poured himself a measure, needing it. The liquor warmed through him, relaxing, and the twitch from his hands diminished at last. O'Farrell lay on the top of the bed, reviewing the evening. He could have done it tonight. Without any specially adapted rifle he could have dropped Rivera as he was silhouetted in that garage, so obvious a target that he could probably have gotten in a second shot before the man hit the ground.

In front of the boy.

In his imagination Rivera seemed to fade into a hazy, indistinct outline, but O'Farrell could remember everything about the child's features and appearance and mannerisms. Older than Billy, obviously, and certainly more sophisticated even for his age, but still a kid. A kid whose father he was assigned to kill, could have killed that night, right in front of him. *Stuff that makes you feel funny*, O'Farrell thought, clinging to a litany. Millions in a Swiss bank. Unquestionably guilty, arms for drugs, drugs for arms.

O'Farrell slopped more brandy into his glass, blinking to clear the picture of the child from his mind. Never like this before. Never seen the victim with his family, doing something as natural as eating dinner. Talking. Being normal. Looking normal. It might have been a constructive, worthwhile evening, but he wished to hell he hadn't gone, just the same. He didn't want to know the kid and the woman. He wanted to remain aloof and impersonal, and he didn't feel that anymore. He'd always know, now, know what the boy looked like and the woman, able to picture them in black, grieving, weeping.

He added to his glass again, waiting for the drink to anesthetize him, but nothing happened, not even drunkenness.

"How much longer is this going to go on, for Christ's sake!" Wentworth protested, outside in the observation car.

"Until we're told to stop, I guess," Connors said.

"I don't like watching one of our own guys."

"You could always quit and become a school crossing guard."

SIXTEEN

O'FARRELL FELT terrible when he awoke, not needing to feign continuing sleep to check his surroundings. The slightest movement was agony. He was sick the moment he reached the closet-bathroom, dry-heaving long after he couldn't be sick anymore, the crushing headache worsening every time he retched until desperately he bunched the thin towel against his face to stop. The ache did ease very slightly but it was still bad, worse than he could ever remember any headache before. Or ever wanted to know again.

Because it was the only one available, he had to swill out the brandy-smelling glass of the previous night, briefly causing a fresh spasm of heaves, before he could get some water, which he carried unsteadily back into the bedroom, lowering himself gently onto the disheveled bed. His mouth was gratingly dry but he sipped the water carefully, not wanting to cause any more vomiting. The brandy bottle was on a side chest—like his great-grandfather's photograph back in Alexandria—and showed just about a third full. So he deserved to feel like he did; he practically deserved to be in a hospital, attached to a stomach pump.

Strangely, ill though he felt, O'Farrell did not actually regret the alcoholic breakdown. That was all it had been, an isolated, unforeseen breakdown like breakdowns always were. And they could always be overcome. Never again, he vowed. A drink or two, sure—and no more of this crap about counting how many or feeling guilty—but never again like last night. Not, as it eventually became, break-neck attempted oblivion. That was wino stuff, like the hair-matted wrecks lying in their own piss on 14th Street or in Union station. O'Farrell shuddered, immediately wincing at the discomfort the slight movement caused. He wasn't heading for 14th Street: never. Last night had been a warning. A release and a warning. Now he'd get on with the job.

Which he could do. He'd been thrown off balance, badly, by the woman and the boy, and he shouldn't have been, but he'd recovered now. Breakdown over. He had to forget the family. Not forget, precisely; that was stupid because he knew they existed. Compartmentalize them; that was the professional phrase. Compartmentalize anything likely to be a distraction, an interference. Hundreds . . . thousands . . . saved, he thought, not just lives. Suffering and hardship . . . Breakdown most definitely over. *Assassination saves lives.*

It took O'Farrell a long time to get ready but he still found himself among the rush-hour workers when he left the boardinghouse. He made his way to a fast-order café and forced himself to consume dry toast he didn't want and coffee he couldn't taste, knowing he had to get something into his stomach if he ever wanted to feel better. It didn't settle easily, but it settled. Just.

When O'Farrell got there, the BMW with which he had become familiar the previous night was still parked outside the Hampstead house. He drove past and concealed himself almost completely in a side street about fifty yards farther on, reminding himself he'd kept this rental car three days, which was long enough. The large package in Rivera's garage would prevent the BMW being put away, thought O'Farrell, an idea flickering unformed. How long would it stay there?

It was just past ten when Rivera left the house. O'Farrell noted the time and the surprising fact that the ambassador was not driven by an embassy chauffeur. He followed, sure of the destination and therefore not bothering to keep close surveillance, but he was able to anyway, because of the freak lightness of the traffic. He was glad he had because he was able to see a uniformed man—the chauffeur, he guessed—and two other men waiting expectantly at the embassy entrance to receive the man. So just after ten was Rivera's routine departure time from home and just after 10:30 his routine arrival time at the embassy. The American sighed in disbelief at the nonexistent security. Rivera appeared so unguarded it almost seemed suspicious.

Rivera went inside. The car was driven off by the uniformed man, confirming O'Farrell's impression. It was a simple around-the-block journey to the rear of the premises, where there was a small, name-designated parking area. Rivera's reserved spot was in the very center, in full view of all the rooms at the rear. Not possible here, thought O'Farrell, whose earlier idea had hardened. The chauffeur got out and went into the building. O'Farrell pulled in just beyond the embassy, on a double yellow line, watching the vehicle in his rearview mirror. Almost at once the chauffeur reappeared in an apron and with a bucket and cloth and started to clean the vehicle. O'Farrell eased out into the traffic again, expecting Rivera to remain within the embassy for the morning at least. It was unimportant anyway; he had other things to do.

Nausea was still a threat and O'Farrell drove tight-lipped, feeling cold but aware that he was sweating at the same time. The headache ebbed and flowed and the light hurt his eyes, causing a different and quite separate pain. His first full-blown, tie-and-tails hangover, he recognized. Even at college and later, in the army, on furloughs or celebrating something, he'd never drunk enough to lose control of himself, like the previous night. And was damn glad he hadn't, if this were the result. He was absolutely sure—and grateful—of one thing about the binge. If these were the aftereffects, there was no danger of his ever becoming an alcoholic.

He was glad to deliver the rental car at Kennington, retrieving the credit-card slip and paying in cash, assuring the counter clerk that the car had been perfect and he would use them again. O'Farrell crossed to Acton by underground, stomach and head in turmoil from the jolting claustrophobia of the subway car, which stank of stale people too close together.

In Acton he chose a dark blue Ford and arranged the same payment method as before, wondering as he drove east toward the embassy and the first contact with Petty since his arrival in England whether he would need all the rental cars he had carefully reserved. Or the boardinghouse accommodations, either. Hardly, if it remained as easy as this.

O'Farrell was lucky and actually found a parking place in Grosvenor Square. At the embassy reception area he identified himself as Hepplewhite, the alias he had used at the first boardinghouse and which was his agreed cover name during any planned embassy visits. The CIA station chief came out at once. He said his name was Slim Matthews, but he wasn't, at all: he was a roly-poly man who smiled a lot and rocked back and forth in an odd, wobbling gait when he walked.

"Been messaged you might stop by," Matthews said when they reached the security of the CIA section.

With a security classification and in a code from which Matthews would know not to ask questions, O'Farrell knew. He said, "At the moment, I just need the communications."

"You look like hell," Matthews said. "You all right?"

"Ate something that came back at me," O'Farrell said, easily. He realized, gratefully, he was feeling better.

"Food in England is shit," Matthews declared. "Hardly had a decent meal since I got here."

It didn't seem to be having much effect upon the man's

weight problem; perhaps it was glandular. O'Farrell said, "There'll be stuff arriving for me, packed, in the pouch. It shouldn't be opened, of course. I'll collect."

"Understood. Anything else?"

"Nothing," O'Farrell said. He hoped.

Matthews escorted O'Farrell through the barred, marine-guarded inner sanctum. His verbal authorization was enough. No note was made in the log in which all entries and exits were supposed to be recorded.

O'Farrell used a priority number to reach Langley and was quickly patched through to Petty. The section chief answered the telephone coughing and O'Farrell wondered if the pipe had been just lighted or extinguished. "How's it look?" the department head began.

"I've decided the way," O'Farrell announced.

Petty grunted. "It has to be coordinated with the move against Belac, don't forget. We haven't heard from the Bureau or from Customs yet."

"The opportunity won't last," O'Farrell said. Jesus, don't say they were going to pussyfoot around when he had the chance to do it and get out!

"It's got to be in the proper sequence," Petty insisted. "Which is Belac first."

"What if it can't be that way!"

"We don't want to spook Belac."

"So what's more important?"

"Both," Petty said infuriatingly. "How much time have we really got?"

"I don't know," O'Farrell admitted. "Not long."

"If it goes, you'll have to find another way," Petty said.

Just like that! O'Farrell thought. "This isn't easy, you know!"

"No one ever said it was," Petty said. "What do you need?"

O'Farrell listed the materials he wanted shipped from Washington. He added, "And I want the watchers withdrawn. I don't want an audience."

Petty went silent for a few moments. He said, "Just the usual precaution."

"It isn't necessary. And they're amateur. Get them off my back."

"Okay." The clumsy sons of bitches, Petty thought. But then O'Farrell always had been good; it was encouraging to know that he still was.

"I mean it," insisted O'Farrell. "No watchers."

"Speak to me before you move," Petty said.

"All right." He was definitely on hold, O'Farrell knew.

"And well done."

"It hasn't happened yet."

"I know it will," Petty said. "How many times do I have to tell you that you're our best man?"

Crap, thought O'Farrell. He said, "You don't have to bother."

"Another thing," Petty said, as if he'd suddenly remembered, which O'Farrell knew couldn't be, because Petty never forgot anything. "Got a query channeled through from Florida. DA's talking deals with the pilot, Rodgers, in exchange for testimony to a grand jury against the Cuban. DA wants to know if we've got a mitigating recommendation, to go with his."

You my man, thought O'Farrell. He said, "What's the District Attorney offering him?"

"No idea," Petty said. "An indictment against Cuadrado has political mileage; it'll make some waves and headlines here in Washington. So I guess it'll be worthwhile."

"Nothing!" O'Farrell announced shortly. "I don't think we should recommend any mitigation at all."

There was a further silence from the other end. Then Petty said, "I thought Rodgers told you all he could."

"He played with me," O'Farrell said. "Acted out some B-movie bullshit. What he told me he's telling the DA. So why does he get the same favor twice?"

"Your decision," Petty said. "Don't move without us talking again, okay?"

"I'll wait," O'Farrell said, resigned.

Back in the outer section, O'Farrell thanked Matthews, and the station chief said he'd like to offer O'Farrell a drink but knew he couldn't. O'Farrell, who would have liked to accept and have someone briefly to talk with, said he would have enjoyed it, too, but he had to decline.

The BMW was still in the rear parking area at the Cuban embassy, and O'Farrell settled himself for an indeterminate wait, which in the event wasn't long at all. Rivera himself came out of the rear door to take the car, and O'Farrell guessed the destination within minutes of the departure. The door of the Pimlico house opened and closed quickly, and O'Farrell thought they had to be pretty anxious to risk a quickie in the afternoon but then remembered they hadn't been together the previous night and guessed it was a case of catching up.

It *was* a quickie. From Pimlico, Rivera went back within the hour to Hampstead, where again the car was left outside. Rivera departed at the same time the following morning—and the morning after that—and again the car was parked outside at night. And again there was a complete absence of security.

All O'Farrell could do was wait, like he'd promised Petty. He was reluctant to do that; he'd gotten through the last few days, but he wasn't sure how much longer he could last.

He attended a church in Kensington on two consecutive mornings, but it didn't help, not like it usually had. On the second occasion a cleric tried to get into a conversation, but O'Farrell cut the man short, although not rudely.

Church visits were an excuse, he decided. Like a lot of other things.

Apart from the very first few months—or maybe weeks—of their marriage, Rivera could not recall things being easier between himself and Estelle. Her attitude towards him changed completely, to one of friendship he had never known from her, and he positively relaxed in her company, as she relaxed in his. They attended two official receptions. At both she was dazzling and attentive to him, and he actually enjoyed them, and when she went to her assignations with the Frenchman, she did so more discreetly than she had before, not flaunting her early departure and late return as a challenge. They talked about Lopelle only once after her drawing-room revelation. Estelle said his wife had agreed to a divorce and Lopelle himself had accepted Rivera's terms, believing it would be better for his own diplomatic position, too. Rivera said he was glad everything was going to work out. Rivera was curious to see what the man looked like but had not asked if he were at the two receptions; he didn't think the man could have been, from the closeness with which Estelle stayed with him.

Estelle even began breakfasting with him, which was something she had never done, and it was at breakfast that she said, "Maxine's ill."

Maxine had come to them as a nanny for Jorge and stayed on to act as housekeeper when the boy had grown older.

"What's wrong?"

"Some flu-type virus," Estelle said. "The doctor says it's contagious, so I'm keeping her away from Jorge."

"Do that," Rivera said, immediately concerned. "How long will she be off work?"

"I don't know," Estelle said.

John Herbeck had worked for them all—Apple and Hewlett Packard and IBM—as a development engineer and still considered himself the best, even though the last of them, IBM, had been a few years ago now. He kept up with everything—all the trade mags and the in-house publications that were slipped to him by friends still in the business—and knew he gave value for money to those who retained him as a consultant on technological innovations. And as a spotter, too, directing buyer to seller. That was the easiest money of all. Less now than there had been, in the halcyon days of Silicon Valley, but still enough to keep him comfortably in the style to which he had become accustomed. But only just. It seemed to be getting more difficult, with every passing month. He was becoming quite anxious to attract new clients.

SEVENTEEN

Too MANY things were going wrong too quickly, and Belac was making mistakes. Which he acknowledged, and which further upset him; that it was all costing him money upset him most of all. By now he should have gained his entire profit but he hadn't, because of that damned ten-percent withholding. And trying to handle the Swedish business by letter—actually trying to save money by not going—was a mistake. It had taken nearly a month of correspondence, Belac using the cover of his Swiss shell company, before it became clear from Epetric that the blocking of the VAX order was not their decision but that of the California company, which refused to supply any more material until they were better satisfied with the documentation, as required by the American export authorities.

Nearly a whole month wasted! And now he had to confront the biggest problem of all. America.

Belac conducted his special trade fully aware of its risks and knew every detail of the indictments outstanding against him in the United States. He genuinely considered

both to be ridiculous, like so much that COCOM prohibited, because each indictment was for supplying the communist bloc with computers that could be manufactured
from components available over shop counters practically
anywhere in the West. Ridiculous or not, however, the indictments remained two very good and convincing reasons
why he should not risk entering the country.

But he hardly had any choice. He'd built a clear
$2.5-million profit into the VAX order alone and laid out
a nonreturnable deposit of $250,000. If he didn't supply
and Rivera had to purchase elsewhere, it meant not only
his losing almost three million. It meant the all-important
word getting around among the other dealers: it meant losing his reputation and possible future customers. The con-
siderations didn't end there. Belac had to *know* why
Shepherd Industries was objecting to documentation that at
this stage was foolproof, whether the objection indicated
that he was definitely being targeted by U.S. agencies.
He'd gone in and out of America, since the indictments
had been handed down; he had enough passports for a
dozen trips. But this time it would be more dangerous;
he'd have to use his own passport at some stage to run
hare to their hounds to see if there *were* a pursuit. It was
time to stop making mistakes, time to start being very
careful.

Belac went three days after receiving the explanatory
letter from Sweden.

A man of habit, which disastrously lulled the CIA
watchers into carelessness, Belac began the evening as he
normally did by going to the fixed-price restaurant in
which he normally ate. But after half an hour, he left
through its rear door for the waiting taxi that took him directly to the railway station, where he caught the Swiss-
bound trans-European express with minutes to spare. He
was fifteen minutes into the train journey before the CIA
discovered that he had left the restaurant, but some days

would pass before they would admit losing him completely.

Belac crossed the Swiss border on a valid German passport in the name of Hans Krebs. In the same name he booked into Zurich's Baur au Lac Hotel. In the morning he flew to London.

Belac flew into the United States by a circuitous route, from London and through Toronto, so that he entered from Canada. It was on the last leg of the journey, into Seattle, that he took the big risk, booking the ticket in his real name of Pierre Réné Belac. But he went through passport and immigration control on the Krebs document, knowing passenger manifests are not compared against the passports of arriving passengers. There was not the slightest hindrance, and within forty-five minutes, his trail having been laid, he was waiting by the boarding gate of the last San Francisco flight of the day. Deciding not to press his luck, he traveled on the German name.

He changed back again to his real identity at San Francisco airport and used his own driver's license to rent a Lincoln Continental from the Hertz office. He stopped in San Jose, parking the car in a shopping mall, and continued his journey by taxi, although not into San Francisco. In Milpitas he found a cheap motel, which, in comparison to his apartment in Brussels, was practically luxurious. At last he slept, exhausted by traveling for so long and drained by the nervous strain as well.

He woke in the morning feeling refreshed. From Brussels he'd carried the names of three consultants known within the arms trade to have responded to hi-tech inquiries in the past. With the first he got an answering machine. The second was John Herbeck, who came on to the line as soon as Belac explained his requirements to the secretary. After a few minutes' conversation they arranged to meet for cocktails at the Mark Hopkins, on Nob Hill.

The consultant turned out to be a swarthy, deeply suntanned man with the tendency to laugh after speaking, as if he were nervous of his listener disagreeing with what he said.

Belac knew his business and was easily able to keep the conversation going about technology developments throughout Santa Clara Valley and the tightness of the industry compared to a few years ago. Then Belac mentioned the restrictive problems of COCOM.

Belac waited for the American to pick up the lead, and Herbeck took it.

"It's a mine field," Herbeck said, in clumsy cliché. "Commerce and Customs seem to change their minds day by day; it's hell keeping abreast of it."

"Which is why I need somebody here, on the spot," Belac said. "In Europe it's impossible for me to keep track."

"A retainer, you mean?" Herbeck pounced.

"If we come to a satisfactory arrangement, then most certainly it would involve a retainer," Belac said.

Spotting, thought Herbeck: what he enjoyed doing most. He said, "I'd like to get some idea of your activities."

So would a lot of people, Belac thought. He smiled his sparse smile and said, "I think it's best summed up as being a middle man between interested parties."

"I see," Herbeck said slowly, believing that he did. "What, specifically, would be my part in the operation?"

Belac shrugged. "Variable, I would imagine," he said. "At the moment I would see myself contacting you if I had a tentative order, to get your advice on the most likely supplier and for guidance upon any export infringements."

"Would you have me become involved in any negotiations?" the American asked.

"As I said, it might be variable. The normal way for my company is to deal direct."

No illegality! Herbeck thought. If all he did was identify companies, he wasn't breaking the law; if he set out the COCOM restrictions every time, he would actually be observing it. "What sort of retainer are we talking about here?"

"Something else I seek your advice about," lured Belac. "What's the normal scale?"

Don't go too high but don't go too low, either, Herbeck thought. He said, "Again it would depend on the work involved, but I would think something in the region of thirty-five thousand a year."

The absurdity of paying anyone money like that! Belac kept any reaction from his face and said, "That would be quite acceptable. I would expect to meet your expenses as well."

Happy days are here again, thought Herbeck. He said, "What more, then, can we talk about?"

"I can't make a positive decision tonight, you understand," Belac said. "You're the first consultant with whom I've opened discussions. I have other appointments."

"I understand," Herbeck said, miserably. "Is there a number where I could reach you?"

"I'll call you in a few days," Belac said.

"I'll be waiting," the consultant assured him hopefully.

Belac left the Mark Hopkins and hailed a cab, bitterly regretting the money he was spending on taxis but knowing it was necessary. He paid the vehicle off in San Jose and went on foot through one of the mall entrances to check for any surveillance upon the car. He gave himself an hour, wandering in and out of stores, and finally decided he would have identified the watch had any been imposed.

He hailed a taxi and returned to his motel, ate watery scrambled eggs and drank gray coffee in the motel diner, and reflected, unamused, that the whole artificial performance could easily be an expensive waste of time.

Belac waited until ten the following morning before ringing Shepherd Industries. There was the briefest of pauses when he identified himself as a representative of Epetric before he was connected to Bernard Shepherd himself. Epetric was sending him from Sweden to resolve the problem of the VAX contract, Belac lied. Could they meet in two days' time? Shepherd agreed, almost too quickly to have consulted a diary. Noon was convenient to both.

Shepherd's immediate nerve-jangled reaction was to call Morrison's San Francisco number, but he had a second thought. The connection to Stockholm was swift, as was the assurance from Epetric's chairman that no executive of theirs was being sent to California.

The number must have been direct to Morrison's desk, because the FBI man answered at once.

"It's worked; he's coming!" Shepherd announced. And you bastards can get off my back, he thought.

"When!" Morrison asked.

"We've arranged a meeting in two days' time."

Customs and FBI had their first planning meeting an hour later.

"Maximum airport watch, everywhere we can think of," said Morrison, addressing the assembled agents. "Let's not lose the son of a bitch this time."

O'Farrell had coped so far with the screwing around in Washington but only just. Like so much else on this assignment, it hadn't happened before. It had always been the same routine: satisfy himself, go in, complete the job, and get out. Clean, expert, no loose ends. Not like this. It was ridiculous for Petty to insist, as the man had insisted on O'Farrell's second contact from the London embassy, that there was a problem assembling the requested material; in twenty-four hours the CIA could gather together enough weaponry and ordnance to start a war.

O'Farrell had found an answer in keeping himself busy. And not by concentrating on Hampstead or High Holborn or Pimlico; he actually reduced his surveillance there, worried that it might cause suspicion. He did ordinary, even touristy things, instead. He visited the Houses of Parliament and took a river trip on the Thames and saw a ludicrous movie about spies. He changed boardinghouses and rental cars and at the end of the week he carefully worked out the time difference to ensure that Jill would be home and called her collect from a telephone box. She asked when he would be returning and O'Farrell said he wasn't sure, but soon, he hoped. Patrick appeared to be contesting the alimony in rebuttal, so it looked like a protracted and nasty legal situation and Jill wished he were home. O'Farrell said he wished it, too, and promised to call again, when he had a definite return date.

Booze was no longer a problem because he did not allow himself to consider it one. He had a drink or two if he felt like it at lunchtime, and a couple more if he felt like it in the evening, and he finished off the brandy, although gradually, over a few evenings. It had to be sensible, the way he was treating it, because after the brandy night he never got drunk. He came close the day of his depressing conversation with Jill, having a couple more than usual, so there was an artificial belligerence to his manner when he got to the embassy. He hurried, although not rudely, the preliminaries with Matthews but began with unusual forcefulness his protests to Petty, who curtly cut him short.

"The stuff's being freighted to you today," Petty said. "You can move two days from now."

EIGHTEEN

MORRISON AND Hoover arrived at Shepherd Industries in the afternoon, as they'd arranged. Morrison said that although every sort of interception was being attempted, the likeliest place to arrest Belac remained the factory complex itself.

"So it's cooperation all the way," Hoover said.

"*Each* way," Shepherd qualified, heavily. He'd actually talked it through with his attorney since that morning's call, suggesting the man be present when they arrived. He wished he'd insisted, despite the lawyer's caution that it would look as if he needed legal protection against wrongdoing.

The FBI man grinned, tight with excitement; the impending bust was good promotion material. He said, "Here's the deal. When Belac's in the bag, I'll make public all you've done, express official gratitude. How's that sound?"

"All right," Shepherd agreed, missing the qualification.

The full planning meeting was the next day at noon, the time they expected Belac to be seized the following day. Eight other men, in addition to Morrison and Hoover, crowded into Shepherd's office, but were not introduced. It was Morrison who called the gathering to order. He had Shepherd recount the telephone conversation, and when the industrialist finished, the FBI man said, "It looks like the best chance we've ever had."

"We hope," Hoover said. The Customs inspector spread out maps on Shepherd's conference table. Upon them a series of outwardly radiating concentric circles were drawn, with the factory at the center. The group made an effort to isolate every road that could in some way or part be used to reach it. The total came to eighteen, and Morrison said, "We'd need an army to cover them all."

"And have to include San Francisco police and Santa Clara county police and the highway patrol," Hoover said.

"Too many," Morrison said, and for the first time Shepherd realized the intended seizure was being confined to the FBI and Customs.

"Which brings us back to the factory, which is why

we're here," said one of the unidentified men, who carried a clipboard, although he hadn't yet written any notes.

At Morrison's request, Shepherd produced the plans of the factory, both internal and external. The man with the clipboard said, "Going to be a bitch sealing the outside, without his seeing it as he enters. The parking lot at the rear is fenced and containable, but this open area at the front is hopeless. He'd spot any concentration of men a mile away."

"So there can't be any," Morrison said. "He's got to be allowed onto the premises and into the elevator before there's any move."

"Don't we need that anyway?" Hoover asked. "Don't we need Shepherd wired to get some discussion between him and Belac, linking Belac to the VAX order, to go with all the documentary stuff?"

Morrison shifted, annoyed at Hoover suggesting it first. To the industrialist, Morrison said, "You feel okay about that?"

"What do I have to do?" Shepherd asked.

"I fit you with an undetectable microphone; it's voice-activated so everything either of you say is automatically recorded," said another of the FBI team. "It'll tie Belac in absolutely, with everything."

Shepherd guessed that each man within the room was some sort of section chief or expert. It seemed vaguely dangerous, but with no alternative Shepherd said, "Sure, I'll do it."

To Morrison, the electronics man said, "As we're pretty sure where the conversation is going to take place—right here—why don't I rig this office as a backup? By noon tomorrow I could get this place live enough to record everyone's thoughts."

"Good," Morrison said. "What about photographs?"

The man squinted professionally around the office and said, "Noon's a perfect time, and the light looks plenty strong enough. . . ." He turned, locating a door. "That a closet?" he asked Shepherd.

Shepherd nodded.

"Ideal," said the man. "I can fit a fish-eye lens in there that'll take in just about the entire room."

To the man with the clipboard, Morrison said, "So here's how we'll back up. We'll have someone in the foyer, overalls, stuff like that, tending the plants like those contract people do. As soon as he hears Belac say he's from Epetric and sees him inside the elevator, he walks out of the building. Just that. It'll be the signal for your people, who've held back, to move in with vehicles, sealing every ground floor exit. . . ." To another man, Morrison said, "From nine A.M. tomorrow morning we'll have the elevators staffed by our officers. Belac going up in the elevator will be the bell for more people to move in, sealing the building at each level. The supervisor of each unit will be wired. If Belac smells a rat and runs for it—and even if he manages to clear one floor—it won't matter because we'll all be talking to each other, following him down from level to level. And every way out at the ground will be bolted, barred, and locked." Morrison smiled around at the assembled group, as if he were expecting congratulations. "How's that sound? Anything left out?"

There were looks and headshakes among the men. The electronics officer said, "I'd like to get started as soon as possible. I'll do the office first." To Shepherd, he said, "I'll fix you up tomorrow morning. Eight o'clock all right?"

"I'll be here," promised Shepherd. He'd been doing some private reconsideration; within yards of where these men were standing had to be half a dozen ledgers that could get him at least five years in a penitentiary.

The section leaders filed from the room but Morrison and Hoover remained, watching the electronics man. Shepherd was determined he wouldn't leave either of them alone in his office if he could help it.

"You know something that makes me uneasy?" Hoover asked. "How easy it suddenly all seems. It's like he's walking up to us with his hands outstretched to have the cuffs put on."

"If he came, which it looks as if he has, then how else could it be?" Morrison demanded. "This is the only place he could come to."

"I guess," Hoover agreed. "But it just doesn't seem to fit with how he left those CIA guys in Brussels looking like Mr. Magoo."

"You got a better idea than going along with it?" the FBI man asked aggressively.

"I'm just expressing an opinion, is all," Hoover said.

The technician reappeared from the closet and said, "Since you're still here, give me a voice level."

"Abandon all hope, you who enter," Morrison recited.

"Perfect," the man said.

"With luck," Hoover qualified.

Belac rented another car, a Pontiac compact, under a false name this time, and drove it to San Jose to check the Lincoln Continental again. He waited in the mall almost an hour, until he was sure, and this time opened the vehicle and hid the ignition key beneath the mat on the driver's side.

Back in the Pontiac, Belac continued on down Route 208 and detoured to drive past Shepherd Industries, imprinting the layout in his mind. He knew there would be another opportunity on the return journey. At San Francisco airport, he found three internal flights—no need for passports—all leaving within an hour of each other the following afternoon. Constantly aware of the money he was spending, Belac bought tickets for each, to Phoenix, Salt Lake City, and Las Vegas, from three different clerks. If he were taking unnecessary precautions, at least he could recover his money, Belac thought, driving northward again.

He went slowly by Shepherd Industries again, checking his initial impression, and got back to Milpitas by midafternoon. From the parking-lot pay phone, he made a reservation for the following day under his proper name at the Mark Hopkins hotel because he remembered it from his meeting with Herbeck. Afterward, still at the telephone, he wondered how the consultant would react to his approach when he made it. It was a good feeling to be the manipulator instead of being manipulated, Belac decided. Irrationally he began blaming Rivera for all the trouble he was having and pulled his mouth back into his ugly smile as the idea came to him: the Cuban would have to pay. It would be enjoyable, ensuring that the man did. The decision cheered him.

Back in his motel room Belac slumped in the only easy chair, a displaced spring driving itself uncomfortably into his leg, reviewing every precaution he had taken and trying to think of anything he had overlooked. There was nothing, he decided. It was going to be a long evening.

Morrison and Hoover imagined the same thing until the call came for them, in Hoover's office.

"Seattle!" Morrison yelled to the Customs man, the telephone still cradled at his ear. Morrison outstretched his free hand, commanding silence while he listened. He was beaming when he replaced the receiver. "Came in on an Air Canada flight from Toronto three days ago under his own name. Immigration identified his photograph, but he must have used one of his Mickey Mouse passports." The FBI man paused, looking at Hoover. "Well?" he demanded. "Still doubtful now?"

"I guess not," Hoover conceded.

NINETEEN

AT THE first attempt Belac got an answering machine and paced nervously up and down in front of the booth, counting the minutes, keeping the relief from his voice when he got Herbeck's secretary at the second attempt and was connected immediately to the consultant.

"I think I'd like us to work together," Belac announced. He went along with the small talk about what a worthwhile relationship the other man knew it was going to be and the benefits that were going to result for both of them, before cutting in with his demands. Herbeck listened without interruption but repeated the important details when Belac finished.

"I'm sorry to have to ask you to do this," Belac said. "But there's no way I can get up from Los Angeles in time and I want the appointment kept."

"I understand," Herbeck said. "But you'll be here by this afternoon?"

"Three at the outside. I've got a reservation at the Mark Hopkins. I'll call from there."

"What time do you think you could get to Shepherd Industries?"

"Four-thirty. Stress that I want the meeting today, if he can possibly manage it."

"I'll fix it," the American promised.

"It's an imposition, before we've really started working together. I know that," Belac said.

Herbeck took the opening. "We only talked around the relationship."

"Your suggestion is fine by me," Belac said.

"With expenses?"

"Naturally," Belac said. "We'll settle it all contractually this afternoon, when I get up."

The urge to arrive early at the back road from which he had a view of Shepherd Industries was very strong, but Belac resisted it, knowing that a car stationary for too long a time would attract attention. Still, he checked out early and drove along 208, from near the factory to the airport; the journey took within five minutes of what it had taken him the previous day. He considered a late breakfast but decided to save the money, reckoning that he could safely return to the factory complex now.

When Belac reached the back road, he spotted the vehicles at once. They would have been concealed from the normal approach but from his position he could see them and their occupants clearly; two of the vans even had the heavy-duty aerials for radio equipment. Belac refused to panic, remaining where he was and picking out the Lincoln Continental the moment it turned into the approach road.

Herbeck parked it neatly within the painted lines of the designated area and considerately locked it. The men assembled around the sprawled building moved as soon as Herbeck entered it, as if one were linked to the other, motivating them into action. There were men running on foot as well as vehicles swarming to seal the building off. From a place he could not see earlier came two small-windowed armored vehicles.

Belac was exactly a mile down the highway by the time Herbeck finished his explanation to Shepherd and the listening Hoover and Morrison burst into Shepherd's office from the anteroom. Morrison was beside himself with fury, swearing and yelling so much in the first few minutes that he was unintelligible. He yelled at Herbeck to tell him everything, from the beginning, but quickly, and before the man finished, another FBI officer had confirmed that the Lincoln had been rented in Belac's name and that there was a waiting reservation at the Mark Hopkins.

"We've got to stake it out. I know it's a waste of time and that the fucker has snowed us again, but we've got to stake it out. . . ." More controlled now, he beckoned other agents, to include them in the conversation with Hoover. "Let's go for the international departures. He came in through Canada, so let's second-guess he'll go out that way, too."

The electronics expert emerged from the anteroom and said, "I was here until nine last night; this room is like a film studio! You telling me it's all wasted?"

"Every goddamned bit of it," Hoover said bitterly.

Shepherd moved awkwardly from behind his desk, restricted by the equipment strapped to his body. To the electronics man, he said, "Get me out of this crap, will you?"

The industrialist stood with his shirt undone to the waist, feeling foolish as the wires were released. He said to Morrison, "I did everything you asked. We had a deal."

Morrison wheeled on the man, as if he had forgotten him, his face white and tight with fury. "Time you listened to the words, Mr. Shepherd," he said. "I told you we had a deal when Belac was in the bag. He ain't in any bag."

"That's no fault of mine!"

"You know what I think, Mr. Shepherd? I think we'd better have a closer look at your whole operation here. Make sure everything is kosher. You get the idea?"

Belac had taken the Phoenix flight. He spent the entire journey tensed for any sudden interest from the crew and was wet with apprehension on arrival, but there was no check at the debarkation gate. He moved on immediately, waiting only an hour for a flight to Mexico City, where for the first time he felt able to relax. From Mexico he picked up the overnight service to Madrid, where he rested properly before moving on to Paris.

He'd thought everything out by the time he reached France. He'd lived well, by his own frugal standards, and successfully even with two American indictments outstanding against him. And he could continue to do so in the future, providing he did not again attempt to enter the United States. For the moment, maybe for a long time until he built up the proper connections, he'd better stay away from American hi-tech, which was distressing because it was most profitable.

If the Americans were investigating him and the VAX order, which they clearly were, then they had to know of Rivera. Belac wished he could say nothing and let the bastard sink in whatever morass he was in. But there was too much money outstanding. Rivera had to be told, told the VAX was impossible. He, Belac, would agree to refund the sum advanced for its purchase if Rivera would agree to a settlement for everything. And that would be the end.

Belac tried to make the telephone conversation fittingly businesslike. Overwhelming problems had arisen, he said, when he was connected to Rivera in London. They had to meet at once, and Rivera had to come to him in Paris; Belac was confident he'd escaped surveillance, but was unsure about the other man. Rivera attempted to question but Belac refused to answer, repeating the need for a personal meeting. Rivera stipulated the George V and the still nervous Belac agreed at once, despite the price.

"And be careful about being followed," he warned.

Rivera took no precautions at all, angrily suspicious of Belac's melodramatic approach, but the CIA watch had already been suspended, on orders from Washington. The flight was on time and Rivera entered Paris against the outflow of rush hour and reached the hotel ahead of the hour arranged. They met in the ground-floor bar.

The ambassador sat without drinking, letting Belac recount what had happened over the preceding few days, his disbelief becoming positive conviction. Clearly unimpressed, Rivera said when Belac finished, "So where does that leave us with our arrangement?" without any expression of concern.

"The VAX is impossible," Belac said. "I'm not sure now about the tank auction—"

"I *must* have the tanks!" Rivera cut in. The indispensable middleman who always delivered ahead of time, he thought. He wasn't that anymore. By relying absolutely on Belac, who'd failed him, he had no way now to buy elsewhere and still meet the deadline, even the Havana schedule of six months. The fucker of pigs!

"I'll try for the tanks," Belac said. "I have fifteen Stinger missiles. . . . The third ship, the *City of Athens*, is chartered to pick up from San Diego, if the tank deal comes off." For a brief moment Belac was warmed by a private thought.

"So I don't get the VAX!"

"That's all," Belac agreed, hurriedly. "But there's the money you're keeping back. As well as the percentages; and there's four million I'm owed on the transportation costs. It comes in total to fifteen million. At the moment I am something like five million out of pocket—my own money." He felt something like heartburn having to say the words.

"And three million *in* pocket from the money already advanced for the VAX purchase," Rivera pointed out.

"No!" tried Belac, reluctant to sacrifice anything. "I had to pay that for the portions of the system that were supplied, before the ban."

"Rubbish," Rivera said. "You might have had advances and staged payments to other dealers, for most of the stuff, but the VAX was from a bona fide supplier and you would have dealt with them in the normal way, payment on completion at ninety days."

"I have a proposal," Belac said, retreating. "I *will* refund the VAX money, as a gesture of good faith. In return

I ask you to relax this penalty situation; release the other money."

Rivera did not respond at once. It was unthinkable that he should trust the man. Thank God he *had* withheld the money and retained a lever to get the tanks. Just yesterday he'd received detailed delivery instructions. He said, "We had a deal. You broke it."

"I didn't know I was under investigation, did I!" Belac said, exasperated.

"*Are* you under investigation?" Rivera asked quietly.

It was Belac's turn briefly to remain unspeaking. "I see," he said, controlled himself. "Let me return your question. Where does that leave us, with our arrangement?"

"Short of forty tanks, fifteen Stinger missiles, and a computer," Rivera said.

"I will supply the tanks and the missiles," Belac said.

"I have specific instructions," Rivera insisted. "After loading in San Diego, the *City of Athens* has to sail direct to Lobito; it's a port in Angola, West Africa. The American departure must be reported by the master direct to Havana. When I receive confirmation of the sailing, I'll release the money you are owed. Less the VAX payment. So, how long?"

"A week," said Belac. He knew the way to screw the bastard! Screw him and end up with more profit than he'd imagined possible!

"The fifteenth, then," Rivera said. "On the fifteenth I shall have the final money transfer ready, awaiting my authorization, into your account. If I do not receive that sailing confirmation, no money will be transferred. Is that all fully understood?"

"You won't be able to contact me," Belac said. "I'll know where to contact you."

"Have you ever heard of such a screw-up!" Sneider demanded.

"Not for a long time," McCarthy agreed, accepting the sixth coffee of the day. "We didn't actually emerge smelling of roses in Brussels, though, did we?"

"There seems to be enough to move against Shepherd."

"Small change," McCarthy said. "Little more than petulance."

"O'Farrell goes ahead?"

"Petty wants to talk. But I think so. I'd still like it to be the other way."

"Can we afford to take any more chances?"

"I'd go for it if I thought it stood a chance."

TWENTY

THE TRAINING—the professionalism—was there when O'Farrell called upon it, and he hoped it would last. There was a long day and an even longer evening to get through, but he didn't have a drink. He concentrated on his surroundings, satisfying himself that the surveillance had been withdrawn. He kept one boardinghouse reservation, as insurance, but canceled the rest, as he did the remaining rental cars. Desperate as he was to get back to America, he booked a flight for the following afternoon, nonstop to Washington. He wouldn't have to cancel it, he knew. Everything was going to go fine.

The urge to go ahead—to get it over with and get out— had been enormous the day Petty said okay. But he hadn't. Just. There'd been the necessary break in his intense surveillance and the pattern he'd established, so O'Farrell forced the self-control and checked again that what was important to know hadn't changed. He watched Rivera go in and out of the Hampstead house, confirming by the continued casualness that neither the gate nor the front door was alarmed. The BMW was as usual parked outside at night, and the police foot patrol went by at predictable forty-five minute intervals. The night of the clearance, a police car surprised him by passing in between the regular patrols. It appeared to slow outside Rivera's house as well. Of course, O'Farrell had to guarantee over a further two nights that the car's presence was an accident and not an increase in police presence. The car didn't appear again. He spent the days shopping for the necessary, disposable equipment, always in crowded supermarkets where there was no chance of his being remembered: rubber gloves, electrical leads and clamps, magnetic-headed screwdrivers, adhesive tape, a penknife, and a small, concentrated-beam flashlight. The final purchase was a cheap, cardboard briefcase to carry everything. The other things he needed had arrived from Washington.

And now he was ready. Tonight. After tonight it would all be over. Finished. Thank God.

Incredibly, after all the inner turmoil, he felt no apprehension and he was actually surprised. He felt the heightened awareness there always was when the moment came close, the adrenaline surge he positively welcomed because it made him more alert, but none of the gut-churning emotions of the previous weeks, which had, he accepted, brought him close to collapse. And he seemed to have succeeded in putting aside in his mind and consciousness the wife and the child as well, so they were no longer a factor in his reasoning.

Now, he thought again. Tonight. Still no apprehension. The uncertainty, the self-doubt, had to have been a passing phase then, brought on by God knows what. O'Farrell was glad it had passed. He hoped it didn't come again.

O'Farrell set out late, past midnight, allowing time for Rivera to be home and for the BMW engine to be cold. He drove more cautiously than usual, acknowledging this to be possibly the most dangerous part of what he intended to do; he was driving a doubtfully roadworthy rented car containing Czechoslovakian-made explosives and Soviet detonators. And other materials that could, without too great a stretch of a policeman's imagination, be described as housebreaking equipment. *Unquestionably* the most dangerous part. He waited, expectantly, but there was nothing like the uncertainty he'd known recently. It was virtually always like this at the last moment, he reassured himself, just the same: always, in these last few hours, holding a gun or working with explosives that could take a human life. There was a flicker of unease when the phrase "human life" went through his mind but it was very slight and didn't last.

O'Farrell drove by the house on Christchurch Hill—the BMW was there—but didn't slow. He continued on to a turn, turning again and then again, completing the square, parking farther away than he had before. He wanted the concealing protection of the other cars that lined the road there, where his vehicle would be one of many, not isolated for a registration check by a cautious policeman. The lights extinguished, O'Farrell remained behind the wheel, checking the time against the unseen but scheduled passing of the police patrol. At the precise moment he knew they would be going by Rivera's home, he left the car, a smooth, quick movement. Whatever he carried in this area at this time of night would have aroused curiosity, but O'Farrell thought the briefcase was the most acceptable. It bulged heavily, but so did a lot of briefcases; he wished he had been able to age it more successfully. He was glad of the darkness.

O'Farrell walked alert to everything around him, not consciously using the shadows—which in itself would be suspicious—but ready to withdraw into them if necessary. He did, after about fifty yards, when outside lights abruptly blazed ahead of him and there was a noisy, shouted parting between guests and hosts. But when a car suddenly came around the corner, filling the road with its headlights, he did not withdraw. He realized he would have already been seen and that to do so would clearly be suspicious. The vehicle was unmarked and there was no obvious interest from anyone inside. He pulled into the cover of an overhanging tree after it had passed, to watch for the glare of suddenly applied brake lights, but none came. At the corner of the road upon which Rivera's house was built, O'Farrell paused, checking the police progress. Twenty-five minutes before their next patrol, allowing five minutes for any unforeseen change in their pattern. And he had about one hundred yards and a gate to negotiate. Time to spare, he calculated, walking on. O'Farrell saw car lights far ahead. He would easily have been able to dodge, but trees did not overhang in such profusion as before and there was less shadow. He decided it was better to walk on, as if he had every right to be where he was. There seemed to be a perceptible slowing but the car didn't stop; he didn't immediately look back, as he'd done before, worried of their watching him in their rearview mirror. He waited until he was two houses from Rivera's official residence. There was no sign of any vehicle. People either. Ahead, the road was deserted. He checked the time again. Still ten minutes.

He consciously slowed when he reached the edge of Rivera's property, ears strained for any movement or sound—guards, dogs, whatever he had missed in his surveillance. There was a dog barking but it was far away; nearer, and louder, water was running. A fountain, O'Farrell guessed; it might have been in Rivera's garden but could have been in that of a neighbor. He stopped just short of the gate so as not to be silhouetted by it, but able to reach out to test if it were locked after all. As he did so, far up the road, he saw the black, moving outlines of two pedestrians—it had to be the returning policemen. He did not hurry. As close to the wall as he was, he would merge completely with it. The latch lifted with barely an audible click and there was no sound at all as the gate gave inward, on oiled hinges. O'Farrell opened it only enough to ease through, closing it just as soundlessly before moving sideways to the protection of the shrubbery, and off the crunching gravel. He dropped, perfectly comfortable, into a squatting crouch, waiting for the police to pass, ears again tensed to hear a voice or a footstep. Unaccountably he was swept by a feeling of déjà vu and searched for the memory. It came very quickly. How he'd learned to crouch, for hours if necessary, and how he'd listened on deep reconnaissance missions behind the lines in Vietnam, he recalled: in Vietnam, where for the first time he— O'Farrell closed his mind to the recollection.

The sound came indistinctly at first, meaning the officers were a long way off, and O'Farrell was pleased; if he'd been unaware of their approach, the warning would have been more than early enough to evade or avoid. Overhead an airliner growled toward London airport and O'Farrell was able to see the triangle of its landing lights. Less than twenty-four hours, he thought, this time tomorrow, in fact, he would be home in Alexandria, with the newly preserved archive to go back to and the cars to clean on Saturdays and only the problems—the seemingly easier, ordinary problems—of Jill and Ellen and John to worry about. Normality, blessed normality.

". . . know she's screwing around," came a voice, at last.

"What are you going to do about it?"

"I've got nothing to confront her with," came a policeman's reply.

"So you're going to wait until she gets pregnant or catches the clap?"

" 'Course not," said the voice, fading.

"What then?"

The reply was too indistinct to hear. Forty-five minutes, O'Farrell calculated. The BMW was not directly in front of the house, as it usually was, but to the side near the garage. It was a doubtful advantage. The vehicle was out of the direct line from the road, making it easier to work on undetected either from the house or by any passerby, but increasing the distance, he had to move across the noisy gravel. O'Farrell used the grassed garden border until there was no more and hesitated with each seemingly echoed step toward the car. Around him everything slumbered, undisturbed.

O'Farrell squatted again, this time with his back against the vehicle's fender, to prepare the charges. Before separating the plastic into three, he put on the rubber gloves, flexing his fingers against their thickness, wishing he had the thinner surgical type. He didn't attempt to get into the car to reach the electrical system from the front; it would have brought the light on and meant lifting the hood, both impossible. O'Farrell waited until he was beneath the vehicle before turning on his flashlight. The gas pump was clearly visible, about eighteen inches from the fuel tank. O'Farrell taped the charge into the space between the two, and then, with the penknife, stripped the gas-pump lead back to its wires; the positive was the nearest to him. He scraped away the blue covering, attached the contact from the detonator to the bare wire, and sealed the join with adhesive tape. From this detonator he trailed a lead tightly along and beneath the car to a point directly under the driver's seat, where he attached against the chassis his second charge. From it O'Farrell brought his continuous lead up through the engine housing to meet with the explosives he had already introduced through a bigger access and strapped in front of where the driver sat. A perfectionist, O'Farrell checked the placing and the connections from the rear to the front. The ignition activated the gas pump and the gas pump activated the detonator-placed charges. The entire vehicle was one huge bomb.

O'Farrell, finally satisfied, came crabwise from beneath the car. He was not hurrying, knowing he had to wait an-

other passing of the police before he could leave. This was
the first time, he reflected idly, that he had used his knowledge of cars and engines professionally, and wondered
why; what he'd fixed up tonight was infallible. But this
was no place for idle reflection. O'Farrell gathered everything back into the briefcase, propping it against his legs.
There was absolutely no question of his being allowed to
pass any police with it in his hand, he decided; it might be
sufficient to cause an insomniac resident to raise an alarm,
too. O'Farrell carefully cleaned the handle, the only part
he had touched with his bare hands, and went beneath the
car again, strapping it tightly to the fuel tank in the recess
available around the exhaust-pipe arch.

He settled down on his haunches in the shrubbery,
where he had before, for the police return, unable to see
but using the time to brush off the grit and dirt that stuck
to him from being beneath the car. The cleanup wouldn't,
he knew, withstand any close scrutiny, but he didn't expect
there to be any.

The police pacing approached, as monotonously repeti-
tious as their conversation.

". . . why not ask the wife to have a word with her?"

"What if I'm wrong?"

"So you're mistaken."

"Not something I like talking about to the wife."

"Don't talk about sex to your wife!"

"Rarely a subject that comes up between us, as a matter
of fact."

O'Farrell was against the gate as the sound faded, edg-
ing into the road as soon as he felt it safe to do so; they
were a blurred, moving blackness, as they had been when
he first saw them. O'Farrell went in the opposite direction,
walking just short of the pace that would have attracted attention, eager for the first corner. He slowed slightly when
he rounded that and relaxed further when he turned into
the road where the rental car was parked. For several

moments, when he got inside, he sat without firing the ignition, letting the tension seep away.

The car started, first time, and O'Farrell drove a roundabout route, not taking the roads that would bring him past Rivera's house again. The constables might note the number of a car driving so late. And he had a feeling beyond the need for such caution. He didn't want any association, not even the association of driving by again. It was over. Finished. He was going home.

Petty considered the FBI debacle reason enough to suggest another meeting with McCarthy, although he didn't say that when he called to arrange it. The Plans director of the CIA said he thought they did have things to talk about, although his schedule was blocked out for lunch for a month. Petty suggested the rooftop bar of the Washington Hotel for an evening drink, and McCarthy agreed at once; had Petty seen what the *Post* had written after its summer reopening a few weeks back? Petty said he hadn't.

Petty arrived early, to get a suitably private table near the rail before the usual cocktail invasion, wondering if his ulcer would resist the happy-hour snacks that were available. Those he could see seemed to be in a fair amount of sauce, so he postponed any decision. He asked the waitress, hopefully, if pipe smoking were permitted and was told no. He ordered mineral water.

McCarthy arrived late, bustling expectantly past the line that had formed, confident Petty would have a table and ignoring the hostile looks from the people waiting.

The wickerwork seat creaked under his weight. "Kept you long?" he asked, the nearest he'd get to an apology.

"Not at all," Petty said.

The Plans director signaled for a waitress, ordering a Bloody Mary. Gesturing to the Treasury Building and the White House beyond, and then encompassing the monument as well, McCarthy said, "Great view, isn't it? That's one of the things the *Post* said. Great view."

"Great," said Petty. He could actually see the spot where he'd briefed O'Farrell; it seemed a long time ago.

Their drinks were served, and the waitress left. McCarthy said, "Didn't work out at all well in California, did it?"

"Many recriminations?" Petty asked.

"Practically a permanent tribunal," McCarthy said, drinking noisily. "We can't feel very good over it, though. Our guys fell on their ass in Brussels."

"Picked him up yet?"

McCarthy shook his head. "He'll have gone back into the woodwork now."

"What about O'Farrell?" Petty asked. "I could have one of the surveillance teams make contact if you wanted to call it off; we've let him run, but we know from the early days the places where he's staying."

McCarthy gestured for refills, shaking his head against the suggestion as he turned back to the other man. "That's why I wanted to see you. So far the score for our side is zero. . . ." He nodded in the direction of the White House. "At the moment everyone is down the toilet together; a success would be good for us. You spoken?"

"And cleared him, in anticipation of California working as it was supposed to."

"Remember Makarevich?" McCarthy demanded, without warning.

Petty didn't, not at first. Then he said, "Of course."

"Been running a check, the last few weeks," the Plans director disclosed. "That put the Soviets back a lot; a hell of a lot."

"So?" Petty queried, frowning.

"Just think it's interesting, that's all."

TWENTY-ONE

THE BOARDINGHOUSE in Queens Gate Terrace proved the worst—professionally—that he'd chosen. It was run by a widow who insisted that all her guests call her Connie and who set out to be a mother figure to the unattached and a what-I-remember-about-London landlady to all. O'Farrell had stayed aloof and guessed she was offended, but didn't think it mattered, now that he was leaving.

He had refused any meals, as he had in those before, but the last morning was different. He needed a news broadcast, and the television ran permanently in the breakfast room, which would normally have been sufficient reason to avoid the meal anyway.

O'Farrell was up and packed early, downstairs to pay her ahead of anyone else, and asked if he could change his mind and have coffee and toast maybe. Connie beamed and offered eggs, but O'Farrell said toast would be fine.

All the morning papers were displayed on a table just inside the room and O'Farrell flicked through them, apparently unable to choose. He guessed it would have been front-page and there wasn't a report in any of them: too late, he guessed. He chose the *Times* and then orange juice, nodding to the four people already in the room, who, thankfully, ignored him. O'Farrell took a table near the wall. He went through the motions of reading the newspaper, seeing nothing. Predictably the television was on; the set was attached to a support arm suspended quite high on the wall, so the lift of the watchers' heads gave them all an attitude of piety. O'Farrell supposed it was fitting, for the awe in which television was held.

A rock group plugged their latest release, a trade-union leader insisted some labor dispute was the government's fault, and a tongue-tied gardener tried to explain how he grew prizewinning produce. Then the anchor person started ". . . extended news because of last night's horrific incident in Hampstead . . ."

The first picture on the screen was a long shot of Rivera's house from the far side of Christchurch Road. The house itself had sustained hardly any damage apart from broken windows, but the front of the garage was completely blown in, with firemen still dowsing the embers. What remained of the BMW, a pressed-flat piece of metal attached to one wheel and a few engine parts, was propped oddly on its edge against the garage wall, and a large area of the gravel was scorched black.

The camera panned in closer. A reporter stood at the gate next to a policeman self-consciously aware of being on camera.

". . . no explanation yet for the outrage," the reporter was saying. "What is known is that because of this morning's rain Mrs. Estelle Rivera"—here the screen was filled with a still photograph of the woman, obviously at a reception with Rivera—"wife of the Cuban ambassador, José Rivera, went to their BMW car to get it closer to the house to pick up their son, Jorge, to deliver him to the lycée. I understand the explosion, which in turn created a fireball, was immediate. Death would have been instantaneous. Forensic and bomb-disposal experts have recovered parts of an explosive device but are disclosing no details, although one expert has told me it was clearly planted by an expert to cause . . ."

A swirl of dizziness engulfed O'Farrell, so much so that he could not clearly see the television screen, and a sickness rose through him, like it had after the stupidity of the brandy, and a coldness, a chilling, shivering coldness tight-ened around him, taking his breath. Mouth clamped, he tried to push the sensation back, wanting to see and to hear everything before the newscast finished.

"We have learned," came the voice distantly, through a fog, "that the housekeeper who normally drives the boy to school in her car has recently been ill and unable to do so. Jorge, twelve, was at the rear of the house at the time of the explosion and was fortunately uninjured, although he is being treated for shock. Señor Rivera is also said by the household to be deeply shocked. . . ."

With the promise to report further as information became available, the remote broadcast returned to the studio. O'Farrell let the screen recede into a blur again, trying to think—to create another order of priority as he had so very recently done—but nothing rational came through the cold sickness.

". . . shocking. Absolutely shocking . . ."

O'Farrell blinked up at the landlady. How long had she been standing at the table, talking to him? She handed him the toast and said, "Here you are. Eat it while it's hot."

O'Farrell nodded, unable to speak, accepting the toast he didn't know what to do with.

The woman gestured toward the television. "Can you imagine the mentality of anyone able to do such a thing!" she demanded.

"No," O'Farrell managed.

"Shot," the woman insisted. "That's what should happen to him when he's caught. Stood up against a wall and shot."

"Yes," O'Farrell agreed shortly. He'd killed—murdered—an innocent person! The awareness flooded in upon him, and his need to vomit worsened. That first morning's surveillance had begun too late to monitor any school run; he'd only been interested in Rivera's pattern. Yet he'd seen the wife and child! Should have considered how he got to school! Slipshod. Careless. So because he'd been slipshod and careless, he murdered an innocent person; come close to murdering an innocent kid as well. Unprof— O'Farrell stopped himself even completing the word, refusing it. What the fuck was professional about what he did! Where was the profession—the art—in killing? Innocent, he thought, unable to get the word out of his mind. Completely innocent; beautiful and poised and innocent. Christ—oh dear Christ—what had he done! No turning back, no putting together what was destroyed, no expiation. Innocent.

Now he had to run. Run like a rat would run, away from something it had fouled or contaminated. Destroy but don't be destroyed, judge but avoid judgment, catch but don't get caught. Innocent.

O'Farrell felt suspended, almost as if he were outside his own body, watching himself perform. He crumbled the bread to convey the impression of having eaten and forced some coffee down. He went through the charade of farewell and drove the rental car without any conscious awareness back to its garage, remembering to get the credit-card slip back for cash. He canceled the remaining boarding-house, in Crossmore Road, and took two taxis to the embassy, finally approaching Grosvenor Square on foot from Park Lane. Petty spoke first when the connection was made.

"It's very bad."

"Yes."

"Any risk of our involvement becoming known?"

"No."

"Sure?"

"Positive."

"Everything cleared up behind you?"

"Everything."

"Get out."

"The reservation is for two this afternoon. TWA."

"Don't tell your wife."

"Why?"

"We'll meet you."

* * *

Rivera had no difficulty displaying the attitude the police and the Special Branch and the Diplomatic Protection Squad expected. He was, after all, genuinely frightened for himself and it showed, and he let it, unashamedly. And he was frightened, maybe more, for Jorge. He'd insisted upon hospital observation of the child, although the doctors disagreed on the need, and insisted further that members of the embassy staff, in reality officers of the Dirección Generale de Inteligencia, guard the child in addition to the British protectors now assigned.

He had some feeling, too, about Estelle. Whatever he'd felt, or rather not felt, it was difficult to conceive of her being blown apart as she had been, so that identification had to be made from items of jewelry. So he cried, although not for long.

It was the afternoon before he had any proper interview with the authorities, who told him more than he was able to tell them. The forensic experts believed both the explosive and the detonators were from the communist bloc, almost certainly Czechoslovakian; they'd know definitely after more tests. The materials had been placed throughout the vehicle, not concentrated in one spot; it was undoubtedly the work of a professional assassin. It was impossible to be sure, until they caught whoever did it, but they were working on the theory that the bomb had been intended for him, not his wife.

"Have you any idea, Excellency, who might want to do a thing like this?"

Rivera spread his hands, a gesture of helplessness. "I haven't the slightest idea," he said.

He had, of course. He'd never imagined Belac would go this far.

Havana predictably labeled the attack a capitalist conspiracy, but with some irony accused America of being the originator. A State Department spokesman in Washington said the claim was too ridiculous to be treated seriously.

TWENTY-TWO

O'FARRELL DRANK steadily throughout the flight and by the time the plane landed at Dulles had attained that frowning, carefully moving I-know-but-nobody-else-does level of drunkenness. He high-stepped his way off the aircraft onto the elevated debarkation bus, and in the terminal he missed his bag the first time it came around the carousel. He thought that was funny and giggled, grinning back at people nearby who stared nervously at him.

Erickson was waiting inside the customs hall, on the other side of the checkpoint. Somebody had spoken to somebody, because O'Farrell was passed through without any hindrance. He swayed in front of Erickson and said, spacing his words, "Didn't expect you; didn't know what to expect, but didn't expect you."

"You're drunk," the deputy said.

"Still standing."

"Only just," the man said. He steered O'Farrell down to the lower level; the limousine was right outside the entrance, the driver reaching out for his bag. Tobacco smoke swirled out like fog when the door was opened and O'Farrell was further surprised.

"Didn't expect you, either," he said to Petty. "And Erickson's already told me I'm drunk, so you needn't bother. . . ." He'd perched on the jump seat of the limousine and turned back to the door. "Where is Erickson?" he said. "With me a moment ago."

"He won't be long," Petty promised. He coughed

thickly and said, "Not really the circumstance to ask how you are, is it?"

O'Farrell twisted, ensuring that the driver's compartment was sealed off from the rear, and said, "For the record, I'm absolutely fucking awful." He'd never sworn at Petty before, never shown the man any disrespect at all. Didn't matter now; nothing seemed to matter now. The damned pipe smoke was making his eyes water.

"We'll get you better," Petty said.

O'Farrell thought the remark funny, like missing his luggage had been funny, and he giggled. "I'm not sick!" he said.

"Sure," Petty said infuriatingly.

The passenger door opened, admitting Erickson and a welcome draft of unfogged air. To his deputy, Petty said, "Everything okay?"

"No problem," Erickson said. "No one at all."

O'Farrell's drunken frown returned as he looked at the two men, and then his face cleared, in understanding. "A baby-sitter! You gave me a baby-sitter from the embassy for the flight over, in case I got confessional."

"Just a precaution," Petty confirmed.

"You think I'm that fucked up!" There was a schoolboy pleasure in saying rude words to the section head.

"You're tired; had a few drinks," Petty said. "We'll talk in a day or two."

"What if I had spoken to someone on the flight?" O'Farrell persisted, with alcoholic bravado.

"Couldn't have happened," Petty said conversationally. "You'd have been interrupted, diverted. Forget it."

Although the limousine was already almost to the Beltway, O'Farrell said, "Shouldn't we tell the driver . . . ?" and then trailed away, in belated awareness. "Where am I going?"

"Fort Pearce," Petty said. "We need to debrief you. Give you a few days' rest as well . . . just a few days."

O'Farrell knew Fort Pearce; years ago—he couldn't recall exactly when—he'd attended a couple of advanced training courses there on behind-the-lines survival. It was officially designated an army installation but in reality it was a CIA complex, mostly for warfare and sabotage instruction. He said, "So I'm being locked up in the stockade?"

"Of course you're not," Erickson said without conviction. "It's a debriefing, that's all. And the people at Fort Pearce have the highest clearance, so it's the most obvious and convenient place."

O'Farrell didn't believe it. He wondered, although without any fear, what was going to happen to him. Whatever, he deserved it. He said, "How long is a few days?"

"Two . . . three . . ." Petty started.

"Whatever. A few days . . ." Erickson said.

"What then?" O'Farrell demanded.

"Let's get the debriefing over first," Petty said.

Erickson indicated the liquor cabinet recessed between the jump seats. "You want a drink?"

"No," O'Farrell said at once. He squinted through the darkened windows of the car, but could not gauge where they were. "I'm not going to become unreliable," he said, and at once regretted the remark. It sounded as if he were scared, which he wasn't, not yet.

"We know that!" Petty said.

"Not even a consideration," Erickson added.

"Just important to get you fit again," Petty said.

The back-and-forth delivery seemed to be ingrained, thought O'Farrell. Annoyed at being patronized, he began, "I'm not . . ." but stopped, deciding it wasn't worth the bother. He wished he'd taken Erickson's offered drink, although he was proud that he'd held back. Would Fort Pearce be dry? He couldn't remember from his previous visits, although he doubted this was going to be anything like his previous visits. He said, "You debriefing me?"

Petty shook his head. "There are experts at Fort Pearce."

"Specialists," Erickson finished.

"In what?" O'Farrell demanded pointedly.

"Everything." Petty was avoiding him once more.

How much O'Farrell would have liked, just once, to have trapped the man, talked him into a corner and pinned him into some definite commitment. Feeling it was time— and surprised they hadn't prompted him into it in their ventriloquist's act—O'Farrell said, "It was a disaster. I know it was a disaster. . . ."

Petty raised his hand, stopping the apology. "Not now . . ." the section head said.

"Better later . . ."

"More appropriate . . ."

"I just wanted you to know."

"We do . . ."

"Completely . . ."

The vehicle slowed and O'Farrell saw they were at the gates of Fort Pearce, the driver already going through the identification and entry formalities. O'Farrell would have expected the passengers to be checked, but they weren't. The car went on for quite a long way inside the complex, wending along roads between barracks-type buildings, before stopping. When O'Farrell emerged, it was into an area he did not know from his other visits. They stood before a white-painted, clapboard building styled like barracks but taller, two storeys. The bottom floor was encircled by a covered veranda reached by steps wide enough for two or three people to climb abreast. But they didn't. Petty led, O'Farrell followed, waved forward, with Erickson at the rear. The prisoner was under close escort, thought O'Farrell. There was a guard at the entrance, and Petty made the identification before leading on with apparent familiarity down the wide, polished-clean corridor. All the doors leading onto it were closed and there was no noise from behind any of them. Halfway down was a bulletin board forlornly bare of any notices. O'Farrell realized that after all the drinking he needed a bathroom. He looked around for one; none of the doors were designated or marked, not even with numbers.

Petty entered one practically at the end. It led into an unexpectedly expansive office whose occupant was already standing, smiling, in front of his desk. O'Farrell stared at the man curiously. He looked impossibly young, practically college age. He nodded to Petty and Erickson, previous acquaintances, but held out his hand to O'Farrell. "Lambert, John Lambert," he said. "And you're Charles O'Farrell. Is it Charles or Chuck?"

"It varies," O'Farrell said. It sounded like a cocktail-party greeting and Lambert actually seemed dressed for one in his subdued Ivy League suit, pin-collared shirt, and inconspicuous club tie. Lambert wouldn't be his real name; probably adopted just for this encounter. The man's nose wrinkled against the pervading tobacco smell.

"Want you to understand something," Petty said. "John's cleared for everything. He knows what you do and all about Rivera and the accident with his wife."

"It wasn't an accident," O'Farrell said quietly. He knew now why the two men had met him at Dulles Airport. Lambert had to be personally introduced and guaranteed, by people he trusted, for the debriefing to progress at all. He guessed Lambert was a psychologist more highly cleared than Symmons, one of the get-your-head-right brigade. The man really did look young.

"We'll get to that in time," Lambert said dismissively. "Not now. You'll be bushed after the flight."

How much of the tiredness was genuine fatigue and how much was alcohol-induced? O'Farrell wondered. He said, "I'm okay."

"Tomorrow's soon enough," Lambert said. "Let's get settled in first."

Petty and Erickson, their function fulfilled, looked at each other, and Petty said, "We'll be getting back. We've got a drive."

"A few days," O'Farrell said, sufficiently sober now to

be unsettled by what was happening. It never had before, after any previous mission. But then, he reminded himself, no previous mission had ended like this one.

"That's what we're talking about," Petty said.

Why *was* the talk like this: the casual chitchat of a cocktail party! Why weren't they talking about a blown-apart woman named Estelle Rivera who had a well-mannered, cute little kid who'd missed being blown apart with her only by a fluke, because a car had been parked in an inconvenient place and it was raining?

"I killed someone!" O'Farrell yelled, so unexpectedly loud that Erickson, by the door, jumped. "I murdered an innocent person!"

"Easy now, easy," Lambert soothed. "Not tonight. Later."

"Why's everyone avoiding it, as if it never happened! Why later?"

"No one's avoiding it," Lambert said, still soothing. "We'll talk it all through, you and me, tomorrow."

Another twenty-four hours—twelve at least—for them to discover if he'd left any trace? A possibility, O'Farrell knew. What would they do to him if he had, if there were the likelihood of the whole mess becoming a public disaster? He shifted, unsettled; the business of these men was killing potential embarrassment, wasn't it? Wrong, perhaps, to erupt as he had. Could he back down without appearing to do so? He said, "What will the result be, after we've talked it all through?" and wished he'd thought of something better, something stronger.

"We won't know that until we've talked, will we?" said Lambert, making a perceptible gesture for the other two men to leave. "Let's go see where you're going to bunk down."

Despite the suggestion, it wasn't a bunk. It was a bed in a single room a little farther along the same corridor. There were built-in closets and a private bathroom, a remote-controlled television, and *Newsweek* and *Time* on a table separating two easy chairs. Like every motel room in which he'd ever stayed, O'Farrell thought. He was glad to see the bathroom.

"Anything you want—food, booze, anything—just pick up the phone and tell the operator," Lambert said.

There were two phones, one beside the bed, the second on the magazine table. O'Farrell saw that neither had a dialing mechanism. He wasn't sure, but he thought the man had just slightly stressed the word "booze" when he'd made the offer. Testing, O'Farrell said, "It was a long flight. I wouldn't mind walking around a little."

Lambert grimaced, a man imparting rules he hasn't made and doesn't approve. "There's not been time to get you any authorization documents," he said. "You know what the security's like here; the mice carry ID!"

The man who looked too young to be here at all was trying his best, O'Farrell conceded. He said, "No walks?"

"Afraid not."

O'Farrell indicated the telephones. "What about outside calls? I need to speak to my wife."

"Not just yet," Lambert said apologetically. "Maybe tomorrow."

"Or the day after," O'Farrell said.

"Maybe," Lambert agreed.

"You going to lock the door?"

"No."

"There's a guard at the back as well as at the front of the building?"

"Yes," Lambert confirmed.

"Where I would be stopped, forcibly if necessary, if I tried to go by."

"It's the way they're trained in a place like this."

"So I'm under arrest? Imprisoned?" O'Farrell demanded.

"I wouldn't have described it as that."

"Describe it to me your way," O'Farrell insisted.

"Protected," Lambert said. "Extremely well protected. I would have thought you'd be grateful."

The men rode for a long time without speaking to each other. Petty contacted an emergency number from the car phone and had himself patched through to McCarthy for a brief, monosyllabic conversation. When he replaced the instrument, Petty said, "Our antiterrorist unit at the embassy has been allowed access by the British. More theories than you can shake a stick at. Current favorite is that it's political, Latin American–based. Forensics has identified the explosive as Semtex and the metal left from the detonator as of Soviet manufacture."

"Looks good, then?" Erickson was pleased to get in first with a question rather than having to provide an answer.

"Exactly as it was planned, apart from the victim," Petty confirmed. Before Erickson could speak again, he said, "So what about O'Farrell?"

"I think we need to get the result of the debriefing to be sure," Erickson said. "He looked as flaky as hell when he came off that airplane. And there was the booze. There was quite a bit of it in London, too."

"He seemed to sober up quickly enough," Petty said. "But there's a lot of guilt there. He's supposed to be trained to control guilt."

"Retire him?"

"McCarthy wants to talk to me about it."

"What's there to talk about?"

Petty shrugged. "Who can tell? You know what a devious bastard McCarthy is. He's had quite a conversation with Lambert, apparently."

"This time we seem to have gotten away with it," Erickson said. "I think to risk using O'Farrell again would be madness."

Petty gave another shrug. "Who knows?" he said again.

"In the immediate future we don't have to get within a million miles of José Gaviria Rivera."

Back in Fort Pearce, O'Farrell actually considered kneeling by the bedside, like a kid, but shook his head against the idea, looking around the empty room in positive embarrassment. He tried to pray, lying in bed in the darkness, but shrugged that attempt off, too. There could be no forgiveness, no absolution, for what he'd done. Had there ever been?

TWENTY-THREE

IT WAS an odd room. Because of the construction of the building, it should have had an outside window, but it didn't. Neither did it really look like a proper office. There was a desk and a telephone, but books were haphazardly stacked all over it, and more books spilled over from the bookcase beyond. The television was on, showing a game in which men and women who were supposed not to know each other were romantically paired, and Lambert was propped on the edge of the desk, watching it. At O'Farrell's entry, he turned like a man surprised and then waved him in.

"Good to see you," Lambert said, as if their last meeting had been a long time ago. "Don't these programs blow your mind! Can you imagine making yourself look stupid in front of millions of people!"

"I've never seen it before," O'Farrell said. "But no, I can't imagine it."

Lambert held the remote control in his hand for several

moments before reluctantly switching the television off and turning his full attention upon O'Farrell. "They fascinate me," he said. "Just fascinate me."

Definitely a psychologist, O'Farrell thought. He supposed it had been obvious but he'd hoped Lambert wasn't. He looked around for shapes to fit into holes but couldn't see any. There were couches and chairs around a dead fireplace and two extension telephones on side tables. There were a lot of large plants in pots. O'Farrell recognized a rubber tree; its leaves were very dirty and dry. All the plants sagged from lack of water.

Lambert gestured vaguely toward the easy chairs and couches and said, "Make yourself at home. You like some coffee? I've just made some fresh coffee."

"Thank you," O'Farrell said. He was indifferent to the coffee but it pleased him to have Lambert fetch and carry for him. Why? he asked himself at once. Careful; he wasn't the psychologist.

Lambert served the coffee with powdered cream and sugar in little pots on the side. With his head still bent, the man said, "So you killed her? The wrong target?"

O'Farrell blinked at the abruptness. "Yes," he said. His headache wasn't too bad, considering the previous day's intake, but he felt tired, although he'd slept.

"It was an accident."

"How the hell can you say that!"

"You intend to kill her?"

"You know I didn't!"

"So what else can it be but an accident?"

"I wired the car, for Christ's sake, turned it into one fucking great bomb! How can planting a load of explosives in a vehicle, which blows up and kills a person, be minimized as an accident!"

Lambert had been standing. Now he took his own coffee to an opposite chair. "What about Rivera? What if he'd turned the key and he'd been the person killed?"

O'Farrell frowned. "What about it? I've gone through

all the evidence against him. He's guilty; involved in criminal activity against the interests and security of this country."

"So it's okay to blow him away! No conscience problem there!"

This was like getting into the ring with a far superior boxer constantly able to jab past your defenses. O'Farrell said, "That is the function I am employed to carry out on behalf of the United States of America."

"Well recited!" Lambert mocked. "You comfortable with that?"

"Of course I am."

"Why of course? Where's the natural consequence come in?"

O'Farrell was sweating and put his cup down before he spilled it. This man was bewildering him. Hopefully he said, "There are some people, a few, who are beyond normal parameters; beyond the law, if you like. People capable of great harm, great hurt. The judgment against them is not reached by a court of law, but it is as fair and impartial as if it were."

"Hitler . . . Stalin . . . Amin. Killing saves lives," Lambert completed. "I'm familiar with the list; it's a cliché. You know what? I don't think you believe that. Maybe once, but not anymore."

O'Farrell was glad he was sitting down because his head was swirling. The ache was worse, too. He thought he saw an escape and went for it. "It's an academic debate anyway, isn't it?"

"Why?" asked Lambert.

"I'm hardly likely to be used again, after this debacle, am I?"

"Whose choice not to be used again? Yours? Or the Agency's?"

Jab, jab, jab, O'Farrell thought. "The Agency's, I would have thought."

"Why?"

"This record seems to be stuck." O'Farrell chanced the sarcasm but was unsure if he should take the risk. Speaking overly slowly, he said: "In London, England, I made a bomb that killed someone who should not have died. As of yesterday, I became an operative too unreliable to trust anymore."

"Who said that?"

"Nobody *said* it. It's obvious." It was the first time since the disaster that O'Farrell had thought fully about it. And its personal implications. So he'd lose the hidden salary. So what? The value of the house in Alexandria had to have increased twofold at least over what he'd paid for it. If the allowances to the kids became too much of a burden, he could always sell it and buy something cheaper, cheaper but still a damned nice house.

"How would you feel about that, being taken off the active roster?" Lambert persisted.

O'Farrell came close to smiling at the absurdity of the expression; was that a cosmetic name for Petty's department, the active roster? Slowly again, but for a different sort of reason this time, he said, "It would be wrong—morally and mentally—for me to enjoy what I do. I'd be some sort of psychopath. I have sincerely considered every mission I have undertaken to be justified, like Rivera's removal. I have never thought of being taken"—he stopped at the phrase, then pushed on—"off the active roster in the middle of an operation. If that's the way it ends . . ." He shrugged, struggling for words. "Then it ends," he finished badly. Toward the conclusion he'd been floundering, O'Farrell admitted to himself. Worse, it appeared as if he'd been trying to convince Lambert about his function, about the whole existence of his department within the CIA.

"A soldier, obeying orders?"

"I find that a good analogy."

"And you were a professional but special soldier before

you joined the Agency, weren't you? And professional soldiers are taught to kill. Especially your unit."

"Under proper rules of engagement," O'Farrell qualified.

"Was that how you saw your missions? Obeying orders like a professional soldier, following unusual but properly established rules of engagement?"

"I said I felt comfortable with the analogy. Perhaps that's how I felt sometimes." Nothing was coming out as he wanted; he felt hopelessly inferior to this man, who had to be at least ten years his junior and seemed to know everything that had ever gone on in his mind. Lambert was far more formidable than Symmons. O'Farrell realized for the first time that Lambert was wearing the same suit and shirt as the previous evening; perhaps there really had been a party where he'd gotten lucky and not gone home.

For a long time Lambert stared at him, blank-faced and unspeaking. Finally the man said, "Charles O'Farrell, that marshal ancestor of yours, never did that, did he? Never quit or got taken off anything before it was properly ended. Before justice was done."

That wasn't a jab; that was practically a knockout blow. "I don't think so; not that I have been able to find out." The words strained out, dry-throated.

"What about him?"

"I don't understand the question."

"Didn't you see some comparison there, between yourself and your great-grandfather?"

O'Farrell gulped some coffee to ease his throat. "Not really," he lied knowingly. "Maybe there's a similarity. I never thought about it."

Again there was a long, silent stare and O'Farrell read disbelief into it. Lambert said, "What do you think of the booze in London making you careless? A factor in the accident?"

Another body blow, worse than before. O'Farrell breathed in deeply, as if he had been winded. Had to fight back, he thought, stop appearing so helpless! He said, "You seem to have carried out a pretty deep profile."

"Normal precautions, like every assignment," Lambert said. He smiled. "A rule of engagement."

Which was true, O'Farrell knew. He'd spotted the watchers himself. As forcefully as he could, he said, "What's this all about?" and thought it was a demand he should have made before now.

"Didn't you expect there to be an inquiry?"

"By Petty and Erickson certainly. Maybe others, from my section or Plans. Not being held a virtual prisoner in any army camp and interrogated by a psychologist!"

"That's interesting!" Lambert said, as if he'd located an odd-shaped fossil on a stony beach. "Is that what you consider this to be, an interrogation?"

It had been an exaggeration, O'Farrell conceded. This wasn't really an interrogation, not the sort he'd been trained to resist. Why then was he so unsettled by it? He said, "Perhaps not quite that," and hated the weak response, just as he disliked most of his other replies. Trying to recover, he said, "You didn't answer my question: what's it all about, this interview?"

"Your state of mind," Lambert announced disquietingly. "And you didn't answer mine. What about the booze?"

"I had a few drinks," O'Farrell said, stiffly formal. "I never endangered the operation. It had no bearing whatsoever upon the accident."

"Well done!" Lambert said, congratulatory.

"I don't . . ." O'Farrell started, and then paused. "I won't—I can't—consider it an accident. I never will be able to."

"You just called it that."

O'Farrell shook his head wearily. "I didn't think sufficiently. It's the wrong word; will always be the wrong word. It was murder. We both know that."

"Innocent people get killed in wars."

"What the fuck sort of rationale is that!" O'Farrell erupted. "We're not talking about a war! Stop it! The professional-soldier pitch won't get to me. I've thought it through; it doesn't fit."

"So you're quitting?"

"We've gone down this road as well," O'Farrell protested. "I'm unacceptable."

"Your judgment," Lambert reminded him. "What if other people . . . Petty and Erickson and people in Plans, all of them, think like I do? What about if they all consider it an accident and don't contemplate terminating your active role?"

"What about it?" O'Farrell knew the question was coming, but delayed it with his own query to think of an answer better than those he'd so far offered.

"You going to resign?" the man asked bluntly.

"I don't know." What the fuck was he saying! He'd thought of nothing else, waking or sleeping, for months; had thought about it this very day in this very room, working out the logistics of selling the house! He wanted to quit—needed to quit—more than he'd wanted to do anything else in his entire life. So why didn't he just say so! Easiest word in the language: yes. Yes, I want to quit. Get away from all this mumbo-jumbo psychology and these ridiculous briefings in ridiculous places, immerse myself in my boring figures in my boring office and truly become the boring clerk everyone thinks I am, catching the adventurers manipulating their expenses and being despised by my wife for not intervening in squalid public arguments.

"Not even thought about it?" Lambert persisted.

"Of course I've thought about it; haven't you thought of chucking what you do?"

Lambert genuinely appeared to consider the question. "No," he said. "I never have. I like what I do very much."

"What *is* it? I mean, I know your job, but why—and what—here, in the middle of a CIA training facility?"

"Talk to people with motivational doubts, like you," Lambert said.

"Is that the diagnosis? Lacking motivation?"

Lambert's expression was more a grin than a smile. "Nothing so simple," he said. "You know what professional medics are like—three pages of bullshit, complete with reference notes and source material, to express a single idea."

"Which is that I am lacking motivation?"

"Aren't you?" Question for question.

"I don't think—"

"You do," Lambert said, blocking another escape.

O'Farrell refused to answer, caught by a sudden, disturbing thought. "How did the Agency find out about my family archive?"

"Didn't you have some work done on it?" Lambert asked casually.

The copying, O'Farrell remembered. So it hadn't been some Agency break-in squad poking through the house, prying into everything, maybe sniggering and joking over what they found, while Jill was at work or in Chicago. O'Farrell was relieved. Lambert was lounging back comfortably in his chair, apparently waiting for him to say something. "Well?" O'Farrell said.

"We were talking about motivation."

"You were," O'Farrell corrected, deciding how to continue. "And you seemed to think I'd lost it."

"Haven't you?"

"Yes," O'Farrell said bluntly. He'd said it! And he had the acceptable explanation ready. If this sneaky bastard took it, this debriefing could end and he could go home to Jill.

"A breakthrough!" Lambert said.

"Is that surprising, after murdering someone?"

Another of the long, silent stares, broken this time by a slow headshake of refusal. Then the psychologist said, "Is that how you intend to use the accident?"

"I'm not using it for *anything*!" said O'Farrell, knowing

he had lost, too exasperated to deny Lambert's choice of word.

"You began assembling all that stuff on your great-grandfather, making the lawman comparison, long before the Rivera assignment," said the man. "Drinking too."

O'Farrell shook his head, genuinely weary. "Think what you like. I don't give a damn."

"You just want to go home, go to bed, and pull the covers over your head."

O'Farrell went physically hot because that was exactly what he had been thinking. "Maybe just that."

Lambert rose from his seat, but halfway toward the coffeepot he hesitated. "Would you like a drink? Something stronger than coffee, I mean."

O'Farrell ached for a drink. He shook his head. "Not even coffee."

"You do that, do you?" Lambert asked conversationally. "Set yourself limits and feel proud, as if you've achieved something, when you stay within them?"

Like everything else during the meeting, it was a small but complete performance to make another point, O'Farrell realized. He was still hot but now with anger against the man it seemed impossible to outtalk. "No," he said.

Lambert smiled, with more disbelief, and continued on to the coffee machine. Standing there, he said, "I don't blame you. I'm surprised the doubts haven't come long before now."

O'Farrell frowned, further bewilderment. "Whose side are you on!" he said.

Lambert, smiling, walked back to his chair. More to himself than to O'Farrell, he said, "There have to be sides, good or bad, right or wrong. . . ." He looked up, open-faced. "I'm on your side, if that's the way you want to think about it. That's why I want to get the truth, everything, out into the open, so we can talk it all through, lay all the ghosts."

"Why?" O'Farrell asked suspiciously.

"Why!" Lambert echoed, surprised. "You were flaky before England. With all the guilt after the accident you're going to become a pretty fucked-up guy, aren't you? And the Agency worries about fucked-up guys, particularly in your section."

"Okay," O'Farrell said, not really knowing to what he was agreeing.

"You're out of balance," Lambert said. "For months, maybe longer, it's been difficult morally for you to go along with what you've been doing, right?"

O'Farrell nodded. There was a vague feeling, too vague for relief but something like it, at the admission, at talking at last to someone who understood.

"Why not?" Lambert said, not wanting an answer. "Within the strict lines of morality, how can you justify taking another life? It's difficult to fit, whichever way you twist it."

"More than difficult."

"Is it, though?" Lambert demanded at once. "I said earlier they were clichés, but wouldn't millions of lives have been saved and the suffering of millions more been avoided if Hitler and Stalin and Amin had been removed? *Isn't* there the need for that sort of justice?"

"Decided upon by whom!" O'Farrell came back. "Who are these unknown wise men with clairvoyant powers that can't be appealed! What gives them the right to sit in judgment!"

Lambert sat nodding, as if he were agreeing, but said, "That's a weak argument. Won't stand examination. Have you, personally, ever been asked to move against anybody in *anticipation* of their evil?"

O'Farrell did not reply for several moments. "No," he admitted begrudgingly.

"Have you, personally, ever had the slightest doubt of the guilt of the person in any mission you have been asked to undertake?"

"No," O'Farrell conceded.

"If any of them had appeared in a court of law and the evidence against them had been presented, what would the judgment have been?"

"Guilty," O'Farrell said. Hopefully he added, "Although it's debatable whether the verdict would have been death."

Lambert was ready for him. "Let's debate it then. According to the judgment of their own country, was it more than likely that the sentence would have been death?"

"I suppose so," O'Farrell said.

"Judged according to their own standards?"

"Yes," O'Farrell capitulated.

"You were in Special Forces?"

"Yes."

"Ever had any difficulty carrying out a morally objectionable order in the army?"

"No."

"Why not?"

"I . . . it was . . ." O'Farrell stumbled.

"Because you had the right," Lambert supplied. "You had a service number and a rank and usually a uniform and that gave you the right. More than that, even. If anything went wrong, as it went wrong yesterday in London, the ultimate responsibility wasn't yours—"

"But it was yesterday," O'Farrell broke in. "I didn't have any right to kill Estelle Rivera."

"So you didn't try to kill her!" Lambert said, equally insistent. "It was an accident."

O'Farrell sighed, but with less exasperation than before. He definitely did feel better talking to this man, convoluted though at times he found the reasoning. He supposed that by a stretch of the imagination—a stretch he was still unprepared to make—the London incident could be considered an accident. He wasn't prepared to dispute it anymore. "And I don't have a rank or a serial number, either."

"Part of the same problem," Lambert said. "No official

backing or support. Minimal, at best. Guess your great-grandfather operated that way a lot of the time, though."

O'Farrell thought it was the first time the psychologist had strained too hard to win a point. He said, "A dogtag or a badge. I can think of them as the same."

"So where are we?" Lambert appeared to feel the same as O'Farrell about his earlier remark.

"You tell me," O'Farrell said, enjoying the temporary supremacy.

"Talked through for today, I guess."

"I want to go home," O'Farrell announced. "There's nothing left for us to talk about."

"Give me another day, to sort a couple of things out in my mind," Lambert said. "Just a day or two."

"One day just became two," O'Farrell said.

"Evening of the second day. My word."

"If it's not, I'm going to test the quickness of the guys on guard," O'Farrell said.

"Sure you are," Lambert said, and O'Farrell regretted the bravado; he had sounded like a child protesting that he was unafraid of the dark when really he was terrified.

In addition to the genuine mourners, there was a large contingent from the Cuban security service and more from the Diplomatic Protection Squad. Rivera didn't object, although he disliked having so many guardians constantly around him. "Highly professional and skilled" was the forensic description of the assassination; so Belac had gone to a lot of trouble, employing the best. But then, it was logical that the arms dealer would know the best. It was his business to know things like that. Beside him Rivera felt a slight movement, as Jorge clutched his leg. Rivera put his arm around the boy's shoulders and pulled him closer. Jorge had cried a little in the church but had recovered now, in the churchyard, and Rivera was proud of him. At the touch Jorge looked up through filmy eyes and smiled slightly, and Rivera hugged him again.

Rivera kept his head bowed because it was expected but managed to look quite a way beyond the priest saying whatever he was saying over the coffin, which was resting on the lip of the grave. Rivera hadn't expected there to be so many people. They were crowded together, solemn-faced, and the immediate grave area was a blaze of flowers; some of the wreaths were quite elaborate. He was glad he'd deputed a secretary to make a note of the names so he could write later.

The coffin was lowered. Rivera felt a nudge of encouragement from someone and took the offered trowel, casting earth into the grave, giving it in turn to Jorge. When the boy moved, there was a chatter of camera shutters. Rivera wondered if the photographs would appear in the papers belonging to Henrietta's husband. After the bombing they had described him as a playboy diplomat, and he'd made a mock complaint to Henrietta.

Rivera thanked the priest, whose name he could not remember, and hesitated on the pathway back to the cars for people to murmur their regrets as they filed by. He murmured his thanks in return. Some of the women patted Jorge's head as they passed. Rivera wished they hadn't and knew Jorge would feel the same way, too.

The cortege had left from the embassy and not the Hampstead house because it still bore the burns and damage of the explosion, so it had been easy for Rivera to give the instructions to his First Secretary.

The man was beside him now. Rivera said, "Well?"

"No, Excellency."

"You sure?"

"Quite sure."

Rivera was disappointed. He had quite expected the man to attend.

The line was almost over before the First Secretary leaned toward Rivera and said, "Here, Excellency," and Rivera stretched out a limp hand to accept that of Albert Lopelle, Estelle's French lover.

The formality over, Rivera hustled Jorge into the car but remained outside himself. To his First Secretary, he said, "You have to be wrong. That can't be Albert Lopelle."

"I assure you it is," said the man. "I have met him several times."

Rivera looked in disbelief after the Frenchman. He was so fat he walked with a rolling gait, and he was short, not much over five-five, and visibly balding. The handshake had been wet with perspiration, which was perhaps understandable, but Rivera guessed the man perspired a lot.

"Incredible," Rivera said, finally entering the car. He felt offended that Estelle should have considered leaving him for such a man, empty though their marriage had been.

TWENTY-FOUR

RIVERA HAD never imagined that Pierre Belac would try to kill him, no matter how acrimonious their dealings became. Now, after the attempt, it was very easy to do so. Rivera remained frightened. No longer for himself. But for Jorge, who had almost died as it was. Jorge had to be protected. Permanently, not temporarily by all these squads milling about, squads who'd eventually be withdrawn.

Safety would be easily enough achieved. All he had to do was pay over the withheld ten percent, which he'd agreed to do in Paris and which he'd always intended to do anyway. He'd like to be able to tell Belac that. But he didn't know where Belac was. And if he were to do so, it would make him appear scared. And that couldn't be allowed. Rivera wished, fleetingly, there were some way he could go on withholding the outstanding money to teach Belac the lesson the bastard deserved. But he had to think of Jorge. He'd settle everything as soon as the *City of Athens* left San Diego.

Rivera apportioned Estelle's death into advantages and disadvantages. An unquestionable advantage was how he came to be regarded by his government. Predictably Havana overreacted, immediately drafting extra bodyguard officers from the Dirección Generale de Inteligencia, some of whom entered the country unofficially because the diplomatic complement at the embassy was already complete. With them came the deputy director of the DGI, a sympathy-offering general named Ramirez, to head their own investigation. The apparently grieving Rivera showed the proper and expected caution, checking first with Havana that the man was cleared to discuss the arms shipments before offering his carefully prepared story. Arms dealing was a close-knit, jealous, and violent business; the general surely knew that? Here a modest shoulder shrug, eyes sadly averted. Rivera'd known and accepted the danger to himself, never imagining it embracing his family. The attack had only one logical explanation; arms dealer against arms dealer, eliminating the source of such lucrative contracts. Another shrug. Perhaps it was fortunate that the order was so close to completion, removing the reason for jealousy, for murder. Rivera smiled the sad smile of a man bereaved. He had suffered, Rivera offered, the sacrifice a loyal servant of the State was sometimes required to suffer. He was heartbroken. But still—unshakably—the same loyal servant.

Ramirez probed for the possible identity of jealous arms dealers. Rivera, determined that his hidden Swiss bank account stay very hidden, said he didn't know, but intended to find out through the network of contacts he had established. Ramirez said that if a name or names could be confirmed, the DGI had been ordered at the highest level in

Havana to match the retribution to the crime and that the
DGI had every intention of carrying out that order if it became possible. The extra bodyguards would remain,
Ramirez promised, under the control of the local station
chief, Carlos Mendez. The official ambassadorial residence
was to be fitted throughout with an extensive security system. In the immediate future, dog handlers would be employed to patrol at night. Rivera again smiled his thanks,
resenting the protection even more. It was important, he
stressed, for him sometimes—quite frequently, in fact—to
move about unescorted: arms dealers were secretive men,
nervous of identification. For the moment, the general insisted, such encounters had to be restricted. Rivera accepted the edict, realizing it would be wrong to press the
argument.

The protection created the biggest disadvantage. In addition to his own people, the British assigned men from
the Diplomatic Protection Squad, building a virtual wall
between him and Henrietta. And her initial distancing reaction when he telephoned the day after the funeral wasn't
what he had expected, either.

"Maybe it's a good thing, for a while," said the woman,
almost casually.

"What!" he said, surprised.

"Someone tried to kill you, that's what you said. What
if they try again?"

Rivera sighed. It had been a mistake, trying to impress
her. He supposed it was natural she should be frightened.
"I don't think there's much chance."

"How can you say that!"

Because Belac will be too scared himself to make another attempt, Rivera thought. "They'll know the security
that'll be in place now."

"That doesn't sound a very convincing reason to me,"
said Henrietta. "Who's trying to kill you? And why?"

It was an obvious question, and Rivera was prepared for
it. "You know the opposition that exists against Castro?

And what my family were—aristocrats—before the revolution? I'm regarded as a traitor, for joining Castro instead of the opposition."

Henrietta was quiet for so long that Rivera thought they had been disconnected and said, "Hello?"

"You saying the anti-Castro people tried to kill you for that!"

It hadn't sounded as good as he'd expected, Rivera conceded. Improvising, he said, "There've been threats in Havana, apparently. I wasn't identified, but the government thinks it all fits. It's another reason for thinking there's not a lot of risk now; having failed here, they'll choose another target somewhere else."

"What's it feel like, knowing people tried to kill you?" Henrietta was a complete sensualist, and for the first time her voice sounded normal.

"Strange," he said, improvising further because he knew her need. "I felt suspended to begin with, numbed—"

"What about excited!"

"Yes, later. Very excited."

"Excited like you know I mean?"

"Yes," Rivera said. There were occasions during their lovemaking when Rivera was nervous about what she'd wanted to do much as he was uneasy now.

"I wish we *could* meet," she said, soft-voiced.

"I'll find a way," Rivera said emptily. He'd tried for a long time, before telephoning her, to think of something and failed.

"What would it matter if the security people knew we were together anyway?" Henrietta demanded.

It was a valid question; where, precisely, was the problem? "That's really more of a difficulty for you than for me now. You're the one who's got the husband."

"Only in name, dear." Henrietta giggled. "I don't see why it should be a difficulty. They won't be in the room with us, after all, will they? As far as they are concerned, you're simply visiting friends."

It was certainly a way, Rivera realized. And he wanted a way, because already he was missing her. He wished he could gauge how she really felt. Now that Estelle was gone, there were a lot of possibilities they could consider together. Rivera tried to find the drawbacks to Henrietta's suggestion. Very few, he conceded. Mendez would obviously report to Havana, using the newly restored authority so long denied him, which might possibly prompt a query, but an explanation was easy. He was cultivating Sir William Blanchard, an influential newspaper magnate, in the hope of getting articles favorable to Cuba in the man's publications. He could, in fact, send his own report to Havana, in anticipation of it being demanded. He said, "I think you've found the answer."

"When?" she demanded instantly.

For the first time Rivera remembered how recently Estelle had died. "Not for a day or two."

"William's away all next week."

"Certainly next week then."

"Before if you can."

"I promise."

That night, in that part of the diplomatic pouch only Rivera was allowed to open, came the confirmation: the master of the *City of Athens* was scheduling his departure from San Diego in two days' time. The ambassador was relieved that the lading had gone uninterrupted. It meant, he realized, that $12 million should be transferred to Belac, to complete their deal. Rivera smiled, less frightened than he had been immediately after Estelle's assassination. He'd hold on to it for a few more days. He was well enough protected, for the time being. It would be good, showing Belac he was unafraid.

It was a sprawling complex they could enter separately without any suggestion of a meeting, and inside the security was absolute, so McCarthy and Sneider traveled to Fort Pearce separately from Petty and Erickson for the meeting with Lambert.

There was a game show on the television when the group entered Lambert's office, and for several moments the psychologist kept it running, gesturing toward it.

"Do you know that in half an hour of a show like this, you can see most of the theories of Freud with a few of Jung's, for good measure?" he asked.

"If you say so," McCarthy said, unimpressed.

Lambert took the hint and switched the set off. "Coffee or booze?" he invited.

"Booze." McCarthy's coffee drinking ended promptly with the beginning of happy hour. "You got Wild Turkey?"

"Yes," Lambert said; he stocked it for this meeting, knowing McCarthy's preference.

"Two fingers, with a little branch water. No ice," McCarthy stipulated.

"The same," Sneider said.

Petty declined a drink. The ulcer was giving him hell and the medication wasn't helping a damn. "Mind if I smoke?"

"Do you mind if I fart?" Lambert asked.

Petty already had his hand lifted hopefully toward his top pocket. He stopped, frowning. "What's that mean?"

"Means I find pipe smoking offensive in public, like farting," Lambert said.

McCarthy chuckled, accepting his drink. "We're all of us going to wear you down in the end, George. Why don't you just surrender?"

Petty dropped heavily into a chair, leaving his pipe where it was. He said, "O'Farrell gone?"

"About two hours ago," the psychologist said.

"Tell me in simple words, no inside-the-head crap," McCarthy said.

"There was a great deal of guilt about wrongly killing

the woman; I got rid of a lot of it," said Lambert. "At the
end he was calling it an accident as a matter of course. But
that really just provided a focus for the real problem. He's
started to question the morality: what right have we to decide upon life or death? I think I got him back more or
less on course there. He's proud of his army service, the
medals and the recognition for being a gung-ho, behind-
the-lines bastard. Which is another problem: he doesn't
have the security blanket of knowing there's someone or
something behind him if he fouls up. That was his real
emotion coming back on the plane. Plenty of guilt, sure.
But terror for himself, too. The ancestral archive is him
grabbing out for some sort of justification, wanting to
imagine himself the lawman."

"What about the mother and the father and the Russian
thing?" Sneider asked.

Lambert shook his head, going to his coffee machine.
"No particular trauma there. He regrets not visiting them
more when they got older, thinks he might have seen some
change in his mother in time to get her treatment and prevent it happening, but it's not a big problem for him."

"It did happen though, didn't it?" McCarthy pressed.

"What?" Lambert frowned.

McCarthy gave a dismissive head movement. "Talking
to myself," he said. "He mention Makarevich at all?"

"Never," Lambert said at once.

"So what's the bottom line?" Petty asked. "Can he
work again or not?"

"Depends how you wrap the package," Lambert said.
"O'Farrell's got a lot of pride, about his house and his
family and looking after everyone; about doing everything
right. Proud of not being a quitter; that was a phrase that
came out several times, as we talked. And then there's the
flag and the country and patriotism. I'm pretty sure it's
genuine, but of course it makes it easy for him to think of
himself as the soldier he once was."

"So how the hell do you wrap that up in a package that doesn't leak!" Sneider demanded.

"I don't know," Lambert admitted. "Everything would depend on the assignment. He'd have to believe it absolutely—more absolutely than the checks and balances he's previously been allowed—even to consider it."

"Let's skin the cat another way," Erickson said. "Let's say we did all that, proved that the devil had made it back in human form. What are the chances of O'Farrell's nerve going or his motivation failing and everything going splat, right in our faces?"

"Always a possibility," Lambert said unhelpfully. "Always has been, always will be, unless you employ psychos. O'Farrell said something like that himself."

"I'm not getting a lot of guidance here," Petty protested. "None of us are."

"I'm giving you my opinion," Lambert said. "Not what I think you want to hear. Aren't we trying to prevent everything going splat, right in our faces?"

McCarthy grimaced. "Didn't you ask him outright if he wanted to quit?"

"A few times," Lambert said. "I never got a full answer, on any occasion. First he'd say yes, then he'd say no."

"What did that signify?"

" 'I'm not a quitter,' " Lambert quoted.

"I don't think it's sufficient, any of it," Erickson said. "So far we've lost nothing. We've been lucky. Let's cut loose while we're still ahead."

"That's my feeling, too," Petty said.

McCarthy held out his glass to be replenished, and when Lambert returned with it, the Plans director said to the psychologist, "What decision would you make in our position?"

Lambert stared down at the man for several moments. "It's possible," the psychologist said. "Possible but dangerous. On balance, you're going to need a hell of a lot of luck."

"It's always dangerous," Sneider said.

"I've got an idea," McCarthy said. "A hell of an idea."

"We cut adrift from O'Farrell?" Sneider anticipated, for once wrongly.

The Plans Director frowned at his deputy. "Christ, no!" he said. "Whatever made you think that?"

TWENTY-FIVE

JILL WASN'T there when he got back to Alexandria. Three or four days earlier, before the sessions with Lambert, it would have thrown him for a loop, because he'd telephoned from Fort Pearce hours ahead, telling her of his supposed return on the afternoon British Airways flight. As it was, he contained the reaction to mild surprise. Jill was conscientious and often worked late at the clinic; hours sometimes, although he didn't think she would tonight because she knew he was getting back.

He made a drink and wandered about the house, feeling its familiarity wrap comfortingly around him. He felt safe, secure. The impression reminded him of what Lambert had said, at one of their sessions; the first, he thought, although he wasn't sure. The man had been right. Climbing under the bedcovers was just what he'd wanted to do; hide for a long time in the darkness, where no one could find him. Know he was there, even. He'd needed Lambert, needed the man more than he could calculate at this moment. Not that he could forget what had happened in London. It had been appalling and would always be with him. But Lambert had put it into perspective for him; he didn't have any problem with the word "accident" anymore. Because that was what it had been: an appalling, ugly accident. But accidents happened. How had Lambert put it? The very fact that this was the first, ever, showed how careful he was, how professional. Something like that.

It had been an incredible relief to be able to talk as he'd talked to Lambert. He knew the feeling was ridiculous, after so short a time, but he found it easy to think of Lambert as a friend, the way the man had asked him to. *Think of me as a friend, someone you can call and talk about anything, anytime.* O'Farrell wasn't sure that he would. It was all right this time, because of the circumstances. He'd needed the man. But to want to talk through things again might make Lambert think he was some sort of goofball, one of those goofballs who kept regular weekly appointments with a shrink and couldn't function without them. Then again, he might. It wasn't something he had to decide right now.

The tour inevitably ended in the den. The copied archive and the fading photograph that Jill had collected for him were still packaged, waiting to be refiled. He'd known the Agency kept tabs on him—it was a logical precaution—but he'd never guessed it was so complete. O'Farrell jerked his head up at a thought, gazing around the bookshelves and the furniture, at everything. Would the house be wired? With Jill out every day, the technical people would have had every opportunity to set a system up. O'Farrell started to move and then stopped, sitting back in his chair. He'd be wasting his time. The micro-technology now was so advanced that even an expert, like he was supposed to be, wouldn't find anything. It was an eerie thought; unsettling. He didn't bother with the files. The copied photograph was disappointing; his great-grandfather looked different, oddly, absurdly, more like the gunslingers he'd hunted than the lawman he had been.

O'Farrell checked his watch. He'd been home for over an hour. Where was Jill? An emergency, perhaps? But why hadn't she called, or had a secretary call?

The clinic receptionist was a bouncy black girl named Annabelle who said hi and how was London and she wanted to go there someday. If there *were* an electronic monitor, Langley wasn't going to be pleased, O'Farrell thought. Annabelle, confused, said Jill had left hours ago, around lunchtime, without saying where she was going. O'Farrell's immediate thought was Chicago, and he was relieved that Ellen was in the apartment. Ellen was as surprised as the receptionist at the clinic; she'd spoken to her mother the previous evening but there'd been no arrangements for her to fly up. O'Farrell said there had to be some misunderstanding at his end and it was unimportant, carrying on the conversation that was necessary. Billy was fine and Patrick had promised to clear up the arrears and maintain both the alimony and child support in the future, so she didn't think it was necessary to start any legal pressure at the moment. Patrick had gotten a job as a car salesman and the commissions were good and wasn't that terrific? O'Farrell sadly decided that Jill was right, that their daughter still loved the bastard, and agreed it was terrific if the payments kept coming. They would, said Ellen. This time Patrick had really promised. He was seeing Billy again, too. The previous weekend he'd bought the boy an electrically controlled car.

"So how was your trip?"

O'Farrell waited for the stomach drop, but there was nothing. He said, "Just work," and his voice stayed perfectly even.

"Nothing exciting at all?"

O'Farrell swallowed. "Nothing," he said, with more difficulty.

"I love you, Dad."

"I love you, too."

O'Farrell gratefully replaced the receiver, filling his

mind with the immediate problem. So where was Jill? She was a woman of habit, of regularity, someone who didn't take afternoons off without saying where she would be. He felt the beginnings of concern. And then of helplessness. He could try the police covering the district where the clinic was, to see if there'd been any reports of an accident, but what then? Ask for the car number to be posted and circulated, maybe, but they wouldn't do that, unless he had cause to think she'd been involved in some crime; there had to be dozens of husbands and wives late home every night. He was right, he told himself; there *were* dozens of husbands and wives late home every night, for all sorts of perfectly understandable reasons. So why the hell was he panicking! *Every night* wormed its way into his mind; Annabelle had said Jill left at lunchtime. Maybe Lambert would— O'Farrell started to think and then stopped, closing out the thought.

He went back to the kitchen and mixed another drink. He'd give her a little longer, another hour maybe. Then the police. Call other people at the clinic to see if she'd said anything to them. Who? O'Farrell squeezed his eyes shut, trying to remember the names. Jill always seemed to be talking about people she worked with, so much so that he usually switched off, and now he couldn't remember the names. There was a Mary, he thought. And an Anne. Or was that the same person, Maryanne? And what about surnames, to look them up in the book? They wouldn't be at the clinic, not this late. The night staff would tell him, once he'd satisfied them who he was. Just another hour. Then he'd start calling around.

O'Farrell carried his drink with him to the front of the house, where he could look out onto the street. It was very quiet, fully dark now, all the parking spaces used up by returning residents without garages. There'd be the cars to clean over the weekend. O'Farrell looked forward to doing it; mundane, certainly, but familiar, secure by its very ordinariness.

Their garage door was electric, operated by an impulse from a control box in either vehicle, and it was the unlocking click and then the operational whir he heard, seconds before he saw Jill's car. The inner door from the garage led into the kitchen, and O'Farrell was already there when Jill came through. She seemed taken aback to see him and said, "Where the hell have you been!"

"Where the hell have *you* been?" he said. In his concern he sounded angry, which he wasn't.

"All the way out to Dulles is where I've been," said Jill. "I decided on a surprise, so I went to meet the plane. And you weren't on it, weren't even booked, when I checked."

O'Farrell reached out, pulling her to him, to gain time to think. And not just to think. He wanted to feel her, hold her close and know the reassurance of her being there. She'd always been there. Always would be. What would he do if Jill went out one morning and fired the ignition and literally exploded, simply didn't exist anymore!

She broke away from him. "Darling!" she said. "You're shaking! What's the matter? What's happened?"

"Nothing," he said, recovering. "Tired, that's all. Would you believe it! I set out to surprise you!"

"What?"

"After I telephoned I realized I wasn't going to need as much clearing-up time after all. I got to the airport in time for the TWA flight through New York, so I canceled the original reservation and switched. Got here two hours earlier."

"You know what?" said Jill, smiling and believing him. "We must have passed each other on the way to and from the airport."

O'Farrell hugged her again, anxious for the closeness. Mouth in her hair, against her ear, he said, "That's what must have happened." It hadn't occurred to her to disbelieve, to doubt.

"You're still shaking."

"It isn't anything. Tiredness, like I said. Plane was crowded; tour groups."

Jill moved farther into the kitchen, perching on a breakfast stool. "I had another idea, after the first surprise," she confessed. "If you'd felt like it, I was going to suggest dinner somewhere instead of coming straight home."

She was dressed in her newest suit, the one she had picked up at a Saks sale. "Great idea!" he said.

She shook her head. "You're tired."

"Nothing a shower can't fix in five minutes."

"Nonsense," she said. "We're home now. I'll make something here."

O'Farrell didn't want to disappoint her, but he thought it would be dangerous to press too hard. So much for the woman who never did anything unexpected! He said, "You quite sure?"

"Absolutely positive," she said.

He didn't think she was. Effusively he said, "Tomorrow night! Anywhere you like!" knowing it wouldn't be the same, because there wouldn't be any spontaneity.

"We'll think about it," she said.

It had to be a Lean Cuisine lasagna and she joined him in some wine, and O'Farrell gave the prepared account of what he was supposed to have done and seen in London. Telling her of his call to Ellen made the opening for Jill to talk of her time in Chicago while he had been away. Like O'Farrell, she wasn't impressed with Patrick's sudden responsibility. She put at three months the time it would take the man to lose the job or fail with the payments or possibly both. The drug scare at Billy's school was so long ago they didn't even talk about it anymore.

It was obvious Jill expected him to make love to her that night and he did, although it wasn't easy and he had to fake it. He didn't think she guessed and he was fairly sure she climaxed.

The following night they did go out, combining an orchestral recital at the Kennedy Center with dinner at the restaurant there, the river view making up for the food. The outing really did lack spontaneity, but Jill said it was wonderful. Abruptly O'Farrell said he really didn't know what he'd do without her, and Jill laughed and said he'd never have to find out, would he?

O'Farrell tried hard for the normality he craved. He found a reference to his great-grandfather in a history of western American exploration to add to the collection and on the first Saturday cleaned the cars, disturbed at how dirty and neglected they had become. There was even a rust stain on the Ford.

The normality didn't last long. The summons from Petty came the second week, a summons to Lafayette Square itself, which was unusual. When O'Farrell entered, he saw that Erickson wasn't present, which was even more unusual, but he hoped he knew the reason. The air was thick with the incenselike smell from the perpetual pipe.

"Just wanted to see how you were," Petty announced at once.

"I'm fine," O'Farrell said. Thinking that sounded too short, he added, "Thank you."

"How did you get on with Lambert?"

It was a professional question, and O'Farrell thought the psychologist could have answered that more satisfactorily than himself. "I appreciated the advice, the chance to talk. It was very helpful." Everything was coming out very stilted. Why was Petty delaying?

"You expect an official inquiry?"

At last! O'Farrell said, "I would have thought it automatic."

"It isn't," Petty said brusquely. "And there isn't going to be one."

"Nothing!" Lambert had made it possible for him to live with himself, to accept the accident and justify what he'd done in the past, but O'Farrell still believed what he had told the man, that the Agency would from now on consider him unreliable.

"The circumstances are obvious," the section chief said. "Nothing happened to embarrass anybody. So it's a closed matter. Over."

O'Farrell's thoughts were disordered, refusing to form, and it was several moments before he could speak. Finally, stilted still, he said, "What then, precisely, is my position?"

Petty frowned, as if the question were difficult. "Your position?"

"Am I considered to be still"—O'Farrell stopped, seeking the laughably absurd description Lambert had used—"considered to be on the active roster?"

Petty's frown remained. "Of course. I thought I just made that clear."

Once more there was a long pause, from O'Farrell. Then he said, "I see."

"Something wrong?" Petty demanded.

"No ... I ... no, nothing."

"What is it? You seem unsure."

"Nothing," O'Farrell reiterated. "Nothing at all." A soldier, a lawman; that's what Lambert had called him. That's what he *was*.

That night Ellen telephoned from Chicago and asked them to come up at once.

Rivera had gone to Henrietta's twice under escort and the sex had been sensational. He guessed he had been right, that she was stimulated by the thought of the guards being outside. The British detectives remained courteous and formally interviewed him again, admitting they weren't making any progress and once more pressing him to suggest a reason for the attack. Once more he claimed it to be a mystery to him.

Rivera considered the very absence of any demand from Pierre Belac for final settlement of the arms deal a confirmation, if any confirmation were needed, of the man's involvement in the bombing. Rivera was curious why the man hadn't waited until after the last delivery, to get the last of the money.

The ambassador had changed his mind yet again about that final payment, forever conscious of the daily accruing interest. He *wouldn't* settle automatically. With every passing day he became more convinced there was no physical risk. So he'd wait and give himself the satisfaction of making Belac ask.

Henrietta telephoned on his private line at the embassy at five, to check that tonight was still on, and Rivera said it was. He intended coming straight from High Holborn to collect her after the arrival of the daily communication from Havana. They were dining at the Gavroche.

"Will they be round us all the time, these bodyguards?" Henrietta demanded.

"All the time," he guaranteed.

The diplomatic pouch was on time and Rivera sat staring down at the official Foreign-Ministry letter. In view of his outstanding ability, he was being considered for promotion to the central government. To that end he was to prepare himself to attend a forthcoming international conference.

TWENTY-SIX

O'FARRELL AND Jill caught the late-afternoon flight and from O'Hare telephoned the number Ellen had given them. She was still there. They drove straight over. It was obviously an official building, although no one wore uni-

forms and there was definitely no indication of any association with the police.

Ellen looked strained, which was understandable, but
there was no sign of crying. She was alone in an office
with a man she introduced as McMasters; she apologized
for not remembering the first name. The man said it was
Peter. He stood politely to greet and to seat them, his attitude and expression sympathetic.

"Where's Billy?" Jill demanded at once.

"He's okay," Ellen said. "He's with a counselor."

"How bad is it?" demanded O'Farrell.

"Bad."

"That's an exaggeration, and it's important not to exag-
gerate," McMasters said gently. He was a naturally big
man who gave the impression of fatness, which was mis-
leading. The checked shirt clashed against the tweed of his
suit; the tie hung abandoned from a coatrack but that
didn't coordinate, either. The man said, "Your daughter
has been very sensible. Billy's been arriving late at the
after-school day-care center. And then she found money, a
fair amount, hidden in his room. I don't know if you were
aware of it, but there seemed to be a drug problem at his
school a while back. We left a hotline number, if any
parent wanted to talk about anything—"

"Billy's taking drugs!" Jill said, aghast.

"No," the man said, quiet-voiced, reassuring.

"Worse," Ellen said.

O'Farrell had expected his daughter to be crushed, de-
spairing, but she wasn't; she seemed to be tight, flush-
faced with anger. She must have been here a long time, he
reasoned. The despair and the helplessness would have
come and gone a lot earlier.

"We don't know that, either," McMasters said, calmly.
"Billy was picked up outside school this afternoon. He
was carrying crack, in a sealed package. Quite a lot. And
some loose, uncut cocaine."

"Crack!" O'Farrell exploded.

"In his backpack," McMasters confirmed. "Sealed, like I said. And cocaine."

"But what. . . ?" stumbled Jill.

"He says he didn't know what it was," Ellen broke in. "That some people asked him to take it to another man who gave him ten dollars for doing it. He's done it before. That's where the money I found in his room came from."

"My vote is that he's telling the truth," McMasters said. "What he had was a street dealer's stash; no way a user's purchase. We're talking big thousands; he'd have been stealing, not saving. And we've had a doctor check him out. There's no evidence at all that he's a user: no urine trace, no nasal irritation."

"You're not saying Billy's a dealer!" Jill said. "He's short of being nine years old, for Christ's sake! That's preposterous."

"I don't believe it is so preposterous," said McMasters. "But no. I think Billy was a courier, an innocent but ideal courier."

O'Farrell was trying to clear his head of all the easy reactions, the shock and outrage and the refusal to believe. He said, "Does that happen?"

"A lot," said McMasters. "If a dealer's been busted, he's a face. From that first arrest we've got him marked and at any minute one of our people can come out of an unmarked car to see what he's got in his shopping bag. And his supplier knows that best of all; needs to protect himself from association. So what's better than getting some nice innocent kid to complete the run? Just a few blocks, that's all; just sufficient to break the chain."

"But a kid that young!" Jill protested.

"The younger the better," McMasters said. "The supplier doesn't go away; he stays around to see if the delivery is completed. He's known for hours that we've got his stuff off Billy. Probably already replaced it by now, through some other child."

"What's going to happen to Billy?" O'Farrell asked, the bottom-line question he should have asked before.

"We need to know more at this stage," McMasters said. "Billy's the child of a single-parent family, he's not yet nine years old, and he's become associated with drug dealers. And innocent or not, he's known something isn't right, because he's hidden the money he got for doing what he did."

"You didn't quite finish," Ellen said.

O'Farrell looked briefly at his daughter and McMasters, and to the drugs officer he said, "What?"

"Billy won't tell us about it, not properly. Just how much he got; nothing about the people."

"He doesn't know them!" Ellen pleaded. "How can he tell you what he doesn't know. And you know anyway that wasn't what I meant!"

"There's got to be something more," McMasters said. "We agreed on that before your parents came in."

To O'Farrell, not to the investigating officer, Ellen said desperately, "They think I was involved, that Billy might have been carrying for me!"

"What!" O'Farrell said. He was too incredulous to be angry.

"I've asked your daughter to take a drug test," McMasters announced flatly.

"No!" O'Farrell said. And then, in immediate contradiction, he said, "Yes! Why not! Prove that's nonsense!"

Ellen hesitated for a moment, and O'Farrell felt the horrified flicker of doubt.

Then Ellen said, "Of course I will. I've already agreed." She sat upright and strangely isolated, the unshed tears at last flooding from her. Jill reached out, pulling Ellen to her, and Ellen gratefully put her head on her mother's shoulder. She made an obvious effort to stop crying but sobbed on, instead, dry, racking sobs.

"It's all right, it's all right," Jill kept repeating, looking imploringly over their daughter's slumped shoulders at O'Farrell, expecting him to do or say something.

To the other man, O'Farrell said, "Can I see him?"

"Yes," Jill picked up eagerly. "We want to see him—"

"Alone," O'Farrell finished.

Jill looked at him, stiff-faced, but didn't protest.

"Sure," McMasters agreed at once. "No reason why not."

O'Farrell left the office slightly behind the other man, following him down the gleaming, buffered-clean corridors. Underfoot there had to be some rubberized material, because there was only a faint squeak of movement as they walked. In fact, this section of the building was very quiet, no sounds of people or telephones from other offices. They only passed two people, both of whom greeted McMasters by name and smiled at O'Farrell. They pushed through two firescreen doors and went halfway down a corridor to the right before McMasters halted outside a door set with wire-reinforced glass. McMasters said, "You should know the room is covered by video cameras and sound; really there for child sex and molestation cases."

"I've read that it works," O'Farrell said.

"Sometimes," McMasters said.

It looked like a child's playroom. There was an enormous tub of overflowing toys near a wall-mounted blackboard, upon which some stick figures paraded in a neatly chalked line. Beanbag seats were strewn around the floor and there were assorted desks and chairs, without any order. Billy was at one of the larger tables, head bent in concentration over a large sheet of paper on which he was crayoning something. A very young and pretty girl whom O'Farrell didn't think could be long out of her teens was sitting opposite, providing the colors as Billy asked for them. Billy's legs were too short to reach the floor; he'd tucked his feet around a cross support, halfway down. One of his laces was undone.

The girl rose from the table, shaking her head at

McMasters in an obvious signal that Billy had disclosed nothing.

"Hi, Gramps!" Billy said with forced bravery. "Come and see what I've drawn!"

"Why don't we take a coffee break?" McMasters suggested to the girl. She smiled her way from the room ahead of the man, without any introduction.

O'Farrell stood slightly behind the child, gazing down at a spill of colors vaguely resembling some humanoid shape. There was a lot of body armor, something he guessed to be a ray gun and a spaceship, in the background. "It's great," O'Farrell said. "What is it?"

"A Zirton."

"What's a Zirton?"

"A space warrior. I just made him up."

"A good guy or a bad guy?"

"Not sure," the child said, head to one side. "A good guy, I guess ..." He pointed to the chest armor. "That's red. Red's a good color, not a bad one."

O'Farrell took the chair vacated by the girl. "So what happened here, then?"

Billy bent over his drawing, to avoid O'Farrell's eyes. "Some men looked through my backpack and found a package. They brought me here."

The history of the world, written on a postage stamp, O'Farrell thought. "That's it, huh?"

"Guess so."

"You know what was in the package?"

"Nope." The denial was immediate.

"Didn't you want to know?"

"Not really."

"What if it had been something nasty? Mushy? Had leaked out all over the place?"

"Knew it wouldn't." There was a lift and then a drop of Billy's head, bottom lip between his teeth at being caught.

"How could you tell, if you didn't know what was inside?"

"Hadn't leaked out before."

"There'd been other packages, then?"

It was becoming difficult for Billy to find anything more to do to his picture. He nodded his head and said, "Uh-huh."

"How many?"

"One or two."

"Let's do better than that, shall we?"

"Can't remember."

"You've got to remember, Billy. I want you to."

"Five," the child mumbled.

"You quite sure?"

"Uh-huh."

"No more?"

Billy shook his head.

"How did it start, the first time?"

"I dunno."

" 'Course you do, Billy. That's silly, to say you don't know."

"A man came up to me one day, before the school bus came. Asked me to run an errand. Said I'd get money for it."

"Didn't you wonder if you should do it?"

"It wasn't to get into his car or anything. Mommy told me not to do that."

"What did he want you to do then?"

"Just put the package in my backpack, that's all. He said when I got off, I was to wait for a man to come up and say did I have a present for him? When I gave it to him, he would give me ten dollars."

O'Farrell felt hot, his collar restrictively tight, at how exposed Billy had been. An image came into his mind that he didn't recognize at first and then he did: it was a boy eating dinner in an exclusive London restaurant with his beautiful mother and ambassador father. O'Farrell blinked it away. He said, "Is that how it happened, all five times?"

"Kind of," Billy said. "Sometimes I had to wait around."

"But you always did?"

"Sure, always."

"They must have liked that, knowing you were reliable, a good guy."

"They did!" Billy said, smiling up, proud again.

"You become friends?"

"Kind of."

"What did they call you? They call you Billy or maybe something else? Just kid or something?"

"Always Bill, after that first time," the boy said, still proud. "Sometimes Billy-boy."

"What did you call them?"

"I used—" The boy stopped and his face closed, as if a curtain had been drawn across it.

"What, Billy?"

"Nothing."

"You were telling me what you called them."

"Didn't call them anything. Never knew their names."

O'Farrell turned Billy's drawing around so that he could see it better. "What's that again?"

"A Zirton," the boy said. He was cautious now against relaxing at an apparently casual question.

"They make Zirtons in those things I bought you, a few months back?"

"I just told you. I made it up."

"So you did," O'Farrell said easily. "That was a good weekend, wasn't it?"

"It was okay," Billy said stubbornly.

"I enjoyed that hamburger and fries we had, near the lake," O'Farrell said. "You remember what we talked about then?"

"Yes," Billy said, unexpectedly direct.

"And the promise you made me?"

"Yes."

At last the child's lips were trembling, the first sign of

giving way. O'Farrell was surprised Billy had held out so long and thought his grandson was a plucky little bastard. Just as he thought of himself as a shit, for coming down on him like this, and hoped it would all be worthwhile. Relentlessly he went on, "I don't think you've kept it, Billy. I thought we were friends, loved each other, but I don't think you've kept your promise."

"You said I was to tell Miss James or Mommy if anyone tried to sell me drugs at school," Billy said.

It was a lawyer's escape and bloody good for a kid so young. O'Farrell said, "You knew what was in those packages, didn't you, Billy?"

"No!"

"Or didn't you want to know?" O'Farrell asked, changing direction with the idea. "Was that it? You thought you were safer if you pretended not to know what was in them? Even though you did, all the time."

Billy couldn't hold his grandfather's eyes. He looked down into his lap and O'Farrell thought the tears were going to come then, but still they didn't. "I didn't know," the boy mumbled.

"It was cocaine, Billy. That stuff that makes you feel funny, the stuff we talked about. And crack is cocaine in crystals, which is even worse."

The boy shrugged, saying nothing.

"You do know some names, don't you?" O'Farrell persisted. "Not all, not even complete. But you know some."

"Can't."

The word was so quiet that O'Farrell feared he'd misheard. "What? What did you say?"

"Can't," Billy repeated.

"Why can't you?"

"Frightened."

"You mustn't be frightened," O'Farrell urged. "People will look after you. *I'll* look after you. It'll be all right."

The tears came as abruptly as Ellen's had earlier. Billy suddenly sobbed and fell forward on his arms and

O'Farrell sat in helpless indecision, wanting to go around the table and hold him and stop the tears but pulling back against halting the outburst with kindness before it all came out. He compromised, reaching across for Billy's outstretched arms and stroking his hand. It was a long time before Billy looked up, and when he did, his eyes were red-rimmed and his nose was running. O'Farrell gave him a handkerchief and Billy wiped himself. His mouth moved, unsurely forming the words. At last, broken-voiced, he said, "I've kept it all. The money I mean."

"I heard," O'Farrell said, still anxious not to block the flow.

"It would have been sixty dollars, today."

So at ten dollars a delivery, he hadn't lied about the five previous deliveries. "Yes," O'Farrell said.

"Wanted a hundred," Billy said. "There's three months, to Mom's birthday, so I guess I would have gotten it easily. She hasn't had anything new, not for a long time. I was going to give it to her on her birthday so she could have something new. Hadn't worked out a way to say how I'd gotten it, but I'd have thought of something, by the time. I didn't want to hurt anybody. Honest."

"I know that," O'Farrell said thickly. "We'll find something for Mommy, you and me, for her birthday. Okay?"

"Okay," the boy said.

"They're not your friends, Billy. Not these guys for whom you've been carrying packages."

"I know that, really. They pretended to be, but when they said about Mom, I knew they weren't."

O'Farrell went from hot to cold. "What did they say about Mom?"

"That they knew where we lived and that they'd make her ugly—like me, said Rick; he's got a big scar right over his nose—if I told her what I was doing, if I told anyone what I was doing. If I got caught, I was to say it was just an errand and that I didn't know what it was and there was nothing wrong. That I wouldn't get into trouble."

"Was Rick the guy who took the stuff when you got off or who gave it to you near the school?" coaxed O'Farrell.

"He gave it to me, showed me first time how to put it in my backpack."

"By himself?"

"No, he—" Billy stopped, looking pebble-eyed at his grandfather.

O'Farrell held the child's hands tightly across the table, to reinforce what he said. "He can't hurt you; none of them can hurt you now. I won't let them."

"They said."

"They were trying to sound big. Important. It wasn't true."

The child stared across the table, his mouth a tight line, and O'Farrell could feel the fear shaking through him. "Have I ever told you something that wasn't right? Wasn't true?"

It was still some time before the boy spoke. "Guess not," he said.

"So trust me now, Billy."

"Felipe," blurted the boy, looking down into his lap again, as if he were ashamed. "There was a man called Felipe. Sometimes he stayed in the car."

"Was it a big car?" O'Farrell asked, imagining a block-long Cadillac with chrome and fins.

"Like Mom's," Billy said. "Gray too."

"Just Rick and Felipe? Never anyone else?"

Billy shook his head.

"You ever hear their other names?"

The headshake came again.

"Remember anything else about them?"

The third headshake began and then, an afterthought, Billy said, "There was a ring. . . ." He extended his left hand, isolating the index finger. "Here, like a big bird. It was black and had its wings out. Rick said he might give it to me one day."

"What about the man you gave the stuff to? He have a name?

"Boxer," said Billy, not hesitant anymore, actually smiling in recollection. "Had a nose all squashy, like a boxer's. He was different from the others. He was funny. Said that's what he was doing when he was late sometimes, playing hide-and-seek."

He probably would have been, literally, O'Farrell decided, watching from some vantage point to ensure Billy wasn't under observation and that it was safe to make the pickup. "He have a car?"

"A bike!" Billy said enthusiastically. "A racing bike with lots of gears and drop handlebars. Blue. He let me touch it once."

O'Farrell recalled that a lot of the houses in Evanston were unfenced; a bicycle, capable of cutting through backyards from house to house and street to street, was a better vehicle than a car in many pursuits. "You never called him anything else but Boxer?"

"Nope."

"What sort of person was he? He have any rings or stuff like that?" O'Farrell felt exhausted; damp from perspiration and aching in his shoulders and legs.

"He wasn't American," Billy said flatly. "Neither was Felipe. It wasn't the same as us when they talked. And Boxer had a picture on his hand."

"Whereabouts?" O'Farrell pressed.

Billy offered his left hand, the middle finger outstretched. He pointed near the knuckle and said, "A flower, just there. Red."

It was enough, O'Farrell decided; it *had* to be enough. If he were exhausted, how must Billy be feeling? He said, "You've been very good."

"You pleased?" The child smiled uncertainly, eager for the praise.

"Very pleased," O'Farrell said.

"Can we go home now? I don't want to stay here any-more. I don't like it here anymore."

"I'll see," O'Farrell said.

McMasters and the girl were waiting directly outside the door. O'Farrell closed it carefully and started, "Okay, the suppliers . . ." but McMasters raised his hand, stopping him. "I watched it live, in the control room. You did damned well."

O'Farrell was impatient with the praise but didn't show it. He said, "He wants to go home."

"I heard that, too."

"So what about it?"

"It can't end just like this."

"But can he go home, now!"

"I think he needs to," McMasters agreed. "And what-ever happens, I think he's going to want help from a child psychiatrist. He's one scared kid."

"What about the descriptions? Enough for any identifi-cations?"

McMasters studied him curiously and then said, "Not yet; there's a lot of work to be done."

O'Farrell was caught by the tone of McMasters's voice, just as the other man had recognized the meaning in his. O'Farrell said, "And if you had an identification, you wouldn't tell me?"

"Personal vengeance and vigilante stuff are for the movies, Mr. O'Farrell."

It's as good a description as any for what I do, for Christ's sake! O'Farrell thought. He said, "I didn't mean anything like that."

"My mistake," McMasters said, clearly not believing it was.

O'Farrell collected Billy, and then Jill and Ellen, and they rode home strangely embarrassed, no one able to find any conversation. O'Farrell tried baseball talk, but Billy didn't respond. In the apartment there were the sleeping arrangements to make, moving the bedding, which gave them some activity, and at dinner O'Farrell decided to get the clouds out of the way. He did so entirely to and for Billy's benefit, openly talking about drugs and the child's part in what had happened but making it sound as if Billy had knowingly acted like some undercover agent, exaggerating McMasters's reaction to the information the boy had finally provided. Ellen and Jill caught on to what O'Farrell was doing and openly praised the boy, and Billy started to relax, even smiling occasionally. O'Farrell was intent on everything the boy said, for any scrap of additional information, but there was nothing.

O'Farrell was ready for the going-to-bed request, agreeing at once that he should be the one to take Billy, and Ellen behaved like it was the expected thing. The story was predictably about some galactic exploration but Billy clearly wasn't interested.

"They won't come, Rick and Felipe, during the night!"

"No."

"How can you be sure?"

"I'm just sure."

"How long are you staying?"

"A few days."

"Who's going to look after us when you've gone?"

"I'll work it out."

Billy insisted on holding O'Farrell's hand between both of his and several times opened his eyes, accusingly, when O'Farrell tried gently to withdraw. It was an hour before O'Farrell got away. The dinner things were cleared and Jill and Ellen were sitting side by side on the couch, like hospital visitors waiting for a diagnosis they didn't want to hear. O'Farrell told them everything, and Ellen began to cry when he got to the reason for Billy saving the money, the threats that the men had made, and McMasters's thought that Billy might benefit from seeing a psychiatrist.

"Well?" O'Farrell demanded.

Ellen looked uncomprehendingly up at him, red-nosed and wet-faced. "Well what?"

"I want direct, honest answers."

"About what?"

"About a lot of things. Let's try drugs first."

Her lips quivered afresh but Ellen didn't break down. "No!" she said. "How many times have I got to say no!"

"Until I'm satisfied," O'Farrell said.

Ellen opened her mouth to speak but then apparently changed her mind about what she was going to say. She said, very quietly, "No. I don't do cocaine! No, I don't do crack! No, I don't deal. No, I haven't turned my son into a runner! There! Satisfied?" It was very difficult for her to hold on and Jill reached out to her as she had in McMasters's office, in support.

"What about the day-care center?" O'Farrell persisted relentlessly.

"You knew about that!" Ellen said defensively. "Thousands of single parents use the system. It works. Don't look at me as if I've done something wrong!"

"How long has he been there by the time you collect him?"

"Usual time."

"What's usual time?"

"I told you about the extra work, when we had the first scare at the school," Ellen said. "Billy was always okay at the center until I collected him."

Jill pulled away from their daughter. "It took them long enough to realize he was arriving late."

"But they *did* realize it," Ellen said. "And as soon as they did, they told me."

"How about another direct, honest answer?" O'Farrell challenged. "Tell me, directly and honestly, how much Patrick's caught up with the payment arrears. And how promptly the regular amounts have come in?"

Ellen gave a helpless shrug. "He promised," she said.

"He hasn't paid up a goddamned cent, has he!" O'Farrell said.

Ellen shook her head, not looking up at her father.

"For God's sake!" Jill said, finding something at last to be angry instead of sad about. "What's wrong with you! You're working full-time and extra when you can—and you let him get away with this?"

"That's going to stop, right here and now!" O'Farrell said. "I'm going to sort everything out with Billy and I'm going to sort everything out with that bastard ex-husband of yours. . . ." He stopped, caught by a sudden thought and remembering Billy's bedroom pleas. He said, "You called Patrick, about the drugs business?"

Ellen nodded. "Before you. He said he had some important appointments running through until well into the evening, that he'd get over if he could. I guess he couldn't. This new job is pretty demanding . . . worrying. . . ."

"I just can't believe this! I just can't believe I'm hearing this—" Jill started to protest, but O'Farrell took over, careless of interrupting his wife and careless, too, of the fury he was supposed never to feel.

"Billy was pretty worried today, too, holding my hand and pleading not to be hurt. You're more than a damned fool. Don't you realize you've actually *neglected* Billy, letting Patrick off the hook like you have?"

There was a listless shoulder movement from their daughter. "I guess," she said.

O'Farrell was gripped by a feeling of helplessness, helplessness and impotence. Abruptly he stood and announced, "I'm going out for a while. A walk."

"But . . ." Jill started.

"I need to get out."

There was a chill coming off the lake and O'Farrell set out toward it, knowing there was a lakeside walk through a park but thinking after two blocks that in the darkness he didn't know how to find it. He turned back toward the township, knowing he could really have found the park if he'd wanted, knowing, too, why he'd changed his mind. Evanston wasn't big; sprawled awkwardly, with a mall he knew he couldn't reach tonight on foot, but definitely not big. Boxer was an identifiable enough name, if it were how the man was normally known. Foreign accent and a broken nose and a red-flower tattoo on his left hand. And a racing bicycle, although O'Farrell guessed that was reserved for pickups, not nighttime cruising. Sufficient to go on: to look at least.

O'Farrell reached the main highway, running parallel with the railway line, and began to walk its full length, taking in the side roads when he came to them. At restaurants he checked through windows, on the pretext of reading the menus, and he went into every bar he came to, for the first time in months using a drink to justify his presence rather than because he needed it. Drink in hand, he walked around them all, looking, and at one tavern—one of the ones he thought most likely because there was live music and everyone was young, far younger than himself—there were some sniggers and someone behind the bar asked if he needed any help. O'Farrell chanced asking for a man called Boxer and got headshaking blankness in reply.

What in the name of Christ did he imagine he was doing! The question came in a bar just beyond the railway bridge over the Chicago road, a shabby place where the regulars examined him like the intruder he was, resenting his examination of them. What would he have done if there'd been someone here—or anywhere else—matching Billy's description? The tattoo was pretty distinctive but not unique, and the broken nose certainly wasn't. Was it enough evidence to justify killing a man, which is what he'd set out to do? What about the usual, professional criteria? *Personal vengeance and vigilante stuff are for the movies.* Was that what he would have done, dragged the man into some darkened parking lot and beat a confession from him, just like they did in the movies? And then killed him? Killed someone? Hadn't that been the agony, over the last few months, *not* wanting to kill anyone? Hadn't that been what he'd told Lambert? The demands flurried like snow through his mind and like snow blocked up, so that he couldn't separate question from answer and more often couldn't find answers to the questions.

O'Farrell left his drink and hurried from the bar, as if he had something to be guilty about, which he supposed he had in thought if not actually in deed. The apartment was in darkness when he got back. He groped his way through it without putting on the light, not wanting to awaken anyone. He undressed in the dark, but as he was lowering himself cautiously beside Jill, she said, "I'm not asleep."

"I didn't mean to be so long."

"Did you find him, the supplier who got Billy to carry the stuff?"

"No." O'Farrell detected the movement and then Jill's hand took his.

"Would you have tried to kill him, if you'd found him?"

"I wanted to," O'Farrell said.

"I'm glad you didn't," Jill said. "These people are very vicious. You'd have probably gotten hurt yourself."

It was the nearest she'd come openly to questioning his manhood. She wouldn't have believed him capable, of course.

TWENTY-SEVEN

RIVERA DECIDED it was time he emerged from his period of mourning. He accepted that there were some who might consider it premature but he was unconcerned; he was an ambassador, a public servant, and such people were expected to cope with grief better than ordinary people.

Conversely there were others who might consider him brave, trying to rebuild something of an existence after the shattering experience.

Objectively Rivera recognized that he had taken a chance going to the Gavroche with Henrietta so soon after it happened, but they'd gotten away with it; there had been no recognition and therefore no resulting newspaper comment.

Tonight was different. A thoroughly acceptable public affair: how better to emerge gently from a period of grief than at a charity premiere at Covent Garden? Then a diplomatic function or two, more public appearances. Followed by the acceptance of some private social invitations to which he'd delayed replying.

From his customary vantage point Rivera saw the arrival of the diplomatic delivery and turned back into the room to receive it, hoping after the care with which he had planned the evening that no personal communication would delay him. He was at once alarmed by the size of the wallet but just as quickly relaxed: the Foreign-Ministry material could as easily have been enclosed in the general pouch to be processed first by secretaries. It was all the accreditation and documentation for the international assignment of which the Foreign Ministry had already advised him in the promised letter, a conference in Madrid to reinforce trade links with Latin America, despite Spain's presence within the European Community.

There was nothing else, so he was actually ahead of time now, because the arrangement was for him to go direct to the opera house from High Holborn. Idly Rivera flicked through the instructions. There was a general policy document to guide him, from Havana, and two other, more detailed guidance papers from the Trade Ministry. Arrangements had been made for him to stay at the official residence of the ambassador to Spain, whom he remembered as a tiresome man constantly boasting of a close friendship the Che Guevara that only he seemed able to remember. Rivera was expected two days before the commencement of the conference and particularly to attend every official Spanish ceremony, because Cuba wanted to strengthen its ties with the Spanish-speaking country that formed part of Europe.

Rivera descended to his new car and his escorts, nodding absentmindedly at the assembled men, his mind remaining occupied by what he'd just read.

He'd go to the conference, of course, but certainly not allow the promotional recall to progress any further. Now was an excellent moment to announce his diplomatic resignation, in fact, with Estelle's death providing a fortunate coincidence. He could plead that he was distraught by her loss, unable from the shock of being the intended victim to function as he properly should, how they would expect him to function. Quit with sympathy and understanding. And then Paris! Vibrant, sophisticated Paris. It was all simple and straightforward but for one thing. Henrietta. He didn't want to be without her, wouldn't be without her. It was time to talk it all through with her. There were things she would have to sort out and settle. The divorce, for instance.

Rivera's performance at Covent Garden was equal to any upon the stage. The assassination had made him a recognizable figure and there was a burst of flashbulbs as he left his vehicle, the picture made dramatic by the escorts grouped around him. He remained grave-faced, head bowed, bypassing the champagne gathering to go directly to his reserved box. There he chose a rear seat, in shadow from the rest of the theater. He withdrew even further with the arrival of the others in the party, shaking hands with the men who offered pleasantries and holding back when Henrietta positioned her face to be kissed.

The production of *The Barber of Seville* was not as good as Rivera had hoped, and the tavern scene was particularly disappointing, people shouting at each other rather than singing. There was champagne arranged for the break, of course, but again Rivera declined. Henrietta held back briefly, accusing him of taking things too far, and flouncing off when he still refused to accompany her.

The dinner party afterward was at the Dorchester. Briefly Rivera thought of avoiding it, and when he got to the hotel he came close to wishing he had. Henrietta clung to him, holding his arm and sharing every conversation, and Rivera recognized the retribution for his earlier distancing himself from her. The seating plan put him next to her—because Henrietta had arranged it that way—and she sat with her hands obviously beneath the table, blatantly straying across to his thigh and crotch.

He complained, when they were finally alone in the car with the glass screen raised between themselves and the driver. Henrietta said, "For Christ's sake, darling, don't be such a boring bloody hypocrite! There's not one person at that table tonight who doesn't know we've been screwing each other for ages."

Henrietta was right, and it upset him to concede it. He said, "It wouldn't hurt to be a little less obvious for a couple more weeks."

She put her hand in his lap and he moved to make it easier and she said, "You're not worried about propriety now!"

"We're not in front of a hundred people in a hotel dining room now."

Henrietta twisted to look out of the rear window at one of the escort cars. "Do they carry guns?"

"Some," Rivera admitted. "They're not supposed to, under diplomatic convention, but they do."

"How long will it last? Will you always have to be guarded as closely as this?"

"For a long time, I suppose," Rivera said, believing he was stimulating her excitement.

"Even when you're transferred somewhere else?"

It was an opening to start talking about Paris, but Rivera held back, deciding the rear of a car was not the right place. He said, "I would imagine so; I haven't really thought about it."

"I would think it's all right for a while but not all the time; too claustrophobic," Henrietta said, discarding a novelty.

"I don't want it to go on forever." The chauffeur was a member of the GDI, like all his other Cuban protectors. Rivera hoped the vehicle was not equipped with the listening devices that spies were supposed to utilize. He was sure that everything he'd said so far was innocuous enough.

At Pimlico, Rivera followed her familiarly into the house and on to the drawing room, which was on the first floor with veranda windows overlooking the illuminated patio at the rear.

"I'll have brandy," she ordered, flopping onto a love seat.

There were times, like now, when Henrietta could be profoundly irritating, treating him like a servant whose name she didn't even know. Rivera was sure he'd correct the attitude quickly enough, although Henrietta was strong-willed to the point of willfulness, far stronger than Estelle had been. There was still so much each had to learn about the other. Rivera was very sure about one thing. With Henrietta as his wife, he wouldn't consider a mistress; he'd never need to consider a mistress.

Rivera was uncertain, oddly shy, about breaking the news of Paris. "I've got some news," he set out. "I'm going away soon."

"Uh-huh," she said. She seemed suddenly occupied with a pulled thread on the seam of her dress.

Was that the best reaction she could manage? He said, "Spain. I am to be an observer at an international conference." Rivera thought, discomfited, that he sounded like a child hopefully boasting a better holiday destination than anybody else in the class.

Henrietta seemed to treat it as such. She said, "I don't

like Spain. I always feel nauseous there; something to do with the oil they cook with, I suppose. I much prefer France."

The opening hung before him, beckoning. He said, "So do I. In fact I've been thinking about France quite a lot, lately."

Henrietta frowned across the room at him. "*Thinking* about France?"

It had been an awkward way to express himself, Rivera realized. "I want Jorge at the Sorbonne eventually. It would be convenient to live in Paris, better perhaps for the remainder of his preliminary education to be there."

"How could that work, with your embassy being here?" asked Henrietta, still confused.

"I'm going to resign," Rivera announced.

"You're going to do what!" She came forward on her seat, wide-eyed.

"Quit," he said, enjoying the sound of the declaration.

"Give it all up, just like that!"

"There's not actually a lot to give up, compared to a return to Havana," Rivera said. "That appears the alternative."

"But what are you going to do in Paris!"

"Nothing," Rivera said. "Just sit back and enjoy myself."

"When?" she demanded.

So far her reaction had not been quite what he'd expected. He said, "I haven't worked out definite dates. But soon; quite soon."

"Oh," Henrietta said.

The tone was empty, and small though it was, it amounted to the first sound of sadness. Rivera said, "Well?"

"Well, what?"

"You don't sound very upset."

Henrietta offered her glass to be refilled. "Give me a chance, darling! It's something I never expected. I thought we'd go on . . . oh, I don't know . . . I mean, I didn't imagine it ending."

"Has it got to end?"

Henrietta looked steadily at him over the top of the glass he returned to her, then smiled coquettishly. "No reason at all!" she agreed brightly. "Paris is only an hour away by plane, after all!"

"I wasn't thinking of your commuting."

The smile went but the direct look remained. "I'm not going to guess what that means," she said. "I'm going to sit here and listen to you tell me."

"I want you to come to Paris with me," Rivera blurted finally. He'd not meant it to be as clumsy as this; he *was* stumbling about like an awkward schoolboy.

For a long time Henrietta remained staring at him, as if she expected him to say more. When he didn't, she looked away, around the room, as if she were inspecting what he was suggesting she give up. "Divorce William? Marry you, d'you mean?"

"Yes."

She sniggered, at once clamping her mouth shut, her free hand to her face. "Oh darling!" she said. "Oh my darling!"

The word was right but the tone was wrong; it was more sympathetic than loving. "What?" he said.

"We don't marry, people like you and me. Not each other. We marry other, nice people. And cheat on our wedding night, because it's fun. I couldn't marry you! I'd never be able to trust you and you'd never be able to trust me. It would be a disaster. What goes on here—or doesn't go on—between William and me is unimportant, to both of us. I've got *respect* as his wife. I get invited to Downing Street to dine with the prime minister . . . to Buckingham Palace. You're asking me to abandon all that. . , !"

Rivera regarded her with astonishment for a few unguarded moments and then hopefully concealed it. He'd never imagined, ever, that Henrietta would reject him! It was inconceivable; it still was, despite her arrogant, spoiled words. Every consideration had always been *when*, not *if*. Rivera felt foolish, abjectly foolish; he recalled her giggled outburst—*Oh darling, oh my darling*—and realized she had been laughing at him. Actually laughing! At him, José Gaviria Rivera! As she must have laughed before, when he didn't know she was doing so. Those at the dinner table tonight had doubtless laughed at him, knowing his function. A gigolo. He would have been perfect for the jokes, ideally qualified according to the tradition. A Latin, tango-dancing gigolo. Had she seen his brief, honest reaction to her dismissal? He hoped not—worried now about later jokes, among her friends—but it was too late. Only one thing mattered now. Getting out with as much dignity as possible. He tried an uncaring laugh, not sure if he fully succeeded, and said, "Of course I'm not asking you to abandon all that, not if it's important. I just thought I'd give you the chance. . . ." Striving for lightness, he added, "It might have been a different sort of fun, for a while."

"That's just it, my darling: for a while. But where would we go from there?"

You could go to a whorehouse, where you're naturally suited, thought Rivera. He didn't try to laugh again but he smiled and said, "But you're right; Paris is only an hour away." It wouldn't be much of a victory, but he was trying to grab what he could and he'd enjoy turning her down when she suggested coming. And she would call, he knew. Flying to Paris for an assignation would be exciting to Henrietta—fun, like traveling with armed bodyguards.

In immediate confirmation Henrietta said, "I'd like that! And we'll have all the time in the world, won't we?"

Where was his dignified exit line? "Nothing to do except have fun!" he said. The bitch, he thought, in a fresh flush of rage, treating him like a gigolo!

"On the subject of fun," said Henrietta, coquettish again. "Is this a late-night-drinks party or do we fuck?"

This was the moment, Rivera thought, the moment to dismiss her and haughtily walk out. And then he paused. That would be turned into another joke, if he did. *The poor darling was so crushed that he scuttled away with his tail—or maybe it was his prick—between his legs.* He hoped she'd realize later he'd treated her like the whore she was, for that one last time. "We fuck," he said.

The *City of Athens*, upon which the tanks and the Stinger missiles had supposedly been loaded in San Diego, together with acceptable End-User Certificates naming France as their destination, was a rusting, engine-strained hulk of a freighter chartered by Belac because it was cheap and because he had gained $40,000 on the budgeted transportation costs. A day after sailing, one of the turbines failed, and the freighter put into Manzillo for make-shift repairs. It was there that the master received the expected instructions from Havana, rerouting the tanks direct to Angola. By return, the captain advised Havana of his engine troubles and warned of a delay.

It took a further four days for the *City of Athens* to cover the comparatively short distance to Balboa, almost at the mouth of the Panama Canal, and there the engines failed again. This time Havana cabled that the *City of Athens* should not attempt the Atlantic voyage.

It should make for Cuba.

A message advising Rivera of the unexpected detour was sent that night from Havana.

TWENTY-EIGHT

O'FARRELL HAD no idea how long everything would take, so he called Petty on the man's outside, insecure line and said he was being held in Chicago on family business for a few days; all the bookkeeping was up to date and there was nothing outstanding. Petty said he appreciated being told and solicitously asked if there were anything he could do. O'Farrell said he didn't think so.

O'Farrell went to see McMasters on the second day. Billy's description had rung some bells with people in the narcotics division. There was a blank on anyone named Rick, but there was a rap sheet for narcotics dealing on a Felipe Lopez Portillo, who was known to drive a Toyota. He was gay, so Rick was probably the current lover; Felipe got them through their drug dependence and could always take his pick. Boxer had been identified. There were two possession and three supplying convictions against a Rene Ibañez. He'd fought flyweight and briefly been considered a Golden Gloves contender in his class. He'd started living the good life before the good live arrived and had screwed up: he'd fought so badly in his last official fight that there'd been a drug test that had proven positive and he had lost his license. He still fought sometimes on the fifty-dollar-a-night circuit, so he kept himself in shape; particularly by bicycling on a racing machine. And he had a red rose tattooed on the middle finger of his left hand.

"Portillo?" O'Farrell asked. "Ibañez? What nationalities?"

"Portillo's Colombian. Ibañez is Cuban-American."

O'Farrell waited to feel something, but nothing came. The anger—the forbidden emotion—of that first night had gone now, and he knew although he had an identification he wouldn't go seeking them, tonight or any other night. It was still difficult to believe that he'd done that, someone with his supposed control. He said, "You going to pick them up?"

McMasters shook his head. "They're not on the streets, won't be, I guess, until they think the heat's off. And we won't, even then. Not for what happened with Billy."

"What!"

McMasters frowned. "You think we're going to arraign streetwise drug dealers on the word of an eight-year-old kid? Their lawyers would suck us up and blow us out in bubbles."

"Then what the fuck was it all about?" O'Farrell exploded. "Why'd you have me drive Billy so far into the ground that he'll need a psychiatrist, if it was all one great big waste of time!"

"It wasn't a great big waste of time, Mr. O'Farrell," the other man said calmly. "We didn't know Portillo and Ibañez were operating. Now we do. And we know how they're operating, which is something else we didn't know. There's a marker sheet on both of them and we wait and we watch. We watch until they try it again and this time we catch them, only we have more than the word of a kid who believes spacemen exist. We have the evidence of an equally streetwise, hairy-assed narcotics officer who won't be sliced up like chopped liver in the witness box."

"Bullshit!" O'Farrell said. "They won't try a kid from Billy's school again, if they're as streetwise as you say. So what have they got? The choice of a hundred schools, all over the city. You got enough officers to stake out every likely school, for as long as it takes? Your way they could go on operating for months! Years!"

"What's your way, Mr. O'Farrell?" McMasters asked.

"Pick them up off the streets, when we do see them, or bust into wherever we find they're living? Take them to some back lot and tell them they don't deserve to live, which they don't, and blow them away? Summary justice, quick and neat and tidy, no need to bother a judge or jury? That's not the way justice works in this country, sir, irritating though it is sometimes."

O'Farrell swallowed, gazing at the other man, any response jumbled and clouded in his mind like those children's toys that instantly become an obliterating snowstorm by being turned upside down. Finding them and killing them had been *exactly* what he'd been thinking, what he still thought. Justice—the justice of courts and attorneys and measured argument—didn't come into it, had no place. At last he said, "And so it goes on?"

"And so it goes on, although we try to stop as much as possible," McMasters said. "And I agree; it's not enough."

There was no purpose in discussing the philosophy of drug prevention on the streets of Chicago and its suburbs, O'Farrell thought. He said, "Ellen's clean, according to the drug tests. We got a copy today."

"So did I," McMasters confirmed. "I'm glad."

O'Farrell came close to asking the man's recommendation, for a child psychiatrist, but at the last moment recalled that he knew someone else far better qualified. When he telephoned, Lambert listened without interruption, promised to get back to him, and did so within the day. He would, he said, recommend a female over a male and the best in the area was Patricia Dwyer. She turned out to be a motherly, big-chested woman whose office was like the toy-cluttered interview room at the police station. From her fees O'Farrell decided she had to be the best, but she and Billy developed an immediate rapport, so O'Farrell judged whatever it cost to be worthwhile. Before Billy's first session he and Ellen spent an hour with the woman, answering every question. On impulse, because she told them of frequent involvement in matrimonial cases, O'Farrell asked her to recommend a lawyer through whom he could pursue Patrick.

Steven Giles was a nervously thin, stripe-suited man with rimless spectacles and a marine haircut—although he hardly looked robust enough to have served. Giles was peremptory and impatiently aggressive, which O'Farrell decided might be a good attitude for them.

Halfway through their first interview Giles said to Ellen, "So your reason for working late sometimes was that Patrick repeatedly reneged on alimony and child support?"

"Yes," Ellen said, subdued.

"What took you so long to try to get the payments made through the court? The system exists."

"He kept promising," Ellen said emptily.

Giles sighed. "That doesn't say much about your judgment."

"Not a lot does," Ellen said, depressed into self-pity.

The attorney took Ellen through the details of her job, the hours worked, and her income and expenditures and then said, "You don't live a life of luxury, do you?"

"I'm giving her an allowance," O'Farrell said. "She'll be able to manage all right if the alimony and child-support arrears are paid up and then maintained."

Speaking directly to Ellen, Giles said, "I can do my part, and if the facts are as you've outlined them, I don't see we've got a great problem. But you've got to help yourself more if you want to stay ahead in the future."

"What do you mean?"

"The moment he tries to duck, you've got to tell me so I can go back through the courts," the lawyer insisted. "And I mean duck on anything: if he misses more than one visit with Billy without a proper excuse, you tell me. Likewise if there's any job change, I want to hear that, too. . . ." The man hesitated, looking briefly at O'Farrell. "Your father's right. Patrick left you; he's responsible for you. He doesn't deserve any breaks."

"I know," Ellen said sadly.

"So stop being a wimp," Giles said. "Start standing up for yourself. And for Billy."

"Well! well! well!" McCarthy said, putting aside the documentation that had been collated. "Here's some more ingredients for the pot. O'Farrell *has* got some personal involvement with drugs, through what's happened to his grandson. And José Gaviria Rivera is an official delegate to a conference in Spain. What can we make out of that?"

Sneider said, "Spain could be an excellent opportunity. O'Farrell's the one we can't anticipate or second-guess."

"Yet the one who's got to do it," McCarthy said. To the third man in the room, the Plans director said, "So could he be persuaded?"

"Providing the argument was carefully enough prepared, I think he could," Lambert said.

McCarthy smiled at his deputy. "You still got the Makarevich file out of records?"

"Yes," Sneider said.

"It could all come good," McCarthy said, distantly. "Then let's see what people say about Soviet freedom and *glasnost* and all that other shit."

TWENTY-NINE

THE WARNING that something particularly important was arriving by diplomatic courier came in code through the intelligence service's supposedly secure electronics link with Havana, so Rivera was prepared. And worried. It was a method that had never been used before—openly connecting him with the DGI—so the risk had to have been judged acceptable even if the communication channel wasn't secure from the British after all. *Very* important, then. Well aware that speculation was fruitless, Rivera speculated anyway, convinced there could only be one thing to justify it. But what could have gone wrong! His excuse about the VAX—that highly classified, state-of-the-art technology would take much longer to obtain—had been accepted, and everything else had been supplied. There'd been congratulations, the promise of the unwanted promotion. Which left only the siphoned-off bank account. But it was impossible for that to have been discovered! Or was it? If Belac had bypassed him about the held-back payment and complained or sought settlement direct from Havana (Why in God's name hadn't he paid! Why had he been so greedy!) it would have been possible to locate it by working backward, from Belac's Swiss account to the other account from which the earlier money had come.

The pendulum swung, from pessimism to optimism. So what? Because of the Swiss bank secrecy regulations, Havana could only have gotten, at best, an account number. No amount. No evidence of what he'd been doing. And he would have known if Belac had approached Havana, Rivera reasoned. Havana didn't *know* Belac was the supplier: Rivera's refusal to disclose his or any other arms dealer's identity had been essential to his remaining the indispensable intermediary. If Belac, someone completely unknown to Havana, managed somehow to penetrate the governmental layers demanding money, Rivera would receive a query. Could this, in fact, be that query? Unlikely, Rivera reassured himself. This wasn't the level of first inquiry; this was far more serious.

Since Estelle's death, Rivera had established a new routine with Jorge, arranging his ambassadorial commitments so that he could spend three evenings a week with the boy, and they ate together as often as possible. Tonight had been one of the three evenings, but whatever was coming from Havana took priority. He telephoned Maxine to tell her there was a possibility of his being delayed for dinner. She was to apologize to Jorge and hold the meal as long as possible, but perhaps no later than 8:30. He'd call again if he could.

Rivera had made the call on his private line; that phone sat now on his desk, a taunting reminder. Where the hell was Belac? Why didn't the bastard call, to be told that everything was going to be settled between them? Indeed, why wasn't it? It was infantile, an empty victory, wanting Belac to come to him. Rivera had the Belgian's account number and the bank address: all he had to do was authorize the transfer, from one account to the other. Not yet, he decided: not now. He needed to know first what was coming from Cuba: to know if Belac *had* gone to Havana direct. To move money about, on the day of a signal from Havana so important that they'd gone through the intelligence network, could prove to be a mistake. Time enough tomorrow, early, if the incoming message were something completely and uncomplicatedly different. Definitely— without question—do it then. Tell the man everything was final between them. Would Belac still be in hiding in Paris? Somewhere at least away from his Brussels office? It wouldn't matter. If Belac were not there, Rivera was sure the man would have established a procedure to get and convey messages. That's what he'd do: make the approach himself. He hadn't wanted to—infantile!—but things were different now. Very different. Too different.

The diplomatic wallet was hurried immediately to him. Surprisingly it contained only one envelope, but the seal was that of the president's secretariat. His hands shaking, Rivera opened it, dry-throated with nervousness, and it was difficult for him at first to read.

The last shipment of Angola-bound tanks on the *City of Athens* had been off-loaded in Cuba. Eight had proven to be completely inoperable; in four, the engines were so useless that they could not move the vehicles onto their heavy loaders from the dockside. None of the accompanying spares had been for the correct model or make of the tanks. A lot weren't even tank spares at all: they were heavy-duty truck parts. Alarmed about everything in the consignment, the military had tested two of the Stinger missiles. Both were duds, making the rest doubtful.

For a long time Rivera sat unmoving, the still-trembling paper in his hands. His first cohesive reaction was toward Belac, putting against the man all the worn obscenities, but in the middle of the mental tirade Rivera stopped, a smile forming. Incredible! he thought. The opportunity was absolutely and utterly incredible! The tremble now was of excitement. Rivera went fully through the idea that had come to him, thinking it was all so simple, and his smile widened when he decided it could work. Completely.

Handled another way, he remembered. The precise words of Ramirez, the DGI general who'd flown from Cuba immediately after the explosion. *If we discover who did it, everything could be handled another way.* Now it would be. To everyone's satisfaction, but most of all to his. He'd produce Belac as the man who'd cheated on the last consignment, desperate enough to try to kill the one man who could name him to Havana. There would need to be a meeting between himself and Belac, ostensibly for the benefit of the DGI but in fact for Rivera to be sure it was all settled without any revealing interrogation. And the meeting had to take place away from England, because in England the Diplomatic Protection Force was still assigned to him. That would be no problem, either. He was scheduled to travel to the Spanish conference accompanied only by his DGI professionals. There was even an additional explanation, as far as his own intelligence service was concerned, for his meeting with Belac: a payment refused. Because he had been so successful, Havana had trusted him and had no idea what had been agreed on for the faulty tanks and missiles, because he had not yet rendered the doctored accounts. Now they would be doctored even further. But not excessively so; maybe by two million. That sounded about right. Two million for himself, ten million repaid to Havana, and a very final settlement for Belac.

Rivera examined his proposal from the other side, to locate the faults. There weren't many. The greatest would be the DGI wanting to interrogate the arms dealer independently, but Rivera was reasonably confident he could maneuver that. Which left Belac himself. And the necessary meeting. Again, Rivera reasoned everything to be in his favor. Briefly the ambassador read part of the letter again and got up to consult a map on his conference table, trying to make a calculation. Three weeks. He guessed Belac would have allowed three weeks for the shipment to get from San Diego all the way across the Atlantic before it was discovered to be worthless scrap upon its East African arrival. And maybe that discovery would have taken another few days. Whatever, it gave the unsuspecting Belac a fairly tight time schedule if he were to get the money before Havana learned what he'd sold them. There'd be contact, Rivera assured himself; sooner rather than later. He found it difficult to conceive how completely perfectly everything had resolved itself.

Rivera was tempted to respond in full and at once to Havana, but he realized it would be premature. He had to allow himself sufficient time in their eyes supposedly to investigate. Instead he formally acknowledged the message and said he was immediately commencing inquiries and went home for dinner with Jorge.

Rivera had come genuinely to enjoy their increased time together, time he supposed would have been more difficult if he had still been involved with Henrietta. Her, he tried to convince himself, he missed not at all and ignored his pride to concede that she didn't miss him, either. After that humiliating night in Pimlico he had not bothered to call her. She'd telephoned him three times, the first time accepting the message that he was occupied with official duties, the second asking what the hell was wrong, and the third telling him to go fuck himself. He said it would probably be more exciting than fucking her. And so it had ended. Deep down he still wished it hadn't.

Jorge seemed to enjoy their evenings just as much. Rivera listened to the boy chatter on about the lycée and its schoolboy feuds and factions and how well—and sometimes not so well—Jorge believed himself to be doing. Because the opportunity was obvious, Rivera asked his son how he would feel about moving to Paris and Jorge solemnly considered the question before saying that he wouldn't mind, and was it a possibility? Rivera said it was, uncomfortably aware that the whole idea seemed less attractive now that Henrietta was not coming. Paris provided a conversation for much of the meal, although Rivera kept everything vague, making no commitment. How long *would* it be? There was no benefit in remaining much after the Madrid conference, which now had added, essential importance. But Rivera thought—without bothering at that moment with any detailed consideration—that his resignation had to be timed properly. Too soon after the Belac episode might not be the right timing at all. It would be better if there were an interval between the two, as he had imposed an interval between Estelle's death and his reappearing in public.

About Estelle an unspoken agreement had formed between them. She was never mentioned. Ever. Rivera accepted it to be Jorge's way of coping with the horror of his mother's death and did nothing to disturb it; if they were to talk about her, it had to be at Jorge's choosing, no one else's. In the immediate days after the assassination Rivera had even considered removing Estelle's photographs from the house but didn't, again taking his lead from the boy, in whose bedroom two pictures were still on display. From the first day, when it might have been expected, Jorge had never shown the slightest interest in the new security at the house or in being escorted to school by bodyguards. To the boy the arrangements seemed not to exist. So Rivera never remarked upon them, either.

There was a reminder from Havana within twenty-four hours that the inquiry was urgent. Despite the temptation, Rivera sent only a brief acknowledgment and late in the afternoon was actually considering ringing the Brussels number when the sound came on his private line. For a few seconds Rivera gazed at it, contemplating the pleasure and hoping it was not someone else. It wasn't.

"There's some unfinished business," Belac declared at once, glad they were not face-to-face because he was sure his relief at Rivera taking the call would have been obvious.

"I know," Rivera said. There was no uncertainty in the arrogant bastard's voice, no hesitation with the words.

"I made allowances for the death of your wife, but I can't understand why the settlement is still outstanding." Belac began to relax.

"How could I have completed the settlement!" Rivera demanded, every move worked out.

Belac's confidence faltered. It couldn't have been discovered already! The *City of Athens* had days at seat yet. Weeks even. "What do you mean?"

"You didn't think the payment account could remain open under the sort of investigation I was under, did you!"

A reasonable explanation, thought Belac. There was no friendliness in the ambassador's voice, but then there never had been; friendship had not come into their association. But there was no suspicion, either. Which was the important thing. The fool still thought he was getting what he wanted; instead of which he was getting what he deserved. Belac grinned to himself, enjoying his play on words. "I hadn't thought of that," he admitted. "How are you going to settle?"

"A letter of credit," Rivera said smoothly.

"What's wrong with another money transfer from a different account?"

"*Any* account with which I'm associated is too danger-ous," Rivera said. Referring to the American episode, he added, "I thought you were being very cautious."

"Upon whose account is the letter of credit to be drawn?"

"Government," Rivera said. "No traceable link with me at all."

"I'm still keeping away from Brussels, away from any-where the Americans might be looking," Belac said. "I'll give you an address—"

"It must be handed over personally," Rivera said. With-out having to be tricked into it, the Belgian had just re-solved the one remaining obstacle. If there had been a risk of U.S. surveillance, he couldn't have moved against the man.

"Why?" Belac demanded, instantly apprehensive.

"Think of it!" Rivera urged. "It's a government letter of credit. Going to someone under American investigation, someone whose name is on official files. Think about the result of it being intercepted and discovered. Besides, it's an openly negotiable document, and we're not risking that to any postal service; the idea is absurd."

It was, Belac conceded. But the prospect of a personal meeting meant further delay. He'd have to find out the whereabouts of that damned freighter. It wouldn't be diffi-cult; he knew the way. Belac said, "What chance do we have of a safe, unobserved meeting?"

"I'll come to you, in Europe," Rivera offered. "Out of England I shall only be escorted by people who know, people who will actually provide protection!" The retri-bution became sweeter by the minute; there was just a minimal distortion of the truth.

"Where?" Belac demanded. "And when?"

Rivera had expected far more objection—why not trans-mit the letter through a one-off bank transaction, for instance, a question for which he'd prepared an answer—and was surprised at Belac's apparently easy acceptance.

And then he remembered that the arms dealer was in a hurry, and why. Flatter the sow's ass, Rivera thought. He said, "I've got an official reason to come to Europe. The place and the time can be your choice. I don't need more than two or three days' warning."

Time enough to find out about the *City of Athens*, Belac calculated. The arms dealer, who was staying in a small commercial hotel on Amsterdam's Rozen Straat, near the Prinsen Canal, lied and said, "I am still in Paris but I'm moving on. I haven't definitely decided where. I could call you in four days; arrange everything then."

"That sounds fine," Rivera said. In those four days there was going to be a lot of highly classified traffic between London and Havana.

"But no longer than four days," Belac stressed.

"Definitely not," the ambassador agreed.

Rivera was glad that he'd been able to dine on the promised night with Jorge because it would have been impossible now. He wrote a very full report, a duplicate copy to go to the DGI general. The uselessness of the final cargo made sense of the assassination, he argued; it had been an attempt of his supplier to remove him, the one person who could have provided the man's identity when the fraud was discovered. He had spoken to the man and become further convinced by his evasiveness. There had, of course, been no open admission; all the blame for the worthless tanks and missiles had been put upon the American nominee purchasers. But there had been a hurried agreement to refund the purchase price, so hurried that Rivera took that as further indication of guilt. During his London visit, Rivera wrote, DGI General Ramirez had indicated a course of action that Rivera considered appropriate; to that end, he had arranged a meeting between himself and the arms dealer, to recover the money and to provide the necessary identification to DGI personnel who would anyway be accompanying him to Europe. He was sending a duplicate of this message to the DGI for its formal approval and asked for that approval, if given, to be communicated direct to the intelligence *rezidentura* at his embassy. Rivera concluded by deeply regretting his choice of supplier.

The response was as swift as Rivera hoped it would be. There was complete acceptance of his explanation. And approval that the matter be resolved according to the DGI general's suggestion. The *rezidentura* was being separately advised. He, Rivera, retained the absolute confidence of the government.

The same day Carlos Mendez, the embassy head of the Dirección Generale de Inteligencia, sought an interview.

"I have been told there is an assignment," he said. The man was pleased. He'd never liked being excluded from monitoring what the ambassador did.

"Yes," Rivera agreed. There was no nervousness, no reluctance, about what was going to happen. He was going to be involved in killing a man, he thought. He felt nothing.

Lloyds of London is the largest ship insurance organization in the world and for that reason maintains a global record of every vessel's movement and position. It is a record to which the public has access, as Belac knew from previous experience of switching ships around the oceans. It took only minutes to learn about the *City of Athens*. Its last reported position was four hundred miles west of Puerto Rico. Because the record is updated daily there was no reference remaining to the emergency stop at Cuba several days before.

He was safe, Belac decided; quite safe. All that remained was to find a convenient meeting place in Amsterdam.

Patrick entered the court hesitantly, slightly behind his attorney, as if he were seeking protection from the man who was, in fact, protectively big, a fat, overflowing figure who waddled rather than walked.

O'Farrell and Jill were already there, in their turn protectively flanking Ellen on either side. O'Farrell was intent—and dismayed—at Ellen's reaction to her ex-husband. Until Patrick entered the court she had been closed-face, but at once she smiled, hopefully. Patrick stared back, stone-faced, dismissive.

O'Farrell switched his attention fully upon Patrick. The suit was polyester, too sharp and too bright, an odd shade of blue. The undulating black hair had deeper waves and was longer than O'Farrell remembered and shone from some hair preparation. There was a heavy gold band on the same wrist as an even heavier watch, which was also gold, and as O'Farrell watched the man sit down at a table with his fat attorney, a yellow-metaled medallion attached to a neck chain slipped through his shirt. O'Farrell's contempt increased: more fucking gold than in Fort Knox, yet the man couldn't maintain payments to his first wife and child.

The two lawyers looked across the courtroom at each other, Giles nodding to the other man, who nodded back. Giles leaned closely to O'Farrell and said, "His name is Gerry Pallister."

"Good?" O'Farrell asked.

Giles smiled. "That's what we're going to find out, aren't we?"

There was a demand for them all to rise, which they did. The judge was a woman, a round-faced, motherly person. As the appellant Giles rose at once to outline Ellen's application, but almost at once Pallister got to his feet, announcing that his client sought for the alimony—although not the child support—to be reduced on the grounds of hardship and that it was excessive.

O'Farrell gazed directly at Patrick, who studiously ignored the attention, and thought at that moment, despite all his training, he did not know if he could have kept his hands off the man if they had been in different surroundings.

A lot of the early part of the hearing came down to legal technicalities, the two lawyers close to the bench arguing procedural points, so it was some time before Ellen was called to give evidence. O'Farrell was impressed at how well she did. She was clearly nervous, but there was no tearful collapse. She gave her answers in a firm, respectful voice, following Giles through the questioning on unmade payments and unkept promises. O'Farrell was aware of Pallister frequently looking to Patrick, as if seeking clarification or confirmation, and O'Farrell wondered what bullshit story Patrick had fed his attorney before the hearing.

Ellen stood up well under examination from Pallister. The lawyer challenged her about payments she said had not been made that Patrick was insisting had, but Giles had anticipated that. Forewarned, Ellen produced her bank statements covering the disputed period, which clearly showed no deposits of either the alimony or child-support figures. The further attempt, after a hurried, head-bent consultation with Patrick, to insist that the payments had been made in cash, clearly did not impress the judge. Pallister tried several different ways to get Ellen to admit she could manage to keep herself and Billy on a reduced income and O'Farrell sat hot with concern that Ellen would misunderstand and agree, but Ellen didn't, and when she returned to sit with them, O'Farrell squeezed his daughter's hand and whispered, "Well done."

Patrick tried hard in the witness stand, and O'Farrell couldn't make up his mind at first whether the man was impressing the judge. Patrick admitted not paying some—but not all—of the arrears and pleaded remarriage and the commitments of a new family. It was not that he was unwilling to pay; it was that the lowness of his uncertain, commission-based income made it impossible for him to pay. If his income improved, he was willing, in fact, to advise his former wife, return to court, and have any new order increased. He was not intentionally neglectful. He sought to honor his responsibilities, as best he could.

Giles was absolutely brilliant, although not immediately so, and O'Farrell looked up worriedly at the man's questioning. Giles's stumbling, hesitant queries and practically servile demeanor at the beginning bewildered and shocked O'Farrell, because it was so alien to what he knew of the man.

Patrick, a bully, immediately discerned an imagined weakness. He seemed to grow in stature, as if he were being inflated, and the replies snapped back, sometimes before Giles had completed his wavering inquiry. There were times, once or twice, when Patrick actually smiled, an artificial expression like a clip-on bow tie. He was smiling when the trap opened and shut, engulfing him. The hesitancy and servility went as Giles repeated word for word an early answer from Patrick, comparing it as an obvious lie against some later response. He challenged the income figures produced by the man, and when Patrick argued that he had been telling the truth, Giles produced salary information from the car firm for which Patrick worked. Pallister made a token protest at Giles's approach to Patrick's employer, but it was only token, and O'Farrell suspected the burly lawyer was annoyed and displeased at having been so obviously lied to by his client.

Giles even asked about the gold watch and bracelet and got an admission from the supposedly impoverished and now groping Patrick that he'd bought both during the time he'd told the court he could not afford to keep up the payments.

By the time Giles finished, Ellen was shown to be a struggling devoted mother, Patrick the callous former husband, careless of her and of their child.

The court ruled that Patrick should pay off the full arrears that Ellen claimed at fifty dollars a month—through the court—and made an order that all future alimony and child-support payments should also be made through the court. The ruling was accompanied by the warning that the court would take a very critical view of any failure on Patrick's part to meet his obligations.

Giles came to O'Farrell and said, "He was damned lucky he didn't get hit with perjury."

"So Pallister wasn't so good after all?"

"I felt sorry for him," Giles said. "You get a client who bullshits, there's no way you can win."

O'Farrell hurried from the courtroom ahead of Jill and Ellen, wanting to catch Patrick, which he did at the door leading out into the street. Patrick pretended not to hear the first shout, only stopping when O'Farrell overtook him and stood in front of him.

"You get all that, shithead!" O'Farrell demanded.

"Get out of the way, for Christ's sake," said Patrick, trying to push by.

O'Farrell didn't move. He said, "But that's just the point, shithead. Getting out of your way is something I am *not* going to do. I'm going to be in your way all the time, from now on. You be so much as an hour late, just once, in looking after my daughter and Billy, I'm going to have you back in court so fast there'll be skid marks. There won't be a moment when I'm not watching and waiting for you to fuck up. You hear me!"

On the way back to the apartment, Jill said, "I never imagined it would be possible to show Patrick up quite so clearly for what he is."

"You were right, both of you. He is a bastard, isn't he?" said Ellen. O'Farrell hoped that at last she believed it.

When they got back, the blips on the answering machine indicated there had been some calls without messages being left. O'Farrell had made the drinks, handed them around, and was saying, "I think we can celebrate," when the telephone sounded again. He answered it with his glass in his hand, thinking it might be something or someone to do with the hearing, Giles for instance.

"I've been trying to get you all day," said Petty.

"There's something I'd like us to talk about fairly urgently. You can get away, can't you?"

It was a brief conversation. O'Farrell agreed, without any questions.

As he replaced the receiver, Petty said to the man with him, "You absolutely sure about giving him the position?"

"Of course I'm sure," McCarthy said. "O'Farrell's a loyal operative, proved over a number of years, isn't he? What could be more fitting than promotion?"

THIRTY

"It *is* an emergency," Erickson stressed, in immediate support of the division chief's proposal. "You can understand that, can't you?"

There were black scuff marks on the wall by the radiator, as if the deputy sat there a lot, swinging his leg back and forth like he was doing now. O'Farrell said, "I wouldn't have used the word 'emergency.'"

"Come on!" Petty said from behind the desk of the Lafayette Square office, his voice that of a reasonable man being misunderstood. He went on, "We wouldn't be putting it to you if there were any alternative! But there isn't. You're the only one who's studied completely the Rivera file, who knows and believes the assignment should be carried out—"

"There's no time to prepare anyone else. . . ." Erickson picked up.

"The Madrid conference starts in a week," Petty said. "It can't be anyone else. . . ."

". . . really no time . . ."

The only one who knows and believes, O'Farrell thought. He wasn't sure he knew or believed anything anymore. He tried to remember the leisurely, logical conversations he'd had with Lambert at Fort Pearce, but couldn't. Not the actual words and arguments. There was just the impression at the end that what he did—what he'd done in the past—was right. O'Farrell said, "What's so important about it being done in Spain? Why not allow the time to brief someone else? There are other places."

"After what happened in England, Rivera is wrapped up tighter than a baby," Erickson said. "In England it would never work."

"Why should security be any less in Madrid?" O'Farrell persisted.

"Because in Madrid the security people will have *all* the conference delegates to protect," Petty replied at once.

"He'll still have Cuban protection, presumably?"

"Not as complete again as in London," Erickson said. "We've checked the Cuban delegation. There are only four security personnel."

"I have a family problem, in Chicago. I don't want to be out of the country at this time," O'Farrell said. He hesitated. "In fact, I said this was going to be a turnaround trip. I'm expected back tomorrow."

"You mentioned family difficulties when you called," Petty said. "Anything we can do? Not just personally; the Agency as well, I mean."

O'Farrell was surprised at the offer. And at the apparent sympathy. "I don't think so, but thank you," he said. "My grandson is caught up in a little bother." *Little* bother? O'Farrell questioned himself at once. It hadn't seemed little over the past few days. Still didn't. Which was why Jill had been astonished when he'd announced he had to return to Washington. They hadn't argued—because, of course, they never argued—but O'Farrell knew it was the closest they'd come for a long time, on Jill's part at least. That's

why he'd promised to fly back the following day, to minimize the upset.

"Kids!" Erickson shrugged, as if he knew all about it
and was having the same problems himself.

"The conference starts in a week," Petty said. "Due to
last just four days. So the whole business can't last any
longer than twelve days. America is sending an official
delegation, so we have access to all the security arrangements being considered by the Spanish: routes, timings,
everything. It won't need the usual reconnaissance."

"Operation," "assignment," "business," O'Farrell noted:
all the meaningless ambiguities to avoid the real word,
"murder." Flatly he said, "I don't want to do it." He
waited for an emotion: fear, at the awareness of how the
refusal would affect him, relief, at finally saying it after so
much agonizing, so much doubt. He didn't feel anything at
all and was positively disappointed. Petty was not looking
at him. Instead the man's attention was entirely upon
Erickson.

Petty said, "You were right."

Erickson shrugged a so-what shrug but didn't say anything.

O'Farrell, misunderstanding, supposed it was obvious
that the two men would have discussed his reaction before
his arrival that morning. Wanting to fill the strangely embarrassing silence, he said, "After what happened in London, what else did you expect me to say?"

There was an odd expression on Petty's face when he
looked back to O'Farrell, as if he had forgotten that the
man was even in the room. The blankness went, but there
did not appear to be full recognition. Petty said, "This
isn't going to sound right . . . not sound right at all."

"I don't understand," O'Farrell said, confused.

Petty gestured toward his deputy. "He warned me it
wouldn't sound right if I did it this way. But I didn't want
to make it seem like a condition. I thought you'd agree,

you see. Then it would have come out altogether differently. Now it won't; no way."

"I really don't understand a word you're saying," O'Farrell protested, bewildered.

Petty selected one of the carved-bowl pipes tidily racked on his desk, lighted up, and emitted thunderclouds of smoke. O'Farrell thought what a useful ploy it was for delaying a discussion. The pipe going, Petty said, "There is no other way of saying it, except straight out."

"I'd like that," O'Farrell said.

It wasn't, however, Petty who began. From his windowsill perch Erickson said, "There's been a big personnel review at Langley, covering all the departments. . . ."

"Including ours . . ." Petty said, on cue. "There's going to be a lot of changes: dead wood cut away, a lot of reshuffling. . . ."

"And you feature on the list. . . ." Erickson said.

The speed of his being dumped surprised O'Farrell. He knew that it was to be expected, because of his refusal, but he'd imagined there would be some cosmetic interim period, a week or two before the hidden privileges began to be stripped away. He tried to think of something to say but couldn't.

"High on more than one list," Petty said. "For all our secrecy and deniability, there's a lot of respect for you . . . a lot of respect."

It sounded just like the enforced-retirement speech O'Farrell suspected it to be: before presenting the much-deserved gold watch, the managing director talked at length of dedication and loyalty over many years. . . . The difference here was that the speech was in stereo, from two speakers. And there wasn't going to be any gold watch. Feeling he should contribute something, O'Farrell said, "That's nice to know."

"Which is going to be recognized . . ." Erickson announced. The man's swinging heel scuffed another black smear among all the others, a shape vaguely resembling a question mark.

"How'd you feel about working here?" Petty asked. "Permanently here, I mean. With Don and me."

O'Farrell looked from one man to the other, his initial, irrational thought how unusual it was to hear Petty refer to the other man by his Christian name. Frowning, he said, "But I *do* work with you both."

Petty smiled. "Ever wonder why Chris Winton was never replaced as second deputy?"

The asthmatic bachelor who'd been the third member of the group when he'd first joined the department, O'Farrell remembered. He said, "A long time ago. I supposed there was a good enough reason that was none of my business."

"There was a good enough reason. . . ." Erickson started.

"And now it's very much your business," Petty finished. "Winton wasn't replaced because there was no one good enough, no one with the necessary mental strength and qualifications to fill the position. The feeling at Langley is that there is, now; that you should get the job."

O'Farrell was astonished and had to call upon every last bit of his training not to show it. His mind raced. He would no longer be in the field, no longer required to kill. The most important consideration. No reduction in his income. Essential, with all the family demands. No abrupt overseas trips, so he'd always be available to sort out Ellen's problems. What about drawbacks? He didn't think . . . And then he did, brought up with a jolt. He said, "No, it doesn't come out right at all, does it?"

"I explained!" Petty insisted.

"So explain it some more," O'Farrell said. "Has my promotion already been decided? Or does it depend upon my finishing the Rivera assignment? No Spain, no promotion?"

The looks were very obvious between Petty and Erickson. Petty poked into the bowl of his pipe with a pointed metal spike he took from the pipe rack. He said, "We've both been interviewed, separately and together. Both made it clear we very much want you on board. . . ."

"You've got to believe that!" Erickson said. "We really do want you here. It would be a terrific team. . . ."

"But no decision has been reached?" O'Farrell asked.

Petty shook his head. "No."

"Nor will it be if I refuse the Rivera assignment?" Why had he been so contemptuous earlier of the ambiguities? Why didn't he say "kill" or "murder"?

"That doesn't necessarily follow," Petty said. "It shouldn't affect any decision."

"Shouldn't," O'Farrell said. "But it will."

"Not if I explain it properly. Which I will," the division director promised.

So what was it? O'Farrell demanded of himself. A genuine although badly phrased invitation, for which Petty had already apologized? Or the ultimatum he'd accused them of presenting? As an ultimatum it had to be the clumsiest, most heavy-handed ever put forward in the history of ultimatums. So bad, in fact, that it practically supported the director's apology for making the offer the wrong way around.

A loud silence built up in the room. Petty let his pipe go out and Erickson stopped swinging his leg. Both looked at O'Farrell, obviously expecting a response. O'Farrell looked back at them, wishing he could think of one but not able to, because there was so much at so many different levels to consider and decide upon. It was Petty who broke.

"That's the best I can do." The man shrugged. "I'll make the strongest pitch I can. Okay?"

"When?" O'Farrell asked, speaking at last.

"When?" Petty frowned.

"When do you have to make this strong pitch?"

"There's a meeting penciled in for Friday. I guess that's when it'll be. I haven't heard any differently."

Three days' time, O'Farrell thought. "I just can't do it; not after what happened in London. It's—" He stopped, seeking the right way to express himself. "I don't know. I just can't do it. . . ."

"Your personal decision," Petty said. "That's the way it's always been. . . ."

"Always will be," Erickson said. "You going back to Chicago tomorrow?"

"Sometime," O'Farrell agreed. Why the vagueness? He had a confirmed reservation on a noon flight.

"Hope everything turns out all right," Petty said. "Don't forget: if there's anything we can do, just ask."

O'Farrell didn't catch that noon flight. After the interview at Lafayette Square he drank more than he had for a long time. He took the martini pitcher into the den of the Alexandria house and sat in head-sunk reflection, making and unmaking decisions until it became difficult to rationalize at all. But not because of the booze. O'Farrell still felt in complete control of himself when the pitcher was empty. His difficulty was the difficulty that always existed: his complete and utter aloneness, never having anyone with whom he could discuss anything. And then he remembered that there *was* someone.

O'Farrell used the unlisted number that John Lambert had given him, feeling a positive stomach lurch of relief when the psychologist answered at once. Lambert said of course they could meet—that had always been the understanding—but not until the afternoon of the following day. O'Farrell agreed that would be fine. He canceled the Chicago flight and didn't book another and reached Jill at their daughter's apartment at the first attempt, too.

The same brittle tenseness there'd been in Jill's voice when he'd announced the Washington visit came back when O'Farrell apologized for having to extend the trip. There was a lot of "what the hell" and "for Christ's sake" (and "fuck" once or twice) but O'Farrell remained level-voiced and very calm. There was something important that had come up, jobwise, and he had to see it through. There was no practical purpose in his being in Chicago; everything that had to be done had been. She asked how long and O'Farrell hesitated and said he wasn't sure; just one day later than she'd expected him back, maybe. When Jill had worked the anger out of her system, she asked suddenly if there were anything wrong and O'Farrell hoped she missed the hesitation in his reply. There was nothing wrong, he assured her. He promised to tell her all about it when he got up to Chicago; there'd be more than enough time to create some fantasy about embezzlement inquiries or clerical mistakes. After so much practice, he'd become expert at such stories. Jill said she loved him and he said he loved her, unusually anxious to end the conversation. She sensed the keenness, asking if there were anything else the matter apart from work, and O'Farrell said of course there wasn't.

He decided against any more to drink, leafing instead through the mail that had built up. He dumped the circulars and slipped the bills into his diary for payment. The only letter left was from the historical society that had provided most of his ancestor's archive. There was a lot of photocopied material. A cover letter explained the society had been bequeathed several storage boxes of records kept until now by a family who'd researched their own ancestor's arrival and subsequent career in America. The man had been a judge who'd actually sat upon some of the first O'Farrell's cases. From their past dealings the society had known, without the need for an offering letter, that O'Farrell would want the copies, for which they enclosed their bill. They hoped O'Farrell would find the shipment useful.

O'Farrell flicked through the shipment without actually reading any of it, which was as unusual with such new and potentially exciting material as wanting quickly to terminate a conversation with his wife. There had to be about fifteen to twenty legal-sized sheets and other pages of different sizes. O'Farrell put them tidily upon the top of his bound archival books, which he didn't bother that night to open. Which was the most unusual deviation from habit of all.

O'Farrell arrived early at Fort Pearce but Lambert had already given the authority for his entry to all the checkpoints. The psychologist actually came in person to the last guardpost to sign him through.

Lambert appeared to have walked down because he rode in O'Farrell's immaculate Ford back to the barracks-type building in which the man had his office.

"So how are things with Billy?"

Momentarily the question startled O'Farrell, and then he recalled the telephone call for help from Chicago. He said, "I was going to thank you. The psychiatrist you recommended, Mrs. Dwyer, has been tremendous."

"Ms.," Lambert said. "It's Ms. She's not married. So what's happened?"

O'Farrell told the other man, and Lambert said, "Sounds like Patrick is a contender for the shit-of-the-year award."

O'Farrell stopped carefully in the parking lot behind the building, choosing a space where he thought the Ford would be least likely to be hit by another motorist. He said, "There'd be no contest, believe me."

As they walked side by side into the building, Lambert said, "Do you think all that you threatened will keep him in line?"

"I don't think the bastard is capable of being straight if he wanted to be. At least we've got the court order now; we can pressure him. And Christ, am I going to pressure him if he screws up!"

Lambert led the way into the windowless office. O'Farrell, his previous visits in mind, saw that again the impossibly young-looking man was as always dressed with Ivy League smartness, the willing guest always ready for a party invitation. Without asking, Lambert filled a plastic mug from the permanently steaming coffeepot and handed it to O'Farrell. For once the television wasn't on.

"So what's the problem?" the psychologist asked.

He didn't know how to begin, O'Farrell realized; not in a way that would properly convey his conflict of feelings to the other man. He looked around the room, trying to sort out his thoughts. There appeared to be several new rubber trees since last time, neatly planted in individual pots, but their leaves still looked dry. Near one stood a watering can. O'Farrell hadn't thought rubber trees had to be watered very much.

"I asked what the problem was," Lambert said.

"I want to explain it all so you'll get the true picture, so that you'll understand," O'Farrell said. "It's important that you understand how it all fits together."

Lambert grinned openly at him. "Why not stop trying to think for me?" the man suggested. "I've got degrees that say I can understand things pretty well."

"I wasn't being offensive."

"Just let it come out whichever way it comes."

Which was what O'Farrell did, and he wasn't happy with how it sounded. Several times he backtracked, explaining parts of the meeting with Petty and Erickson quite differently on the second attempt than on the first; at other times he petered out in the middle of a sentence, unable to find an ending. At last he stumbled to a halt and said, "I didn't get that across at all, did I?"

"I got most of it," Lambert assured him. "It certainly looks like an ultimatum. I just can't believe anyone could make it as awkwardly as that."

"That's something I find hard to believe," O'Farrell agreed.

"He's your boss; you've worked for him for a lot of years," the psychologist said. "Is he normally as half-assed as that?"

"The opposite," O'Farrell said. "Ours isn't a division that can allow any misunderstanding."

"So let's turn it over the other way," Lambert said. "If it's not an ultimatum, then Rivera and Madrid don't matter. And you're still in line for the promotion."

"Unless the panel or the director or whoever is making the final decision change their minds *because* of my refusal."

"Good point," Lambert agreed. "This promotion means a lot to you?"

O'Farrell paused before replying; he wouldn't try to explain it because he was unsure if he could. He said, "A hell of a lot."

"All the hidden extras, able to go on supporting everyone in the family and no longer having to be the executioner?" Lambert offered.

How was it that Lambert could sum it all up in about twenty words when he'd thrashed about for hours and still couldn't put it in a comprehensible sentence? O'Farrell said, "I hadn't thought about it as simply as that."

"You'd still be involved, of course," Lambert pointed out. "You wouldn't be pulling the trigger or whatever, but with Petty and Erickson you'd be agreeing to the targets and initiating the operations."

"I know that," O'Farrell said.

"Still killing, then?" Lambert pressed. "The only difference would be that you wouldn't be doing it yourself. You don't find any difficulty there?"

"I thought we agreed on the need—and the justification—when I was here after the London mistake?"

Lambert nodded. "I thought we did, too. I was curious whether you'd changed your mind."

"No," O'Farrell said. "I haven't changed my mind."

"Not easier, perhaps, to be the judge rather than the man carrying out the sentence?"

Lambert hadn't summed it all up, not in those first twenty or so words. It had taken him just a few more. Now he'd succeeded: everything laid out in the open, like items on a display stand. With that realization came another, the awareness of why he'd had so much difficulty expressing himself. It had all been so much bullshit the previous night, slumped in the den, pretending to examine all the options. He hadn't examined anything, apart from the bottom of his martini glass. He'd refused to let himself think the thoughts that Lambert was making him examine now. O'Farrell said, "I would think both are equally difficult. It isn't easy to kill a man. Or deciding if he should be killed."

"I never supposed it was," Lambert said.

The other man appeared briefly discomfited, and O'Farrell couldn't understand why. As if in reminder, O'Farrell said, "I've definitely told them I wouldn't do it: go to Spain and eliminate Rivera." He detected an old petulance in his voice.

"You've already told me, several times," Lambert said.

It seemed to be a moment—and a matter—for long and heavy silences, thought O'Farrell. As with Petty the previous day, it was Lambert who broke it.

The psychologist shook his head and said, "I'm not going to do it."

"Do what?" O'Farrell asked. Now it was he who was discomfited.

"Make your decision for you. That's what you want me to do, isn't it? Tell you what to do. And I won't do that."

There was the temptation to argue, to insist that wasn't why he'd sought the meeting, but O'Farrell knew it would have been a hollow protest, impossible to maintain. His reliance upon Lambert, a man he scarcely knew, was something else he had refused to admit to himself until this very moment, and he was disturbed by the awareness. It was a reversal of everything to which he was accustomed. Everyone—all the family—relied upon him. He was the strong one, the person who provided the guidance and the answers. He didn't like the opposite, the implied weakness. He said, "I wanted to talk through the options. You were the only person I knew with sufficient clearance." He even sounded reliant!

"And we've done just that, talked through the options. All of them," Lambert said. "Now it's time to decide. For *you* to decide."

"I told you—" O'Farrell began, but Lambert interrupted him.

"If it *were* an ultimatum, absurdly put though it was, you can change your mind," the psychologist said. "Petty's meeting isn't until Friday. And Petty can't have given the assignment to anyone else, because you told me yourself there isn't time to brief anyone else."

"You sound as if you think I should do just that: change my mind," O'Farrell said.

Lambert shook his head. "I told you I'm not going to do it, not decide for you," he said. "It doesn't matter a damn to me whether you change your mind or not. My official association with you ended when you left here the last time. What I am trying to do, because you asked to see me, is show you the way to face up to the reality of the situation. You've already made it clear you're not going to do it, which would normally effectively retire you from the department. Fine, if that's what you feel like doing. But there's the promotion possibility. And I know all the reasons why that's personally important. Petty says he'll do his best for it not to be affected. I don't know him well, but from what I do know he seems to be a pretty straight guy. So let's trust him. Again, fine. You wanted all the options? There they are, spelled out for you again."

O'Farrell used the psychologist's phone to call Lafayette Square, using Petty's direct and unlisted line. "I'm prepared to do it," he announced.

"I'd hoped you would be," Petty said.

"Amsterdam!" Rivera echoed, to the arms dealer's announcement.

"And I want the money," Belac insisted.

"You know it's available," the ambassador assured him. "Are you there now?"

"Not yet," Belac lied. "Listen carefully: take a note. Six-eight, three-two, four-four."

"What's that?" Rivera asked, although he already guessed.

"A telephone number you are to ring, in three days' time," Belac said. With the *City of Athens* and its load of shit still miles from anywhere on the high seas, the Belgian thought, gloating.

"What's wrong with an address?" Rivera queried.

"I told you already," Belac reminded him. "I'm not having you lead the Americans to me."

He'd questioned sufficiently, Rivera decided. Belac was on the hook once more and he didn't want the man slipping off. "In three days," he agreed.

"Don't try and cheat me," Belac said.

The cocky bastard, thought Rivera. He said, "I've never tried to cheat you. It's been a misunderstanding."

"I don't want any more misunderstandings," Belac said.

Rivera summoned the DGI chief the moment he disconnected from the Belgian's call. Carlos Mendez listened intently to Rivera's edited account of the conversation and said, "We'll need to leave tomorrow, early. I'll make the travel arrangements. And speak to Havana."

Rivera frowned. "Belac isn't expecting me for another three days."

Mendez gave a palm-up gesture. "I don't mean to be presumptuous, Excellency," he said. "But this has to be my way. All of it."

Rivera's frown deepened. Presumption was precisely the attitude of the other man. He had to let it pass without correction for the moment, but he made a mental note not to let it continue.

Rivera left the embassy early, wanting as much time as possible with Jorge. He got to the Hampstead house just after the boy's bath. Jorge came down the stairs still warm, smelling clean. And smelling of something else. It was the soap Estelle had used, Rivera realized at once. Had Jorge used it accidentally, picking up a piece that had been over-looked after Estelle's death? Or had he intentionally ransacked some bathroom cabinet, searching it out?

They went through the established ritual of such evenings, Rivera sitting with a drink while Jorge recounted the events of the day, and then Rivera talking of anything that had happened at the embassy that he thought might interest the boy, which was not very much.

Rivera announced the following day's departure, without saying where he was going, and apologized for the suddenness of the trip. Jorge, already warned of the Madrid conference, accepted the news quite contentedly. He asked his father when he would be returning and Rivera said definitely the day the conference ended, the sixteenth.

"Three days before school lets out," Jorge said brightly.

Rivera knew of the extended, August-into-autumn holiday, of course, but he'd forgotten the precise dates. "We'll really make it a vacation!" he promised. "You choose the place."

Jorge was briefly silent with the seriousness of a twelve-year-old. Then he said, "Why not Paris, where we're going to live?"

It made perfect sense, Rivera thought. They might even look at likely property, although house hunting was a fairly boring activity for a boy of Jorge's age. "Paris it is," he agreed. "I'll have the arrangements made while I am away."

"Did you talk to Mama about our going to live there?" asked Jorge.

The introduction of Estelle almost off-balanced Rivera. Aware that to show any surprise would be a mistake, he said at once, "No. I hadn't decided about it."

"I think she would have liked it, don't you?"

"Yes," Rivera said, with difficulty. "Yes, I think she would. She was fond of Paris."

"Will you take me to the places you went to with Mama? I'd like to see them; know that she'd seen them, too."

"Yes," Rivera promised. "We'll go to every one."

"I loved Mama," the child declared.

"I loved her, too," Rivera said, for Jorge's benefit.

THIRTY-ONE

NOTHING WAS as Rivera expected. He'd anticipated flying direct to Amsterdam, but they didn't. They went—just he and Mendez—by train and cross-Channel ferry, and again not directly. From Calais, on a journey that required two changes, they traveled through France, going into Luxembourg at Namur and into Germany at Aachen. It was late into the evening before they reached Hannover.

The hotel was very small and dirty, halfway along the Davenshedterstrasse. They went out to eat, choosing a restaurant at random. It was bad. Rivera started to feel vaguely unclean; his skin itched, particularly on his arms, and he went twice to the toilet to wash his hands.

"Has all this really been necessary?" he demanded. Throughout the day he'd had to follow Mendez's lead and he hadn't enjoyed that, either. Mendez clearly had, every minute of it.

"If it weren't, I wouldn't have insisted upon it," said Mendez, almost insolently. "There are far more checks at airports than at train border crossings and you've no reason, official or unofficial, to be in Holland anyway. Isn't it better for your presence to remain completely unknown?"

"I suppose so," Rivera said begrudgingly. "I expected more than just yourself."

"I'm not alone," Mendez said. "There are to be others in Amsterdam."

"From London?"

Mendez pushed away his largely uneaten meal. "Cuba itself. It's safer that way."

Rivera felt the first flicker of apprehension. There might be a mistake and he, José Gaviria Rivera, might get caught up in an apparently squalid incident. Which wouldn't remain squalid at all, once the investigation started.

"You mean they're special. . . ?" Rivera's voice ebbed away, in his search of the word.

"Yes," Mendez said helpfully. "What about protection? Belac, I mean. Does he have a lot of people around him?"

Rivera considered the question, recognizing its implication. "Never," he said, surprised now that he thought about it. "We've only ever met alone, just the two of us. And according to what he told me, he's staying away from Brussels, where he might have some protectors, because of the American investigation. That's why we're meeting in Amsterdam."

Mendez gave a teeth-baring smile. "That's good," he said. "We'll have to make sure, of course. But that sounds good."

The hotel sheets, white in a long distant past, were gray, and the narrow bath was stained and actually dusty from lack of use. Rivera slept remarkably well, the pillow covered with a clean shirt and the one towel between himself and where he lay. When he showered the following morning, the water created an instant grime scum around his feet from the dirt in the bath.

The hotel in Amsterdam was much better. It was a *pension* on Wolvenstratt run by a Dutch doll of a woman, white-aproned, big-busted, and with a polished-apple face permanently creased by smiles. She allocated them adjoin-

ing rooms and hoped they found everything they wanted in
Amsterdam. Rivera said he hoped so, too.

It was a day of pale, near-autumn sunshine and warm
breezes, perfect for a country of gardeners and flower
growers. Rivera and Mendez found a pavement café between the canals, but the intelligence man insisted upon
their sitting inside and at a table at the back.

"Belac's somewhere in Amsterdam," Mendez said.
"You're not due to be here yet. Coincidence really does
occur, sometimes. I don't want to risk your being accidentally seen by the man."

Irritating though it was to be subordinate to Mendez,
the man did appear to be consummately professional,
Rivera admitted to himself. The diplomat nodded understanding and said, "So we're here. What now?"

"For you, very little until the meeting with Belac," said
Mendez. "I have to locate the others already here, although there's little preparation we can make until you
speak with Belac and make your arrangements."

"Shall I be involved in the planning?" Rivera tried to
make the question natural enough, but he was anxious for
the answer. What if the professionals from Cuba seized
Belac, instead of what he expected them to do! The truth
about the withheld money would emerge in minutes. *How*
could he have been so stupid as to have tried to manipu-
late it as he had!

"I'd prefer it if you weren't, but it's necessary," Mendez
said. "They have to follow your lead; they've got to know
you."

The warmth of the day, and their sitting inside rather
than out in the air, could account for the perspiration bubbling on his upper lip, Rivera decided. He said, "What
about the reason for their being here at all? And what they
have to do? Do they know I have to recover something,
before they move?"

"They've been told Belac has cheated us, severely. But
not how. Nothing at all about arms shipments. And noth-

ing, either, about Belac's part in what happened"—Mendez hesitated, considerably—"what happened in London."

Nothing about the money! Rivera thought hopefully. Nothing, that is, providing Mendez were telling the truth. He said, "Will our meeting be today?"

"Tonight," Mendez disclosed. He pushed a slip of paper across the table between them. Written on it was the address of a restaurant on Rapenburgerstratt. "There is a private dining room at the rear. Meet me there at seven."

An order instead of a request, Rivera thought. "Where are you going to be until then?"

"Making contact," Mendez said dismissively. "I'd like you to go back to Wolvenstraat and stay there, until it's time to meet. And don't shop on your way back, buy a gift or a souvenir for Jorge, for instance. There must be no visible record of your ever having been here."

Rivera did exactly what he was told. Back at Wolvenstraat he stood at the window of his room, staring out at the tree-lined street, watching the early buildup of the rush-hour traffic. After that he sat in the only easy chair until he became bored, which was very quickly, so he went back to the window again. The traffic was heavier, a line stretching back from what he assumed to be a canal bridge.

Because of him—at his instigation—a man was going to die in a few hours, Rivera thought. It was an unreal feeling, now that the moment was almost here; difficult to rationalize. There was no guilt; no doubt, either. What then? He didn't want to be part of it, not this close a part; he was a diplomat, not a thug. It made him feel dirty, like he'd felt in the German hotel. He was sweating again, too. Dear God, how glad he'd be when it was all over. Not just this. The ambassadorship and the London embassy and arms purchases: everything.

The run of thoughts led him back to the last evening with Jorge. The totally unexpected reference to Estelle was important. It had been more than reference, in fact: a normal conversation. Rivera was relieved. He took it to mean that the shock, the need to block every memory out, was easing at last. He wouldn't remark about it, of course. He'd continue letting Jorge set the pace. Rivera thought it was important, too, that Jorge wanted to go to Paris for his vacation, knowing it was to be their new home. Perhaps it wouldn't be boring for the boy to house-hunt. Perhaps that's what Jorge wanted, a decisive break from a house and from a city that held so much horror for him. Just as he wanted a decisive break. Rivera couldn't think of anything he wanted to retain from his time in London, apart from his polo. He'd have to put some serious thought to that. Choose the appropriately prestigious club to approach, get the right sort of stabling for the ponies, ship them across well in advance of the season. He didn't want to enter a new club with animals that were below form, unsettled by their trip.

Rivera became claustrophobic long before the scheduled meeting and impulsively set out to walk to Rapenburgerstraat. Obedient to Mendez's warnings not to buy anything, Rivera had no street map, but he found a public one on the side of a tourist stand near the canal bridge. It took him several minutes to locate the street he wanted; it seemed to be a long way away. He began walking purposefully, enjoying being out in the open again despite the onset of the evening's chill, the canal a marker to guide him. Paris would be the place for shopping; Paris would be the place for many things.

Rapenburgerstraat *did* appear to be a long way away, a much greater distance than he'd calculated from the map. He was beginning to feel the effort of unaccustomed walking and abruptly remembered Mendez's further remark about a chance sighting by Belac. He looked almost nervously around for a taxi, relieved when he saw one near the Amstel Bridge.

The traffic had eased by now, so Rivera arrived early at the restaurant. For a few moments he remained uncertainly on the pavement, feeling it would be a mistake to enter the private dining room early, to appear in the role of receiving the others. Instead, on the spur of the moment, he posed himself a personal, private test. There was a tree-shadowed bench just past the junction with the main road. Disregarding the chill, Rivera sat there, in the growing dusk, concentrating absolutely on the brightly lighted restaurant entrance, a Cuban sure he could identify other Cubans as they arrived. He remained there for half an hour, until 7:15, without picking out anyone. The panic was quick to grow. He had the name of the restaurant written on a piece of paper (have to destroy it later) so he couldn't be mistaken. Where were they, then! Had something happened, to make it necessary for everything to be changed? What possibly *could* have happened, at this early stage? Nothing, Rivera thought, grasping for reassurance. Mendez had known where he was, until the last hour at least. The man could have telephoned if there'd been any change. Unless . . . Rivera stopped, his nervousness running ahead of his conjecture, unable to think unless what.

There was an obvious way to find out.

He hurried across the street and entered the restaurant. It was a huge, cavernous place so brightly lighted it made him squint, with all the tables jammed close together. It was already full, because the Dutch habitually eat early, and loud from the clatter of plates and bottles and glasses and the babble of everyone talking and laughing at once. The reservation desk was just inside the door, in front of a zinc-topped bar that stretched the entire length of the right-hand wall. A large section of that was given over to food, too, with most of the stools already occupied.

Rivera was waved cursorily toward the rear and had to ask again before finding his way to the private room. Outside its door he hesitated, unsure whether to knock and then angrily dismissing the doubt. He entered without any warning but stopped again, just inside.

An oval table, set for dinner, stood at the far side of the

room. It had only one vacant place, at the very end. Mendez sat at the other end, the top, clearly in command. There were four other men, two of whom appeared to have stood hurriedly at the sudden opening of the door. All were completely nondescript, bland-suited, blank-faced. Rivera was sure none of them had entered while he'd watched from outside. He hadn't seen Mendez, either. It didn't matter. It had been a ridiculous, meaningless test.

An intricately carved Dutch dresser dominated the wall to Rivera's left. It was stocked with bottles, wine as well as liquor. Also displayed were salads and cheeses and cold meats. Being kept hot on a hot plate were four covered serving dishes.

"We were wondering where you were," said Mendez. "We've been waiting for you. To eat and to talk."

There was an obvious rebuke in the man's voice. Rivera said, "I'm sorry," feeling he had to, but wishing it were avoidable.

There were no introductions and none of the men appeared the slightest bit interested in him. Mendez indicated the place at the far end of the table but at least poured Rivera's wine. At the intelligence chief's suggestion they served themselves food—Rivera declining anything. The talk quickly became a monologue, from Mendez. Rivera inferred as the man spoke that unlike himself and Mendez the four nameless men had flown directly into Amsterdam to spend time becoming familiar with the city's geography. Whenever Rivera's function entered the explanation, Mendez always referred to the ambassador as "him," never once using a name or title.

"Have you done anything about the telephone number he gave?" asked a man to Rivera's right.

Mendez shook his head. "It'll be a public kiosk, easy enough to find," he predicted. "Passersby usually answer a ringing telephone, and we could get the location that way. But it's also a safeguard for Belac, although it's pretty basic. All it takes is a few dollars to some kid to hang around to see if a call *is* made, to find out where it is, and Belac knows someone's looking for it. And for him. It's not worth the risk of frightening him off."

Looking between Mendez and Rivera, the same man said, "What if the meeting is somewhere very public?"

"It doesn't matter where it is," Mendez said. Nodding in Rivera's direction, he said, "You'll be watching him. Once Belac gives him an envelope and leaves, you just follow the man: deal with him at the best time."

That wouldn't work, Rivera realized. Belac was expecting an envelope *from* him, not the other way around! And wouldn't go from the meeting without it. He said, "What if Belac asks me to go somewhere with him instead of making the exchange in the open?"

Mendez gestured around the table. "They'll be with you all the time. But don't remain a moment longer than you have to; you have to get away, to distance yourself, as quickly as possible."

"I know that," Rivera said. He was sweating again, the familiar hollowness deep in his gut. It wasn't going to work! he thought. It had seemed so easy, so plausible, in London. But not now. And there was nothing he could do about it now! He was trapped!

"Are we to move if there is no exchange?" asked a man nearer to Mendez.

Rivera at once saw that the possibility had not occurred to the intelligence chief and he enjoyed the other man's discomfort, despite his own. At the same time he saw a wisp of hope, a way to extricate himself. Before Mendez could reply, Rivera said, "No! That's to be the signal. No one is to move until the envelope is passed over." It was still a desperate gamble, probably impossible if Belac wanted to meet during the day, but it was a chance and he had to seize any chance he saw. Or imagined he saw.

Mendez was slightly flushed at a decision being taken away from him. Rivera stared at the man, waiting for the challenge, but eventually the intelligence chief said, "That's right. No move until that's done."

There was more general discussion in which Rivera took no part, talk about contact procedures and methods of recognition, and Rivera sat listening and looking at the quiet men grouped around the table. I'm sitting with killers, he thought, men who take other men's lives, as a job. More unreality. The voice of Mendez broke into his reflection: "There's nothing more to discuss until tomorrow."

The four showed no sign of leaving, but Mendez rose, and Rivera rose with him. There were nods among them, but otherwise no farewells.

"That wasn't how I imagined something like this being done," Rivera said. He hadn't known how to imagine it.

"Something like this?" Mendez asked, not understanding.

"Planning . . . planning the sort of thing that we were."

"Why not?" The man shrugged. "What better way to gather a group together without suspicion than at a party in a restaurant?"

"Party?"

"The manager, the staff, were told it was a retirement celebration." Mendez looked both ways along the street, waving for a taxi. As they went by the bench upon which Rivera had sat, trying to identify the Cubans entering the restaurant, Mendez said, "Weren't you cold, sitting there as long as you did?"

Rivera, his face burning, didn't reply. There was nothing to say.

There had been a lot of unexpected changes in a very short time, most of them to the good. The tense farewell conversation with Jill, in Chicago, had been the only practical upset and O'Farrell didn't feel as badly about that as he normally might have done. He would have liked, somehow, to tell her why he'd made the decision to go away at this time; how important it was to her and the family. To all of them. But as with so much else it would never be possible. Not completely. He guessed he could talk about the most dramatic development, his official and impressive-sounding promotion ostensibly within the State Department. Special Financial Adviser.

O'Farrell fastened his seat belt for the Madrid landing, letting the title echo in his head, enjoying it. With every reason for enjoyment. Tinged with relief, although that was vague in his mind and he was letting it stay that way. This wasn't another meaningless title, like so many in Washington. This represented an official, provable position within the government, something he'd never had before. Not with this job, anyway. He'd had it in the army, even when he was attached to Special Forces. Known there was authority, legality, behind him. Now he had it again. He wasn't on his own anymore; no longer deniable. It gave him the same rank and the same financial grading as Petty and Erickson. According to Petty, at the meeting just before he'd left Washington, his elevation to join them in Lafayette Square was inevitable, although it still had to be confirmed.

The arrival was announced. O'Farrell gathered up his flight bag and ensured that his briefcase was secure. It contained one of the other surprises, possibly that last revelation he'd ever expected about his great-grandfather. O'Farrell had stuffed the latest material from the historical society into his briefcase at the very moment of walking out of the Alexandria house, to read during the flight, and come across the article very near the top of the pile. He'd thought, initially, it might become the centerpiece of his collection, because it was the only full interview with the man he'd ever discovered.

The astonishment—and O'Farrell genuinely had been astonished—came halfway through. There it was, in black and white, in the man's own words: he'd grown to dislike the role of lawman. The explanation was rambling and badly formed—but then wasn't his own?—and O'Farrell was chilled by the uncomfortable parallels. The old man had talked about the unsound laws of the time. And evidence he considered insufficient to obtain safe and proper convictions under those laws. The most chilling disclosure of all was the one O'Farrell found the easiest to understand. The fear that maybe once—and once was all it had to be—the wrong man, an innocent man, might be sentenced to death.

O'Farrell collected his bags from the carousel, passed unhindered through Customs, and quickly got a taxi to the city. He'd never had that problem, he thought, the familiar reassurance. Never an innocent man. The Vietnamese had been guilty, and the PLO hijacker had been guilty—convicted out of his own mouth—and Leonid Makarevich had been the most guilty of all. With Makarevich the cliché really did fit: that time assassination really had saved lives.

As he began to enter the city, O'Farrell felt the first stir of unease but was not perturbed by it. It wasn't like the London uncertainties. Or even before, when he really started drinking. There was an objective, professional reason here. This time it had to be hurried—everything planned and completed in less than a week—without the normal allowance for preparation. And O'Farrell, the pattern-and-habit man, didn't like any departure from normal. He hoped it would all be okay when he became accustomed to the place: became acclimatized.

Even the usual changes of accommodation wouldn't be possible. His hotel was the Tirol, on the Calle de Princesa, a wide, horn-echoing highway; O'Farrell wished it were quieter. The last time, he consoled himself; just a few days and then never again. He was a Senior Financial Adviser now, a man with an accredited position.

The CIA station chief at the American embassy was a cheerful man, red-faced from obvious blood pressure, named Dick Lewis. He acknowledged Washington's advice of O'Farrell's arrival but carefully scrutinized

O'Farrell's documentation before handing over the material Langley had instructed him to collate.

"Been working for weeks on this goddamned conference," said the man. It was a complaint without any real feeling, the predictable moan of the local operative against faraway headquarters who never understood. "Can't understand what's so important about it."

"You know what Washington bureaucracy is like," O'Farrell commiserated, entering into the required performance. From Petty he knew there was a twenty-strong contingent coming from the Commerce Department, with some observers from the World Bank. He said, "I very much appreciate your getting all this together for me."

Lewis flicked dismissively at the manila package. "What you wanted was easy," he said. "You very much involved, or shouldn't I ask?"

"You shouldn't ask," O'Farrell said. "Actually I'm only caught up peripherally. I'm going to have to use communications later. Ship some stuff in, too, in the diplomatic bag."

"That's my job," Lewis said. "Postmaster to the free world. You gonna have time for a drink or dinner while you're here, maybe?"

"Maybe. I'll let you know," O'Farrell said, avoiding the outright refusal. He said, "What's the Spanish security like? Adequate?"

"I'd choose another side to fight a war with," Lewis said. "I feel sorry for them, though. There're the Basques, in the north, fighting a separatist campaign. Virtually the same thing with Catalan, in the east. With this international conference in the middle, like a ripe plum."

"You expect trouble, then?" O'Farrell asked.

"I'd lay odds," Lewis said. "They're calling on the army and Christ knows what else, but they still can't cover everything. The shit'll hit the fan somewhere, believe me, or Mama didn't call me dick after the size of my appendage."

Lewis was telling him nothing he had not learned from the final meeting with Petty. It was another reason for O'Farrell to be worried. He hadn't operated in a situation like this before, with security authorities anticipating an outrage. He hadn't *ever* operated with security authorities on alert, in fact. He said, "I'll be in touch."

"Anytime," Lewis said. "Don't forget that drink."

The local embassy package consisted entirely of maps and plans and sketches and memoranda, most included to disguise those with which O'Farrell was truly concerned: the plans of the Cuban embassy, and those of the official residence of the Cuban ambassador to Spain, where Rivera was to stay; the protected routes to and from the conference hall; the plans of the conference hall itself; and the timings for the delegates' movements. It was fortunate, O'Farrell supposed, that America's participation had given them access to all this advance information. O'Farrell added a detailed map of the center of the city and with it traced the routes, thoroughly acquainting himself with the locations of the buildings.

Even before reconnoitering on foot, O'Farrell instinctively knew it was going to be difficult, the most difficult yet. Everything was too wide open, too public. *Not enough time to prepare* chanted through his mind. Security everywhere. Army contingents too.

O'Farrell stored and locked all the documentation in his briefcase and sat for several moments staring at it, the doubts jostling for importance in his mind. Abruptly, without warning, he was convulsed by a shudder, his arms and legs visibly vibrating. It hadn't gone, he knew. Despite Lambert's reasoned arguments and logical persuasion—the arguments and the logic he'd said he could accept and really thought he had—O'Farrell recognized the fact that he hadn't been convinced at all.

That he couldn't do it.

But he *had* to do it. All he had at the moment was a title, three fatuous words. And he wouldn't get it, not until

he completed this assignment. However much Petty might
protest and posture, it had been an ultimatum; was still an
ultimatum.

O'Farrell sighed, very deeply. With so little time he
should go out now, tonight, to begin the reconnoiter at
once. He decided upon a drink instead. Maybe two.

THIRTY-TWO

THE LINE was engaged. Rivera stood in the public kiosk, tightly controlling his nervousness, the busy signal
mocking in his ear. He'd tensed himself to hear Belac's
voice, half thought of the words to say in reply to finalize
their meeting. He had never considered a busy signal. It
was an understandable setback if he were calling a public
kiosk as Mendez guessed, but it disturbed him. As frightened as Rivera was, everything had omens and this was
not a good one. He replaced the receiver and pressed the
lever to regain his money, shrugging to Mendez beyond
the glass. The intelligence chief was the nearest to him,
with the others close at hand: two sat in a café just across
the road, drinking coffee, and two were leaning against the
canal rail, but were looking back toward him. Rivera's
most vivid childhood memory was his reluctant appearance in a school drama production, exposed upon a stage
before what at the time had seemed hundreds of people.
He'd hated it and forgotten his lines and made a fool of
himself; he could remember still his embarrassment and
felt it again now, the object of attention from an audience
judging his performance.

He dialed again, fleetingly wondering whether he'd called the wrong number on the first occasion, although he didn't think he had. It was still busy. Every digit had been correct that time. He recovered his money again and shrugged once more at Mendez.

The intelligence chief came right up to the kiosk, frowning. Before the man could speak Rivera said, "It's engaged."

"Engaged? Or out of order?"

Rivera's stomach lurched at the thought of not being able to establish contact at all; there were too many implications in that for his disordered mind to assimilate. "Engaged," he said uncertainly.

"Try again."

Rivera did, and this time it rang clear. Rivera's feelings switchbacked from apprehension to relief and immediately back to apprehension. Mendez remained close to him, close enough perhaps to hear the conversation and Rivera wasn't sure he could risk that. Telephone in hand, he looked pointedly at the intelligence man, who stared back challengingly. He didn't move.

"Yes?" It was Belac's voice.

"I rang at the arranged time," Rivera said. With Mendez so near he *would* be performing: to Mendez, if the man could hear, he had to sound demanding—the wronged and cheated person recovering millions—and to Belac he had to appear misunderstood, even conciliatory, wanting to hand the millions over. Rivera turned his back upon Mendez, trying for a position that would make what was said as indistinct as possible. And then thought of another escape; the switchback climbed toward relief again. He'd never liked switchbacks, even as a kid: they'd made him feel sick then, too.

"Someone was using it," the Belgian said, not bothering with any fuller explanation.

Belac had spoken in English and Rivera had responded automatically in English. But they'd usually conversed in

French! And throughout the journey across France and then here Mendez had shown no knowledge of the language. Reverting to it at once, Rivera said, "This cloak-and-dagger business is absurd."

"I'm imposing the rules," Belac said, confident he was able to do just that. "You got the letter of credit?"

Thank God the man had answered in French! Rivera said, "I want to meet and get the whole thing settled." He decided that sounded sufficiently aggressive, even if Mendez could understand.

"I'm glad to hear it at last," Belac said.

Rivera's nerves were too tightly stretched for the other man's arrogance to upset him; he was scarcely aware of it. He said, "We're supposed to be fixing a meeting."

"I've got to be careful, like I told you," Belac said. "I can't risk the possibility that you might have been followed by the Americans, to get me."

If only you knew, Rivera thought. He managed a definite sigh into the mouthpiece. "I wasn't followed to Paris and I haven't been followed here. What do you want, for Christ's sake!"

"Not for you to lose your temper, for a start," Belac said.

"I'm waiting," Rivera said, refusing to be goaded.

"Don't you think Amsterdam is a beautiful city?"

"Yes," Rivera said flatly, accepting the fact that he had to go along with the other man.

"I've decided we should see it, you and I. The way the tourists see it, that is. There's a canal-boat dock near where Nieuwe Spiegel Straat goes over the Keizers Canal. Make the six o'clock departure; we can see the city lit up for the night."

"Yes," Rivera said, shortly again. He'd tried to guess how Belac would stage the encounter, of course; a canal trip had never even entered his mind. It could hardly be more public, encapsulated with God knows how many others! It would definitely be impossible for Mendez—for any of them—to make a move against the man in surroundings like that! He said, "How long's the trip?"

"Why's that important?" Belac snapped back at once.

"No reason," Rivera stumbled, regretting the careless
question. He was finding it difficult to hold single, sensible thoughts; three or four words would come into his
mind but then drift away, and others, unconnected, would
get in the way when he tried to call them back.

"You in a hurry to keep another appointment?"

"I wasn't thinking," Rivera said, retreating further.
Please don't let Mendez speak French, because this wasn't
forceful or demanding at all!

There was a silence from the other end of the line, so
protracted that Rivera suddenly thought the other man had
disconnected. He said, "Hello! You there!" and wished he
hadn't when Belac said, "Yes, I'm still here."

"I'll be at the dock at six o'clock," Rivera said briskly,
trying to recover.

"A little before six o'clock," the other man stipulated.
"It's a popular trip this time of the year. Don't want to find
we can't get on, do we?"

"A little before," Rivera agreed.

They gathered around the café table, all of them listening in various attitudes of attention as Rivera set out the
arrangements.

"Careful bastard," Mendez said when the ambassador
finished.

"Could be clever, too," said one of the others.

"Nothing will be possible aboard a packed canal boat,
will it?" Rivera said.

"It will still provide an identification," Mendez reassured him. "That's all that matters."

Desperately Rivera wished that really were all that mattered; he'd never be able to spend any length of time with
Belac—a few minutes even—without Belac demanding
some sight of the money draft.

"These boats don't let passengers off during the tour,"

said one of the Cubans, showing the benefit of their extra day's reconnaissance, but further unsettling Rivera. "So he'll disembark at Nieuwe Spiegel, where he started."

"Good area?" Mendez queried.

"Adequate," the spokesman said. "I've known better."

"We need to look at it in detail, now we've got a definite location," Mendez said. "Divide into two pairs, positively no contact with each other. Tourist cover: cameras, travel bags, maps, stuff like that. I'll split separately again."

Rivera let the planning talk swirl around him, only half listening. There was so much that could go wrong! So many assumptions that could be mistakenly drawn. Why had he—Rivera stemmed the familiar demand, the mental whine of self-pity; it wasn't a question to which he'd find any better answer than he had already. Rivera was aware of everyone except Mendez standing up from the table and brought his attention back to the group, but again, as on the previous night, there were no farewell gestures.

"There's not a lot for you to do for a few hours," Mendez said. "You might as well get something to eat."

"I'm not hungry," Rivera said. The sickness was in fact bubbling within him, threatening to erupt. He hoped he could control it.

"You all right?" Mendez asked solicitously. The concern was not for Rivera himself but for any difficulty arising in the part the ambassador had to play.

"I'm fine," Rivera said, wishing he were.

He remained at the table after the other Cuban left, forcing another coffee upon himself to claim occupancy. After that he wandered without direction or awareness of his surroundings, occupied entirely in the self-justifying inward debate necessary to steel himself for what was to come. It shouldn't be difficult pinpointing Belac for retribution, after what the bastard had done. Wrong to be nervous. Wrong to be frightened. Positively dangerous, in fact, because if he were frightened he'd make mistakes he

couldn't risk making. Fumble the supposed exchange, to make Mendez curious maybe. Or worse, by his
attitude, alert Belac that he was being targeted. Give the
man the chance to escape. He couldn't let that happen; it
was inconceivable that Belac should escape. So he had to
stay calm. Calm and controlled. Not difficult, he told himself again. Belac was a killer. The man had murdered
Estelle; arranged it at least. Thrown Jorge into shock. And
cheated. Or tried to cheat. Been caught, though. Now
came the punishment. Not, actually, his decision. Havana's
decision. The correct one, of course. Belac deserved everything that was coming to him, everything and more.

It was a clock striking that brought Rivera out of himself: the sound, reminding him that time was important,
not the hour itself, which he was too late to catch. He
checked his own watch, saw it was a quarter past five, and
stared around, with no idea where he was. The taxi driver
spoke bad English but better French, although there was
still some difficulty before the man properly understood
the destination. Rivera rode on the edge of his seat, arm
held so he could constantly see the time. He shouldn't
have left it so late! Stupid to have wandered so long and
so far, without concentrating upon what he was doing! He
should have— Stop it! he told himself. No panic. Plenty of
time. Remain calm. Controlled.

It was past the half hour when they reached the landing
stage, a well-organized tourist attraction with metal rails
arranged to channel customers into an orderly line toward
the tickets and the glass-roofed boats beyond. Except there
was no line. A board promised a six o'clock departure,
and as he entered the metaled walkway Rivera saw there
was a boat already waiting. It appeared moderately filled,
perhaps slightly less than half the seats occupied. Rivera
purchased his ticket and had it punched at the gangway
and bent forward to enter the viewing deck. It was entirely
upon one level, benches and seats running the complete

...un apart from the aisle breaks. The glass canopy spanned from rail to rail, giving a panoramic view apart from the thin support ribs, which caused hardly any obstruction.

Mendez was in a rear seat, immediately inside the door, so that he had a full view of the observation area. Another Cuban whom Rivera recognized was three rows ahead, on the same side. A second was much nearer the front.

Rivera edged forward to a seat five rows short of the leading Cuban, liking the layout of the boat. He put his coat down to reserve the seat beside him. Any conversation or exchange between himself and Belac would be more difficult for the others to monitor than he'd imagined!

"It was good of you to reserve me a seat."

Belac spoke in French, taking his lead from that morning's conversation. He was hatless but wore a light raincoat and carried a tourist map. Rivera nodded his head and moved his coat. Belac sat without removing his.

"I watched you arrive," the arms dealer said.

"By myself," Rivera said. Was his feeling revulsion? Or fear? Revulsion, he assured himself. He had nothing to fear from this man.

"It would seem so."

"How long are you going on like this, dodging around Europe?" Rivera asked.

"For a while yet," Belac confided. "I know the system. At the moment they're trying to make a case for another indictment. So they want to know where I am, hoping to lure me somewhere to be arrested. The search will slacken off when someone else becomes more important."

"You're certainly very careful."

"Didn't I tell you I was when we first met?"

"I don't remember," Rivera said. "Maybe."

"What happened to your wife was terrible," Belac said almost formally. "You have my sympathy."

How could he do it! Rivera thought, incredulous; how

could Belac sit there and parrot the words when he'd been the instigator! There wasn't the nervousness he'd feared; no threatening sickness, either. Rivera decided it was going to be easy leading this man to his destruction. He said, "Thank you." His voice was calm, controlled, just like it was supposed to be.

Through the glass canopy Rivera could see men moving among the mooring lines, preparing to release the boat. A sound—he wasn't sure if it were a bell or a horn—signaled what he presumed was their departure.

"Let's go!" Belac demanded with sudden urgency.

"What!"

He turned to see the Belgian already standing, looking down at him. "Go!" Belac repeated. "Come on!"

Rivera hesitated, not knowing what to do, and then stumbled up after the man. He was confused, conscious of everyone looking at him. Mendez's face was a mask, but its very blankness showed his fury as they swept by. Rivera actually did stumble, following the other man back up the gangway. Belac was at the top, near the rails, engaged in a shoulder-shrugging apology to the ticket collector by the time Rivera got there.

"What the hell. . . !" Rivera erupted.

Belac turned, smiling, and settled with his arms against the rail, gazing back at the canal boat. "Elementary caution," he said. "You might have thought you traveled here without company, but the Americans would hardly have announced their presence, would they? You'd be a suspect as well. They would have followed us onto the boat, though. And now, if you were under surveillance, they'll follow us off again. So we'll know, won't we? And I can laugh in their faces because here in Holland they can't touch me!"

Neither would anyone else be able to touch the man, Rivera realized, the first cohesive thought to come through the bewilderment. He could actually see Mendez and the other two Cubans he'd earlier identified, each in clear profile because all three were sitting gazing straight ahead, refusing to look toward the shore. Rivera strained to see through the glass, to pick out the others who would have boarded after Belac, but couldn't. It didn't matter; nothing they could do now if they were going to remain unsuspected. *Could be clever, too.* That had been the remark from one of the Cubans. Rivera hadn't known what the man meant then but he did now; knew it horrifyingly well. In one simple move Belac had reversed everything. Saved himself from the planned retribution. Worse, Rivera assessed, he'd been separated from his protectors, the men who were going to keep *him* safe! Rivera gripped the rail, beneath the concealment of his coat, needing to stop the shaking. Alone; he was alone with a man prepared to kill! Armed too; of course Belac would be armed! Wasn't that his business! Armed and prepared to kill, like he'd been prepared to kill before.

Could he refuse to pay? Declare that he knew all about the worthless cargo and say their deal was off? He'd confronted the man before. But before he hadn't known how far Belac would go. He couldn't do anything but pay, to get the man away. Rivera was terrified.

The gangway was withdrawn, and the boat edged away from the canal wall. From where they watched they heard, although not clearly, the beginning of the guide's commentary. A girl, Rivera saw; quite pretty.

Belac turned to him, still smiling, and said, "So! All's well!"

"I'd already told you that," Rivera said. "It was completely unnecessary."

Belac led the way through the zigzag of railings; because they were spaced narrowly, to maintain a single file of people, Rivera had to trail behind, follow-my-leader fashion. Over his shoulder, Belac said, "It would have been a boring ride anyway. And I don't like boats."

The man appeared very sure of himself, Rivera thought; cockily so. With much more reason than he knew. To extend the conversation, although he didn't know why, Rivera began, "What did—" and then stopped because he saw them. The Cuban who'd actually made the remark about cleverness was standing on the far corner, his companion at his elbow. Both were studying something the first man carried, a map or a pamphlet. Safe! Rivera thought, euphorically. He was safe after all! It could still work, still be all right. He could still win! Up went the switchback of emotion.

The Belgian was waiting at the end of the delineated walkway. "Yes?" he said curiously.

"What explanation did you give for us leaving like that?" Rivera improvised. Only two of the squad. So a lot would depend upon him now. He would have to lead and hope they followed properly, anticipating him. Safe! he told himself again, his mind held by the single, most important fact. He was safe!

"That we'd realized the trip wouldn't allow us the time necessary to catch our flight home," the Belgian said. He extended his hand, palm upward, offering the money. "I got a refund on the tickets. Take it. That's what we've met for, isn't it? To settle debts."

Rivera took the florins, saying nothing. Belac was gloating, he knew, imagining himself very much in charge. Enjoy, Rivera thought; gloat on. Not much longer now. To gloat himself, Rivera said, "Yes. We're here to settle debts."

He set off along the canal-bordering road, wanting the Belgian to follow him now, determined to reverse their roles. As he walked he put on his coat, using the maneuver to glance behind. The two Cubans were following, but very casually, and farther behind than he would have expected.

"Hey!" Belac protested. "Where we going?"

"Walking awhile," Rivera said. He guessed he was vaguely circling the center of the city, through the part crisscrossed by canals. Would it be quieter, ahead? He didn't know—why hadn't he listened to their planning, the previous night!—but it was logical that the two following wouldn't move unless it were quiet, with few people around.

"What's there to walk for?" Belac demanded. "Just give me what you owe me. Now!"

The man stopped, which gave Rivera another opportunity to turn. He was relieved to see the two Cubans had moved quite a good deal closer. He said, "Don't we have things to talk about?" and continued on.

The Belgian remained unmoving for a few seconds and then had to hurry to catch up. Rivera enjoyed having the other man running after him. How it had begun and how it was going to end, he reflected. It was very satisfying.

"What's there to talk about?" Belac demanded, coming alongside.

For the first time Rivera caught a note of uncertainty in the man's voice and decided he had to beware of it. Rivera had intended to humiliate Belac absolutely, openly letting the man know how he'd failed abysmally, in everything. But now he reconsidered. He couldn't predict how Belac would react if taunted too far. Rivera refused to deprive himself completely, though. He deserved some triumph. It was quite dark now, and the cafés and shops had given way to canalside houses, so it was quieter, too. He knew it would only be a brief gap before more cafés and brighter lights near the next bridge. He said, "Debts, like you said. Value for money might be a better way of putting it."

"You're not making sense," the Belgian said. His voice was frayed by further doubt.

There had to be the apparent exchange for the benefit of the following men. Rivera took the envelope from inside his jacket, completely concealed from behind but so that Belac could see it. The Belgian reached out, greedily, and at that moment, Rivera opened a space between them and turned, so the impression was of his receiving from the

Belgian's outstretched hand rather than offering it. Just as quickly he put it back and Belac said, "What the. . . !"

"That was it," Rivera said, refusing to stop, carrying the Belgian along with him. "That was the twelve million dollars you were owed, the twelve million you're not going to get."

"I warned you—" Belac started, but Rivera talked over him, hurriedly now, anxious to get it over because he could see the next bridge ahead, with its shops and restaurants.

"I know about your warnings. Like I know about those tanks." Now Rivera stopped, turning to face the man, praying those behind would understand. "You tried to cheat me, Pierre," he said quietly. "You loaded rubbish, shit, on that ship in San Diego and thought you'd get the money before it was discovered. That's what you did, didn't you? You treated me like a fool. . . ." Enough, Rivera knew; he'd risked more than enough, unable to stop himself.

"No, listen . . ." Belac said, all the bombast gone now. "I didn't know. Don't know . . ."

Where were they! Why weren't they here! "Liar!" said Rivera, as loudly as he believed he dared risk. He saw them at last, from the corner of his eye, still yards away.

Belac seemed to become aware of them at the same moment. He snatched a look toward the men, then back at Rivera, and for a moment stood utterly still. Then he began to turn, toward the sanctuary of the bridge ahead, and was actually moving when Rivera stepped forward. It wasn't in any way an attack upon the man—not as he was later to convince himself boastfully that it had been. He did nothing more than collide with the Belgian, but it impeded the man long enough for the Cubans to reach him.

Belac was bulge-eyed with terror, like a rabbit caught in the beam of a poacher's torch. He whimpered, not able to make a proper cry, and started scrabbling beneath his coat. But they were on him now, not hitting the man or showing any weapons. They seemed merely to close around him, like people crushed together in a crowd.

Rivera stood watching, transfixed himself, until one of the men said, without looking at him, "Get out!"

It broke the mood, but only just. Rivera started toward the bridge but kept glancing back, wanting to see. Nothing appeared to be happening; they remained close together, almost comically so. But then the figure in the middle, Belac, slumped, but he didn't fall because of the support of each man on either side. Just before Rivera got too far away to be able to distinguish what was happening, he thought he saw them moving toward the water's edge.

Rivera just managed to regain his room at the Wolven straat *pension*. As soon as he was inside the locked door the emotion gripped him and he had to support himself from collapse by clutching a chair back. He crouched against it, rocking back and forth, but peculiarly glad it was happening now, before he confronted Mendez. It was just shock, he knew, shock that he hoped was being literally shaken out of him.

It took a long time for the sensation to subside, and when it did it left him aching. Cautiously he lowered himself into the chair but sat with his arms wrapped around his body, as if he were hugging himself in self-congratulation. Which, largely, he was. He'd succeeded! Somehow, miraculously, he'd avoided all the snares and all the potential hazards to rid himself of Belac. The familiar, comforting word presented itself: to be *safe*. Forever. There was a brief return of the shaking, at that awareness, but not so severe as before.

By the time Mendez returned, Rivera was quite recovered, contentedly waiting.

"You got the money?" the intelligence chief demanded at once.

"Knowing the boat had to come back to where it started, at Nieuwe Spiegel, it wasn't such a good idea to concentrate three people aboard, was it?" said Rivera. He wasn't dependent upon this supercilious whoremonger any longer; nor would he be, ever again. He wanted very quickly to relegate Mendez to the position he had held before, the clearly defined subordinate to the clearly defined superior. Mendez visibly flushed, and Rivera knew he had jabbed a nerve.

"Two were ashore just for that eventuality," Mendez said defensively. "I asked about the money."

"I heard you," Rivera said. And stopped.

Mendez stared back, the redness increasing. Finally he said, "Well, do you have it?"

It had been incredibly fortunate—another miracle—that Mendez had been trapped aboard the boat and not involved in the ambush. "Yes," Rivera said.

"I think I should see proof of its return," the man insisted.

"Why?"

"There were two purposes in this operation," said Mendez. "Recovering the money. *Then* dealing with Belac. I'm sure of one. Not the other."

"I have told you the money has been returned," said Rivera. "That is sufficient."

"I may tell Havana that, upon your authority?" Mendez fought back, weakly.

"No you may not!" Rivera said at once. "You will tell Havana nothing in my name. Confine yourself to your own service and your own authority."

The following morning Rivera expected to see the other men, but they did not appear, and he refused to give Mendez the satisfaction of asking. Their train to Paris, from where they were to fly to Madrid, did not leave until midday, so they were able to read all the newspapers. The most comprehensive account of Belac's death appeared in *Der Telegraph*, the story newsworthy because the man had a .375 Magnum still in his shoulder holster and was identified as an arms dealer for whom two indictments were outstanding in the United States. A Commerce Department spokesman in Washington was quoted as saying Pierre Belac was a much-wanted criminal under other investigations at the time of his death. There was a further statement from an Amsterdam police spokesman. An autopsy was still to be carried out, but at that stage there was no evidence of foul play; the death appeared to be either an accident or suicide.

"How was it done?" Rivera asked.

Mendez sat regarding him and Rivera knew the man was debating whether to tell him. In the end Mendez said, "A concentrated gas, from a capsule gun. Forces the heart muscles to contract into the appearance of a heart attack. It dissipates completely from the body in minutes: nothing suspicious will show up during any postmortem examination."

"Clever," Rivera said.

"A Russian invention," Mendez disclosed.

"Well, now!" Petty said. The U.S. indictments had automatically placed Pierre Belac's name on the watch list of Interpol, the international police communication organization, so the death in Amsterdam and all its circumstances were relayed to Washington within hours of the body being dragged from the canal.

"Intriguing," Erickson agreed. Getting in first with the question, he said, "What odds do you give on there being a Cuban connection?"

"No bet," Petty said. "It's an obvious thought, but people like Belac are mixed up in too many things." He picked up and put down a pipe, unlighted. "I couldn't give a shit how or why Pierre Belac died," he went on. "What I am worried about is it spooking Rivera in some way."

"I'll signal Madrid for us to be told the moment the Cuban group gets in," Erickson said.

"Wouldn't that be a bastard, after all the effort that's gone into it!" said the division chief bitterly.

"What about O'Farrell?"

"Nothing more than the local man's confirmation that he's arrived," Petty said.

"Belac's death is being publicly reported," Erickson pointed out. "What if O'Farrell reads about it and gets spooked as well?"

Petty lighted up at last. His face obscured, he said, "I'd like something to be easy! Just once I'd like something to be fucking easy!"

THIRTY-THREE

BY INCREDIBLE coincidence O'Farrell witnessed Rivera's arrival; saw the man through the car window, autocratically gazing straight ahead from his seat behind the chauffeur, a second escorting limousine tight behind. The barred gates of the embassy opened—presumably from some advance warning radioed from the car—and then snapped shut again, swallowing up the cavalcade like a devouring mouth.

O'Farrell strode on up the incline. A perfect target, he thought, ironically; just what he needed, and just what he had been searching for, for hours. Guided by the information he'd picked up at his own embassy, O'Farrell had on foot explored the conference hall approaches and the designated link roads and the ambassador's official residence and finally this, the embassy itself. And there Rivera had been, impossible to miss. Not that he could have done anything, of course; exposed himself, making his arrest inevitable. How—or when—could he act, then? The conference area was impossible. It was already obvious that the security would be at its highest there, army units and police and militia moving themselves and their vehicles into position, all main and side roads cordoned off with crash barriers. The routes to and from the Cuban embassy and the official residence appeared out of the question, too; they were largely closed off by more crash barriers, and from the documents he'd collected from the U.S. embassy he knew traffic lights and intersections were going to be police-controlled to enable all the delegates' vehicles to travel at high speed.

At the top of the incline O'Farrell paused, hot from exertion, gazing back in the direction from which he'd come. It had to be here, somehow, he decided. Or at the residence. Both walled and both guarded, by Cuban as well as Spanish security. But possible, O'Farrell calculated, making his way back to the Calle de la Princesa through side roads to avoid passing by the embassy again. Just possible. And by virtue of that strict security.

The arrival and departure of each delegation was to be rigidly regulated, timed and distanced and ordered. And from the U.S. embassy guidance O'Farrell knew precisely when it was intended that Rivera should set out and return. The gate operation was extremely smooth, but the limousine had been forced to slow. Just possible, O'Farrell thought once more.

Technically, that is. He recognized that the biggest uncertainty remained himself. He wouldn't get drunk this afternoon, not like he had last night, anesthetizing himself to what he had to do and how he felt about doing it. Had to force himself on, to perfect the planning. It would mean explosives again. In a car parked at the cross street he'd noted and isolated, just before Rivera's limousine swept by. The side roads brought O'Farrell out very close to his hotel, and despite the earlier resolution he went unhurriedly to the bar, his mind busy. It definitely needed a car and explosives. But it wouldn't be possible to activate the detonator by a preset clock, because there was no guarantee that the listed timings would be kept precisely to the second. He had to allow for a variable of up to five minutes. Which meant exploding the device himself, by electrical remote control, from some vantage point from which he could watch and wait until Rivera's vehicle was in exactly the right position.

O'Farrell chose local brandy, harsh to his throat. The glass wobbled with the unsteadiness of his hands as he lifted it, like the glass had the previous night. Watch, he thought; he'd have to watch and see it happen. Hear the roar and see the metal tear and split and know a body was being torn and split and—

No! He wouldn't do it! Never again! It wasn't right; it had never been right, and he'd always known it. Why so long! Why had he for so long postured about patriotism and hidden justice, and sought parallels with a long-dead relative when there weren't any parallels! He didn't know; so much he didn't know. Or want to know. Maybe he could rationalize it, in time. Rationalize but never excuse it. What about now, this very moment? That was the pressing consideration, the problem he had to solve first. There was a way out. Simple, in fact. Easy. Perhaps not the way to conclude his active career in the eyes of a very few people back in Washington—Petty and Erickson and the others he knew existed, although he didn't know who they were—but that's all. Very few indeed. They might suspect, he supposed. It was practically inevitable that they would suspect. But suspicion wasn't proof, and there certainly wouldn't be any proof. He'd ensure that well enough. Nothing they would be able to do. Nothing at all.

O'Farrell gestured for another drink, sure that already there was less movement in his hands. He certainly felt better; felt great. He'd have to make the right moves, in their proper order. Petty first then. Describe the supposed plan and stress the problems as strongly as possible, without making it sound like excuses in advance. Ask for the explosives and timing device at the same time. Then reserve a car. All so easy, so incredibly easy. He was free! It became another word to lodge in his mind. That was exactly how he *did* feel, free of a burden physically grinding him down, like a weight that was too great for him to support anymore. Overly dramatic, O'Farrell decided. But just how it was.

O'Farrell telephoned the embassy to advise that he was on his way, instinctively cautious on an open link, so the station chief was waiting when he arrived. The air conditioner had broken, and Lewis was redder-faced than before, puffing in his distress.

"Sometimes it's days before they fix it," the man complained. "You don't know what it's like to be without it until you don't have it."

"I can imagine," O'Farrell said sympathetically. Preparing the ground for any later inquiry from Langley or Petty, he said, "You were certainly right about security. The Spanish are locking this place up tighter than a drum."

"*Trying* to," the fat man qualified. "Something will happen. Mark my words."

"You warned the State Department?" O'Farrell pressed.

"Three separate memoranda," Lewis said. "The Secret Service increased their escort because of it."

A bonus, O'Farrell reflected. The secure communication area was in the basement of the embassy and the clear telephones were isolated in small cubicles. The lack of airconditioning made it ovenlike. The connection, as always, was immediate. As he invariably did at the beginning of such contact, Petty remained completely silent while O'Farrell talked himself out. This time Petty was waiting for O'Farrell to make some reference to Belac's death, in Holland, but there was nothing. He shook his head to Erickson, on the other side of the room.

"A lot of obstacles," Petty agreed.

"A car bomb is the only way," O'Farrell said.

"Just like London," Petty mused. "That's not a bad idea; it'll send the investigators around in circles."

"Semtex explosive, like before," O'Farrell requested. "And a remote control, like I said."

"In tonight's pouch," the division head promised. "I'm sorry there wasn't time for more preparation."

O'Farrell took the opening. "To be absolutely ·safe I needed it."

"You've got all the routes and timings?"

"Yes."

"Check them thoroughly, every morning and night," Petty instructed. "Those schedules can screw up."

"Of course," O'Farrell said. ·

"You got the job," Petty said.

The announcement was so abrupt and O'Farrell's mind so occupied elsewhere that initially he did not comprehend what he was being told. "What?"

"Your promotion here, to join Erickson and me. It's been confirmed."

"That's wonderful news," O'Farrell managed, his throat working up and down. How could it be! There was no moral difference between initiating a killing in the comfort of a Washington office and carrying it out in some backstreet part of the world. One thing at a time, he told himself; concentrate upon evading this assignment before worrying about anything else.

"Congratulations," Petty said. "We're looking forward to your joining us. You take care now, you hear?"

Practically an invitation for what he intended to do! O'Farrell thought. He said, "You know I will."

"All luck."

"Thanks."

O'Farrell left the embassy, still promising to drink sometime with Lewis, deciding he might as well occupy the afternoon renting the car. He ignored the big agencies, as he had in London. On the outskirts of the city, on the road toward Las Rozas, he rented a Seat from a broken-toothed garage owner grateful for the cash transaction, and considered himself lucky to make it back to central Madrid. The drinking that night was quite different from before. It was for pleasure, relaxation, and not for oblivion, and although he had a bottle of wine with dinner and brandy afterward, O'Farrell went to bed feeling quite sober.

The following day, the last before the conference began, O'Farrell repeated his earlier surveillance and climbed the incline toward the embassy, knowing that the brief moment of Rivera's car slowing upon entry and departure really would have been the only opportunity had he intended going through with it. It would, of course, be necessary to continue making it appear that he was: monitor the daily movements, as Petty advised, and create the bomb and park the Seat in the street he had selected. There was always the possibility of a watch squad that he hadn't bothered this time to locate, and they would have to support his account that he'd done everything possible before aborting the attempt because his own detection and seizure would have been inevitable. The taking care that Petty had insisted upon.

O'Farrell hid himself among a small crowd watching Rivera's departure that first morning and, afterward, in his hotel room, watched the television coverage of the formal opening, although he couldn't understand the commentary. He saw Rivera on three occasions, each time enclosed by security men. He checked the man in and out of the embassy during the luncheon adjournment, saw more television coverage in the afternoon, and was standing on the pavement again in the evening when Rivera returned. It was interesting, O'Farrell reflected, that the scheduled timings had been remarkably accurate, the only difference being in the evening, and that by Rivera being just two minutes late.

The sealed, eyes-only package containing the Semtex and the timer would be at the embassy by now. It would be wrong if he didn't collect them sometime the following day. He'd do it after seeing Rivera away. It would mean his carrying a bomb around a city on full security alert, but by itself Semtex looked like gray cement, and he could leave it in the trunk. The timer he would keep in his room, a rather elaborate alarm clock to anything but the closest of examinations.

O'Farrell was awake early, once more without any discomfort from the previous night's intake, setting out in good time for what was becoming routine. He was attracted by a perfume shop on the opposite side of the road and crossed, spending several minutes looking at the window selection, trying to decide upon a present for Jill. Definitely perfume, because she enjoyed perfume. And something for Ellen, too. Her birthday, he remembered; the birthday for which Billy had been saving. They could say it was from both of them.

The window-shopping had delayed him and the crowd had already formed ahead as he approached. He was still about thirty yards away when the gates of the embassy opened and the diplomatic vehicles began emerging. The timing's off today, thought O'Farrell. Rivera's car was just clear of the entrance when the explosion came, a window-shattering eruption with an immediate after-punch blast of air that knocked him heavily into the bordering wall. Rivera's limousine disintegrated in front of his eyes: O'Farrell was just able, to its left, to see the other car that had formed the bomb, its cratered and burning shell visible through the debris and dust.

O'Farrell's training automatically took over. He rebounded off the wall, already turning to get away from a scene of violence. What the hell! What or who in the name of Christ had—

It was as far as O'Farrell's bewilderment ever got. The shot was perfect, absolutely professional, a spread-on-impact, high-velocity shell that caught him midchest, gouging the life from him. It was too quick for there to be the slightest pain. He was dead before his body landed, half on the pavement, half on the road. But his face was frozen by shock. His eyes were wide open, staring, an expression of astonishment.

THIRTY-FOUR

IT WAS the first bad day of a Washington autumn, gray and sullen with a spiteful wind strong enough to howl through the larger catafalques and burial vaults. There was a lot of security because of the Secretary of State's attendance, secret servicemen with their walkie-talkies and earpieces standing point around the entire grave area. The official cars had been allowed to pull very close, a further precaution, but McCarthy's vehicle, a long stretch limousine to accommodate all the people, had been allowed to park on a promontory separate from the rest. Against the smoke-glassed windshield were attached sufficient passes and official clearances to allow it to go anywhere it wanted.

There were five men in the vehicle. All were dressed solemnly, although just short of funeral black. The elevation of the vehicle enabled them to see everything.

"There's the family," Petty said as a group got from one of the huddled cars and slowly led the way to the grave edge. "Billy's the one to the right."

The boy was in fact holding his mother's hand and weeping bitterly. Ellen was walking with difficulty, trying to support her head-bowed, sobbing mother on her other arm. John was helping on the other side, and Beth was holding tightly to their son. Mother and son were crying, too.

"You put the fix in, with Chicago?" McCarthy asked.

Petty nodded. "Patrick's payments are being computer-monitored. There's no chance of his falling behind."

"That's good," the Plans director said absently.

There was a flurry of movement from cameramen as the Secretary of State and his party came into shot with the family.

"We can't go down there. We could be photographed too easily," Sneider said from behind the wheel. He was driving because of the need for absolute security within the vehicle.

"I'm still not sure that O'Farrell had cracked completely, that he would have fouled up some way," Petty said. "He'd made all the right moves."

"He would have cracked," Lambert said, with quiet, expert insistence. "My guess is that he wouldn't have fouled up; he was still too good for that. My guess is that in the end he wouldn't have gone through with it."

"We owe a lot to you, doctor," McCarthy said, the architect of everything that had happened. "If it hadn't been for you, O'Farrell would have stayed a basket case after London, and none of the rest would have been possible. Not so perfectly as it has turned out."

"He certainly developed a strong dependence," Lambert agreed modestly. "It was too strong for him to continue on his own anymore. The doubt was too deep."

"So often the way it happens." McCarthy sighed.

"He was doing everything he should have done in Madrid," Erickson insisted, coming out in support of his division chief.

"What was the point in taking the risk!" McCarthy said, with strained patience. "This way everything is boxed and tied with ribbon. Rivera's dead, as we intended. The speculation about the who's and why's of that killing will go on for weeks, and every day it'll act as the warning we always planned it to be to Havana. And in Spanish custody is a man provably a Soviet assassin; it doesn't matter a damn that the guy won't talk or admit anything. They got him in the room with the gun still in his hand, for Christ's sake! It fits perfectly with the history of O'Farrell's mother; Moscow pursuing relentlessly the son of a nationalist dissident. We can even seed the doubt that the murder-suicide verdict on the parents was wrong. That their deaths were Soviet orchestrated, too . . ." McCarthy looked at Petty, as the doubter. "You see anything hanging loose from that?"

Petty wished he could. He still believed absolutely in the correctness of what he and his department had to do, but this was the first time they'd turned on one of their own people. It frightened him. He said, "I agree it wraps everything up."

"Maneuvering the Soviet involvement and then alerting the Spanish authorities was brilliant," Sneider said sycophantically, stroking McCarthy's favorite hobbyhorse.

"Didn't I say that's what the Russians would do when we leaked O'Farrell as the killer of Leonid Makarevich?" McCarthy said.

The arrested Soviet assassin was named Vladimir Kopalin, Petty knew. He knew, too, that the Agency had monitored the man's arrival in Madrid and watched him stalk O'Farrell and let it happen: *wanted* it to happen. He said, "We're going to keep O'Farrell's State Department appointment, right? It wasn't just a way to guarantee the media hype by getting the Secretary of State here today?"

"Sure, why not?" The Plans director shrugged. "That way Mrs. O'Farrell collects a nice fat pension as well as the insurance."

"What about the new man, who really took Rivera out?" Lambert queried.

"What about him?" Erickson demanded. He was as unsettled as Petty.

"He okay?"

"He said it was easy; called it a piece of cake," Petty reported. "Actually it was the way suggested by

O'Farrell. . . ." He paused and added defiantly, "The way he was going to do it."

Lambert appeared to miss the jab. He said, "We'd better tell Symmons to keep an eye on him. Let's not recruit someone who enjoys it. That's dangerous."

"I thought everything we did was dangerous," Petty said. He felt oppressed within the limousine and desperately wanted a pipe. Below them, through the protectively black windows, he saw that the interment was almost over. The mourners were shifting, about to leave, and the limousine drivers were standing ready to open the doors. Abruptly Petty announced, "I'm going down to speak to her."

"That's not wise," Sneider said.

"A lot of things aren't," Petty said. "I'll make my own way back."

He left the car before there could be any more objection, shivering at once as the wind cut through his topcoat. It was too strong to attempt lighting a pipe, he realized miserably. He shrugged his collar up further and took a pathway to bring him out by the other official cars, as if he had emerged from one of them.

The family group were still some way away when he got there and he hung back from the media rush as the Secretary of State spoke briefly to them. Mrs. O'Farrell was shiny-faced and very red around the eyes, but she wasn't crying anymore. She didn't appear to speak a lot, hardly at all, but nodded and even smiled faintly at what was being said to her.

Petty waited until the woman had almost reached her car before stepping forward. "Mrs. O'Farrell?"

Jill hesitated, looking toward him, waiting.

"I knew your husband; worked with him," Petty said, awkwardly. "I wanted you to know how sorry I am."

"Thank you," said the woman. Her voice was quite resolute.

"You'll have all the State Department material: telephone numbers and references. If you need any help, please use them." State would automatically channel any communication through to him.

"I'll remember that," Jill promised. "I'm thinking of selling out here and moving to Chicago. I've a daughter there, you know."

"No," Petty lied. "I didn't know. It would probably be a good idea."

"There's a church in Evanston that's been very kind to me since it happened," Jill said, the dam unblocked, wanting to talk now. "We attended church regularly, Charles and I. We both found it a comfort."

Petty's throat moved and he was glad his coat collar was high. "Yes," he said inadequately. Beside her the child he knew to be Billy had stopped crying, too, but the breath was going into him in sobs that made his tiny shoulders shudder. "Please don't forget," Petty urged. "Any problem at all, just get in touch."

"Yes," Jill said.

Petty doubted that she would. He pulled away and watched until her car led the cortege out of the cemetery, eventually following toward the exit. He was quite close before he realized the figure there was Erickson, hunched for protection by the gate pillar.

"I thought we could get a cab back together," the man said.

"I didn't like that," Petty declared. "I didn't like that one little bit."

Erickson began waving for a cab. "McCarthy says he wants to talk. Another assignment, I guess. He said it was important."

"Aren't they all?" Petty queried wearily. It wasn't until he was inside the cab and it was moving away that he realized it was festooned with No Smoking stickers.

Everything was completely alien to Jorge; he could remember none of it. It was very hot and his clothes stuck to him and the streets stank of sewage and gas fumes, making his chest tighten. He'd been escorted from England by a woman as well as a man from the Foreign Ministry. She kept trying to hold him and he wished she wouldn't.

"Your father is a hero," the man said in the car taking them from the airport. "He is to be honored. There is already a place for you in a state academy."

Jorge was taken straight there and he hated it, as he hated everything else. The curriculum was completely different from what he had studied at the lycée, he was bullied, and an older boy sexually molested him the first week. Jorge complained to the housemaster, who dismissed it as a fact of academy life. The master let the other boys know of Jorge's complaint and he was beaten very badly and kept for several days in the academy's sanatorium, with a suspected rib fracture.

The same couple who had brought him from London collected him for the ceremony they had promised. Jorge was allowed to stand on a podium with a lot of important-looking men, one of whom had a beard and appeared to be obeyed by everyone else. The man ruffled his hair once. He smelled of cigars.

Jorge understood little of it. There were a lot of speeches and a lot of cheering and a small curtain was pulled away from a plaque set into a wall. His father's name was written upon it. So were the words FIGHTER FOR FREEDOM.

This time Jorge let the woman hold him and on the way back to the academy told both her and the man how he was beaten and how the older boys kept getting into his bed at night. The man promised to speak to the principal. Jorge begged him not to, because of the beating he had gotten on the previous occasion. The man said it would be different this time.

"Please sir," said Jorge, guessing the importance of politeness. "I would like to go home."

"What?" said the ministry official.

"Home," Jorge repeated. "I don't like it here. I want to go home."

The embracing woman withdrew her arm. The man said, tightly Jorge thought, as if he were offended. "This is your home. This is where you are going to live now."

It took three days for the complaints to percolate down from the principal's office. This time the beating was worse than before and Jorge had to stay longer in the sanatorium because an X ray disclosed that one of his ribs was definitely cracked.

The woman from the ministry visited him at the end of the month. She said, "You've got to start trying harder. It is a great privilege for you to be taught in the academy. There have been complaints about you from the authorities. They say that you are a troublemaker, upsetting the other boys. You want to be liked, don't you? Behave yourself!"

THE BEST IN SUSPENSE
FROM TOR

☐ ☐	50451-8	THE BEETHOVEN CONSPIRACY *Thomas Hauser*	$3.50 Canada $4.50
☐ ☐	54106-5	BLOOD OF EAGLES *Dean Ing*	$3.95 Canada $4.95
☐ ☐	58794-4	BLUE HERON *Philip Ross*	$3.50 Canada $4.50
☐ ☐	50549-2	THE CHOICE OF EDDIE FRANKS *Brian Freemantle*	$4.95 Canada $5.95
☐ ☐	50105-5	CITADEL RUN *Paul Bishop*	$4.95 Canada $5.95
☐ ☐	50581-6	DAY SEVEN *Jack M. Bickham*	$3.95 Canada $4.95
☐ ☐	50720-7	A FINE LINE *Ken Gross*	$4.50 Canada $5.50
☐ ☐	50911-0	THE HALFLIFE *Sharon Webb*	$4.95 Canada $5.95
☐ ☐	50642-1	RIDE THE LIGHTNING *John Lutz*	$3.95 Canada $4.95
☐ ☐	50906-4	WHITE FLOWER *Philip Ross*	$4.95 Canada $5.95
☐ ☐	50413-5	WITHOUT HONOR *David Hagberg*	$4.95 Canada $5.95

Buy them at your local bookstore or use this handy coupon:
Clip and mail this page with your order.

Publishers Book and Audio Mailing Service
P.O. Box 120159, Staten Island, NY 10312-0004

Please send me the book(s) I have checked above. I am enclosing $ _____
(please add $1.25 for the first book, and $.25 for each additional book to cover postage and handling.
Send check or money order only—no CODs).

Name _____
Address _____
City _____ State/Zip _____
Please allow six weeks for delivery. Prices subject to change without notice.

TOR—TOPS IN SUSPENSE

☐ ☐	50168-3	ANGEL OF VENGEANCE *Anthea Cohen*	$2.95 Canada $3.95
☐ ☐	50143-8	A BAD DAY IN THE BAHAMAS *Cullimore*	$3.50 Canada $4.50
☐ ☐	51148-4	BERNHARDT'S EDGE *Collin Wilcox*	$3.95 Canada $4.95
☐ ☐	58794-4	BLUE HERON *Philip Ross*	$3.50 Canada $4.50
☐ ☐	50549-2	THE CHOICE OF EDDIE FRANKS *Brian Freemantle*	$4.95 Canada $5.95
☐ ☐	50581-6	DAY SEVEN *Jack M. Bickham*	$3.95 Canada $4.95
☐ ☐	50720-7	A FINE LINE *Ken Gross*	$4.50 Canada $5.50
☐ ☐	50911-0	THE HALFLIFE *Sharon Webb*	$4.95 Canada $5.95
☐ ☐	50214-0	THE SCHOLARS OF NIGHT *John M. Ford*	$4.95 Canada $5.95
☐ ☐	58784-7	TALLEY'S TRUTH *Philip Ross*	$3.50 Canada $4.50
☐ ☐	50906-4	WHITE FLOWER *Philip Ross*	$4.95 Canada $5.95

Buy them at your local bookstore or use this handy coupon:
Clip and mail this page with your order.

Publishers Book and Audio Mailing Service
P.O. Box 120159, Staten Island, NY 10312-0004

Please send me the book(s) I have checked above. I am enclosing $ _____
(please add $1.25 for the first book, and $.25 for each additional book to cover postage and handling.
Send check or money order only—no CODs).

Name _____
Address _____
City _____ State/Zip _____
Please allow six weeks for delivery. Prices subject to change without notice.

DAVID HAGBERG

☐
☐ 50964-1 COUNTDOWN $4.95
Canada $5.95

☐
☐ 51358-4 CROSSFIRE $5.99
Canada $6.99

☐
☐ 48051-2 HEARTLAND $3.50
Canada $4.50

☐
☐ 50409-7 HEROES 3.50
Canada 4.50

☐
☐ 53987-7 LAST COME THE CHILDREN 3.95
Canada $4.95

☐
☐ 50413-5 WITHOUT HONOR $4.95
Canada $5.95

Buy them at your local bookstore or use this handy coupon:
Clip and mail this page with your order.

Publishers Book and Audio Mailing Service
P.O. Box 120159, Staten Island, NY 10312-0004

Please send me the book(s) I have checked above. I am enclosing $ _____
(please add $1.25 for the first book, and $.25 for each additional book to cover postage and handling.
Send check or money order only—no CODs).

Name _____
Address _____
City _____ State/Zip _____
Please allow six weeks for delivery. Prices subject to change without notice.